Raves for McNamara's previous novel, FATAL COMMAND

"McNamara is an excellent writer of detective fiction, every bit the equal of—and often more in control than—bestselling former L.A. police detective Joseph Wambaugh."

San Francisco Chronicle

"A bloody good book . . . It grabs the reader by the throat and won't let go until the final genuinely moving confrontation."

San Jose Mercury News

"He knows the territory and he can portray the exhilarating and the seamy sides of police work. He also can spin a pulse-throbbing tale with accomplished skill."

Kansas City Star

"McNamara has the magical touch. He knows how to grip his readers with human emotion and raw action. . . . A tough book but an honest one."

Ocala Star-Banner

Also by Joseph D. McNamara:

SAFE & SANE (nonfiction)
THE FIRST DIRECTIVE*
FATAL COMMAND*

Published by Fawcett Books

THE
BLUE
MIRAGE

Joseph D. McNamara

FAWCETT GOLD MEDAL • NEW YORK

A Fawcett Gold Medal Book
Published by Ballantine Books
Copyright © 1990 by Joseph D. McNamara

All rights reserved under International and Pan-American Copyright Conventions. Published in the United States by Ballantine Books, a division of Random House, Inc., New York, and simultaneously in Canada by Random House of Canada Limited, Toronto.

Library of Congress Catalog Card Number: 90-30025

ISBN 0-449-14755-X

This edition published by arrangment with William Morrow and Company, Inc.

Manufactured in the United States of America

First Ballantine Books Edition: November 1991

This book is dedicated to Gordon Silva and Gene Simpson, the loved ones they left behind, and all the members of the San Jose Police Department who carry on their work. I thank the City of San Jose for allowing me the privilege of serving alongside them during the past fourteen years. Liza Dawson's insights and skills helped greatly in shaping the final product. My thanks also go to my son, Don, for his suggestions.

The use of undercover investigative techniques requires a careful balance between meeting law enforcement objectives and the prevention of mental injury and emotional disturbances.

FBI LAW ENFORCEMENT BULLETIN, FEBRUARY 1989

Prologue

COMING IN FROM THE FOUR A.M. BLACKNESS, I FOUGHT OFF the last bit of sleepiness and entered the briefing room. Three times a day platoons of more than one hundred officers gathered here for roll call and instructions prior to going on patrol. Now, the sounds made from the group at the far end of the room echoed eerily off the walls hung with pictures of wanted criminals.

I looked at the twenty large men in combat fatigues milling about aimlessly. The harsh white fluorescent lighting threw shadows across their incongruously boyish faces and bounced dull metallic reflections from the barrels of the assault rifles they carried. These were the elite—SWAT cops—and they dwarfed the three scroungy undercover sting detectives in their midst.

It was only eight weeks ago that I had been unexpectedly appointed acting police chief and this was the first major raid under my command. The men were fully trained, but I well knew that a lot could go wrong. A burly lieutenant also in fatigues waved to me. He was operational commander and a good man at his job, yet I fought my instinct to call him over and take personal command.

Coffee and greasy doughnuts were set out, and the cops clustered around the refreshments played grab ass much the way they had in high school locker rooms before going out to play in the big game. But this morning's game was potentially lethal and I was making an effort to keep my nervousness from showing. Police chiefs were supposed to be like generals, without nerves or doubts.

In my previous position as chief of detectives, I had authorized the sting. For eight months we ran it out of an electronics repair shop. Sting detectives posed as employees eager to buy hot goods. When the crooks showed up with stolen property, they were ushered into a back room where the sale prices were negotiated and money and property changed hands. Of course, the thieves had no idea that the transactions were being recorded by hidden videotape cameras. The crooks wouldn't have a prayer in court, but first we had to get them there. It wasn't always that easy.

A number of them were heavily armed and would kill when cornered if they got the chance. Then too, the criminals and their lawyers had an incredibly efficient communications network. Within hours after one of the thieves' lawyers saw the court papers describing how evidence had been obtained during the sting, word would flash through their ranks and our best "customers" would vanish before we could arrest them. This was our answer, a predawn synchronized operation to nail the crooks who had been caught in our net before they could resist or get away. The sting detectives were there to make sure the people taken into custody were the same crooks who had sold them dope or stolen property. They would identify people after the SWAT guys had rounded up and disarmed the players.

Looking more like street people than solid citizens, the sting detectives were jubilant. Their undercover work had ended yesterday, and they were relaxed for the first time in eight months. Clad in jeans and leather vests, they were skinny, fragile, dirty-looking, and the bright light contrasted them sharply with their younger, clean-cut SWAT colleagues. The dicks now joked among the uniformed cops the way professional football quarterbacks made sure to mingle with their offensive linemen.

"You don't have to be smart to work a sting, all you gotta do is look like a hype," said SWAT team leader Scott Ward with his big paw spread around Detective Nunzio Papa's shoulders.

I smiled to myself. Ward was all of twenty-seven. Old enough, big enough, and tough enough to be a team leader in the SWAT unit. In my NYPD days I would have wondered what a hype was. But California law enforcement's jargon was more precise. After all, you could be a junkie in a number of ways, but a hype was addicted to heroin or other drugs injected with a hypodermic needle.

Papa shook Ward's arm loose and said, "You ain't nothing, Ward. It's too bad they gave you steroids instead of a helmet when you played at State. You mighta been able to make detective yourself."

Ward's team members laughed at the detective's comeback. Nunzio Papa moved nimbly away as Ward attempted to grab the detective under the armpits and lift him into the air. The SWAT team cops in their combat fatigues and flak vests were posturing a bit.

I studied Papa, our star undercover man. He was an intense guy with swarthy skin pitted by acne, and had the bulging eyes of a strung-out coke fiend. It was easy to see why thieves and drug dealers fought to sell him stolen goods or dope. His slight build helped, but he was a natural actor who threw himself into things with an incredible energy. The energy made me uneasy. In high-risk undercover work, it was a short step from super-productivity to disaster.

The lieutenant was moving through the ranks patting backs and urging the cops to take seats. The group around the coffee urn thinned as men squeezed into briefing-room chairs made for average-size cops. Eighteen rows of tables with ten swivel seats attached to each table stretched toward the rear of the room. Five places in the front row had the names of uniformed cops who had been killed in the line of duty imbedded in the desk. The row was left empty by unspoken consent. I leaned against the wall and watched as the lieutenant came to the front of the room.

"OK, listen up, gentlemen . . ." Their lieutenant paused then said, "and members of the sting team." The SWAT guys guffawed. It wasn't that funny, but laughing would show that they weren't thinking about what could happen an hour from now when the raid began.

"Chief Fraleigh," the lieutenant turned to me, "do you have a few words for the troops?" He moved aside from the microphone on the raised podium.

I almost missed my cue. No one had told me I was expected to speak. What should I say? "If you get your balls shot off I'll visit you in the hospital, and if you don't make it, at your funeral I'll hand your badge and the folded flag to your mother." Guys this young couldn't have wives and kids, could they?

Moving up to the front of the room I saw that the detectives were in their thirties. Climbing buildings and hanging off helicopter ropes in antiterrorist and hostage-rescue training was the work of young cops. Most of them sported mustaches, trying to make themselves look older, but all it accomplished was to make me feel ancient at the age of thirty-eight. Once, I had felt that strong and confident, but it had been a long time ago. Two policewomen sat quietly to the side, clearly left out of the camaraderie.

I stood level with the cops, declining to use the podium and microphone for such a small group. "I know you've done this before and know your stuff. Our guys working the sting did a good job. They've got these crooks cold on candid camera. But remember, there are paroled robbers, muggers, dope pushers, and career burglars on this morning's list, and you'll be starting them on long stays in the joint. They'll know that once they spot you, so let's be careful. Good luck."

"Thanks, Chief." The lieutenant moved back to the mike. "We have forty-one felony arrest warrants and sixteen search warrants to be served. We're breaking into three teams— Tiger One, Two, and Three. Five men and a sergeant on each team. The sting cop who obtained the warrant will come in after the arrest team secures the house or apartment. He'll ID the players for you. The general rule is that the warrants give us the right to break and enter. If you spot illegal weapons or stolen goods at the location, bring in everyone present. It should be admissible as evidence against them, but we'll have a deputy D.A. in the command room all morning, in case you have questions on who gets booked. We'll let the D.A. guess what the Supreme Court wants this time. He can cut them loose here if necessary. We've set up a priority list based on the crooks' past criminal records and how dangerous they seemed during the sting. We hope to collar the real baddies first while they're still catching their Z's. Are there any last-minute questions?"

"Yeah, Lieutenant," Scott Ward said. "The sting guys are buying the beer for tonight's party, right?"

"Absolutely, Scott. Unless you want to help them out." The lieutenant got the last laugh. "OK. Let's pick up your assignments and hit the bricks. No mistakes. Follow procedures, and no one gets hurt. At least none of us."

Well, that was it. My work was done for the next couple of hours. The cops went into the moonless night and I crossed my fingers and went home for an early breakfast.

"How many of these turkeys are yours, Nunzio?" Ward held up a fistful of warrants as Tiger One Team's van drove through the sprawling, sleeping, residential neighborhoods of Silicon City.

"Fourteen. Almost all of them sold some dope. The narcs don't like us on their turf. But what can you do? The shit is everywhere. These dirtbags would make us in a minute if we didn't deal dope. Still, it's funny. I don't know why I always feel a little guilty when these assholes see me wearing a badge," Nunzio said.

"You should feel guilty about us instead," Scott Ward growled. The van pulled up at the first stop, a block from the three-story tenement where the arrest warrant would be served. At four-forty in the morning, the streets in the racially mixed low-income area were deserted. "Here we are risking our asses for your pinches. Real cops make their own collars."

"Hey, that's department policy. You guys are expendable. Detectives with high IQs have to be protected."

"Up yours, Nunzio," Ward said, flicking the detective's gold earring as they got out of the van.

"Ouch. Lay off, asshole. Listen, guys. Seriously, this first dude, Hector Gonzales, is bad. He's crazy as hell and likes to hurt people. He's a three-time loser and sold me a lot of dope and guns. I know he's got a whole box of Uzis up there ripped off from a San Jose gun store. Hell, he sold me five of them. He knows he'll be going in for good this time and he'll shoot it out if you give him a chance."

"So what else is new?" Ward said.

The team, welcoming the darkness, moved toward their prearranged positions surrounding the apartment house, all hoping that the demented, and well-armed, Hector Gonzales was fast asleep. But none hoped harder than Nunzio. As a sting dick, he'd stay behind in the van with the sergeant until Gonzales was in custody. Still, he felt sick to his stomach with fear as he remembered his sessions with the tall, slim doper with the schizo eyes. Nunzio was an experienced cop used to dealing with tough and dangerous criminals, but Gonzales was different. Scary. Nunzio puzzled over what made Gonzales unique. Most crooks saw cops as the enemy and hated them, but it wasn't personal. They knew cops were going to try to nail them. But Gonzales was a killer who thought anyone who got in his way had to be eliminated. Nunzio shivered; Gonzales looked forward to trouble so he'd have an excuse to kill. He was a psychopath.

"Shit," Officer Tony Perez said—jumping as a dog in the building began to bark shrilly. His hand had hit the microphone button strapped to his left shoulder. Belatedly, he remembered the sensitive microphone and hoped that the sergeant hadn't identified him as the one breaking radio silence.

Perez was twenty-three. He had been in two previous hostage operations which turned out to be false alarms. This was his first real arrest situation. The garbage dumpster in the building's rear parking lot was his assigned cover and the closest post to the van. The first cop in position, he crouched behind the dumpster, swallowed, and checked his weapon for the third time in the darkness.

The sergeant manning the Motorola radio console in the van smiled slightly and wondered if his rookie Tony Perez had slipped on dog shit. Because Hector Gonzales was so dangerous, the sergeant had reconnoitered the area the day before. He had assigned the newest member of the team to the best cover, a garbage dumpster. Tomorrow was the once-a-week pickup, so it was ripe, but with Hector Gonzales occupying the apartment on the opposite side of the building, Perez's supervisor had put him where he was least likely to see action.

Another dog with a deep bark had joined the first. Tony Perez began to sweat, despite the coolness. Again he touched his earplug radio receiver to make sure it hadn't come loose. *It must be about seven minutes since they had left the van. Time for the sergeant to poll them.* Perez didn't want to take his eyes off the building to check his own watch. He cursed silently when a light went on in a second-floor apartment, and wondered if he ought to report it to the sergeant. *No. Only emergencies got reported.* A gray-haired woman in a bathrobe parted the curtains and looked out from the lighted window. Perez moved behind the bin, catching his knee on a sharp corner. *Damn. He had torn his pants and maybe his skin on this lousy rusty metal. He tried to remember when he had gotten his last tetanus shot. Those fucking dogs. They should be illegal. The whole goddamned building is going to wake up any second. And the suspect had assault rifles. That changed the whole game plan if he knew they were out here. A semiautomatic Uzi could fire two hundred rounds a minute. If it was fully automatic, six hundred rounds. And your flak vest wasn't going to stop slugs with the kind of muzzle velocity assault rifles provided. The gun shops not only sold them to any screwball no questions asked, but they let a crazy like Gonzales steal them. Jesus. It doesn't make sense that cops have to go up against assault rifles. What the fuck do they think we are, marines?*

If the woman started yelling, was that an emergency? What the hell was wrong with the sergeant? It had to be seven minutes. Perez became aware of the terrible smell and gagged. An intense itch started in the small of his back. He touched his earplug. *Was the sergeant OK?*

The sergeant in the van stood and stretched, checking his stopwatch. Three minutes had elapsed since the cops had left. ETA for Ward and his partner at the front door of Gonzales's second-floor apartment was seven minutes. At that time the sergeant would poll the team to make sure they were in place. When everyone was ready, he would clear the two men at the front door to begin the raid.

Something was moving inside the dumpster. Scratching, squeaking. The hair on the back of Perez's neck stood. *Jesus! Rats. The fucking bin is full of garbage rats. You have to get painful rabies injections into your stomach if they bite you. Goddamned sergeant. Why wasn't he doing his job?*

The sergeant looked around when his watch hit five minutes, wondering where Nunzio Papa had gone. *Probably outside taking a piss behind one of the bushes. Although, who knew with these sting guys—maybe he just whipped it out and pissed on the van's tire.*

Scott Ward and his partner had slipped in through the unlocked front door and now stood outside Gonzales's apartment. Ward, on the left side of the door, pushed the safety on his machine gun to off. His partner, on the right side of the door, carried a steel battering ram. The partner held up his right hand to Ward and froze. His eyes widened. He lowered the battering ram to the floor and began to unsling his weapon. Then Ward, too, heard the sound. Someone was creeping up the staircase. What the hell? He swung his automatic weapon to cover the stairs and pushed the safety off.

Detective Nunzio Papa peeked over the top of the staircase and found himself looking into the barrels of two Mac Elevens.

"Nunzio, what the fuck are you doing here? You were supposed to stay back in the van with the sergeant until we got the place secure. Now you're gonna be in the goddamned way," Ward whispered.

Another dog began to bark.

"Come on, Ward. Break the fucking door before Gonzales wakes up. If he hears us and beats it, I'll have to be looking over my shoulder for this crazy motherfucker for the rest of my life. Let's take him." Nunzio stood erect and walked up to Ward, who roughly shoved him away from the door and any Uzi slugs that might come suddenly ripping through it.

Tony Perez realized that he had to take a leak badly. He was also considering using the barrel of his assault rifle to scratch the itch in the middle of his back, but he couldn't remember whether the safety was on or off. His fingers indicated that it was on, but he suddenly wasn't sure and didn't dare take his eyes from the building to look. Something must have gotten screwed up. It had to be ten or twelve minutes by now and every fucking dog in the building was barking. Another light had gone on in the corner apartment. He touched his earplug.

The sergeant's watch hit seven minutes. He pushed a switch on the console. "Report Tiger One," he said.

"Alpha One and Two in position," Ward whispered into his mike.

"Ten Four, Alpha," the sergeant said.

"Bravo One in position."

"Ten Four, Bravo."

"Charlie One in position"

"Ten Four, Charlie."

"David One, lights on back here," Tony Perez said.

"Are you in position, David One?"

"Affirmative," said Perez, blushing in the darkness. *So he should have confirmed his position first. Didn't the damn sergeant even want to know lights were on?*

"Tiger One is ready, Alpha. It's your call," the sergeant said.

Ward, frowning, covered his mike. He pointed at Nunzio Papa. "What are we gonna do with this asshole? Should I tell the sergeant?" he whispered to his partner.

In an upstairs apartment, a man yelled at a dog to shut up and a baby began to cry. Ward's partner shrugged.

"OK." Ward gave Nunzio Papa a last glare, then said into the mike on his shoulder, "Alpha One commencing."

"Ten Four, Alpha," the sergeant acknowledged.

"Alpha One now commencing," he broadcast in case any of the team hadn't picked up Ward's weaker signal.

Ward reached out and pounded the apartment door with his right hand. "Police. Open up," he yelled, satisfying the legal requirement. Without waiting for an answer, his partner smashed the flimsy wood apart with the battering ram.

Nunzio rushed into the living room first, ignoring Ward's curses. The other cop dropped the battering ram and picked his weapon up from the floor and followed Ward.

"Police. Freeze, Gonzales!" Nunzio, in front of the two SWAT cops, shouted as he leveled his 357 Magnum at Hector Gonzales, naked and sound asleep on a pull-out couch. A very young teenaged girl, also nude, slept alongside him in the darkened room. Nunzio's shout awakened her. She sat up in the bed screaming hysterically.

The doper instinctively swung the girl in front of him. In the fraction of a second that Nunzio's eyes focused on the girl's young breasts and scant pubic hair, Gonzales's hands closed on the nine-millimeter semiautomatic Colt pistol that he had under the pillow. His first shot thumped into the chest of the SWAT man, narrowly missing Nunzio, who had blocked the cop's vision. The round didn't penetrate the cop's flak vest, but it took him down and sent his weapon clattering to the floor. Scott Ward, unwilling to blow away the girl, held his fire and tried to flank Gonzales, who was now on his feet holding the girl in front of him.

Nunzio, also unwilling to risk shooting the girl, charged forward and grabbed Gonzales's gun hand. The weapon discharged a round into the ceiling, and Nunzio might have pulled off the gutsy move if the sweet young lady hadn't kicked him squarely in the balls. He collapsed to his knees. Gonzales, yelling *"maricón!"* leveled his gun at the helpless detective's head. Ward, the last cop on his feet, did the only thing he could. He released a burst from his machine gun just over the head of Gonzales and the girl.

Gonzales fired wildly in Ward's direction while keeping the girl in front of him as a shield. He yanked her through the bedroom door and the two of them, balls-assed-naked, fled. Both Nunzio and the other cop were on the floor moaning in pain. Ward checked them quickly. Seeing that they weren't seriously wounded, he radioed for an ambulance and alerted the cops outside about the shooting.

Tony Perez, behind his garbage dumpster, heard the shots and Ward's report of two cops down and his request for an ambulance. He couldn't leave Ward alone with two dying cops and a crazy with an Uzi. Perez bolted from his cover and ran to the rear entrance. He knew that the action was on the other side of the building, and that he'd see anyone fleeing down the rear staircase.

Slowly, he opened the back door. No one was moving, although the shooting had really set the dogs off. He took the stairs two at a time, pausing at the second-floor landing. Hearing nothing on the staircase, he charged ahead up to the second floor and ran to the front apartment.

Meanwhile, Scott Ward moved with care to the bedroom door beyond the living room where Gonzales and the girl had been sleeping. Following his training, he first peered through the crack and then dramatically leapt into the room with his weapon ready. To his consternation, he was surrounded by four wide-eyed little kids who were crying at the top of their lungs while the two youngest tugged at the cop's pants leg. Their sleepy-eyed mother, obviously stoned, stared at him from bed, oblivious to what was happening.

Tony Perez, cautiously looking through the splintered front door, was surprised to see Nunzio Papa and the SWAT cop pulling themselves to their feet. "You guys OK?" Perez said.

Scott Ward had detached himself from the children. He searched the remaining room in the apartment and found it empty. As he was about to report this on the radio, Perez rushed in.

"You OK Scott? Where are they?" The rookie had his weapon leveled.

Ward stared at him. "Jesus, Tony, you didn't leave the back entrance uncovered did you?" he said.

Five minutes later, and three miles away, Officer Jorge Mendez turned a corner in his marked cruiser and met a hail of bullets. Shards of glass from the windshield cut his face, and a burning pain in his chest made him realize he was hit. He slammed on the brakes, but lost control of the car. The cruiser crumpled into the wall of a convenience store and its motor stopped. Customers rushed from the store and found Mendez slumped over the wheel, unconscious. One of the onlookers had the presence of mind to grab the car's microphone and tell communications what had happened. Twenty minutes later, Hector Gonzales's voice was recorded on the 911 line telling the operator that he had just shot the pig in the police car because he had missed the little fag spy in the apartment, but not to worry—he'd take care of him in the future.

Pale and sweating, Nunzio confirmed that it was indeed Hector Gonzales's voice on the tape.

One

LEAVING THE BRIEFING, I DROVE FIVE MILES THROUGH DE-
serted streets to my condominium. I passed a number of
darkened office buildings that Silicon City referred to as
downtown. If I had blinked, I would have missed it. Coming
from New York, it was one thing that I had never adjusted
to— the lack of a center in most California cities. Typically,
clusters of office parks made of two-story modern buildings
with huge parking lots sat next to a large hotel with a huge
parking lot that was adjacent to a shopping mall with a huge
parking lot. This inspirational architecture quickly gave
way to single-family homes going on mile after mile until
you came to another such office/hotel/shopping complex.
Sometimes there wasn't a hotel. Occasionally, two-story
apartment developments popped up on the broad avenues
that connected the ever-present noisy freeways. On the
main drags near the freeway exits, ubiquitous fast-food
places and gas stations crowded each other.

It was easy to get lost if you didn't know where you
were going. Lanes, drives, and circles wound you into one
cul-de-sac after another. By the time you escaped back to a
main street, it was impossible to tell north from south. And,
of course, you never saw a pedestrian who might have given
you some idea of where the hell you were. Silicon City had
a half million population, but driving its streets, you could
have been almost anywhere in so-called urban California.

My complex was an upscale one. The units were designed
to look like expensive town houses. There was a swimming

pool, which I had never visited, a sauna, which I had never visited, and a community room, which I had never visited. The first time I had gone to the office to pay my rent, the gal behind the desk had said, "Ah, our new chief of detectives. We're so pleased to have you here. We can certainly use the extra protection." A gray-haired guy in a baseball cap had overheard and buttonholed me on the way out to tell me a long story about how someone had stolen a brand-new tire from his car parked right outside his unit. Since then, I had mailed my rent check in on the first of each month.

I filled the kettle and set the water to boil, then measured enough decaffeinated coffee into the Chemex filter for three cups. In the bedroom, I tossed my clothes onto the unmade bed, then went to take a shower. Nola's silk bikini panties still hung on the shower door. Two long weeks ago she had stayed the night and washed them in the sink. She was gone and they were still damp when I had rumbled out of bed. She hadn't come back to collect them. Suddenly, the same intense longing for her filled me. I took the panties and rubbed my face against the soft material, but her smell was gone. A number of times I had reached for the phone to invite her back to reclaim her delicate underwear, but somehow I never had completed the call. I shook off the ache of loneliness and got into the shower.

In the kitchen, I zapped a frozen sesame bagel in the micro for twenty-three seconds before putting it into the toaster oven. While it was browning, I followed instructions and shook my cardboard container of real orange juice to improve the taste. I knocked off a glass as I poured water from the kettle into the Chemex filter. I flipped the bagel to do the other side, then tossed the used coffee filter into the sink to drain, and filled my cup with coffee. By that time the bagel was ready and I slapped it onto a plate and spread on low-fat margarine. I was efficient.

My kitchen had an open counter area for eating. I sat on one of the two stools facing into the dining area with its small table. Beyond was the living room and the sliding-door exit onto the semiprivate patio and gas barbecue looking onto the park's jogging-and-par course—my therapeutic center for trying to forget Nola. Eight-mile runs, par-course exercise, and twelve-hour days at work. It hadn't worked.

From the corner of the living room, the old man stared at me from the framed photograph hung on the wall above the desk. He was in his New York Police Department assistant chief's uniform. Strong jaw, bull neck, broad shoulders. It was the photo the New York *Daily News* had used with its front-page story explaining that he was the highest-ranking suicide in the department's history, during a scandal stirred up by a rookie plainclothesman. Me. His number-two son. Nola had asked why I hung the picture—it obviously caused me such pain.

The phone rang and I picked up the kitchen extension. Captain Toll, the acting patrol commander, said, "Chief Fra-leigh, I'm sorry to disturb you, but one of our patrol officers, Jorge Mendez, was shot by a suspect escaping from the sting raid."

I felt the half bagel turning to stone in my stomach. "How is he?" I asked, hoping to hear that it was only a flesh wound.

"It doesn't sound good. He took at least one round in the stomach. He's in surgery now at Valley Hospital."

"OK, Captain. I'll be there in a few minutes." I left my coffee and bagel unfinished and headed for the hospital to find out what had happened.

Toll stood among three grim-faced cops in the corridor outside the emergency room. Toll and I shook hands. I nodded at the other men, somewhat surprised to see the SWAT lieutenant there in his fatigues. Mendez hadn't been one of his men, and the raids were still under way. "Any change in his condition?" I asked.

"No word since I spoke to you on the phone, Chief." Toll went on to describe the botched capture of Hector Gonzales and I felt my face redden with anger. The SWAT lieutenant looking down at his spit-shined black combat boots avoided my eyes.

"Here comes the doctor who's been briefing us." Toll nodded toward a middle-aged doc in a white coat approaching us with a deep frown.

Toll introduced me. The doctor shook my hand. He took off his eyeglasses and began absent-mindedly cleaning them with a handkerchief. "He's young and healthy and they got him here quickly, thank heavens." The doctor was a mumbler, and I strained to catch his words. "Unfortunately, the round entered through his side. Through the flap in his protective vest. The vest stopped two other rounds. He's got some blunt trauma from them on his chest, but that's not serious. However, the bullet that went through tore up his insides. Severed an artery. He's lost a lot of blood. We've already given him sixteen units. The hospital has put out a call for volunteers." His voice trailed off.

I felt like grabbing him by the shoulders and shaking him and saying, goddamn it. Tell us if he's going to make it or not. Before I could speak he was mumbling again. "The trauma team did an excellent job at intake and the surgeons are experienced. They're doing the best they can. I'll keep you posted."

"Doctor?" I tried to form the question.

He sighed. "It's fifty-fifty. He's got one foot on the banana peel." He walked back toward the elevators.

I couldn't stop my eyes from tearing. Mendez was twenty-four. A cop for all of three years. All he had done was drive his patrol car. He'd had no chance at all and the bad luck that one round had found its way through his vest.

"His wife's here, Chief. We told her about the sting and what happened with Gonzales on the raid. She's in the little private waiting room." Toll pointed down the hallway.

They were all looking at me. I took a deep breath. "OK, I'll go talk to her."

"She's pretty upset now. You might want to wait awhile, Chief," Toll said.

"I'd rather talk to her now so I can take a look at the scene. I'll come right back. We probably have a long wait here before we find out how Mendez is going to be."

Catherine Mendez looked to be all of sixteen, probably very pretty, but now her face was swollen, her eyes red from crying. I was startled to see her bulging stomach. She must have been seven or eight months pregnant. Damn it all.

"Cathy, this is Chief Fraleigh."

I was unprepared for the contemptuous look she gave Toll. When she turned to me, she was furious. Her brown eyes were filled with hatred.

"Mrs. Mendez, I'm so sorry." I reached out my hand.

She didn't take it. "You're responsible. All he wanted to do was drive a beat car. Help people. But you have to get fancy with your stings and raids. That's why he was shot. Because of you." She glared at me.

I stared at her. I shivered. Her anger left me totally drained, speechless. She began sobbing. Her sister was ten years older and heavy. Without looking at me, she took Cathy Mendez's arm and led her to the couch against the wall. I watched. Cathy's body shook as she wailed, and I worried about the baby. "She's upset now, Chief. She'll come around. The chaplain is on the way." Toll touched my elbow, gently steering me out of the room, but her words echoed in my ears and my earlier doubts about the risks of sting operations haunted me.

Two

AT ELEVEN O'CLOCK IN THE MORNING THE DOCTOR IN-
formed us that Jorge Mendez had come through surgery
well and his vital signs had stabilized. He was moved from
the intensive care unit into a private room with a twenty-
four-hour nurse and police guard. He would pull through.
His wife was with him. I went back to headquarters.

Late in the afternoon, my aides, detectives Paul English
and the Block, sauntered into my office. "Well?" I said,
trying to hide how pissed I was. They were the architects
of the sting operation.

"Chief, we came to discuss our new sting operation with
you," Paul English said.

"Really? Have you seen the paper?" I held up the afternoon
edition of the *Silicon City News*. The headline read: COP
SHOT. NAKED COUPLE ESCAPES HEAVILY ARMED POLICE. I
threw the paper on my desk. "I particularly like their vivid
description of the keystone cops firing machine guns at four
toddlers . . . Come in, Toll."

Captain Herbert Toll was, as usual, immaculate in uniform. Slim, and lantern-jawed, he could have been a recruitment poster. In fact, he had been during his patrolman days.
Since then he had added spectacles which for some reason
presented people with a magnified view of his eyes. He
saluted me as he always did. I acknowledged by waving
him to a chair.

"Morning, Captain," Paul English and the Block said
pleasantly enough.

19

Toll gave them just the slightest nod. Ordinarily, both of them would have jumped to attention and mockingly joined in his salute. Toll wore a hearing aid as a result of his days as an instructor on the police firing range. The constant repetitive noise had caused a loss of hearing. Paul and the Block had thought it amus- ing to modify their voices from overly loud to almost lip synchronization during their meetings with Toll. They had him constantly fiddling with his earpiece until someone leaked the joke to him. So not only was there the standard interdepartmental rivalry between the detectives and Toll, but he didn't appreciate their wise-ass attitude. All the more so since they were known as my boys.

I had to admit they were the police odd couple. The Block, so named because at five eight and two hundred eighty-five pounds he resembled a block of concrete, had no neck, and a bullet head covered by rapidly vanishing curly fuzz. In contrast, Paul English was a Stanford grad who never let us forget it. Six feet tall, he was slim and hand-some, occasionally being mistaken for Robert Redford. Off duty, he was rarely without a beautiful woman at his side.

I had chewed their asses for baiting Toll, who saw only their insubordination. We had been detective partners for years, going through some tough times together. When they put their minds to it, they were two of the best cops I had seen, but none of us had really adjusted to my rise from sergeant to acting police chief in less than two years. I turned back to my so-called aides. "You have the nerve to talk of a new sting?" I said.

"Chief," said the Block, "these things happen. What the hell, the other arrests went off OK. We got forty felons in custody who ain't gonna see daylight for a while."

"That's great, Block," I said. "City Hall is in a panic about all this shoot-out publicity, but I'll tell them they should be glad we didn't machine-gun-up any other neighborhoods and let naked maniacs and their fourteen-year-old girlfriends make fools of us there, too. And I'll tell Mendez's wife to forget about the shooting. It's just something that happens once in a while."

"Hey, don't forget I got shot in the chest a few years ago," the Block growled at me.

"Don't brag about it," I said.

Toll's face was flushed. "Chief, with all due respect, let me interrupt. That's exactly why I'm here. Detective Nunzio Papa violated procedure. Not only is the entire department embarrassed because he disrupted a roundup, but he could have gotten SWAT personnel killed along with himself. Papa wasn't even wearing a protective vest. And one of my patrol officers was ambushed because of him. It's my recommendation that Detective Papa be suspended for ten days and put back in uniform. He's obviously too unstable for detective work."

"That would kill morale for our dicks. Nunzio Papa is the best we got on the sting. The crooks can't wait to sell him loot. And to tell you the truth, if I thought a crazy asshole like Hector Gonzales would be after me, I woulda wanted to make sure those SWAT youngsters did it right myself," the Block said.

Toll almost exploded out of his chair. Not only had his beloved SWAT warriors been interfered with yesterday, they were being put down today. "Chief, people must be held accountable. The uniformed men are, and when they see detectives escape discipline, it hurts morale."

I leaned back and swiveled toward Paul English who said, "You're right, Captain." Paul was a smoothie. Toll blinked. He hadn't expected agreement.

"Yeah," the Block cut in, "don't forget that the SWAT unit was warned about how dangerous Hector Gonzales was, but they let him and a girl in their birthday suits climb down the back fire escape, wire an ignition, and get away. Someone's ass got to be held responsible for that."

"Officer Tony Perez is new to the unit. He made an honest mistake leaving his post. That will be remedied by training. I'm not going to penalize a man trying to do his job. It never would have happened if Papa hadn't barged into the apartment," Toll said.

I listened Solomon-like to the discussion. Paul English stroked his chin. "That's true, Captain Toll. It would probably destroy Officer Perez if he's disciplined. Training is a positive response."

"Bullshit. The asshole left his post. We're lucky the poor cop on patrol wasn't blown away," the Block said.

Toll's glasses were in danger of fogging up. I had seen Paul and the Block use their Mutt-and-Jeff act before, but this was the first time on a police captain. "Another thing," the Block continued, "Scott Ward is no rookie and he began the operation knowing that Detective Papa was going in with him. And what about the sergeant putting a new man alone in a tough spot?"

"That's ridiculous. You're just like all detectives trying to protect each other," Toll said.

"Nah. That ain't true, Captain," the Block said. "I'm agreeing with you. We gotta hold people accountable, but it's gotta be fair. If a lowly detective is transferred, then you should dump the SWAT lieutenant and sergeant for not taking better care of that poor rookie and for letting Papa leave the van too early. But, it will finish Nunzio Papa. The poor guy's a nervous wreck with Gonzales on the loose. You know, slapping Nunzio on the balls now . . ."

Toll's face was still flushed. His jaw set. "Sir," he said to me, "I don't agree with these men, but I think it imperative that Detective Papa's dangerous irresponsibility be punished. I would be willing to consider action against the SWAT supervisors."

Ah! The Block and English hadn't counted on this. They had agreed on Detective Papa's discipline only because they were sure Toll would back down rather than discipline his own people. "That's very flexible of you, Captain. Don't you agree, men?" I smiled at Paul and the Block.

"Yes. It's more than fair of you, Captain." Paul's smile wasn't quite as full as it had been. "You did make two excellent points earlier. First, that morale in the department has to be considered. Second, that remedial training is necessary all around. Morale in both the detective and patrol bureaus is suffering now because a dope dealer like Hector Gonzales threatened Detective Papa and shot an officer in a patrol car. They want a show of support by management. If the department's reaction is to transfer Papa and the SWAT supervisors, we'll get a real backlash. Maybe your suggestion of remedial training is the best way to go after all."

Watching Toll's face I could see that Paul's participation on the Stanford debating team hadn't been a total waste. The Block spoke while Toll was wrestling with Paul's argument. "Another thing. Nunzio Papa is a minority. The Hispanic community ain't gonna like one of its hero cops being dumped on by management."

"He's Italian, not Hispanic," Toll said in disgust.

"Yeah. I guess you're right, but both his names end in vowels, and a lot of people think he's Hispanic. Then if you only give Perez retraining, they'll figure you let an Italian go, and made an example of the Hispanic."

Toll glared at the Block. "Papa is Hisp . . . I mean, Perez is the Hispanic and Papa is the Italian. Why would anyone think Pap . . . I mean, Perez, is Italian?"

"Well, you know, his first name is Tony."

Toll rolled his eyes at me and started reaching up to scratch his head before he remembered that he didn't want fingerprints on his hat's gleaming visor. "I don't know, Chief. What about Captain Gerhart? He won't lose a chance to exploit this in the press if no one is disciplined."

"Fuck Gerhart. The sting detectives ain't his command. They report directly to the chief's office."

"I know that." Toll had lost all patience with the Block. "I'm thinking of Gerhart's ambition. He'll use anything. And Chief Fraleigh's permanent appointment is up for review next month. This sting and the publicity could hurt."

"I'll take care of that," I said, with a confidence that I didn't feel. Toll had misstated the facts. My appointment was as acting chief. The Board of Supervisors was considering applications for the permanent position, mine included. Captain Fritz Gerhart was well-connected politically and my principal rival for the job.

"Chief, of course, I'll support whatever you decide, but it's important that I know now so that I can spread the news. The grapevine is killing us, and some of the most negative stories are coming from Gerhart's people."

"Well, let me see if I've understood all of you. You've agreed that there were mistakes by both the sting detective and the SWAT unit. And that Detective Papa and Officer Perez are good men, of value to the department. We could destroy that value with negative discipline as well as hurt morale in general, so your recommendation is for remedial training and better coordination on future operations. I can live with that, but what can I say to city hall and the press?" I said.

"The quality of mercy is not strain'd," Paul said, while the Block scratched his privates.

Toll looked like he was about to say that my summation of his views stretched things, but instead he shrugged. "Your office will handle the public statement, Chief?"

"Yes. Thank you, Captain."

As soon as Toll had whipped his salute and departed, Paul and the Block jumped to their feet and saluted. "Thank you, Chief, sir. We'll be off now to communicate your mercy to the subjects," Paul said.

"Like hell you will. Plant your asses. I went along with your scam on Toll, but I want you to know I don't like it.

Furthermore, I can't think of a worse time to start a new sting."

Paul opened his folder. "Chief, look at these stats. Burglary in the neighborhood where we did the sting is down sixteen percent. Larceny is down twenty-four percent. Remember, that's a minority community, the poorest area in the city. And here's why crime is down. Of the forty people in custody, thirty will be prosecuted as career criminals because they sold us stuff from so many burglaries. They'll do ten years. And no trials. The D.A. loves it. We have them on videotape bragging about how they stole the goods. They don't even bother to plead *not guilty*. We know from the stings that they're committing a lot of crime and we're not catching them otherwise."

"How can crime be down if we just nailed them this morning?"

"Don't forget this is the second sting we did. I'm giving you the results of the first one. We used a furniture shop then. This time an electronics repair store. Also, on each of the stings we hit pay dirt on killings, not just burglaries. In both operations we bought guns that had been used in fatal robberies. We didn't even have suspects until we traced those guns, but we caught two murderers."

It was funny. They were right. Stings made a lot more sense than having cops sit around waiting to catch crooks after they had ripped someone off. Our clearance rates were about 2 percent for residential burglaries. This was proactive police work. We caught thieves who would continue to work until we got lucky and someone called 911 after spotting them break in, or a patrol car made a lucky car stop and found a backseat loaded with TVs, firearms, and VCRs. As a cop, I had always complained about brass without balls. Commanders who were more worried about media criticism than catching criminals. Since I'd been named acting police chief though, I found myself sounding more and more like the bosses I had despised.

"The crooks must be getting wise to your operations by this time," I said.

"They are. That's why we picked a bar and grill for the new sting," Paul said.

"What? As if these things aren't dangerous enough we're going to run a bar? Suppose there are fights, holdups? And cops would be drinking on duty."

"We can protect against those things. We want you to come out and see the place in a couple of weeks."

"I don't know, Paul. A bar . . ."

"It's a natural," the Block said. "People in bars are always buying stuff that 'fell off a truck.' And the dirtbags will never suspect the bartender and people working there are cops."

"The other thing to consider, Fraleigh, is that we will run it for about six months. The interview process for chief and your appointment will be long past before we do the raid," Paul said.

I felt my enthusiasm growing. A bar. It was a bold idea. A first in law enforcement. I could see us writing up the results for an article in *Police Chief* magazine. There were many risks, but I didn't want to be a do-nothing chief, cowed by politicians. Why take the job if I wasn't going to take some chances? It wasn't like the old days where I literally risked my life on the street, but I felt a similar surge of adrenaline. Then I thought of Catherine Mendez's look of hatred, and shivered.

"Speaking of the famous raid, Paul, what are you doing to catch Gonzales?" I said.

"We have a western states APB on him and are doing local broadcasts every two hours. And, in your heart, you know the Block is right. Gonzales is a killer. He would have shot an officer sooner or later. The beauty of the stings is that we're apprehending people like him before they hurt someone."

"What else are we doing to nail him?"

"Believe me, Chief, all the cops out there are pressuring their contacts for information. We'll come up with him."

"Yeah, and I hope this time we'll hold on to him. Make sure the detectives stay the hell away. When are you planning to open this new sting?" I said.

Paul hesitated and smiled as they were edging out the door. "Actually, we served a few beers this morning, Chief."

Three

IT WAS TWO WEEKS LATER WHEN I RECEIVED AN URGENT request from Paul English and the Block to visit the bar sting. Nunzio Papa was assigned to drive me there. Hector Gonzales was still at large and I tried not to look at the twitch Nunzio had developed under his right eye. Police humor had asserted itself once it became clear that Jorge Mendez was recovering. And Nunzio had started finding phone messages like: "To: Nunzio. Message: Please return the jockey shorts I left in the room. I know they're too big for you. From: Your friend Hector G." And the SWAT team was now known as the TWAT team.

We parked, and with continuous shifty-eyed glances along the way to see if we were being observed, Detective Papa led me through a mixed area of working-class residences and light commercial development. We passed an auto body repair shop and moved into an alley. A homeless person sprawled against the side of the building. He had pissed in his pants and stank from the cheap red wine in the half-empty bottle he clutched to his chest. His bleary red eyes closed on me in the belligerently vague way common to the species. A month or so ago I would have categorized him as a bum. Now that I was acting police chief, I had purged myself of that word and used the term *homeless*, never quite achieving the right tone of reverence reached by the local politicians. Since Detective Papa had ignored the homeless one, I did the same.

Finally, we came to heavy iron doors and Papa fumbled with his keys while unlocking two dead-bolt locks. Before we went through the heavy swinging doors, he pointed and said, "Notice the posts." There were six thick iron posts sunk into the ground along the side of the building. "They tried to break in three times already. We got good locks and alarms, but we put the iron posts three feet from the walls so the bastards can't crash a truck through the wall and clean us out when the place is closed and none of us is here."

He led me through the beery-smelling cellar and up the stairs to one of the bar's back rooms. The Block, sitting on a bench, made the small room seem even smaller. He handed a telephone message to Nunzio. Looking over his shoulder I read, "To: Nunzio. Message: Let's do lunch. From: Your friend, Hector G."

Nunzio reddened and his normally bulging eyes grew even bigger. "Block, you . . . you. . ." he stuttered, then glancing at me, managed to control himself, slumping into a chair, his eyes fixed on the floor.

Next to the grinning Block sat Paul English. They were looking into the next room through a one-way glass mirror. Luther Banks, a giant black cop, sat in the corner working a videotape recorder with a monitor screen and earplugs so that he could be sure the picture and sound from the next room were being recorded. "Chief." He nodded his puffed-out Afro at me. His kinky black beard was thick, and he weighed almost as much as the Block, although he was eight inches taller.

I nodded back and took off my sunglasses.

"That's a nifty disguise you got there, Chief," the Block said. I had discarded my jacket and tie at the office and put on dark glasses. The Block, paying no attention to my disapproving look, continued. "How about a cold one? We only serve the best here, you know. It's Michelob on tap." He held up a nearly full frosted pitcher. I noticed that his glass was almost empty. It was a quarter to eleven in the morning.

I shook my head no. "The chief won't drink this early in front of the men, Block," Paul English said. "After all, he has to live up to his rank."

Nunzio and Luther watched curiously to see if I was going to tolerate the insubordination. I had been tolerating it ever since I had the misfortune to be made their sergeant a few years earlier.

"What's so important that you guys want me to play cops and robbers with you?" I asked.

"Look at that dirtbag." The Block, ignoring my question, pointed toward the one-way mirror. A skinny Caucasian hype was showing a Panasonic VCR to a heavy, round-shouldered man with a beard and a single long pigtail hanging down his back. I recognized Sergeant Manny Herrera, head bartender, and first-line supervisor of the sting. He shook his head and frowned at the thief who was assuring him that the VCR was the top of the line and retailed for almost a grand.

Herrera plugged in the VCR and turned it on, but nothing happened. "It don't work. Did you drop it on the way out of the guy's house or something?" he said.

"No man. I swear I tried it before I lifted it from the place. It worked. You said one third on these. I ought to get three hundred at least."

"Hey mother, give me a break. I ain't into charity. This thing's broke. Look at it. I got to get it repaired and risk someone shooting their mouth off to the cops," Herrera said.

The Block was chuckling. "This little asshole has brought in six of these things in two days. We were running out of buy money so we rigged up some dummy outlets in the room. Naturally, nothing's going to work. Otherwise we'd have to follow the jerk and have a patrol unit happen to turn the corner when he was walking out with someone's television. He's just smart enough to get suspicious if we do that and blow the sting, so until you loosen up and give us the dough we need, we got to improvise." He laughed again. "Still, I love to swindle these punks."

"Twenty-five bucks and that's only because we did so much business together," Sergeant Herrera said to the crook.

I stared at the hype through the glass. "Why are we allowing this creep to operate if he's doing that many burglaries?"

Paul English said, "His name is Charley Thompson, and he's introduced six other crooks to us, including the interesting one who's coming in any minute. The one we wanted you to see. Thompson really got the word around. He's actually produced even more than any of our scouts, with the exception of Luther. But, you're right, he's a one-man crime wave. We talked with his parole officer, Jack Murphy—he's doing us a favor and waiving him on a technicality."

"Which technicality?" I said.

"Jack is going to stop in for a sandwich tomorrow night and just happen to spot Charley in the bar and violate him for being in a licensed premise. It will take him off the street for a few months. We don't want to do it sooner because we need more info from him."

We watched Thompson grudgingly accept the twenty-five bucks. He reached down to his ankle and drew out a thirty-eight-caliber revolver. My heart skipped a beat and I noticed an almost imperceptible stiffening of Sergeant Herrera's back. Luther Banks reached into the corner and picked up a short-barreled Remington shotgun. He pumped a round into the chamber and moved to the door leading to the next room, quietly slipping the dead-bolt lock. His left hand gripped the doorknob. He was on the balls of his feet ready to go in. The cut-down shotgun looked like a child's toy in his huge right paw. The Block was right behind him, his nine-millimeter semiautomatic in his right hand. He pushed the safety off. Luther kept his hand on the doorknob ready to jerk the door open.

This was what I hated about stings. The potential for robbery and violence. We deliberately attracted professional criminals who knew there was dough around. Our cop "fences" were vulnerable as hell.

Thompson wiped his running nose. "We know he's burning five C's a week of Colombian coke," the Block whispered, even though the room was soundproofed.

"Manny," Thompson said as he hefted the gun in his right hand, "I'll blast you any mother you want for five bills. Anyone, even a fucking cop. What do you say?"

"I'll let you know if anyone asks around about a hit. What kind of piece is that, man? I might be able to use it."

We held our breath watching the junkie decide what he was going to do. He fondled the gun, his finger caressing the trigger. You could almost hear the wheels turning in his spaced-out head. He knew he could blow Herrera away without anyone in the noisy bar even hearing the shots, and he had just seen Herrera peel off twenty-five bucks from the thick roll that he always displayed to keep the crooks motivated.

Finally, the addict handed the gun to Herrera. Luther quietly relocked the dead bolt and I began to breathe normally again. "I ripped it off from a doctor's house. The jerk-off had guns all over the place and one of those NRA signs, you know, THIS HOUSE PROTECTED BY COLT AND REMINGTON. I wasn't even going to do the place until I saw it. We cleaned out his whole collection—three shotguns, an AK forty-seven and six pistols. Since then, I got word he's got a coin collection worth plenty in a big safe in his TV room. It was locked, but me and my brother's going back to make him open it for us, then off him," he said, as casually as if he were discussing the weather.

As expressionless as ever, Luther Banks cleared the shotgun while the Block pushed the safety on his weapon and holstered it. Sergeant Herrera opened the cylinder, emptied the gun, and squeezed the trigger rapidly, checking to make sure the firing pin was clearing the steel plate that separated it from rounds in the chamber until the trigger was pulled. He was so close that I could see that the gun was operative. "When you figure you're going to do the doc? Maybe I can move the coins."

"My brother's getting his bail lowered tomorrow. I figure I can get him out Sunday morning, then we'll go look the place over. The sawbones should be home on Sunday."

On our side of the mirror, Paul spoke. "That's five days. Fortunately, Manny got it out of him. We'll get his parole revoked tomorrow night while his brother is still in custody. We can trace the serial number on the gun and if the doctor reported it stolen, we can warn him and try to find a way to keep Thompson's brother in jail indefinitely."

In the next room, Sergeant Herrera paid seventy-five dollars for the stolen handgun that retailed at over two hundred. It was a little eerie in our soundproofed chamber watching the events taking place and knowing the players had no idea that we were there. Except for Herrera. My guess was that he had been thinking about us when the hype pulled the handgun. On the other hand, he had been a cop long enough to know that as close as we were, it wouldn't have made that much difference for him if the hype had pulled the trigger a few times.

There was no more banter now. Our attention was riveted on Sergeant Herrera. He turned, listening to a soft knock on the street door. When it was repeated twice, he moved to the door and looked out the peephole then unlocked the door. "Come in," he said. We heard some mumbling, but whoever was outside didn't seem to want to come in. After listening for a minute Sergeant Herrera said, "OK, OK." He turned to the hype. "Charley, do me a favor—go on out through the bar entrance, all right?"

Thompson shrugged, wiped his nose once more, and walked out to the bar. Sergeant Herrera turned again to the outer door. A slightly built, pale, balding man in a badly wrinkled seersucker suit came in and slowly eyeballed the tiny room. He scowled at the battered couch and the coffee table overflowing with filled ashtrays and empty beer cans. Turning, he walked to the exit just used by Charley Thompson and cracked the door open a bit, peering out into the bar area. Apparently reassured, he closed and locked the door and walked slowly toward us. He tried the locked door to our room.

"Man, you could have come in. Charley is all right," the sergeant said.

"Yeah, sure he is. That nothing would sell his mother for a line of coke or a deal with the D.A. What's behind the door?" He was only about two feet away, so close that I could see a grease spot on his tie and a shaving cut on his chin. We stayed very still, listening to him jiggle the door handle.

I tried to place him. He wasn't a standard crook type. We didn't see many suits and ties in these kinds of operations. Yet, he clearly was a sleazebag, an angle-worker with the same wise-guy attitude you'd see in the exercise yard at The Q—San Quentin Prison. I had a nagging feeling that I knew him.

"Just a storeroom. Bunch of bar crap mostly. I don't let hot stuff pile up here." Sergeant Herrera cooly pointed to the VCR, the handgun, a stereo set, two television sets, an Uzi, and a shotgun stacked in the corner. "I picked up that stuff this morning. It goes out with me as soon as we finish. I don't let nothing stack up." He wandered over to the pile of merchandise, trying to get the guy away from our door. "Charley brought in this VCR and gun." He held up the weapon.

The visitor walked over to inspect the gun, and we relaxed a little.

"You make this sweetie yet, Chief?" the Block whispered, a sound reminiscent of a truck downshifting gears.

"Let me guess. He's one of Colonel North's Contras. What the hell is going on? I don't have all day."

Paul English spoke to Luther. "We tried through the years to get him to take courses in interpersonal relations with employees, but obviously we weren't successful." Luther showed no sign of having heard Paul. He stared at the recording equipment, careful not to look in my direction. Chiefs were not openly mocked. I turned back to the one-way mirror knowing full well that the Block and English would fill me in on the stranger when the whim moved them and not before. Clearly, this was the mysterious meet for which I had been so urgently summoned.

"I know your friend Charley. Don't bother to tell me what a stand-up guy he is," the balding man said.

"It all depends who he's fucking with." Herrera spoke so softly and ominously that I almost believed he'd blow Thompson away without hesitation. So did the other guy. He started to say something, but after a glance at the smoldering Latin facing him, he shrugged.

The sergeant deserved an Oscar. His threat removed the other man's reluctance to talk. "I got a deal that might interest you. But first I got to know whether you can handle it." He stared at Herrera, who just looked back at him. The man cleared his throat. "Do you know who I am?"

"You're a defense lawyer, right?"

And suddenly I knew who he was and why the cops wanted me as a witness to this meeting.

Four

"FIRST OF ALL, CALL ME DICK BARRY."

We had a real criminal genius here. His name was Richard Bartlow, and like most crooks, when he needed an alias, he couldn't quite get away from his given name and initials. What made him infinitely more interesting was that his brother was a city supervisor on the ad hoc committee which would decide whether or not I would be appointed permanently as chief of police. The cops had gotten me here because he was big game and highly sensitive politically.

"We don't give a shit about names, man. We all got ten or twelve ourselves." Herrera laughed, and Attorney Bartlow fidgeted.

"Yeah. But you have to be careful. Not all the cops are in doughnut shops, you know, and they're not all as stupid as they look."

I was sure Herrera fully agreed with that statement, but he dismissed it with a wave of his hand. "We're careful. I been doing this a long time and I ain't been inside, you know."

"Except once. Four years ago, right, Bolero?"

Manny Herrera didn't have to act now. In the back room we all stared at Bartlow just as hard as Herrera did. As a precaution, all of the cops working on the sting were given false identities and fictitious criminal records which were matched with driver licenses and automobile registrations. This information was entered into the State of California's computerized criminal identification system, which was accessible only to cops.

Herrera was on his feet, angry. "What are you talking about, motherfucker?"

"Relax," Bartlow soothed him, "I just wanted to show you that I can be valuable to you. I've been practicing criminal law here for twelve years. I have good contacts in the police department and I don't care if you like boys or gorillas. I think we can make some big bucks together."

Detective Paul English had been inventive in giving Herrera his "criminal history." He had created a character who had only one conviction—for sodomizing young boys taking music lessons in the school where he had been custodian. Paul's black humor had resulted in Herrera's fictitious file reporting that the subject's favorite time of attack had been during the playing of recordings of Ravel's "Bolero," thus, the moniker. Paul had also added arrests for sale of stolen property, suspected homicide, and assault by firearm, which explained Bartlow's fear. Herrera had been pissed at Paul over the sodomy stuff, but by the time he had seen his "record," there wasn't anything he could do about it, and the rest of the sting cops thought it hilarious and addressed him as Bolero.

I had the familiar painful knotting in my stomach listening to the crooked lawyer. His "contacts" in the police department . . . Only a cop could have run the computer criminal-records check which Bartlow was quoting from.

"Man, if one word of that reaches any of these guys around here . . ." Herrera had picked up the gun he had just bought from Thompson and he was so menacing, I found myself hoping he hadn't reloaded. He was just acting, but I had known cops to get carried away with their roles.

Bartlow was sweating. He extended both palms outward. "Relax, relax. You know everything is confidential with an attorney. I just wanted to establish a good business relationship."

"Well, you ain't doing shit so far."

"Look, there could be a lot of money in this. You wouldn't have to screw around with this petty stuff, televisions, VCRs. I'm talking about millions."

"I don't fuck with any big dope deals. Too many rats and narcs."

"I couldn't agree more." Bartlow wiped his forehead with a handkerchief. "You should have seen some of the cases I handled on dope. You couldn't trust anyone. Even the cops and judges who took the dough would burn you. That's what I meant about Thompson. My question is—can you handle negotiable securities?"

"I can handle anything," Herrera said. "But you got to show me what you got and give me time to set up."

"I don't know." Bartlow sat back and gave Herrera the hard eye. "I know you're not a cop or a snitch, but this is big stuff and I don't want to spend my declining years in Soledad."

The sergeant knew his business. He didn't say anything. Just sat there looking at Bartlow. Not too anxious. At least four minutes went by as we watched, hoping Bartlow would bite. "Man, I got other things to do. You decide you got something to get rid of, come back when you're ready. Maybe we can do business." Herrera stood.

Bartlow got up. "You know, I think we may do some business. I'm going to leave this one bond with you. It's the kind of negotiable instrument I can get in big numbers. And I mean big in millions."

Herrera was cool. Even though he was as intrigued as we were, he bluffed Bartlow. "Man, if it's that big, don't even leave it. I don't want no part of Soledad either, and that kind of stuff is so hot no one touches it."

Bartlow sat down. "I'm glad you said that. If you hadn't, believe me, I'd be out of here. I need to know I'm dealing with someone who's careful. But, the beauty of these babies," he fingered the piece of paper in his hands, "is that they won't be hot for many years and maybe not at all. And by that time, if we do it right, it won't matter."

"Yeah? And how you going to work that miracle, Mr. Attorney?"

"You'll know all in good time if we do business. In the meantime, you can check out this bond with your sources. Out of state would be best, but Los Angeles or San Diego are far enough away."

"Last year some guys come to me with a ton of credit cards, money market checks, and some stock and bond certificates. I got some cousins and a couple of contacts in New York who I used," Herrera said, neglecting to mention that the contact was his cousin, a detective first grade on the New York Police Department's special frauds squad, and that the guys who had come to him were now in the joint.

"Great! Let them look at this." He handed Herrera a piece of legal-size paper. "I'll get back to you in two weeks." Bartlow had been unable to hide his excitement when Herrera had talked of his New York contacts.

As soon as Bartlow left, we went into the next room and examined the document, being careful not to touch it. Luther Banks, using tweezers, carefully put the document into an evidence bag and marked it. Although we had Bartlow loud and clear on videotape, we would also want his fingerprints on the paper so he couldn't later claim that he had handed over something different. In addition, we would try to identify any other prints on the paper.

Now we needed some expert advice on just what we had, and who owned it. One of the major challenges of a sting operation was finding the rightful owner of stolen property. Without an owner, we couldn't prove the goods were stolen and the case would go out the window no matter how incriminating the conversation on video.

"It's a bearer bond, face value five thousand dollars, payable without any questions," Paul English announced.

"The asshole's prints got to be all over it the way he handled it," the Block said. "We got him cold."

"Only if we can find the owner and prove that it was stolen," Paul said.

"Even then," Manny Herrera interrupted, "he didn't ask for any money. And the D.A. wants a number of buys before he's willing to prosecute, especially against one of his brother lawyers."

Paul English said, "He left a five-thousand-dollar bond like it was nothing. Where could he be getting them and why is he so sure there won't be heat?"

"Beats the shit out of me," the Block said, "but it's gonna be a great pleasure to slap the cuffs on that little shyster."

"Chief, you got a question?" Herrera said.

I thought out loud. "No offense Sarge, but you were set up to look like a two-bit fence. If this is half as big and as safe as Bartlow says, why would he be coming to someone like Bolero?"

Five

"YOU'RE PRETTY LAID BACK FOR A GUY ABOUT TO BE HIRED or fired, Fraleigh," the Block said.

He and Paul English had snuck me out the back way and we were now riding toward headquarters.

"He's not laid back. He doesn't want the job and is looking for an excuse to evade the interview," Paul said.

"Yeah. That's the Peter Principle, ain't it?"

"No, Block." Paul was patient. "Although the Peter Principle does apply to the chief. It says that people rise to the level of their incompetence in organizations."

"His level of incompetence was sergeant. Remember how much trouble he caused us when he was our team sergeant in the Dick Bureau? What's the big deal about him being police chief? It's not like he has to do anything." The Block's growl was bad enough on the ears ordinarily, but now he was behind me in the backseat, and my head was splitting.

"You guys are about as funny as an AIDS diagnosis," I said. "Does it ever occur to you that we might discuss police work, like maybe closing down this sting you talked me into, before someone gets killed?"

"Jesus. He does want to be chief. At least he's acting like one. As soon as lawyers and politicians catch their tits in the wringer, he wants to close the sting."

"The Block has a point, Fraleigh," Paul said. "The cops will spread the word that you backed down once you saw Bartlow's brother."

I turned and looked at Paul as he violated the California Motor Vehicle Code by brazenly steering through a group of pedestrians in the crosswalk. He had a smug smile, and when I looked at the Block in the backseat, he was smirking. They had set me up.

"So that's why you wanted me to see the meeting. You figured I couldn't back out of this crummy job without people thinking I had been scared out by the politicians. And if I get the job and discontinue the sting, the cops will figure it was the price I paid for the appointment. But what you didn't know was that they're not going to appoint me even if I groveled before them."

"That's not true, Fraleigh, and you know it," Paul said. "You have three out of the five votes unless you deliberately say something crazy."

"You mean something like, I'm going to keep you two on the payroll?"

Paul ignored me. "Remember another thing, Fraleigh. If it's not you, it will be one of the good old boys like Fritz Gerhart."

"Gerhart," the Block shouted, and I held my head. "He and Petrie were the two captains that crook Middleston made you hire when he was mayor. If the fucking D.A. wasn't in with them, our great 'mayor' would have been charged with being an accomplice in murdering Louis and Raoul. And if Gerhart gets in as chief, the first thing he'll do is fuck up the case so that Middleston will beat everything."

Paul and the Block were more right than I cared to admit. Gerhart was a snake. Recently, he had leaked an investigation of two crack-dealing cops to the media, knowing that publicity about cops selling dope didn't help my candidacy. The subsequent news story had alerted the cops just as they were about to sell to an informant whom we had wired. The dirty cops pulled back and were still on the force, lying low until the heat was off. Gerhart had also leaked an undercover operation just as it was about to take out a ring of industrial burglars. They too had been forewarned by the publicity, and the undercover operation failed. I knew what he had done, but couldn't prove it. It was hard even for a permanently appointed chief to get cops to risk investigating a top commander. It was impossible for an acting chief. I might be gone next week, but, as a captain, Gerhart had civil service tenure. He'd be around to pay back any cops who had investigated him, and I wouldn't be here to protect them.

It wasn't pleasant to think of someone like him becoming police chief, but it didn't bother me that much because I wouldn't be here. The Block's point was more important. We had lost two good friends and I couldn't sit by and watch Gerhart tamper with the evidence against those responsible. Of course, Gerhart himself hadn't been criminally involved, but he had been tight with Mayor Middleston. The mayor had been so dominant in local politics that the D.A. had never prosecuted him, even though there was good evidence that he had been involved in the killings. We had been forced to work with the FBI to get him charged, and even then, all we could get him for was selling computer secrets to an Iron Curtain country. The mayor's closest political ally was Duane Bartlow, who would do his best to get the board to appoint Gerhart as chief. Part of the deal would be that the new chief would pressure cops to change their testimony in the case against the mayor. Who knew? Maybe some of the evidence would disappear from storage. One way or another the case would go down the drain if Gerhart was appointed chief.

Before we'd left the bar I'd told the Block and English that I was to be invited back to witness the next meeting between Sergeant Herrera and the excitable hype Charley Thompson. I wanted to listen closely as Thompson laid out Bartlow's scam, make sure he was pumped dry—and then immediately put him on ice before he killed someone. The Block and Paul seemed much too cavalier about the potential for violence, and I wanted to make sure the sting didn't drift into some kind of cop's *Apocalypse Now*.

Late the following afternoon, Manny Herrera called. "Chief, I thought you would want to know. I heard from Charley Thompson. Said it's important that he see me. He'll be here in about two hours."

"OK, Sarge, I'll be there. What's he so excited about?"

"I'm not sure, but I stalled him. Told him I might be busy to see if he'd open up. He got a little anxious. Said it would be well worth my while to hear about Bartlow and his brother."

"The politician?"

"Yeah, it sounds like him. We'll send someone to pick you up?"

"Thanks."

Detective Nunzio Papa drove me to the bar in an eight-year-old Buick taken from an unsuccessful, continuously stoned, small-time dope dealer. Silicon City's mechanics had protested when we went into federal court to get ownership under the law allowing the seizing of property used in the drug trade. Riding in the wreck, I could understand the mechanics' point. We had ten cars seized from dealers, but they were all expensive new cars in good condition. Mercedeses, Porsches, even Bimmers. The Buick was junk and difficult to keep running.

The left front fender had been replaced because of a collision. It had that dark ugly brown undercoat you get while waiting for a paint job. The rest of the car was faded white. It was hard to imagine that painting it was going to make much difference. One of the front wheels had a distinct wobble when we got up to thirty miles an hour. The windshield had a noticeable crack stretching from the top to the bottom on the right side. There was a hole in the muffler and a couple of cylinders missed noisily. The front-seat upholstery was dirty and torn and a busted spring under me made itself felt every time we hit a bump.

Nunzio, sitting next to me, hadn't shaved in a couple of days and his clothes were filthy. He wore a black leather vest and a short-sleeved shirt which exposed tattoos of a mottled green dragon on his left arm and a large skull on his right. His greasy matted hair was long, but not long enough to cover his gold earring.

I had on sunglasses darker than the kind Chicago football player Jim McMahon favored, and I looked scroungy. I wore the oldest blue jeans I owned, along with a plaid sports shirt that should have been given to Goodwill years ago. We were glaringly out of place as we drove through a mile of broad boulevards lined with bright fancy shops and cute little grassy malls. This was our minor-league Rodeo Drive. It was redevelopment, what the Board of Supervisors deigned to spend money on despite the city's having the lowest police and fire staffing in the state.

The signal light turned amber for the cross traffic, and Nunzio eased the gear back into drive. The car had a tendency to stall out if you didn't shift into neutral at stops. We were driving south. A blue and white going east came to a halt as the amber changed to red in his direction. The uniformed cop behind the wheel gave us the bad eye. We pretended not to notice and looked straight ahead. Getting stopped now would be disastrous. The cop would ID me on sight and since we were only a couple of streets from the sting, he might well put two and two together. The police grapevine would be buzzing within hours and the operation would be blown. And being rousted would make me late for the session with Thompson.

The light turned green, and Nunzio put the car into drive, simultaneously stepping on the gas. Of course, the damned car stalled out. He tried to start the motor as traffic piled up to the rear. The starter kept missing. I hoped he hadn't flooded the engine. A woman right behind us in a bright red Mercedes convertible leaned on her horn, and Nunzio instinctively started to flip her the finger. I grabbed his wrist.

"Careful. The cop is watching us," I said, still staring straight ahead.

Nunzio cursed the woman in the Mercedes. "The cunt. She's probably late for an afternooner with some wetback busboy."

"Just get us the hell out of here, Nunzio." From the rearview mirror I saw the woman behind us spot the cop and immediately let up on the horn. She was an attractive middle-aged blonde. She flashed the cop an embarrassed smile.

Finally, the motor caught and we moved through the intersection just as the light turned red again. Looking in the side mirror, I watched the police car turn right and fall in behind us.

"Shit." Nunzio had his eyes on the rear mirror. "Wouldn't you know it. Dedicated. He's following us instead of trying to get into the old broad's pants. We got great luck. Hope he gets a call—we're too close to the place to explain anything to him."

Old broad? She was probably a year or two younger than me. "Are these plates in the computer as stolen?"

"No. They're under my phony name."

We were out of the chichi area, back into the reality of used-car dealers, secondhand thrift shops, tire dealers, and fast-food holes. It could have been a highway in Paramus, New Jersey, if it hadn't been for the occasional smog-diseased palm tree. I motioned to a dingy-looking coffee shop coming up on our right. "Why don't you pull in there? We can go inside and make believe we came in to take a leak. The cop's checking the registration on his radio. When it comes back clean, he'll probably buzz off."

"He better. We're running late and if I don't get you there by the time the meet goes down, the Block will be all over my ass."

He drove into a space in the parking lot as if he hadn't noticed the cop pulling in behind us. We sauntered into the place. A couple of truck drivers at the counter turned to watch us. They didn't look at all friendly.

We walked toward the men's room. A burly fat guy wearing an apron that may have once been white moved from behind the counter where he had been fooling around with the coffee urn. Dwarfing Nunzio, who was only five seven, the cook barred our way to the restroom. With two truck drivers at the counter and a cop outside, he was tough. I glanced away from his bald head and saw from the corner of my eye that the cop was talking into his car microphone.

Nunzio whined, "Man, we only want to use the men's room for a minute."

"You gotta piss, go do it in that piece of shit you drove into my parking lot." The bald guy wasn't that muscular, but he sure was confident.

I pulled a couple of bucks from my pocket. "Could we sit at the counter and have some coffee?" We needed a few minutes. If we left now, the cop was sure to question us.

"Stick it in your ass. I don't even want you bums in here."

Nunzio said, "OK, OK, man. We hear you." Backing toward the door, he saw that the police car hadn't moved. "Say, is it OK if I get some cigarettes from the machine?" He fumbled with change from his pocket.

The cook didn't hide his disgust. "Go ahead. Then get the hell out of here. I'm sick of guys like you coming around and driving customers away."

The change toppled from Nunzio's hand and rolled along the floor. "Sorry, sorry," he said, scurrying around picking up the coins. He retrieved a quarter then dropped it again and it rolled away from him along the floor. He crawled after it. The cook looked at the truckers and rolled his eyes toward the ceiling.

I watched the police car drive out of the parking lot. Nunzio was on his feet and also noticed the cop was gone. He forgot about his lost quarter and walked back toward me. There was another quarter on the floor near the first trucker. Nunzio smiled and stooped to pick it up. "Scuse me, man."

The trucker put his heavy boot on Nunzio's hand and started to press down. In a blur of movement the detective flipped him off the stool. The truck driver fell heavily against a booth, solidly whacking his head on the side of the table. Nunzio was on him quickly, his foot on the man's throat. "You fucking asshole. I ought to . . ."

"Let's go," I yelled at him. The cook and the other trucker stood as frozen as the man on the floor. I grabbed Nunzio's arm. "I said let's go."

He hesitated, then walked ahead of me out the door.

"Why did you bend over for the second quarter?" I said when we were back into traffic.

"I thought it would have been out of character if a bummy-looking guy left the quarter there. They'd remember me, and you can never tell when that might be bad."

"And now they won't remember after you used a professional martial arts move and almost took the guy's head off?"

"Sorry, Chief. But this stuff can get to you. Every place you go you're shit. My wife won't even go out in public with me for the past three months."

Detective Nunzio Papa was showing the familiar signs of undercover stress. He was understandably jumpy about Hector Gonzales. He had family pressure, and my presence wasn't helping a bit. Like most street cops he wasn't used to being around the police chief. If the uniformed cop had rousted us and the sting got blown just as it started to reel in crooks, Nunzio would have gotten plenty of heat from the other guys. He continued to twitch.

Six

I SAT NEXT TO SERGEANT MANNY HERRERA ON THE COUCH where he did most of his business. On the wall to our right were some of the most pornographic pictures of beautiful women I had seen in my police career. And I had spent two years in the vice squad. In answer to my questioning look, the Block said, "About half of the dirtbags coming in here to do business aren't so doped out that they can't get laid. And most of the others like to pretend that they can still get it up. So these pictures are a good way of keeping them from looking too close at the birdie." He pointed to the goofy mirrored picture on the wall opposite us, behind which the videotape camera rested.

The police artist had painted a scene onto the silvered surface which blocked out the light from the inside room. A bulbous-nosed bum with rosy cheeks and a frayed cigar smiled out at us while a number of bees and wasps flew ominously around him. Wasps and bees sting—cop humor, like the establishment's name: The Blue Mirage Bar and Grill. Warnings that would never be picked up. The camera was focused from the bum's red nose; the microphone was right above us, planted in a phony smoke alarm.

Elaborate efforts to control crime through illusions. I tried to imagine being a burglar and sitting here conspiring about crime with Herrera while secret cameras were recording the transaction. It didn't work. I couldn't really put myself in the place of the thieves and dope pushers who came in with all kinds of illegal drugs, or "controlled substances," as we referred to them in law enforcement, flowing through their veins. Losers who had been stealing, in and out of jail for most of their lives. That was why it was hard for me to identify with what Herrera was doing. Unless you could play the role of your clients, you were useless as a narc or a cop doing a sting. Maybe that's why I had been such a disaster as a NYPD plainclothesman.

"Sarge," I said, "you did great this afternoon. I've done a lot of investigations, but I couldn't have pulled off your act."

Herrera turned to me, his face wooden, unfriendly. "You didn't grow up where I did," he said, conspicuously omitting the "Chief" or "Sir" I was slowly getting used to.

"Hey, Manny," the Block said at top volume, "stop the bullshit about how you walked uphill both ways to school in the barrio. The chief grew up in New York with punks that would have eaten the Cholos for breakfast. Besides, he's not gonna close you down. Right, Chief?"

Herrera's round face broke into a grin. "Hey, Block, fuck you too. So those New York gringos liked to suck cock for breakfast. What's it to me?"

But I noticed he looked at me differently. With respect. There wouldn't be any more bushwhacking the boss. He hadn't seen me wince when the Block mentioned New York.

Herrera turned to me. "You're not going to shut us down, are you, Chief? We're just starting to roll."

"No." I wrenched my mind back from New York and the past to the sting. "I have some concerns about safety, including yours, but I think we can deal with them and keep the operation going."

There wasn't any more kibitzing. They had worked hard for months setting up the operation, actually doing some of the carpentry with their own hands. Police "scouts" had painstakingly created an image of being petty thieves. They pretended that Manny was their fence and that they were reluctant to share him with anyone else. It baited the hook, inexorably luring the real crooks into Manny's lair. Now was harvesttime, and the cops didn't want to lose the crop because of me.

"I want two things to happen," I said. "First, we have to take Charley Thompson off the streets. He's real strung out, and I believe him when he says he's ready to kill. Second, I want the name of the cop who gave Bartlow the details of 'Bolero's' arrest record. It's just a short jump from Bolero to Manny's real identity, and that could be fatal for you guys. Also, I want a minimum of two people in the back room, and the guy with the shotgun goes in if he thinks the crooks are wise to Manny. I don't want anyone getting hurt because we wait too long out of fear of blowing the sting."

"That's three," said the Block.

"What?" I frowned at the Block, who had a habit of disrupting important conversations.

"You said you wanted two things to happen, but you gave us three. That's all."

"You won't get an argument from me, Chief." Herrera's voice had none of the street in it now. "That damn hype gave me a scare when he pulled the gun. He is ready to hit someone. And a cop who gives info to a sleazebag like Bartlow . . ."

"All right, Sarge, when Thompson comes in, I want you to squeeze him about Bartlow and see if his brother on the Board of Supervisors is involved. You know how to do it without making him suspicious. When is his parole agent going to violate him?"

Herrera frowned. "Jack Murphy, goddamn him, we been trying to get him all day, but we did get a message from his office that he should be here later. When I finish with Charley, I'll bring him out to the bar and buy him dinner. Good old Charley told the judge he had a drinking problem when he was getting sentenced. Actually, he was out of his head on crack, but they put in a condition of parole that he stay out of bars, so it works out fine for us. We'll make sure Charley has a drink in front of him. Murphy will notice and violate Charley right back into the can."

It was almost time for Charley Thompson's appointment. The Block, English, Nunzio Papa, and I retreated to the observation room after the Block filled a pitcher with Michelob. I thought it would be good for their morale so I let him pour me a glass—besides which it was getting dark, and I was tired and thirsty.

When Herrera let someone in through the bar door, it turned out not to be Thompson, but a clean-cut, blond, blue-eyed guy about twenty-eight.

"These assholes all carry a line of bullshit about how bad they are," the Block whispered, "but this guy had us laughing. His name is Bright, but bright he ain't. He told everyone around him that he had broken out of the joint in Jefferson City, Missouri, where he was a lifer for killing a family of four who had fucked up his dope deal. We figured he was full of shit like most of these jerks—a two-bit burglar at best. We got his prints on beer cans, glasses, pieces of paper, you name it. We gave them to the latent print guys. They screwed around two days before they got a make on him. Guess what? He's a fugitive from the Jefferson City pen where he was in for the limit for offing a family of four in Kansas City."

"Hey, Manny," the all-American-looking killer said, "I got to thank you for letting me sack out here last night. Since I broke out I haven't slept, you know, with all the heat. The feds got an APB on me. This is the only place I felt safe in two months."

"Hey, no problem, man," nice-guy Herrera said, not mentioning that during the night, cops had been planning Bright's one-way return trip to Jefferson City.

Paul English said, "Bright's driving a Volvo borrowed from a gal in the Friends Outside Movement. He's been with her off and on for a week."

"She's the kind of broad who likes to think she can fuck these cons straight. Heh, heh, into *going* straight, I mean."

Paul continued without acknowledging the Block's attempt at humor. "The car is parked four blocks from here. During the night, we removed the rear license plate. He probably won't notice it when he drives away, but we have two marked patrol units watching it. One unit will stop him about a mile from here and ask him about his missing plate. If all goes well, Bright will be telling a hard-luck story back in the pen about how some crook stole his rear plate and the cops recognized him as a fugitive. He'll never connect it with the sting, and we'll still be in business."

"Is there any chance of losing him?" I didn't like the idea of fugitive killers on the lam in my jurisdiction.

"Just to be on the safe side we stuck a transmitter under the bumper. The units can follow him even if they lose sight of the car."

Bright shook Manny's hand and departed unknowingly for Missouri.

The bar door opened and a young woman entered wearing tight blue jeans and a cut-off blouse which left her slim middle exposed. Her fair hair didn't look any too clean. It was tied back with a piece of red yarn. She came across as tough and attractive—a gal who had been around. Yet, somehow, she also conveyed a touch of feminine tenderness underneath.

She placed two cans of Budweiser beer on the crowded coffee table, then removed a couple of empties so that there would be room for the new arrivals. I had already been informed that the table overflowing with empty beer cans and full ashtrays was never completely emptied, and indeed, the stale musty smell had nauseated me while I sat chatting with Herrera.

In the observation room I was conscious of the total silence around me as I watched the gal in the next room bend over in her tight jeans. It seemed to me that she had cocked her well-rounded rear end at us for an unnecessary amount of time as she messed around with the beer.

Finally, I asked, "Who is that?"

Paul English answered without inflection, "Police Officer Mary Falcone."

Manny Herrera had leaned over and whispered something in her ear as she continued to conspicuously aim her rear end in our direction.

"Oh," she exclaimed, "the chief's in there, is he? Hi, Chief," she said with a big smile, flipping the finger toward us, then bending over once more and rotating her rear end in our direction.

Again, Herrera leaned forward to whisper in her ear. This time I was able to catch some of what he said. "He really is. Knock it off before he closes the whole place down."

"Yeah, Manny. Right on, right on." She laughed at him and gave us the finger once more—but I noticed a slight loss of confidence as she glanced over her shoulder in our direction on the way out.

I had made a superhuman effort to suppress my laughter. Police Officer Mary Falcone would never live this down. The cops in the back room were silently hoping that I wasn't angry enough to close the sting. I tried to look sufficiently pissed to make them sweat, although that wasn't easy with the Block and Paul, who knew me too well.

"Mary's tough, Fraleigh. She's only got two years on the street, and she's a little green, but she's going to be a hell of a cop," the Block said, and I remained silent, staring grimly out into the other room, enjoying their discomfort.

She came back in, bringing Charley Thompson with her and two more cans of Bud. He roughly pinched her breast, and I waited, hoping she wouldn't decapitate him with a karate chop, but she slapped his hand away and looked coy. Of course, this only encouraged him, and he reached around to cup her buttock. "You and me. We're naturals," he said, bearing his rotting teeth in a smile. I watched to see how she defended.

"Hey lover," she had slipped away from Thompson and settled on Herrera's lap, "when you gonna feed Momma tonight?"

"As soon as I get rid of this clown," the sergeant said, looking at Charley Thompson like he was deciding just where to bury him. Thompson got the message and sank into the end of the couch away from Mary, but I noticed uneasily that she lingered a few minutes longer than she needed to on Herrera's lap. And the way they looked at each other should have convinced Thompson to keep his distance, but I wondered how much of it was great acting.

"She married?" I asked.

"To an investment banker. Loaded with dough. They live in Los Altos Hills. Millionaire Row. Manny's married too. Got three kids, but he lives in a dump on the East Side," the Block laughed, as Mary finally detached herself from Sergeant Herrera's lap and headed for the bar.

Herrera continued to look surly, letting Thompson guess how annoyed he really was over Mary. "Hey man, I didn't know she's your bitch. Hell, she sticks her tits out and wiggles her ass at everything in pants out there." He pointed his shoulder at the bar door.

"She gets paid to do that. It don't mean nothing," Herrera said.

"Yeah, OK, OK. I get more gash than I know what to do with anyway," Thompson said, again baring his crummy teeth in a grotesque smile. "What I wanted to show you was what I got when I went back to the doctor's house."

I whipped around to look at Paul and the Block. "Goddamn it. You said the doctor was safe."

Paul held open his hands in a gesture of ignorance. Turning back to look into the next room I heard Herrera say, "I thought you was going to wait until your brother got out?"

"They fucked him over some way. They actually raised his bail when that dickface Bartlow told me he was getting it lowered, so I went back myself. Here." He handed the sergeant two gold coins.

"How many did you get?"

"Those two are all. They were in a drawer, but I know the safe is full of them. Trouble is, the doc wasn't there to help me open the safe. I'm going back now and wait for him to come home, even if it takes all night. I'll have the rest of it here for you in the morning. How much you think it's worth?"

In the observation room we gave a collective sigh to hear that the physician was still alive. The heat began to leave my face. We had to take Charley Thompson out of circulation immediately. Paul picked up the wall phone and called Mary in the bar. "Is Jack Murphy out there?" He listened. "OK. When he comes in buzz us back here so we know."

"Where the hell is he?" the Block growled. "Fucking parole agents. They're on permanent vacations."

"This stuff is valuable, man. I'm going to have to look at some books and talk to some people before I can give you a price," Herrera said.

"Yeah, well what I really wanted to talk about was shyster Bartlow and his big-shit brother. Bartlow was my mouthpiece on my last bust. He really fucked up, but anyway, I'm sitting in his office a couple of weeks ago. He don't even have a secretary and his door is open. I hear him telling his brother about getting the shit kicked out of himself in New York trying to peddle some hot paper."

Thompson got up and put his hand on Herrera's shoulder. "Manny, me and you gonna get rich off those two cunts. Believe me, we'll clean up on them and neither has the balls to do anything about it."

"Yeah, you're right. Tell me about all this hot paper."

"Well, Bartlow hangs up. In his office I can see he's been banged up—bandages on his head, can hardly move, you know, ribs cracked. I go, 'Hey, what happened?' He goes, 'Nothing.' So, I go, 'Bullshit. I heard you on the phone. Whyn't you tell me you got something to unload? I got this great guy, Manny, runs a bar, handles a lot of shit.'"

"You gave your lawyer my name? You sure he's not a snitch?"

"Yeah. I told you I heard him on the phone. Him and his brother pulled a big rip-off of these bearer bonds. How, I don't know. He's being cagey, see. But I let Bartlow chew my ear. Turns out he represents Inky Lee Bronheim—a con man and paper hanger—on a forgery bust. Bronheim beats the rap, but Bartlow picks his brains about where 'someone' might peddle some hot bonds." Thompson paused to wink at Manny. "Yeah, 'someone.' I'm sure slick Bartlow fooled Bronheim. Bronheim gives him the name of a big-shot broker on Wall Street named Christopher MacLeod, s'posed to be a hot-shit bond dealer. According to Bronheim, MacLeod's good people. Helped Bronheim in a con. Then helped launder the dough. My bet is that Bronheim calls MacLeod to tell him he's sending a mark. Anyway, asshole Bartlow went to New York, and Macleod and a Chink named Anthony Wong ripped him off in Chinatown. Took two sample bonds from him and put him in Bellevue Hospital for a week. The last thing he is is a snitch. He pumped me dry about you. He was afraid you was a snitch. Anyway, he musta checked you out because next time I seen him he asked me to set up a meeting here."

"He played it pretty tight during the meeting. I don't know if I should trust the fucker. He don't tell me nothing."

"He thinks he's slick. The jerk don't know shit. He's lucky those New York guys didn't off him. But I think him and his brother are sitting on a shitload of these bonds. Easy picking for you and me."

"Did he ever tell you where he got the bonds?" Herrera asked.

"Not yet, but his brother was in on it, and he's sure that the paper ain't gonna be missed. I figure you and me can set up a buyout, take the fucking bonds, and leave Bartlow holding his cock. What's he gonna do, go to the cops?"

The wall phone buzzed. Paul listened. I could hear Mary Falcone's voice on the receiver, but the sound was too faint to make out her words. "Will they send someone else?" Paul said. "OK, Mary. No. Don't worry. We'll figure out something back here." He hung up.

I turned to him trying to listen with one ear to Herrera and Thompson. "Bad luck. Mary just got a call out front. Jack Murphy was broadsided a half hour ago by some drunken kid in a pickup truck. Jack's car was totaled. He's in the hospital with a couple of broken ribs and they're worried that his back may be broken also. They say it would take a couple of hours for them to round up someone else and get him here."

"Jesus," the Block scowled, "what useless bastards."

Paul thought out loud. "We know from what Charley said that he broke into the doctor's house. Even though we haven't been able to identify the doctor yet, we can follow his car and snatch him breaking in. When we book him, we can tell him that someone had reported the first break and that we were staking it out or just investigating it when he had the bad luck to come back. It's not as clean as Bright's parole violation, but it should fool him. What do you think, Chief?"

"I don't like it. Suppose he slips the tail? We end up with a dead doctor. Why don't we do what we did to the cluck from Missouri?"

"Thompson wouldn't be fooled. He'd smell a setup arrest if it happened right after he leaves the bar. Thompson would spend time in county jail talking about it, and the sting would be blown. You know once one con or lawyer learns we have a sting going, word will spread on the grapevine throughout the entire county. Bright, on the other hand, wasn't here when we ran the other stings and isn't likely to be suspicious. He'll be back in the Missouri prison before he knows which end is up." Paul, protecting the sting, was persuasive. "If it looks like he's going to shake us, we can have a marked unit pick him up as a fallback. I'll call now and have two units stand by on our radio channel a couple of streets from here. I know the Honda Thompson is driving. It's parked around the corner on Broad Street. The Block and I will follow him."

"I'll go with you."

Paul opened his mouth—probably to tell me it wasn't a good idea to have the chief actually involved in a case because then he could be called upon to testify as a witness. Instead, he turned to the phone and told communications what he wanted. He knew I was thinking of having Thompson arrested right in the bar.

Thompson moved toward the door. "I gotta get back to the doc's. We can talk more tomorrow when I bring the coins in. And don't worry. I ain't about to leave a witness to squeal how I made him open his safe."

"Here. Have a beer before you go." Herrera handed him one of the beers Mary Falcone had brought to the table. I knew he was trying to delay Charley to pump him some more about Bartlow, and to hold him long enough so that Jack Murphy would be in place.

"OK. Just one. I want to be there before the doc gets home."

The observation room was silent until Paul said, "We won't have time to go out the back way through the alley. Manny won't be able to talk Thompson into staying for dinner. Let's hustle out through the bar while he's still with Manny. That way, we can be in our car waiting down the street when he gets behind the wheel. Mary will get word to Manny about the change in plans."

We got through the door quickly, leaving Nunzio to dead-bolt it behind us. I glanced toward the bar. Mary Falcone wore a long dirty apron. She was serving a beer to a guy when she noticed us leaving. Her eyes slid over Paul and the Block without expression, but when she saw me, she dropped the beer all over the bar, drenching the customer's pack of cigarettes and change. He started screaming, but she stared at me. I was tempted to give her the finger, but police chiefs don't do that sort of stuff, so I blew her a kiss. After all, she had created quite a diversion to cover our departure.

We were in an electric-blue Trans Am, which the Block told me had been confiscated from a dope pusher. Only in California did it make an inconspicuous trail car. About ten minutes later, Thompson walked unsteadily out of the bar. "The patrol units won't have any trouble busting him for driving under the influence," I said.

"They're not in place yet. They'll signal when they are, and I can give them the description of Charley and the car."

"Yeah. I hope you didn't fuck up again, Paul. The big chief here will have your ass if the sawbones gets knocked off."

"Block, I regret that I don't have time to jot down these sparkling conversational gems that you keep dropping. I could bring them back to my English professor at Stanford— or perhaps my zoology professor who was studying apes would be more appropriate."

"Yeah. The zoo. I bet you and your faggy professors spent a lot of time at the monkey house standing behind all the sweet little boys watching the monkeys."

Resisting the temptation to enter their highly professional law enforcement discussion, I watched Charley Thompson get into his car with only a casual glance in our direction. In the front seat he paused for a moment fumbling for his keys. Rolling down the side window he turned the key in the ignition. There was a pop almost like a gunshot. Then, a flash, and a split second later, the sound of an explosion. In the red glare behind the steering wheel, Charley Thompson was thrown upward and forward toward the windshield and both doors blew outward.

"Holy shit!" The Block grabbed the door handle ready to jump out and run to the car.

"Hold it," I yelled, afraid of what was going to happen next. Sure enough, the gas tank went with a huge *whoosh* and the car became a fireball with oily smoke trailing upward into the night sky.

Paul's hand radio crackled, "P One and Two to Fox One." Paul had apparently set up codes and the patrol units were calling us.

"Tell them the operation was canceled and don't put us at this scene," I said.

"Go ahead P One and Two," Paul spoke into his radio.

"We just got to our station but there's an explosion nearby. Should we respond?"

"Our operation was scratched about ten minutes ago. Go ahead and handle the emergency."

Paul drove us slowly away from the scene. The two marked units raced past us with lights flashing and sirens screeching. I tried not to remember Charley Thompson's brief cry at the first explosion. He wasn't exactly a lovable human being, but for anyone to go up in flames . . . The heavy smell of burning oil and gasoline tainted with the sweetish sickening odor of burning flesh reached our nostrils. An unknown doctor was safe, and Charley Thompson, the cocaine fiend, was gone, along with whatever additional information he had about the Bartlow brothers.

Seven

AT 0900 HOURS THE NEXT MORNING, BEHIND THE CLOSED
doors of my office, the Block, Paul English, and I brooded
over the demise of Charley Thompson.

"One less dirtbag," the Block said.

"No one was thinking of offering him a posthumous
medal, Block. The question is, who did it, and what does
it mean to the future of our sting?"

The Block grunted. "Sarcasm by the chief toward a loyal
officer. I could file a grievance. Still, I got to hand it to
you, Fraleigh, you were pretty cool. If the official record
showed us at the scene, people would have asked questions,
and the next thing, the whole operation would have been in
the newspaper. Of course, it also keeps you out of hot water
until the politicos appoint you."

"Or don't," Paul English said. "Jack Murphy and the
parole people know we wanted Thompson violated in the
bar—sooner or later it's going to get talked about, and I
think if Fraleigh is going to get the chief's job, it had better
be later. It won't look so good in print that the acting chief
and two detectives let someone get blown up right under
their noses."

"How the fuck was we gonna know . . ."

I cut the Block off. "Let's forget my appointment and talk
about who sent good old Thompson to his just rewards."

"Assholes like him have a zillion enemies. Some other
hype that he short-changed on a bag of smack, or someone
he screwed out of their share of the loot. Who knows?"

"Except that those kind of people don't use sophisticated explosives, Block. If they do get up enough nerve, it's a gun or knife and it's quick, not months later. They're usually so stoned they don't remember what happened yesterday."

"I think you're right, Paul," I said. "There's also the nasty coincidence that a short time after Thompson becomes involved in our sting, he ends up dead. Guys like him do have a limited life expectancy—he traveled with people just like himself. People who would kill without a second thought. But, planting a car bomb requires a lot of thought. I want you two guys to monitor the homicide investigation closely."

"That young puppy, Lieutenant Short, who you put in charge of the homicide squad, isn't going to appreciate us looking over his shoulder," the Block said.

"I'll talk to him and clue him in on the sting. How many local people have the know-how to do a blast job like we saw? Two, three, maybe? . . ."

There was a gentle knock on the open door. Sergeant Ken Matsukowa peered in at us. "Come in Ken," I said, hearing my voice take on a false note of heartiness. Matsukowa was short and slim. His plain wire spectacles fit around protruding ears too large for a man of his small size. Ordinarily, someone of his makeup would have been an irresistible target for the Block's macho approach to police work. Yet, the Block moved quickly to pull a chair forward for Matsukowa to join us.

"How ya doing, Ken?" I noticed the same tone from the Block that had crept into my own voice.

"Ken," Paul English waved a greeting with none of his usual wise-ass sarcasm.

Matsukowa nodded with a half smile and slipped into the chair. "Chief, Paul, Block. You called, Chief?"

I cleared my throat. "We'd like to know what you have so far on the bombing, Ken."

Matsukowa was our bomb expert. He had been trained four years ago by Sergeant Daryl Finch. Ken took over when

Finch was blinded trying to remove a bomb from an airport locker. The case had never been solved, although the FBI firmly believed that the bomb had been planted by a rebel Croatian group that had planned a synchronized series of explosions throughout the United States to dramatize their cause. The airport bomb had been discovered by chance the day before the attacks were to take place. They were complex devices with a trigger mechanism which hadn't been seen before. Finch's misfortune had saved lives across the country, but he wasn't watching any more old movies on his VCR.

"I'm afraid we don't have much yet, Chief." Matsukowa spoke so softly that I leaned forward to catch his words. "It appears that a small amount of plastic explosive was triggered by the ignition . . ."

"Small amount? The fucking car looked like Hiroshima." The Block flushed as he realized he hadn't chosen the most diplomatic comparison.

"What you saw, Block, was the gasoline tank going up immediately after the small charge wired to the ignition detonated," Ken said. He was our expert, dismantling 147 explosive devices over the past few years without a mistake. But it only took one mistake, or something new like Finch had encountered. It was only a matter of time, which explained our unease. When you were with Ken Matsukowa, it was hard not to let your mind wander to the day when you would be attending his funeral.

He continued, "I have a hunch that the ignition device was fused right to the gas tank. Very elaborate and unusual. I've never seen that M.O. personally, and I've only heard of it a couple of times. Still, I may be wrong. We'll know for sure in a couple of weeks when we get the report on the fragments from the ATF lab at Treasure Island."

I didn't think he was wrong. Ken wouldn't have spoken of a "hunch" if he hadn't been certain. He was just politely saying that the scientific verification of his finding hadn't been received yet from the Federal Bureau of Alcohol, Tobacco, and Firearms, the agency with jurisdiction over the criminal use of explosives, which served as a central clearing house for bomb information. "Were the bombs you heard about done by locals, Ken?"

"One was, Chief. By Mario 'Boom-Boom' Golta, but he's in for life on a fatal bombing three years ago of a labor leader in San Francisco. The other guy, Mel Zale, works for the mob in New York. I've asked our local ATF people to put a trace on him through their New York office."

We sat considering the possibility of a pro being sent from New York to do a two-bit local hood like Thompson. "Er, Chief, my conclusion is based partially on the Block's verbal description to me, but the field crime reports do not indicate he was on the scene. I was wondering if there was other information I should know. There isn't much in the reports."

"You're right, Ken, and that's deliberate." My respect for Matsukowa went up another notch. As delicate and soft-spoken as he was, he wasn't afraid to question the police chief. I debated how much to tell him. He was an expert in his field. A forensic scientist in his own right who periodically lectured at the FBI Academy in Quantico, Virginia. Yet, he had never interviewed a suspect or witness, or made an arrest. He simply wasn't that kind of cop. Given the sensitivity of the sting—the political tie-ins, a dirty cop—the less people who knew what was going on, the better. Yet, we were asking him to help solve the case and maybe risk his life if other bombs popped up.

"Ken, this case is top secret. I don't want you to share one word of it with the feds or even any of our own people."

"Thanks, Chief," he said after I had told him about the sting, including the possible involvement of the Bartlow brothers. "It doesn't help me on anything right now, but you can never tell when some little detail might be very important. And I can see why it has to be totally confidential. I won't share any of it."

"I don't know how he stays so calm. All those bombs . . ." Paul said, as he and the Block followed Sergeant Matsukowa out of the office.

My phone buzzed.

"What's up, Denise?"

"Sergeant Gus Myers from the records unit said it's urgent that he see you."

Just what I needed. Myers had been in records for five years. But the "chief" had an open-door policy. Somehow, few legit cops used it, but Myers had been to see me a half dozen times on trivia during the short time I had been acting as chief.

He was short, and his blue uniform shirt was having a hard time holding in his belly. "I'm on a tight schedule today, Sarge," I said, trying not to stare at his bizarre attempt to hide rapidly advancing baldness. He had bleached his few remaining strands surfer blond. It went with his forty-four years like pizza à la mode.

"Right, Chief. But I thought this was urgent. We've been hearing rumors for a while that the Hell's Angels chapter on Market Street has started extorting money from merchants. Look at this crime report that just came in. It's a classic example of their techniques."

I reached for the report thinking maybe I had been a little hard on Myers. There *were* stories of bikers leaning on merchants—a potential warning of organized extortion. Sometimes guys like Myers got a jacket from the troops as blunderers; deserved or not, they never lived it down. If he had spotted an extortion pattern before the intelligence or robbery unit did, he deserved a commendation.

He stood in front of the desk, hungry for praise, as I read the report. Two tough bikers had terrorized a coffee shop. They hadn't actually asked for money, but had manhandled a customer as an obvious warning, and had only backed off when the manager and a couple of truck drivers had stood up to them. Then they had fled, but the alert manager had gotten the license plate. I was almost finished with the report when I realized that the descriptions of the vehicle and suspects rang a bell. Sure enough, the address where the crime had occurred was the diner that Nunzio and I had briefly visited.

I looked up at Myers. "This was a sharp piece of work on your part, Myers. I'm going to give it top priority by assigning it to my aide, the Block."

Myers swelled up with pleasure. "I'm just trying to do my part, Chief. I wish my bum knee wasn't keeping me inside so that I could go out there and kick ass, teach those hoods a lesson." He saluted briskly. By the time he got to Curly's Tavern after duty, the story would have grown as to how he had personally spotted these guys in the diner and run them right out of town.

Eight

MY FATE WAS TO BE DECIDED BY THE FIVE PEOPLE FILING solemnly into the chambers. Since I wasn't that keen on the job, I wasn't at all nervous. If I got it, I got it. My challenge would be to keep my temper when a crook like Bartlow started playing word games with me during the interview. I had been told to be in uniform. Now I sat there feeling like a general from some banana republic. Four stars glistened across the blue jacket covering my shoulders. It felt strange. Except for my rookie years, I had been a dick, never even wearing a blue suit—let alone a uniform.

The huge, oak-paneled chamber was almost empty. People are fascinated by the doings of TV cops, but the selection of the city's police chief drew more flies than observers. Three bored reporters sat at the press table, while in seats behind them, two college kids took notes for their political-science class, keeping a wary eye on the two regular nuts who attended all board meetings and were given to loud, incoherent outbursts. Even louder and more incoherent than the politicians holding court.

I wondered if it was insecurity, mediocrity, or the egos they grew after being in office, which caused the politicians to elevate themselves eight feet above us, even higher than that other group of dedicated public servants—judges. Waiting for the supervisors to take their seats, I reflected that it was going to be an interesting session. The media with their typical indifference to facts had made me a local folk hero. They had described how I, as acting police chief, had courageously persevered in my duty with the result that the mayor was under arrest for various federal felony charges, and a couple of crooked cops had been busted.

Actually, the Block, Paul English, and I had muddled through a bloody mess, burying two fellow cops and good friends before it was over. If we had done better police work, we could have prevented a lot of pain. Nevertheless, because of the mayor's arrest, this committee, comprised of the five members of the City Board of Supervisors, had on a three-to-two vote invoked its authority under the City Charter, suspended His Honor, and assumed his authority to appoint someone to fill the vacant position of police chief.

The first to sit down was Duane Bartlow. I looked at him with new interest after so recently becoming acquainted with his charming brother at The Blue Mirage Bar and Grill. The two brothers could have been twins. Supervisor Bartlow, forty-three, was two years older than his brother, but shared his slight build and tendency toward early baldness. His steel-rimmed spectacles made him look like a bookkeeper. The deep frown on his face went with a nasty disposition and a big mouth.

Bartlow's conservative gray business suit looked expensive on a supervisor drawing twenty thousand bucks a year. When elected two years ago, he'd been a run-of-the-mill real estate agent in a small struggling agency. Now, he was a full partner in a booming agency and a millionaire to boot. When a developer needed a zoning change or planning department approval for a new shopping center, industrial park, or residential housing project, Duane was the person to call. California's new laws against conflicts of interest hadn't prevented developers from using Bartlow's agency.

Stuart Kendle, an insurance agent, followed Bartlow. He was sixty, tall and slender, with a full head of gray hair. He hadn't bought his suit off the rack, either. His insurance firm was known to write a lot of insurance for companies involved in construction work, but his rise hadn't been as meteoric as Bartlow's. He had been on the board for ten years and was well-liked by big money developers.

Nola Henderson came next. Walking across the room with a model's confidence, she glanced toward me from under her large tinted sunglasses and I felt my groin muscles tighten. Her long, light-brown hair was pulled back from her forehead and fell naturally, emphasizing her slender, softly attractive face. She wore a simple cream-colored dress. It was belted at the waist, just snug enough to hint at the full breasts and long legs underneath. The dress had cost as much or more than Kendle's and Bartlow's suits combined. As I well knew, the label inside was from Saks Fifth Avenue. She came from wealth, and, unlike her two male colleagues, had dressed expensively before entering politics. Her soft brown boots were by Bally and when I had pulled them off, the faint sweet smell of her perspiration had wrapped an erotic mist around me. I wondered if the electricity between us was apparent to others in the room.

She was a lawyer, twenty-nine years old, and had been launched into politics after chairing the county bar association's committee on control of toxic pollution. She had managed to get a couple of the more flagrant corporate violators prosecuted, and had received great publicity. Her standing in various women's organizations and the legal community was good. She had been appointed to fill a vacancy created by the death of Lawrence Smith, a crony of Bartlow's and Kendle's whose Bentley sedan had locked wheels on a dark curve at two o'clock one rainy morning. The investigating traffic officer had estimated he hit the curve at ninety miles an hour.

"He was no kid. A guy with all that dough. What got into him to drive like that?" the cop had asked the coroner during the autopsy.

"About seven or eight martinis," the doctor had answered.

Nola sat in the middle of the curved dais. Following her was Sally Fenton, a dark-haired environmentalist of fifty, who had survived two elections and five years on the board, despite the efforts of her male colleagues. She turned her large, plain face and looked at me as if I was polluting the air.

The final entrant was Laura Kadisch, who had been elected to the City Board of Supervisors three years ago. She had succeeded by way of her political activism in school politics. Ten years ago, with three children in elementary school, she had fought for less crowded classrooms and more teachers. Mothers and the teachers' union had responded and helped her win two terms on the school board, where she had been highly visible in firing the district superintendent on the grounds of incompetence and discrimination against female employees. Two years ago she had won a seat on the City Board of Supervisors.

All five supervisors ran in at-large citywide elections, which explained why there weren't any black, brown, or yellow faces looking down at me, despite the county's large minority population.

Bartlow spoke first. "Mr. Fraleigh, I have been designated to begin the questioning, and the first thing I'd like to ask . . ."

"Just a moment, Mr. Bartlow. As you know, yesterday I was elected chairperson of this group for the next month, and I have not called the meeting to order yet," Nola said.

"It's only an interview, not a formal meeting. There's no reason for dragging this out forever. We have four candidates to interview. You were the one who set up a format to save time, now you want to turn the whole thing into a pompous waste of time."

While he was still speaking Nola got up and walked to a coffee warmer set up behind them. With her back to Bartlow she slowly poured herself a cup of coffee. I stifled a smile. Bartlow was glaring and ranting on, but Nola courteously filled a cup for Laura Kadisch, who had joined her at the table. They spoke softly to each other, chuckling over something Nola said. Finally, Bartlow shut off the microphone in front of him and swiveled in his chair so that he didn't have to look at them.

Taking her time, Nola returned to her seat and spoke in a full, pleasant voice. "I now call the meeting to order. This committee is charged with appointing the chief of police for our city. We have four final candidates who will be interviewed this afternoon. The first is our acting chief. Chief Fraleigh, let me explain the procedure. In the interest of time, each supervisor will be allowed fifteen minutes of questioning. Mr. Bartlow will start the questioning and when he finishes, the next questioner will be to his right and we shall follow that order, with the exception of the Chair. I will conclude the interviews." She turned a glowing smile on Bartlow. "You may begin, Mr. Bartlow."

"Thank you, Mr. Chairman," Bartlow sneered. He frowned fiercely. "Officer Fraleigh, you were part of a police operation resulting in a number of deaths and which brought great dishonor to this city . . ."

Nola in her well-modulated voice came right back at him. "Mr. Bartlow, I explained to the board prior to this session that the United States Attorney had advised me that we should refrain from questions in this area since a criminal prosecution is pending and our questions and Chief Fraleigh's answers might interfere with the case. Surely, you do not wish in any way to obstruct the process of justice?"

"Yes, and I told you that *we* run the city, not the U.S. Attorney, and we have a right to know what this man was doing in the situation if we are considering him for a permanent appointment."

"Madam Chairperson, I make a motion that the candidate be instructed not to answer any questions pertaining to the pending criminal case," Laura Kadisch said.

"Second," said Sally Fenton.

"Discussion?" Nola looked around at her colleagues. "No? Then I call for the question. Please press your voting button."

A big tally board on the wall to their right indicated the votes. Green bulbs lit indicating *yes* votes next to the names Kadisch, Fenton, and Henderson. Red *no* lights lit next to Kendle and Bartlow.

"The motion passes three to two," Nola Henderson said. "You may procede with that admonition in mind, Mr. Bartlow."

Bartlow was furious. "I refuse to participate in something so clearly against the public interest. I will not be voting in favor of this candidate."

Nola smiled politely at him. "Do you wish to waive your question time, Mr. Bartlow?" Flipping his microphone off, Bartlow got up and strode out of the chambers. "Let the record show that Mr. Bartlow has declined to use his opportunity for questions and has left the room. Mr. Kendle, it is now your turn to ask questions."

Kendle spoke too closely into the mike, causing a whine. "Let me say for the record that I believe, as does Mr. Bartlow, that no questions should be barred, and that I participate under protest. Mr. Fraleigh, do you recognize this body as having the authority and responsibility for the operation of the police force?"

"Excuse me for interrupting, Mr. Kendle, but Chief Fraleigh may be somewhat confused by your question since the City Charter states that we have the authority to appoint a police chief to *operate* the department subject to our policies and the laws of California and the United States," Nola said.

"Madam Chair, we are all aware that you went to law school. It seems to me that it is a simple question and I would like it answered," Kendle said.

"I don't understand it either," said Laura Kadisch.

I was doing great. I hadn't had to answer a question yet. But, I knew what Kendle was getting at. He didn't like the secret investigation we and the FBI had done of the mayor.

"Very well, I'll rephrase it." Kendle's face was red. "Do you believe this body has a right to know what the police department is doing?"

"Yes, sir. Under all lawful circumstances," I said.

"And you determine what is lawful?"

"I don't think that's called for, Mr. Kendle. The candidate is knowledgeable of the various state and federal codes which require confidentiality of criminal matters. Surely, you wouldn't want a police chief to violate the law by disclosing confidential information?" Nola said.

"Madam Chairman, I don't see how I can use my fifteen minutes to ask questions if you keep interrupting."

"As Chair, it is my responsibility to see that the candidates are treated fairly. I will be happy to grant you extra time to compensate for the time I take to remind you of the rules."

Kendle asked a few questions, but never really got off the ground. I answered all of his legitimate questions easily, and whenever he tried to get into the criminal investigation of the mayor, Nola cut him off. Just before his time ran out he asked, "Chief Fraleigh, how do you explain your men shooting machine guns in a recent raid and letting a dangerous dope pusher escape?"

My competitor for the chief's job, Fritz Gerhart, had not been asleep. "Unfortunately, there was a lack of coordination and a new officer made a human mistake. I've conducted a thorough investigation and we're implementing new training programs to make sure it doesn't happen again," I said.

"Yes, but . . ."

Nola cut in, "I'm sorry, Mr. Kendle, but your time is up. Could you please make this your last question."

"It seems to me, Madam Chairperson, that you ladies would have an interest in stopping this kind of violence. But Mr. Fraleigh, if I understand you correctly, you're assuring this board that you will not be conducting these dangerous and violent undercover operations. Is that correct?"

"I'm confident that our training will prevent that kind of violence, sir," I said.

Sally Fenton asked whether I thought environmental laws were equal in enforcement priorities to other laws. The day before, Nola had called me about the department's plans for policing a rock concert the following week. Somehow during the conversation she had casually managed to convey a few areas of special concern for Fenton and Kadisch. It seemed slightly illegal to me, but she was an attorney and I knew how much she hated Bartlow. So I righteously informed Fenton that if I became chief, I would form a unit to pursue toxic spills and other violations that the police ordinarily didn't look into. She had other questions, but it was clear that my answer on that one was well received.

Laura Kadisch asked me about schools and programs for children and was pleased when I told her how much I loved such efforts. She asked me how many female officers we had in the department and frowned when I said not enough. We tussled for a few minutes over whether the special recruitment programs to hire females were adequate, and she seemed satisfied when I said I would review them to see if they could be improved.

Nola followed the special-interest pattern, but startled me by how much she knew about the department. Her questions elicited my support for our training programs taught by judges and lawyers, and the department's emphasis on the gathering of evidence at crime scenes, as well as the procedures we had set up to prevent evidence from being tainted before it was introduced in court.

Then she surprised me by asking how I felt about crime prevention programs. I said that I had started the department's Home Alert, Rape Awareness, and Child Safety programs, and believed that we had a duty to educate people on how to avoid becoming victims. She asked if the department had any school programs, thus allowing me to titillate Laura Kadisch by describing how closely we worked with educators on drug abuse and truancy prevention programs. I discovered that my answers praising our PAL and Neighborhood Watch programs even caused serious Sally Fenton to smile. And my answer to Nola's final question, disclosing that I had hired a female detective lieutenant from outside the department, caused all three ladies to beam at me. I felt a little guilty because Lieutenant Cathy Stevens did a great job and that was the only reason I had hired her.

Finally, it was over and I was grateful that Kendle's jab at "you ladies" had backfired. None of them had mentioned either Hector Gonzales or the bombing of Charley Thompson. Walking back to headquarters, I thought Paul English was probably right. It would be three to two for me, thanks to Nola. I wondered what the vote would have been had they known about Nola and me.

Nine

THE NEXT MORNING MY SECRETARY, DENISE, TOLD ME that the chairperson of the City Board of Supervisors requested my appearance at 1000 hours in the office of the mayor. I knew the actual mayor wouldn't be using it, since he was somewhere in the labyrinth of the federal judicial correctional system. It was the day after my exhilarating interview with the board, and I walked over to City Hall from headquarters expecting Nola to congratulate me with the news that it had been a three-to-two vote.

I waited in the reception area remembering the times I had been summoned by Mayor Middleston, who pumped me for information on an investigation in which he was a key suspect. Now my edginess had nothing to do with him or even whether I had gotten the chief's job. It was strictly related to the long-legged, green-eyed woman waiting inside.

The middle-aged male secretary told me, "She's off the phone now. You can go in."

Nola was behind the beautiful wooden antique desk that almost got lost in the spacious room. On previous occasions I had always made a point of ignoring Mayor Middleston by pausing to admire the top-floor view of Silicon Valley, but Nola was far more pleasant to look at than the valley. This morning, however, she was tense. I felt a surge of relief. She was trying to find a way to gently tell me that they had given the job to someone else. I wouldn't be in the trenches, once more trying to investigate a top politician without him learning about it.

"It didn't go the way I had hoped." She fiddled with a pencil on the desk. "I still think it will be OK, but Kendle used a delaying tactic that I hadn't anticipated."

Nola wore a pin-striped business suit with a soft off-white blouse. Delicate long gold earrings dangled from her pierced ears and I could just make out the color of her eyes behind the big tinted glasses she wore. She knew how to dress, had a great figure and a good face, but that wasn't why people would stop eating to watch her walk through a restaurant. She had an indefinable something. A kind of voltage flowing through her that radiated out and caught other people's attention. Yet, it wasn't there this morning. For a change, her femininity wasn't impairing my ability to concentrate on her words. I welcomed the shift from technicolor to black-and-white.

"Kendle made a point that we hadn't filed the appropriate public notice a week in advance of the hearing. It's a phony argument, but the city attorney wasn't present and I can't make legal judgments as a supervisor. So we filed notice for the meeting three weeks from now," she said.

"Do I have to go through that garbage again?"

"No. There won't be any interviews. We'll probably just convene and name the new chief."

"But?"

"Well, they're really going after Fenton and Kadisch. I had their votes yesterday, but a lot could happen in three weeks."

"You mean that they suddenly decide one of the other candidates did better and vote for him?"

"You don't understand politics. I found out today that Bartlow and Kendle are offering Fenton their votes on establishing a five-hundred-acre wetlands reserve, something she and the Sierra Club have dreamed about for years. That is, if she goes along with their candidate for police chief. And as if that isn't enough, they're also offering Kadisch a funded school-crossing-guard program that will cost over a half million dollars."

"I didn't think the police chief's job was that valuable."

"Fraleigh, I think you know how far they would go to get Middleston's prosecution thrown out of court, and a new police chief could just discover tainted evidence or perhaps damage the case by influencing some of the officers to change their testimony."

"I thought you three gals were pretty tight together."

"Neither of them gives the police department the highest priority. They didn't care for Middleston ramming sleazy development stuff down their throats, but they don't realize he could be back if the case against him is dismissed."

"And if either one of them switches their vote, I'm out."

"Yes. It would be three to two for someone else. It can happen, and I get the impression that you wouldn't be heartbroken if it did." She left her chair and walked to the window.

Once again I realized that Nola wanted me to be police chief. Given our relationship, it would give her an edge over her colleagues. She had actually crossed the line in coaching me for the board interview and there was no doubt in my mind that she had cut herself off from me romantically because she didn't want to jeopardize her political career. I got up and stood next to her looking to the north where a 747 passenger jet was cutting through the smog to land at San Francisco Airport. "This town hasn't exactly been full of delights," I said, staring at the yellow blanket of air beginning to obscure the bay.

Suddenly she turned and was grinning like a college kid. The way she had looked the night we met. "Still, there have been moments, haven't there?"

Her current was back on and it hit me in the usual way. Just a moment before, the cold politician had left me indifferent, but now she pushed her glasses back on her head and put her hands on top of my shoulders. We were very close and her green eyes were looking into mine with a fire that caused me to catch my breath. "Is this some kind of sexual harassment?" I tried to joke, but neither of us was fooled by it.

Lightly, she touched her lips to mine and the fragrance of her perfume drifted past me. I put my arms around her. When she pulled me close I grew hard. She pushed against me. I could feel her breasts against my chest and she swung her pelvis against my erection and began to rotate her hips. Blood raced through my ears. I felt flushed and was almost dizzy.

Abruptly, she pushed me back. "We have to stop meeting like this," she said smiling, but her voice too had broken and she was breathing hard. Her hands still rested lightly on my shoulders and I wanted to sweep her off her feet and take her to the couch and ravish her. Right there in the mayor's office. To drive her deep into the couch until she moaned with pleasure.

Her voice unsteady, she said, "I wondered why you didn't call. It's been almost three weeks."

"I wondered why *you* didn't." I was unwilling to admit that I hadn't called because she scared the hell out of me. What she had just done had been very deliberate. Sensing that I had been about to say, "Screw the petty politics and intrigue," and walk away from it all, she had used the oldest influence in the world on me. What I hated to admit was that it had worked.

"I'm calling now. Can you come to my place for dinner? Eight o'clock tomorrow night?" Her fingers on my shoulders burned through my suit jacket, and her eyes locked on mine slammed down the independence I tried to summon.

"Unless the world ends sooner, I'll be there at eight." I still didn't have full control of my voice or breathing.

"We both know this is crazy, don't we?" My shoulders felt like they were on fire where her fingers lightly rested.

"Let's get you into this job first, then deal with it."

"Yeah. I don't want you to be treated like Gary Hart."

Her little-girl innocence and laugh were back. "But neither of us is married. And whose reputation is more troubled—the righteous police chief or the politician?"

"Being married wouldn't make any difference."

She was serious again. "I know, Fraleigh. You appeal to me too much. It's making me uneasy."

I had been referring to the kind of treatment we could expect from the media. She had misunderstood, but her words warmed me. I had sensed the same passion in her that was driving me crazy. For three weeks I had been like a mad-man fighting myself. Determined not to be manipulated by her. Then today, my resolve had crumbled in seconds. In her presence the memory of us together had overwhelmed me.

Ten

WE FIRST MET IN THE BOWELS OF THE COUNTY OFFICE building. Nola chaired a drug abuse commission for the county bar association, and as chief of detectives I had been sentenced to represent the police chief. Most of the committee members were people running some drug program or another for a living. There were also a couple of rich suburban matrons who had gotten too old for junior league, and three lawyers to make sure the meetings never ended on time and that nothing sensible was accomplished.

My thoughts were on the masked rapist who had attacked six Silicon City women. I was engrossed in planning a way to trap him when I became aware of the silence in the meeting room. Nola Henderson was smiling at me. Nice white teeth. "Well, Chief?"

I realized that she had asked me a question. The silence grew as I sat there hoping someone would give me a clue.

"We wanted to know what the police department's opinion was on the issue," she said.

Her eyes had a twinkle, and I noticed that they were a lovely green. She knew I didn't have the faintest idea of the question. I toyed with the idea of saying that the department wouldn't have an opinion until more research was done. A safe answer, but something about the way she was waiting made me say, "I'm sorry. I missed the question."

"The question was whether this committee should continue to meet around a rectangle or should form a circle," she said.

After the meeting, I went up to her. "I notice the Chair has no respect for law and order. You tried to trap me."

She laughed. "Tried? You were a million miles away."

"Let me ask you—it's Nola, isn't it?"

"Yes. At least you got that right."

"Nola, let me ask you how you keep your own concentration during these sessions?"

"There is an awful lot of bullshit, isn't there?" A college-girl grin appeared and held.

"Will it placate the Chair if I buy you a glass of wine?"

"No, but two might do it."

At her suggestion I followed her BMW down the freeway, getting off at the Hamilton Avenue exit and parking next to her in front of the tower building. We took a window table in Sebastion's top-floor lounge where I splurged and ordered a bottle of Chardonnay from the nearby Lohr winery.

"Um, this is delicious." She sipped the wine. "And a whole bottle. I should have embarrassed you a couple of weeks ago."

"Just good public relations, ma'am," I said.

"Hm, I bet." She raised an eyebrow. Her smile was wide and I found myself grinning. If she had read my lustful mind it hadn't fazed her. "Does everyone ask how your face got so banged up? I won't. You were a boxer or football player, right?"

"Is that the kind of questioning they teach in Santa Clara Law School, Nola?"

"Stanford. By the way, before you cut off my wine, I do want to say that some of us in the county bar association admire what you've done in the department."

"What I've done?"

"Yes. Terminating and prosecuting those two cops for brutality. And implementing training courses on evidence handling, questioning of suspects, and testifying in court. It's long-overdue."

"How do you know all that?"

"I'm fascinated by the government of Silicon City—or I should say the lack of it."

"Thinking of running for office?"

"Why not? Someone has to stop the rape of the city by developers."

"Ah, a reformer. Good luck."

"Listen, cynical cop, you're a bit of a reformer yourself."

"What made you become a lawyer?" Discussing reform of local politics wasn't going to get us anywhere.

"I don't know. I majored in political science in college. Law is a logical way to go. Then too, my dad is a lawyer. You know him, Judge Henderson." She stared at me as if I should have reacted to his name.

"Yes, I know of him. Where did you grow up?"

"New York. Dad was with a Wall Street firm. The firm assigned him to work with start-up computer companies out here. He got in on the ground floor, became an expert, became a member of the California bar, and we moved out here. A couple of years ago he was appointed to the Superior Court."

I had skimmed an article in the paper about Judge David Henderson. Nola hadn't mentioned that her old man had made a fortune and developed a lot of political clout before getting appointed to the bench.

"My mom died in a car accident in New York when I was fifteen." Her eyes misted.

When she was fifteen in New York. I was jolted to realize that she had been there when my police career and family life had crashed to an end. I was a little bit surprised that she hadn't read about me, but fifteen-year-old girls have more sense than to read that stuff.

"I'm sorry. You still miss her," I said.

Soft evening light coming through the glass walls played on her face. The panoramic view of the valley was unmarred this evening. Strong winds had cleared out the smog, and the surrounding hills for miles around us were touched with the same mellow light that flickered over her hair and eyes. It was easy to forget that it was a view of mindless sprawl built by California land-development greed. Coming in from the parking lot, the springtime air had caressed us. Now, at the table, she put her hand over mine and squeezed. "I like you. You were embarrassed when I complimented you. You're tough just like a cop, but I sense something underneath." She left her hand on mine until she was sure I understood.

When we were leaving I asked if she would like to go out to dinner sometime and she said yes. A week later we had a great dinner at Les Saisons in the Fairmont Hotel in San Jose. She was bright, and I enjoyed her irreverent comments about Silicon City politics.

The task force was meeting one night a week then, and we got in the habit of having a couple of glasses of wine at Sebastion's afterward. The third week, as she was getting into her car, I impulsively took her hand and kissed her lightly on the lips. I was startled when she embraced me, hungrily returning my kiss. Her tongue darted between my lips, and my own inhibitions vanished. I pressed hard against her, beginning to caress her breast. She moaned and then surprised me again by shoving me back.

"No," she said, her face as flushed as mine.

"Nola," I took her hand again and she didn't remove it. "We're obviously attracted to each other. Don't you think it's time you showed me your etchings or law books or something in your place?"

She freed her hand and put it gently on my face. "I need more time. I'm not sure you and I should get involved."

"What's wrong?"

"Well, I don't do much criminal law, but . . . I know it sounds weird, yet somehow with your job, I don't know. I don't want to lose my objectivity, my independence."

I didn't get it. I was sure that Nola was as attracted to me as I was to her, yet she had cut the relationship off.

I thought a lot about her during the long days before the task force met again. On one hand, she was the likeable, irreverent, grinning college girl. But she was also a desirable woman whose sex appeal made my knees weak. And then too, there was the bright, insightful, ambitious future politician. The meetings had been held on Wednesdays, but for some reason, that week we met on a Monday night. The four long tables in the meeting room were arranged in a square. She always sat opposite me across the room, and I was disappointed when I saw that she wasn't there. The meeting began and about fifteen minutes later she came in wearing the cream-colored dress and Bally boots. Taking her seat, she gave me a brief smile.

I was more impatient than ever for the dumb meeting to be over. Finally, it ended. I drifted over to her as she picked up her bag and asked as casually as I could manage if she was in the mood for Sebastion's. Her smile seemed a little strained, but she said sure.

It took about ten minutes to get there and I knew something was wrong when I got a space right in front of the building entrance. As she was pulling in behind me I walked into the lobby and saw a sign announcing that Sebastion's closed on Mondays. Damn. I hadn't noticed it on our earlier visits.

"We're out of luck. They close on Mondays. We could go someplace else or if you've got wine chilled at home . . ." I said, giving her my best leer.

She looked at me for a long moment, quite serious, unmoving behind the wheel. "I do have some Chablis. Why don't you follow me, it's only five minutes."

Her condo was small, filled with green plants, very feminine, and much neater than mine. Given its location, I was sure it was also considerably more expensive. She waved me to a couch and went into the kitchen for the wine. She poured it with a smile, but she was tense. Hell, we were both tense. I raised my glass. "To you." She clinked her glass against mine and sipped a little, but moved away when I put my arm on her shoulder. She went over to a stereo and put on some soft rock. She came back and perched on the edge of the couch putting her left foot in my lap. "Be a strong male. Help me get my boots off."

I tugged hard enough to wonder how she did it by herself. When I had removed the second boot I ran my hand over her smoothly nyloned foot. Without a word she got up and went into the bedroom. I picked up the boot and stroked the rich leather still warm from her flesh and smell. I took another swig of the wine, feeling even more uncomfortable. I knew how badly I wanted her and how miserable I was going to be if it turned out to be just a friendly drink and goodnight.

After a couple of minutes she returned wearing a short white terry cloth bathrobe. Getting up quickly, I spilled a few drops of wine on my shirt. When I had put the glass down, she put her arms around me and we kissed. I was aroused as hell, but she was still tense and it affected me. She led me by the hand into the bedroom where I saw that she had turned down the bed. As quickly as I could, I undressed and tossed my clothes onto a chair. She had discarded the robe and gotten under the covers while I was busy undressing.

Under the covers she put her hand on my cheek and looked into my eyes. I kissed her lips and my right hand found her breast with the nipple already hard. My own passion was getting out of control and I covered her with kisses. I knew she needed more time, but I couldn't wait. Within minutes I was inside her, thrashing away, determined to possess her. It was over too quickly even for me to really feel deep pleasure. I knew it must have been a zero experience for her. Feeling crummy, I held on to her while she kept her arms lightly around me, neither of us saying a word.

A few minutes later I said, "Can I at least get you some wine?"

"I'd like that."

I went into the kitchen and found the open bottle in the refrigerator and topped off our glasses. I noticed a tray on the cupboard and put the bottle and glasses on it and threw a cloth napkin over my arm. When I returned to the bedroom, she had fluffed out the pillows and was sitting upright wearing the terry cloth robe. The bed sheets were pulled halfway up, covering her legs. I didn't comment about it, but suddenly was conscious of my own nakedness.

"Is that the latest waiter's outfit?" She raised her eyebrows.

Sitting in bed we chatted easily. She kept her hand on mine, occasionally touching me on the shoulder or thigh as she spoke. We were on court stories and I told her about a dumb mistake I had made on the witness stand on my first homicide case, inadvertently substituting the victim's name for the defendant's. Her eyes shone and her laugh was music.

On our third and last glass of wine I noticed that her cheeks were slightly flushed. She was speaking about her first big criminal trial. Nola had been impressing the jury, dramatically challenging the arresting officer on whether he was sure that *this* was the murder knife, when she dropped it in his lap. I chuckled at the picture, and she bent forward, really laughing. Her hair cascaded over her face. I gently helped her to put it back in place, enjoying its soft texture. I had seen the robe getting looser and looser over the past half hour and when she had leaned over it came fully open. That, and her touching gestures, got me stiff again, and since I had stubbornly refused to pull the sheet up as she had, it was quite obvious.

She placed her nearly full wine glass on the table beside her and tossed the robe on the floor. Turning back to me she took me in her hand and began gently stroking. "Now," she said, covering my lips with hers. "Now."

I thought I'd have total control this time, but she erupted with such passion that I realized I had only taken a couple of minutes longer than the first time. I'm not a counter, but it was still long enough for her to have evened the score with a doubleheader, and it was that excitement that set me off in turn. She clung to me, our breathing slowly subsiding. Then she set her soft hair on my shoulder, keeping her arm firmly around my waist.

After twenty minutes she got up to use the bathroom, leaving the robe on the floor. *At least a ten,* I thought, evaluating her figure in my typically crude male fashion. She came back and knelt in bed. Leaning forward, she supported herself on her arms and gave me a little peck on the mouth. Her firm breasts pointed down toward the bed and I cupped them in my hands. She sighed. "Do you like Chinese?" she asked.

My mind raced. *Chinese?* What kind of stuff was she talking about?

And then, having read my mind, she giggled. "You're terrible." She held her hand to her mouth trying to control her laughter. "Not Chinese *sex. Food.* I want to send out for some Chinese *food.* Then after dinner, we'll find out how insatiable you really are."

For two weeks thereafter we were together almost every night. Like a couple of kids, it was our big secret and we just about wore her bed out, although the other rooms also came in for some fun and games.

She had mentioned a previously scheduled three-week vacation in Europe, and suddenly it was time. We said good-bye at her place. I knew I was going to miss her, and I did.

By the time she got back, the Middleston case had broken, Chief Louis Robinson was dead, and Mayor Middleston had appointed me acting chief to take Louis Robinson's place, never dreaming that I was counting the days until I could give the FBI the evidence necessary to arrest him. I managed to speak to Nola once in the week she got back, but things were so hectic we didn't see each other.

The next week she was appointed to the Board of Supervisors to fill the vacancy caused by the unfortunate mixture of good gin and bad driving by the late Lawrence Smith. Nola had become one of my five bosses. I called her and suggested a celebration dinner. "We better think about this for a while, Fraleigh. I don't want to endanger your job, and I certainly hope you'll get the appointment permanently," she said. She didn't mention that her own appointment was only for four months, then she would have to run for election. I remembered her political ambition. If word leaked of our romance, she might lose an election that should otherwise be a slamdunk.

I couldn't change her mind about us getting together. But, a couple of weeks later we attended a two-day drug task force regional meeting in San Francisco. The group had been booked into the Hyatt Regency in Embarcadero Square, but I reserved a room at the Hyatt in Union Square. I managed to talk Nola into riding with me to have a drink in the top-floor lounge there.

"It is beautiful here," she said, holding my hand and looking out at the Golden Gate Bridge.

"Nola, I'm afraid I got confused over which Hyatt the conference was at. I made reservations here, but my room is only a couple of floors below us and the view is just as spectacular of the bay."

"I bet you just made an innocent mistake," she said, running her nails lightly over my hand.

A few minutes later she agreed that the view was everything I had said. She spent most of the night with me, and it was better than ever.

The next night she came to my place and we made love and I thought we were back together. We had too much wine with dinner. About eleven o'clock we were sitting in bed, both drowsily sipping brandies. I had my arm around her and for some reason said, "It's amazing how the Board of Supervisors spotted your talents running the drug abuse commission. Look how many years it took me to get recognized. I guess not everyone has to work their way up through the ranks."

It hadn't been much of a joke, but I was surprised by Nola's reaction. She took my arm from her shoulder, gave me a contemptuous look, and turned out the light on the side table. She rolled away from me to the side of the bed. No goodnight. Nothing. I sat next to her in the dark, pissed. Finally, I finished my drink. I'd tease her about it in the morning. I don't think either of us slept well during the night, but I fell into a deep sleep as dawn was breaking. I slept so soundly that I never heard her leave. A note on the dresser said, "Dear Chief, Don't call me. I'll call you." It was signed Supervisor Nola Henderson.

That had been it. I had hoped that she had left her panties as a sign she would come back. But neither of us had made any effort to get together since then. Now, in the luxurious mayor's office, she had turned on the charm and I was like a high school kid counting the hours until I would see her again. But it nagged, along with another question.

"Nola, there was something I wondered about."

"Forever the detective. What's on your mind?"

"Well, your interim appointment by the Board of Supervisors was unanimous. I know that doesn't mean much since it's standard form to make such things unanimous once it's clear that the appointee has a majority vote of three. I can see Fenton and Kadisch, given their strong identification with women's rights, the environment, and education, being happy with you, but where did the crucial third vote come from? I can't understand either of those crooked rats Kendle or Bartlow voting for you."

"Fraleigh, they're really not that bad. I've got to run now. Let's discuss it tomorrow night." She sent me on my way with a friendly peck on the cheek and the advice, "Stay away from anything controversial until next week. No more stings and naked suspects escaping. Once the appointment is made, you have a property right in the job under California law, and can only be removed by due process. Right now you're dog meat if you get into any hot public issues."

Walking across the street to headquarters I wondered why she had said no more stings. Was it just an innocent reference to the Gonzales escape fiasco or had word of Bolero already reached city hall? And Nola saying that Kendle and Bartlow weren't really that bad? My evenings with Nola were always fascinating. Tomorrow night might be even more intriguing.

Eleven

AT HER DESK OUTSIDE MY OFFICE, DENISE LOOKED HAR-rassed. "Chief Fraleigh, the phone hasn't stopped ringing. Look at these messages." She held up a thick wad of telephone message slips.

"Chuck them, Denise. Let's you and I go out for a beer. What do you say?"

"Oh, God. You are impossible. And not only the tele-phone, but Captain Toll was here twice, Lieutenant Short once, and Lieutenant Keller twice, Lieutenant Martinez once. They all need to see you urgently. And the reporters from both newspapers and two television stations were here to interview you about whether you think you'll be selected. And if you are, what are you going to do about the racial attacks and the rise in complaints about police brutality? Also, they wanted to know if you'd resign in protest if you don't get the job, and whether or not you think your role in the Middleston case will hurt or help you. And oh, yes, they want to interview you on your position on a civilian review board. You aren't for one, are you?" she asked, frowning, concerned about my reputation with the troops and safety in the building.

The department of over a thousand cops was a shambles. There never had been an assistant chief appointed. Nor a chief of patrol. I had been chief of detectives before being appointed acting chief, so now that slot was also open. People were scurrying around in a frenzy of confusion and ambition.

And, of course, the news media could always be counted on to stir things up. "Next time any of those people call you, just tell them to go to hell, Denise."

Her sincere, pretty young face got even more serious. "And that detective they call the Block was looking for you." She had never lost her initial fear of the Block's ferocious appearance and worried for my safety in his presence. I hadn't been able to convince her that the Block's only danger to me was his eccentric professional behavior.

I mocked fear, raising my hand in alarm. "Did he look angry, Denise?"

"Go ahead, laugh at me for trying to do my job."

I realized she was near tears. "I'm just kidding around a little, Denise. We'll all have to be patient until the supervisors get off their butts and decide who should be police chief. Then things will quiet down around here."

She was horror-stricken. "They're not thinking of appointing someone else?"

I took pity on her. She had enough to worry about around this zoo. "No. Not really. It's just some formality they have to go through." Ha.

At my desk I flipped through the phone messages. Reverend Thomas Phillips from the local NAACP requested an immediate meeting to discuss better police reaction to racial harassment of blacks. There had been three separate incidents in which white screwball kids with shaved heads had planted burning crosses on the lawns of black families. We had an informant in the group and expected to make arrests soon, but couldn't disclose what we had achieved without exposing the informant.

I had met Reverend Phillips a month earlier. He was in his second term as president of the local NAACP. Reasonable and soft-spoken, he was well respected not only in the black community, but throughout the city. His criticisms of the department would bring a reaction from the Board of Supervisors. His message also disclosed that the association was considering asking for a civilian review board because of an increase in police brutality complaints by blacks. In addition, they wanted to know why the department's affirmative-action goals hadn't brought black representation on the force up to proportion with the population, while Hispanics and Asians were hired in much greater numbers. I wrote a note to Denise to set up the appointment with the NAACP, and to ask the head of intelligence to brief me on the skinhead case.

A message from Patrolman William Smith, president of the Peace Officers Association, said that they were considering a vote of no-confidence in me because the Internal Affairs unit was convicting cops of brutality just to appease minority groups, and the personnel unit was implementing an illegal affirmative-action hiring program for the same reason. He had also protested that I had caved in to the Female Officers Association in order to get the chief's job. I wrote a note to schedule a meeting with him.

Lieutenant Cathy Stevens's message said that the Sex Crimes Victims Association was going to file a formal protest with the Board of Supervisors because we had stopped our twenty-four-hour special team response to serious sex crimes. Lieutenant Stevens reminded me that she had warned me of this reaction during budget sessions. At the time, I had told everyone that the city had cut our operational budget by 7 percent and overtime had to be reduced. I wrote, "Do the best you can," and sent the note back to Lieutenant Stevens.

The next message informed me that the Chamber of Commerce was officially complaining about grafitti being scribbled all over downtown. The chamber believed that it was the direct result of my having stopped uniform foot patrol downtown. I wrote a note to Captain Toll, the patrol commander, asking if we had curtailed foot patrol downtown as part of the budget cut.

The district attorney's office wanted a meeting to protest the increase in domestic violence arrests we were making.

They didn't have enough lawyers to handle the cases. And there was a message from the Battered Women's Association demanding a meeting to complain that male officers were not making arrests in domestic violence cases. I scratched a note to Denise telling her to have them call each other. Then, remembering her teary eyes a few minutes ago, I crossed it out and wrote that she should set up meetings for me with the two groups.

The Regional News Editors Association wanted a meeting to complain that the department was illegally withholding news information from the press, especially in cases which reflected unfavorably on the police. I OK'd a meeting.

Denise buzzed that Captain Gerhart was present and had to see me. With less than 100 percent enthusiasm I watched Fritz Gerhart come into my office. He was bulky without being fat, and his round undertaker's face exuded goodwill while he planned my funeral. Gerhart tried to camouflage his receding hairline by combing it over his brow in bangs, like teenage bobby-soxers did in the 1950s. It didn't work any better than his attempts at charming people. He eased his six-foot frame into a chair.

"Morning, Chief. I've been trying to get in to see you for some time." His smile was as sincere and warm as an insurance salesman's.

"Really? I don't have any messages to that effect. Who did you speak to, Captain?"

Gerhart shifted in his seat. "Well, I didn't actually call. Just looked in a few times. Your office was empty or the door was shut. I didn't want to disturb you."

"Never feel that you're disturbing me, Captain, if it's something important." I wondered what he was up to. He'd send his mother to the joint to get the chief's job, so he hadn't come to see me for idle chitchat.

"I'm very concerned about this report, Chief." Gerhart put a crime-complaint form on my desk. Glancing at it, I saw that it was the one Sergeant Myers had brought to me, which elevated Nunzio Papa's scuffle in the diner into the crime of the century.

"Yes?" I said.

"Well, you see, I traced the car license plate and it comes back 'Law Enforcement, Confidential,' under your name."

Looking at Gerhart, I suddenly found myself thinking of shyster Bartlow penetrating the criminal-history computer. I scratched a reminder to myself to have Paul check Gerhart out.

"You know about it, Chief?" Gerhart said, when I just sat looking at him.

I had the growing feeling that Gerhart, sweet chap that he was, might be wearing a wire. "I'm not sure that I understand your concern, Captain."

"The detective bureau is responsible for follow-up investigations of crime reports. I'm responsible, and this appears that it may involve serious misconduct on the part of a member of the department."

"That's commendable of you, Fritz. How did the report happen to come to your attention?" I said, pretty sure that Sergeant Myers had covered his bets in case Gerhart got the chief's job instead of me.

Gerhart ran his hand through his hair. "It's my job to review crime reports."

"True. But, this report indicates a misdemeanor if it's anything at all. And I spoke to you last week about paying attention to priorities. I still haven't received your report on the series of dormitory rapes, the stocking-mask rapist, and the teenage Uzi robbery gang."

"Chief, I have to formally protest. This kind of conduct by police officers can't be tolerated. And I should know about an undercover car. If there is an undercover operation under way, I should be made aware of it."

"Oh, come on, Fritz. Every textbook on police work says that intelligence should be on a need-to-know basis. I would have informed you if it affected your work."

"Officer safety is at stake. Suppose my men ran into undercover people without realizing it? Somebody could get hurt."

"Captain, I took all that into consideration. I'm personally having the incident investigated to see if there was misconduct." I decided in the name of prudence not to tell Gerhart that the Block had been assigned to the job. "I assure you there's no danger, and I take full responsibility. I assume you're not questioning my judgment. Now please tell me why I haven't received your reports."

"You'll have them tomorrow."

Gerhart's voice was pleasant enough, but his red face, angry eyes, and stiff shoulders gave away his mood as he stalked out of my office. I hadn't dismissed him, but magnanimously decided to overlook his abrupt departure. It wouldn't be long before he identified Nunzio. People had seen me leaving headquarters with him. Eventually, one of Gerhart's flunkies was sure to figure out that I was the other man in the report. Even Gerhart was shrewd enough to guess that Nunzio was probably involved in a new sting and bringing me for an inspection. There was no doubt in my mind that Gerhart would bring this information to Supervisor Bartlow in return for his continuing political support. So, we had time pressure on how long we could take to find out what the Bartlow brothers were up to.

Captain Toll appeared in my doorway. His spit-shined shoes made me pull my scuffed loafers back under the desk. He saluted. I waved him to a chair. "What's up, Toll?"

"Well sir, I have a list of things set in priorities."

I groaned inwardly. I was only a quarterway down my phone list, and I absolutely had to see the Block and Paul English about the sting. I knew from past experiences with Toll that every detail of multiple issues would be covered with excruciating thoroughness.

"Sergeant Burton is in a bad way. I couldn't get hold of you, so I placed him on administrative leave," Toll said.

I leaned forward. Toll was great at following orders, but uneasy at making independent decisions. For him to have put a veteran sergeant on administrative leave was a big event.

"You know him, Chief Fraleigh. He's an old-timer, big, redfaced, on motorcycle patrol for years."

"What's his problem?"

"Well, he's got this pretty nineteen-year-old daughter. And now she's going out with Detective Frank Coombs."

"So?"

Toll squirmed a little. "Detective Coombs is black."

"So?"

"Well, you know, Chief, Burton is an old-timer, an Okie. He's taking it pretty hard."

"That's his problem, isn't it?"

"Unfortunately, he was observed running around the locker room with his service revolver drawn, looking for Detective Coombs. It took four men to disarm him and his gun went off and broke a water pipe which soaked around fifty uniforms stored in the lockers."

"Jesus! Is he crazy?"

"Not only that, he may be suicidal. The department shrink, er, psychologist says that it's imperative that you call Burton and reassure him so that he doesn't hurt himself. He's at home."

I buzzed Denise. "Get Sergeant Burton on the phone. He's at home."

Toll continued. "The Policewomen's Association is coming to see you. They're complaining that Training Officer Getty has been forcing female recruits into the sack saying he'll flunk them on probation if they don't comply. They demand we fire him."

"Did he do it?"

"In at least a couple of cases."

"Then fire him."

"You know he's black, Chief?"

"I don't give a goddamn if he's chartreuse, fire the son of a bitch!"

Paul English had entered the office as I yelled at Toll, who shrank back into his chair. The Block was right behind Paul and both were smiling happily at me when Denise buzzed to say that Sergeant Burton was on the line.

I snatched up the phone. "Burton, what's this crap I hear about you running around my locker room and firing a shot through the water pipe?"

Paul said, "He's on the phone, Fraleigh, you don't have to shout. He can hear you."

Burton had mumbled something that Paul's voice kept me from hearing. "Speak up, Burton," I kept right on yelling.

He said timidly over the wire, "I'm sorry, Chief, but you heard about my daughter . . ."

"I heard, Burton, and that racial bullshit went out years ago. People around here think you're acting like an asshole. I don't know whether to fire you, take your stripes, or give you a stiff suspension."

"Chief, I had these stripes for fifteen years. I know I made a mistake. Give me ten days. I promise you I won't fuck up again. And I'll apologize to Detective Coombs."

"All right. A ten-day suspension, but you go and see the shrink before you come back to work."

I thought of how I had spent the last forty minutes. What had Nola said, "avoid controversy"?

"You'd be a natural on the suicide hot line, Fraleigh," the Block said. "The undertakers would have a boom."

"I'd be great if either one of you called the hot line," I said.

Denise stuck her head into the office. "Captain Toll, communications just called. They have a sniper barricaded out at Sixteenth Street."

Toll jumped up. "Excuse me, Chief, I better get on it."

He was in such a rush, he almost forgot to salute. "Let me know what's happening," I yelled after him. The Block and English stood at attention saluting Toll on his way out. He glared at them, but kept going, thank God. The Block had a brown paper bag in his lap, which he nearly dropped in saluting Toll. "You don't need an administrator in this job. You need a psychiatrist with a big goddamned net," I said.

Paul spoke softly. "Beware the *Tender Is the Night* syndrome, Fraleigh. It's very common among police chiefs."

"What the hell are you talking about?"

"In Scott Fitzgerald's famous novel by that name the hero is a psychiatrist who manages to cure his wife's madness only to find that being so immersed in her sickness has driven him insane."

"Well, if that's true, I must really be screwy having been around you and the Block all these years. What's in the paper bag, Block?"

"A couple of bottles of champagne. We figured they voted you in as chief and a little bubbly would be a nice celebration."

"You know there's no drinking in headquarters."

"Yeah. But you're the chief. You can suspend the rule."

"OK. Close the door and get three glasses out of the cabinet."

He popped the cork and we hoisted our glasses. "Pretty good, ain't it?" the Block asked, loudly smacking his lips. "What was it, a three-to-two vote, Fraleigh?"

"Right. Three to two, but I didn't get the job."

The Block spilled some wine onto my phone messages. "What! Those rotten bastards. Who'd they give it to?"

"Nobody. They voted to postpone the vote three weeks."

"You're always so smug, Fraleigh, when you play one of your childish pranks on us," Paul said.

"Yeah. I spent six ninety-five a bottle on this stuff in Liquor Barn and you didn't even get the lousy job." The Block stuffed the unopened bottle back into the bag as I refilled my glass.

"You had the job description right, Block, *lousy*," I said. Yet, I had to admit I now wanted the chief's job. Supervisor Bartlow's determination that I shouldn't be chief made me stubborn. I would hang on to the job, at least long enough for him and his shyster brother to take a fall in the Blue Mirage sting. "Another thing," the Block lectured me in his growl, "you shouldn't be drinking. You gotta be careful for a couple of weeks."

I told them what had happened at the Board of Supervisors meeting, and then we got down to police work. I didn't glance at the pile of "urgent" messages I hadn't gotten to.

"I want the top priority of the sting shifted to get the cop who's feeding confidential information to that shyster Bartlow," I said.

They both frowned at me. "There's a lot of heavy stuff going down, Fraleigh. We got word that an armored-car heist is in the works, and we ain't hardly started to nail the neighborhood burglars."

"Not only that," Paul added, "we need to let Bartlow play out his scheme. If we move too quickly, we'll lose him. We're just beginning to trace the bond he gave us."

"You guys aren't thinking clearly. If the cop who's feeding info to Bartlow gets word of the sting, it's all over. Last week you asked me to get the uniformed cops to ease up on The Blue Mirage, because they've spotted all the crooks going in and out and are starting to lean on the place. And intelligence has some tips too, remember? We had to stop them from busting the bar. Each week we've had to tell more and more people in the department. It's only a matter of time until the dirty cop or cops hear about it."

Twelve

I SAT THROUGH THE WEEKLY MEETING OF DETECTIVE
squad commanders. I might have been a defense lawyer,
for all the information the lieutenants were willing to give.
Fritz Gerhart was at the opposite end of the long table and
it was clear that he had an iron grip on the detective bureau.
The squad commanders gave brief reports, volunteering
nothing.

I asked a couple of questions, trying to get them to loosen
up. Gerhart cut in, giving the answers, and the lieutenants
looked out the window. Fritz was notorious for paybacks.
No one wanted to cross him. They read the newspapers and
made weekly bets on whether or not I would survive.

"Give me a more detailed account of where we are on
Zorro," I said.

Fritz Gerhart nodded at Lieutenant Cathy Stevens, head
of the sexual assault investigation unit. Gerhart didn't dare
talk about cases that required detailed knowledge.

I had brought Cathy Stevens into the department as a
lieutenant. She was a good-looking woman in her early
forties. She wore a conservative dark-blue dress with a
wide white belt. She could have been head of personnel
at one of the nearby electronics companies, except for the
gold badge fastened to the left side of her belt and the Smith
& Wesson Magnum on the right side.

Cathy had been a sergeant in the sheriff's department,
and despite having won a shootout in which her male
partner had been killed, and having subsequently run the

best rape investigation unit in California, she had been stuck in sergeant's rank in the male chauvinists' sheriffs' organization. Lucky for me. She knew her business better than most men, and didn't tolerate any crap in sexual assault. Two months after Fritz Gerhart had taken over the detective bureau, Cathy Stevens had requested a transfer to patrol. Gerhart had approved it. I had denied the transfer. It was painful for Cathy, but I couldn't let Gerhart drive out the competent and loyal squad commanders.

"Well, Chief, as you know, he's unique. He's good for at least eight attacks that we know of. Only about half of rape victims report in the first place and with him, probably less. He's called Zorro because of the large black mask and the old-world courtesy he uses. Some of the victims describe him as handsome and needing help." A few smirks appeared on the faces of Cathy's male counterparts. The only female in the room, she paused. The smiles disappeared as her gaze circled the group.

Cathy continued, "Despite his charm, he's dangerous, possibly Fifty-one Fifty, and always gains entrance by using a gun."

Fifty-one Fifty was a section of the California Public Health Law which allowed us to take mentally disturbed people into custody for psychiatric examination. "Cathy, what kind of evidence do we have?" I asked.

"Great evidence once we know who he is, but right now it's not helping us find him. He wears gloves, so we have no prints. Because of the mask, we have no eyewitness ID from the victims other than that he is a male Caucasion, from twenty to thirty years old, medium build, from five eight to six feet tall, and wears Old Spice shaving lotion. On one job he accidently cut his hand. We have a good blood sample and have his DNA profile, which matches the pattern taken in the vaginal swabs. Also, we have a couple of pubic hairs and some clothing fiber. If we zero in on the right suspect, we should have him cold."

"Any leads?"

"Yes, Chief. He always takes jewelry and credit cards from the victims. We're canvassing all pawnshops and secondhand dealers and we have the various credit card companies alerted. But he pistol-whipped the last two victims for no reason. That's why we think he's a dangerous whacko. He brutally sodomized the last woman anally. She's seventy-one years old. We better nail Zorro soon. We're working closely with patrol on M.O. and possible locations."

Ordinarily I would have put Fritz Gerhart on the spot, warning him that publicity about these cases was creating panic among women throughout the city, but I knew Cathy was running a good investigation, and making Fritz nervous would only cause him to get in her way. The meeting ended and I went back to my office.

As usual, there was a new pile of phone messages. I dropped the first three in the wastebasket. The fourth message was from Nola. Our dinner date was off. She had suddenly been called to New York to attend a drug symposium. What the hell was going on? There was nothing sudden about drug symposiums. Nothing that interesting either. I called Denise to find out what Nola had actually said. Naturally, Denise was at lunch.

Impatiently waiting for her to return, I went over my ups and downs with Nola. During the first weeks of our relationship she was all allure, beautiful, bright, entertaining, and . . . yes, ambitious. And, at first, ambivalent about getting involved with me. Yet, she had been up-front about her ambition. Nola wanted to get into politics in the worst way. To reform the world. I had heard it all before. Maybe I shouldn't have been such a wet blanket about her reform ideas.

But it hadn't seemed to matter. The weeks of our romance had been as sweet as a love song in spring. Nola and I couldn't get enough of each other. Then, with her appointment to the Board of Supervisors, she cut me cold. I had to elaborately seduce her in San Francisco to get close to her again for just a couple of nights. On the other hand, I had to admit she was probably right. If our relationship became known, we were both finished in public office. I was willing to risk it. She wasn't. To be fair, she loved the chance she had been given. To me, the chief's job sucked and I wasn't even sure that I wanted it. If it weren't for not wanting to let the Bartlow brothers and Gerhart win, I probably would have looked for a job elsewhere doing what I liked, investigation.

Then yesterday, after two weeks of separation, Nola senses that I'm about to throw in the towel and turns on the charm setting up a date which she is now breaking. And when I question how she had gotten a vote from crooks like Bartlow or Kendle, she says they're not that bad. It hadn't taken Nola long to ease into betrayal and compromise, the essential skills of politics.

Denise came in. "Did you want to see me, Chief?"

"Yes, Denise. I wanted to ask about this message from Supervisor Henderson. Did she say when she was leaving for New York and how long she was staying?"

"No. The message was from her secretary, George."

I dialed Nola's office and asked for her. "I'm sorry, Chief, but she took off an hour ago."

"OK, no problem. She wanted me to call her. I'll give her a call in New York. What hotel is she staying in?"

There was hesitation on the other side. Had he been instructed not to tell me? I decided to find out. "George, Nola wanted me to give her some information relative to local drug problems that she could use at the symposium."

"Oh yes, Chief," he said, relieved at not having to stonewall me. "Supervisor Henderson's at the Walton Hotel in Manhattan."

Something kept me from calling her. Maybe it was because I wanted to so badly. Instead, I immersed myself in the budget. Unit commanders had requested twenty-one million dollars in additional personnel and equipment. At a staff meeting a month before they submitted their reports I had told everyone that the city had mandated a one-million-dollar cutback in police department operating expenses. My two captains in command, Toll in patrol and Gerhart in the dick bureau, had passed on their subordinates' requests without comment. I was to play the bad guy.

I dictated a memo ordering Toll and Gerhart to give me their recommendations for a half-million-dollar reduction in each of their bureau's operating budget. It was unfair to Gerhart, since his bureau was only a third the size of patrol, but making tough decisions would hopefully keep him busy for a while.

The papers blurred before me. Unsuccessfully, I fought against visions of Nola's long hair and memories of her touch and smell in bed. It was getting dark when I gave up. Pushing the paperwork aside, I considered the long, empty evening. I called the sting. Paul English answered. When I told him I was coming out he said, "It's always an honor to have you at our side as we act as our brothers' keepers."

I parked the suggested two blocks from the sting and made my way through the streets to The Blue Mirage's back entrance, apparently unobserved by foreign espionage agents, international criminal cartels, or local crooks. The streets were quiet, deserted.

In the back room the Block handed me a sandwich overflowing with ham, swiss cheese, lettuce, tomato, and mayonnaise. "Our cholesterol special for the chief," Paul English said.

The cop manning the monitor was Art Estrada. He shifted his eyes when he looked up and saw me watching him. He had been assigned to the Narcotics Squad until two weeks ago when I had flopped him back into uniform over Fritz Gerhart's objections. We had information from the feds that Estrada had screwed up two big cases being done in a joint operation with us. Estrada's sloppy preparation and questionable relationships with informants and a fairly big pusher in the region had led the U.S. Attorney to decline prosecution. Once again it appeared that my assistants the Block and Paul English had overridden my personnel decision without bothering to mention it to me.

I hadn't realized I was starving. Wolfing down the sandwich and a couple of Michelobs provided by the Block from his ever-ready pitcher, I half listened to Manny Herrera and Mary Falcone working a young white guy in the next room. The Block said, "This kid isn't even in the minors. He's been hanging around Mary Falcone in the bar for the past week. All he's selling is some cheap jewelry, probably from purse snatches. It's a slow night so Manny's talking to him—you never can tell, he might give up someone important."

The kid was handsome, and judging from the way he looked at Mary, I figured the Block was probably right. "Señorita, it would be a pleasure to provide this jewelry for you. It would match your beauty."

"How much you want for it, Quenton?" Manny was brusque.

Quenton frowned. "Have I offended you, señor?" His voice was soft, unlike the usual thugs we dealt with.

"We do business here. We ain't into exchanging Christmas presents."

"Please pardon me, señor. I meant no insult." He took back the gold necklace that Mary had been examining. "I have no need to sell these. With plastic, who needs money?" With a wide smile he flashed open a leather credit card case.

"Wow! Manny, look at these. How about buying a couple from Bill, here? I could do with a couple of new outfits, and there's nothing like doing it on someone else's plastic. How did you get all of these? Are they hot yet?" Mary was smiling back at the crook.

Manny leaned back on the couch, silent, refusing to respond to Mary's raised eyebrows.

Quenton looked from Manny to Mary and shrugged. "I have no wish to cause trouble, perhaps another time." The crook got to his feet. He bent down and kissed her hand. Mary Falcone smiled at him while Manny Herrera gave him the bad eye.

Bill Quenton, the gallant one, walked out. Mary turned toward Manny on the couch. "You fucking asshole. You let him go without getting the jewelry or credit cards. You know they're hot. What the hell's wrong with you?"

Paul was already moving into the next room to tell them you-know-who was in the back room.

"He's a punk. Small time. If you want to put out for him, do it on your own. Don't get romantic with these creeps around me."

We were our brothers' keepers, but not above the green serpent of jealousy ourselves.

"You son of a . . ." Paul English interrupted her.

I couldn't hear what Paul was saying to them, but Manny stood and said sullenly, "I got to piss." He walked out.

I went into the next room. Mary was angry. Her arms were folded across her chest. She gave me just a brief nod. "Mary, what did you think of that guy?" I said.

"I think he's wrong. Very wrong. Of course, I'm just a woman and don't know shit compared to the rest of the heroes around here."

I held up my hand, palm outward. "Hold on, Mary. I think you may be right. Did you notice any scent from him?"

Paul English whistled, "Hey, who knows? A red-hot hunch from the boss. It would be great if we nailed him through the sting."

Mary frowned, not following. "How can you smell anything back here? It stinks." She pointed to the table with the full ashtrays and half-full beer cans.

It did stink. Damn it. And we hadn't gotten either the jewelry or credit cards. "Which hand did he kiss, Mary?" I said.

She held out her right hand. I took it and lifted it to my nose. My heartbeat quickened as I smelled the faint scent. "Paul?" I asked, and he also sniffed Mary's hand. He shrugged as she brought her hand to her nose and took a deep breath.

"Old Spice?" she said.

"That's what I got. How about you, Paul?"

"I'm sorry. The allergy season has my olfactory sense out of action."

"Why don't you just say you're stuffed up?" Mary, back in good humor, laughed. "What's with the Old Spice? What does it mean?"

"It could be important, Mary. Let me ask you this. When he flashed the credit cards were you able to see any names?"

"Not really. But they seemed to be all women."

I took a deep breath. "Mary, to reach that conclusion you must have seen some names. Try to recall."

Her mouth set. "If I remembered I would have told you."

"Mary, there's an outside chance that the guy is Zorro."

"Jesus, and Manny let him . . ." She paused, realizing that she wasn't mad enough at Manny to make him look worse than he already did. She put her head down in concentration, covering her eyes. "A couple of names were simple, Alice, Jean, Mary, and such. Only they weren't the names, but one was a little unusual. It's just on the tip of my tongue."

"Paul, why don't you check to see if Quenton is still in the bar out front while Mary tries to remember?"

Paul went out the door to the bar.

"I got it." Mary looked up. There was color in her cheeks and her fists were clamped to her sides. "One card had the name *Melissa*. That's all I can remember."

I went back into the recording room and called sexual assault investigations. To my surprise, Cathy Stevens was still there. "Cathy, please give me the names of Zorro's eight victims."

"OK, hold on." She shuffled some papers then said,
"First was Ann Brett.

"Second was Elizabeth Sawyer.

"Third, Marion Huber.

"Fourth, Maria Santos.

"Fifth, Jackie Irvine.

"Sixth, Melissa Ross.

"Seventh . . ."

"Hold on, Cathy," I interrupted. "That last name was Melissa Ross?"

"Right. What's up, Chief?"

"I think we just got lucky." Briefly I told Cathy what had occurred.

"Damn, I sure hope he's still there, otherwise we're nowhere, unless he was dumb enough to use his own name, which I doubt. Good luck."

Paul came in shaking his head. "He had one drink then left. We don't know if he has a car or not."

"Let's see. He left the bar about fifteen minutes ago. Pull in patrol units and order a search. Maybe we'll stay lucky. I'm going back to headquarters to look through mug shots after I describe him to Cathy Stevens. We don't have much more than the coincidence that he was polite, one of the victims was named Melissa, and he may or may not have been wearing after-shave. But it's more than we had this morning."

"I'll get right on the search," Paul said.

It would take a few minutes before the first units showed up and organized the search perimeters. I cruised up and down the streets knowing that the odds were that Bill Quenton or whoever he really was wouldn't still be in the neighborhood, but stranger things had happened. I was peering down an alley when a car horn made me jump. My car was moving slowly, but with my attention focused to the side I had gotten close enough to annoy the driver of a green Mazda pulling out of a convenience-store parking lot.

I waved an apology and got a polite wave in acknowledgment. I hadn't seen the driver's face, but it had been a guy. I stayed behind him for a couple of blocks still watching the streets. I had been dumb. I paid more attention to my driving. All Gerhart needed was for me to have an on-duty accident that I couldn't explain. But, how many people frequenting convenience stores were that polite? It was crazy, but why not pull up to get a closer look at him?

The car was now a considerable distance ahead of me. We were way out of the area around The Blue Mirage that would be searched. I speeded up, but got caught by a red light at a big intersection. The Mazda had turned off the avenue by the time the light turned green. I gunned forward. Another light went red in front of me. I took it. A truck's horn blared at me. I waved, but this time the response was a normal California flip-off. The Mazda wasn't visible. I took a guess at which intersection it had hooked left on, made a turn, and slowed down, looking into the streets on each side of the broad avenue. It was a shipping and manufacturing area, barren of people at this time of night.

I passed a street, then braked and backed up. A green car was parked a couple of blocks down the side street. I turned and approached. A number of cars were parked and as I got closer, I saw why. Tucked into an alley around the corner was a bar with a noisy jukebox and a neon sign promising dancing. I drove slowly past a green Mazda. It was unoccupied. I wasn't even sure it was the one I had followed. Pulling to the curb, my hand reached for the microphone. My radio was on and I heard a sergeant organizing the search around The Blue Mirage. What could I report? Someone had been polite instead of flipping me off? I had nothing. A wild hunch. As chief, I'd look like an asshole to pull people out of the search area. I got out of my car and walked toward the bar.

It was one of those dismal places that every once in a while is in with one crowd or another and does a good business until the group moves on to someplace else. It was big enough to have a small dance floor and about twenty or so tables opposite a long bar. The lights were dim, but I could see that except for two guys hunched over the bar, it was empty. They were in between crowds discovering the place.

I decided to sit in my car. My polite subject might have gone someplace else. I'd wait a few minutes and if he didn't show, drive to headquarters. I was already feeling a little foolish about wasting so much time.

Before I got to my car I heard someone in the bar holler, "See you."

Turning, I saw the guy who had been in the back room of The Blue Mirage pause in the bar's doorway, wave to the customers, and say, "Have a good night."

He sure was polite. He must have been in the john when I looked into the bar. I stood on the sidewalk and watched him approach. He would have to pass me to get to the Mazda. His pace slowed as he got near. He was watching me and there was just the slightest tension in his walk. That didn't mean much in a deserted area like this. I'd feel the same way if someone was waiting near my car. I smiled and he did too.

"Hi," I said. "The place pretty dead tonight?" I nodded toward the bar.

"Afraid so." He was going to walk right past me.

I moved slightly into his path. "Say, didn't we have a couple of drinks together in The Blue Mirage the other night?"

"I don't remember," he said, slowing.

I wanted to get close enough to see what kind of after-shave lotion he wore. He was slender, an inch shorter than I and slighter, but he moved with the suppleness of an athlete. "Sure," I said. "You remember that barmaid? Man, I thought you were going to screw her right there."

"She's a fine-looking woman," he said, moving a step closer. My nostrils filled with the scent of Old Spice. "But I don't remember meeting you." His politeness had diminished a notch as he studied me.

I said, "Sure you do. You're Bill Quenton, or maybe I should call you Zorro."

I had taken him too much for granted. He had gotten close and his kick was so quick that I just managed to turn and take it on the thigh instead of the groin. I was slightly off balance, but I blocked his left hook so that it sailed harmlessly past my head. I hit him in the eye with a right hand but wasn't able to get much into it because we were so close. He bounced backward more than the punch deserved and I saw his own right hand coming up with a semiautomatic pistol. Jesus! I lunged at him, just managing to get my hands on the gun as it went off, sending a round into the sky. He kneed me in the groin and the pain made me momentarily ease my grip on the gun. Alarm shot through me as he swung the weapon toward my chest. With a surge of adrenaline I tightened my grip on his wrist and the gun and jerked in opposite directions. Another shot thudded into the street.

He was fast. Knowing he was losing the gun, he let it go. Setting himself, he hit me with a solid right to the chin. My knees buckled as the gun clattered to the sidewalk. Then he made a mistake. Aware that he had shaken me, he moved to finish the job with his fists. By the time I had made him miss three haymakers, he knew he was overmatched. But it was too late. My knees had steadied and I ripped him with a combo of a left to the head, a left to the gut, and as his hands went down to protect his stomach, I hit him with a right to the jaw. He went down on all fours, but he took a good punch. He wasn't out. I saw him spot the gun. It was six feet away on the sidewalk, but I wasn't taking any chances. He had come a lot closer to winning than I was comfortable with. As he raised slightly to dive for the gun, I remembered what he had done to his last seventy-one-year-old victim. I kicked him in the chest like I was trying for a forty-yard field goal with two seconds left in the game. He collapsed and was unconscious when I put the cuffs on him and picked up the gun.

Thirteen

ZORRO WAS TAKEN TO THE HOSPITAL UNDER GUARD AND admitted. My jaw ached, my thigh was black and blue, and my knuckles swollen, but I declined invitations to the hospital. It was late when I finished my reports on the arrest. The exhilaration of Cathy Stevens and the sting cops hadn't reached me. The sound of Zorro's forty-five semiautomatic in my ear was too recent. I had the shakes, but couldn't show it. Finally, I dragged myself home and into bed. I had left a note for Denise that I would sleep in.

The phone woke me. My clock read 0830. It was four rings before I brought my achy body upright to answer it.

"Chief?" It was Paul English.

"No. It's George Bush. Who the hell did you expect."

"God. You're a grouch."

"Yeah. Well it's nice to get your observations of my character, Paul, but did you have something else in mind to wake me up this morning?"

"I do, but I think it can wait until the Block and I get to your place. Take a shower, and make sure you shave before you read your morning paper. We'll be there in half an hour."

I hung up and went to the door to pick up the newspaper. The front page read: POLICE CHIEF BRUTALLY BEATS SUSPECT. Under the byline of Brad Fellows the story went on in small print to say that the attorney of one Bruce Hyer had alleged that Acting Police Chief Fraleigh had brutally beaten his client in an unsuccessful attempt to obtain a confession. Valley Hospital confirmed that a prisoner by the name of Bruce Hyer had been admitted under guard and was in stable condition with multiple rib fractures, contusions of the eye and face, and a fractured jaw, in addition to a possible concussion. Reporter Brad Fellows went on to say that although the police report stated that the suspect's injuries were inflicted while resisting arrest, Acting Chief Fraleigh had apparently been unscathed and had not been examined in the hospital despite alleging kicks to the groin and blows to the head, causing injury. Also, although two shots had been fired, it was unclear as to who had fired them. Chief Fraleigh was unavailable for comment and his secretary said she had no idea when he would be. The story finished by saying that the police hinted that Hyer was Zorro, a suspect in multiple rapes.

I was dressed and finishing my coffee and the sports section of the newspaper when the Block and Paul English arrived.

"I told you to shave before reading the paper," Paul said, eyeing the three nicks on my chin.

"Who is this Pulitzer winner Brad Fellows?" I asked. "Didn't anyone ever talk to him about Zorro's victims?"

"Brad Fellows has been supplied a number of good stories by Fritz Gerhart and it is safe to assume that information about Zorro's victims has been of low priority to the chief of detectives. On the other hand, if you hadn't decided to John Wayne it, we could have had the hospital substantiate the injuries you received," Paul said, pointing at my swollen jaw.

The Block added his advice. "Yeah, Fraleigh. Just because you're chief doesn't mean you don't have to cover your ass like the rest of us. Any suspect is going to lie like a bandit to the hospital. We've got to hype it up too, or at least half as much as those bastards do."

"Don't forget that the present D.A. is not overly fond of you," Paul added.

"I'll go out to the hospital this morning. Get a photographer to take pictures of my face and thigh. I can hardly walk."

"Good idea, Chief," Paul said.

I braced myself. Whenever Paul had a compliment, you could bet that you wouldn't like what came next. "Have you considered the preliminary hearing tomorrow?" he asked.

"What's to consider? If Cathy Stevens is right, we got Zorro in the joint for the rest of his life."

"I think she is right. Thanks to you, Zorro won't see daylight again, but remember Hesiod: 'Observe due measure, for right timing is in all things the most important factor.'"

"For Christ's sake, Paul, make sense," the Block complained, although I was beginning to understand what Paul was getting at.

Paul spoke slowly. "There's a subpoena for Fraleigh waiting at the front desk of headquarters. They haven't accepted it officially, but unless it's returned as unservable within twenty-four hours, it's considered served. At the preliminary hearing, the defense attorney will question the chief on how he came to follow Zorro. Unless the chief decides to commit perjury, the sting will be exposed."

"Well, what do you suggest, Paul, that I defect to the Soviet Union?"

"They wouldn't accept you. What I suggest on a more modest scale is that you find a plausible reason to get the hell out of town."

"Out of town? And what would I find when I get back—that you'd put five more misfits into the sting? How long has Art Estrada been working at The Blue Mirage?"

"A couple of weeks is all," the Block said.

"You mean just since I ordered him back into uniform. He's probably the source of our leaks both to Bartlow and Fritz Gerhart. You remember that Gerhart defended him, wanted to keep him in the bureau."

"I looked into it. Art got a bum rap. He'll be good in the sting. We need an expert on dope, we're buying so much of it. Don't worry about it."

"Sure, Block. That's what you guys told me when we started this sting. Don't worry. No problems, and the Board of Supervisors won't find out about it for months. Another thing. What the hell is going on with Manny Herrera?"

"Manny needs a few days off, Chief," Paul said. "These stings can get a little stressful after a while."

"Yeah. I'm no one to argue with that. Just remember, I don't want those politicians closing down the sting. Let's get over to the hospital." I winced as I finished my coffee.

Fourteen

AFTER WASTING TWO HOURS IN THE HOSPITAL, I FOUND that I had to put up with Denise's ministrations when I got to the office. Finally, to get rid of her, I dictated a letter and told her it was urgent. A couple of minutes later she buzzed me on the intercom. "Chief, a man named Assistant Chief Seymour Gross from the New York Police is on the phone. He says he knows you and has something important to talk to you about."

"Hello, Seymour, how are you?" I said into the phone.

"The same as ever. How are you, kid?"

"Ups and downs. You know how it is."

"Yeah, listen. I have something sensitive to talk to you about. Have you heard from your brother lately?"

"Jack?" I felt my heart clutch. "No. Not since I left New York."

"Tch—all those years. Well, your brother Jack has been hitting the juice real hard the last few months. He's been whip of the Fifth Squad for two years. They're getting ready to dump him. And I mean out of the job, not just the bureau. I thought I owed you guys one for old-times' sake, but Jack won't even talk to me. I figured if you came back, maybe you could get him to take the pledge before it's too late."

I felt a surge of relief. Jack and I didn't speak to each other, but he was a cop, and while Seymour Gross wasn't giving me good news, it wasn't a "killed in the line of duty" notification either. The squad whip was the commander. My brother had risen from sergeant to lieutenant. I wondered if he had heard that I was acting chief. "The last time I saw Jack was twelve years ago and he slugged me," I said to Gross. "I don't think he'd appreciate my advice."

"Yeah, yeah, I know. He may not listen to you either, but he's your brother. You better get back here if you care about him at all."

"Let me think about it, Seymour. I'm not sure I want to bring back all those memories."

"You come back. I have something to tell you. Something you never knew, but I can't tell you on the phone."

I thought about the subpoena for me out at the front desk and Nola at the Hotel Walton. "Seymour, maybe I could come back for a few days. We're working a sting here, and some leads came up that are in New York."

"Like what?"

"Well, we got a shyster named Bartlow who's peddling hot bonds, but we don't know where he got them. We found out that he tried to peddle them in New York last March to a broker named Christopher MacLeod and a guy from Chinatown, Anthony Wong. Reportedly, they beat the shit out of him and took a couple of bonds and he ended up in Bellevue. We think he probably told them where he ripped the bonds off."

"I'll reach out to some people. It's likely there's a Sixty-one on Bartlow's assault, but I'll lay you odds the detectives shitcanned it. Just another john getting taken in Chinatown. But we should have something for you by the time you get here. Give my secretary, Fran, your flight time. Some of my people will pick you up."

UF61 was the NYPD's basic crime report, and I was sure Gross was right. Assault cases came in the hundreds of thousands a year. Few that weren't easily solved—routine domestic cross complaints—ended up in arrests. There would be a perfunctory DD5, the detective bureau's basic investigation report in which the squad detective catching the case kissed it off. Despite all the mayor's righteous prattling about equality, law enforcement in Chinatown had never been a top priority of New York's Finest. Still, the crime report would be a starting point to trace Bartlow's trail in New York.

"Could you run a check on MacLeod and Wong?"

"Sure."

"Oh. And one other thing, Seymour. We had a fatal bombing here and one of the suspects works for the Gambino family. His name is Mel Zale. Could you see what his status is?"

"Jesus. Are you sure that's all? You don't want me to send the tactical unit out there for a month or so? I call to see if you want to save your brother's ass and you pick my pocket."

I laughed. "Hey, Seymour. I read the papers—I know how dangerous it is back there now. You got to make it worth my while to visit."

"All right, already, give my secretary your flight and arrival time. I'll talk to you when you get in."

I gave his secretary the flight time and she assured me in a strong New York accent, "Not to worry. You'll be met at the gate."

"As much as I dig a free trip to New York, Fraleigh—Paul was wrong. It's no time for you to take a junket."

The Block was driving us to an early nonstop to New York out of San Francisco Airport. Paul was staying behind as my eyes and ears. He didn't have the rank to be left in command, but Captain Toll in charge of patrol was cautious enough to sound Paul out on any major decisions to be made. I'd been forced to leave Fritz Gerhart in charge of detectives, since he was the only detective captain. I was counting on Paul to torpedo any of Gerhart's sabotage efforts in my absence.

Since the bar sting was being handled out of the chief's office, it was possible to maintain secrecy from the other commanders. It was tough, though. There was Lieutenant

Short's investigation of Charley Thompson's bomb murder. And Short, as well as Ken Matsukowa in the bomb squad, were in Gerhart's chain of command, but I had cautioned each of them individually to report only to me, and in my absence, to Paul English.

Despite the fifty-five-mile-per-hour speed limit, the Block was cruising at seventy-five on the 101 freeway, which was noteworthy since most of the day 101 traffic permitted only the kind of speed possible in crowded shopping mall parking lots. On the other hand, it was five-thirty in the morning. I turned on the radio hoping it would shut the Block up, but he just upped his volume.

"You better hope Paul doesn't pick this week to get pussy fever or do one of his famous cloud-nine blackouts. Watching Gerhart is a fulltime job."

"Block, will you shut the fuck up? I can't even think straight." I wondered if I could get a seat away from him. Six hours to New York . . .

"You bet you can't think straight. That's what I'm telling you."

I stopped listening. We boarded what the stewardess had warned us would be a full flight. I took a window seat and the Block sat next to me. I noticed that a graying clergyman wearing a roman collar occupied the seat behind the Block. I hoped for his sake he was prepared to spring four bucks for the earphones the stewardesses were hustling for the movie. My scant sleep the night before made it easy for me to curl up after telling the Block not to wake me for food. Charitably, I warned him, "Don't eat the airline crap. New York has great restaurants. We'll get some good chow tonight."

The Block's grating voice finally recalled me from a dream of violently exploding automobiles, and a somber Nola saying sternly that she couldn't see me again because of a conflict of interest.

"So this young punk, John, who couldn't be more than eighteen, is stringing me a line of shit. I said, look kid, stop the I-was-robbed bullshit—you came downtown looking for hookers. You wanted to get laid, instead you got fucked! They take jerks like you all the time." His laugh boomed.

Drowsily, I assumed he was telling cop stories to some right-wing business fascist who had taken the aisle seat to his left. I stared for a moment at the remains of a tray of food with three crushed, empty Heineken beer cans in front of me. Looking to my left I saw the same setup in front of the Block. He had knocked off my food as well as his own along with six Heinekens. No wonder he was so talkative. Then I blinked. Sitting next to him was a diminutive lady with gray hair and granny spectacles, not some bozo. I slunk down in my seat trying to pretend I didn't know the Block.

"Young man . . ." *Oh, oh, here comes the Rev from the rear seat,* I thought, closing my eyes again and turning toward the window. The clergyman's self-righteous voice climbed. "Young man, your language is disgraceful for anyone, but if you really are a policeman, it's doubly shocking."

The reverend apparently hadn't purchased earphones.

"Mind your own business, you Jesus wimp."

I sat up with a start, looking toward the woman on the Block's left. Sure enough, her face was red and she was glaring back at the astonished clergyman. "If more people supported men like this we'd be able to go out at night."

"Yeah. Lighten up, Rev. Who's meeting you in New York, anyway, Jessica Hahn?" Both the Block and the lady enjoyed a good chuckle at his witticism.

"Block, what's all this junk doing in front of me?"

"Hey, Fraleigh. You came back to life. Meet Patricia." He nodded at the woman to his left. "Patricia, this is Fraleigh, the boss I got to put up with since he shot up in the world."

I returned her smile hoping she wasn't going to chew my ass up the way she had the clergyman sitting behind us. "You're lucky to have such a loyal person working for you, Chief." She sipped from what appeared to be a double scotch. "The Block has told me how fearless you are, and how you protect the men from political pressure. You must be under enormous stress."

The Block's face had turned red. "Well, I didn't tell you how grouchy he is all the time, Patricia. We bear quite a cross." He let out a sigh which shook us in our seats.

I dozed again and when I woke up, the empty trays had been cleared and the Block was pouring another can of Heineken for himself. Patricia's seat was vacant, and the reverend was nowhere to be seen.

"So, who's this old buddy of yours that we're going to see in the NYPD? Do you think he can really help us to find out what Chink Wong and MacLeod were up to with Bartlow and to check out on the bomber—what's his name, Zella?"

"The bomber is Mel Zale, and the other guy was called Anthony Wong, Block. And my contact is Chief Seymour Gross. If the department has anything on any of them we'll get it. Hopefully, we'll also get to chat with them." Old buddy, Gross! That was rich. I wondered what the Block would say if he knew what my relationship with Gross had been.

Seymour Gross had gotten a few more promotions since I'd left New York and was now one of the top-ranking people in the department. He was in charge of Internal Affairs investigations for the entire New York City Police Department. I knew he would try to help me, although probably no one else in the department would.

Fifteen

"CHIEF FRALEIGH?" A VERY ATTRACTIVE BRUNETTE WEARing a snug, navy-blue business suit stood in front of us.

I nodded.

"I'm Captain Stephanie Ferrari from Chief Gross's office. I've heard a great deal about you. It's a real pleasure to be able to work with you." Her eyes were deep brown and friendly. "We have a car outside. Do you have luggage?"

We were in a large black Lincoln. The luggage was stored in the trunk. The Block sat in front next to the driver, who from the rear could have been his twin. A closer look revealed that in contrast to the Block, a lot of the chauffeur's bulk was fat. Ferrari had introduced him as Detective Paddy Fitzgerald. He and the Block had in common size seventeen-and-a-half shirt collars. A detective whose name I hadn't caught sat next to me in the rear seat and Stephanie Ferrari faced us on a pull-down seat which made it impossible to ignore her very good legs. She smoothed her stockings.

"Aren't you awfully young to be a captain?" I said. Ferrari didn't look a day older than thirty. Her sharp features, brown eyes, and smooth olive skin could have belonged to a fashion model. Yet, I knew it was rare for anyone to make captain in under fifteen years on the job.

"Some people think so." She didn't even bother to smile back at me.

"Still, that's an impressive rank for a woman. How long have you been on the force?" I moved in.

"Long enough. It's a civil service system here, Chief Fraleigh—you remember that I'm sure." A mocking smile played around her lips. She had testified against a lot of lawyers and wasn't about to give up any information that she didn't want to. "Detective Fitzgerald helped investigate the assault in Chinatown," Ferrari continued. "Chief Gross has had him temporarily assigned to our office this week. He will set up meets with MacLeod and Wong."

Bits of conversation floated back to us from the front of the car. Fitzgerald was telling the Block, "Can you believe I grew up in this neighborhood?" He pointed his fat paw out the window at the dreary brick apartment buildings. "Look at it. It's all niggers and spicks. Your life ain't worth shit here now."

Ferrari flushed and started to say something to Fitzgerald, but instead turned toward me. "Do your officers talk like that?"

"No, we're pretty professional in California," I said, just as the Block boomed out his answer to Fitzgerald.

"Yeah. It's the same fucking deal out our way. Whites are an endangered species."

Another small smile played about Captain Ferrari's lips, and her brown eyes rested on mine for a moment before shifting toward the bumper-to-bumper traffic. We were on the Van Wyck Expressway, the last term being a sadistic New York joke.

When we finally arrived at our hotel, Stephanie Ferrari said, "Chief Gross has instructed me to have Fitzgerald check you into your rooms while I bring you right to his office."

I turned to Ferrari. "I think maybe I should go up and freshen up. How about giving me an hour?"

"Chief Gross specifically instructed me to tell you that he has to meet with the police commissioner in an hour and it's urgent that he talk to you about this investigation before he gets tied up with the P.C."

I shrugged. I needed a shower after the long trip, but when a beautiful woman beckons . . .

Stephanie Ferrari opened the door, getting behind the wheel vacated by Fitzgerald, who had gone into the hotel with the Block and the other cop. I moved up to the front seat.

"I'll drive us to One Police Plaza. Chief Gross is looking forward to seeing you again."

Ferrari hadn't blinked as she steered past at least two dozen insane New York cab drivers and hundreds of suicidal, jaywalking pedestrians while I hung white-knuckled to my seatbelt. Somehow we swerved through midtown into lower Manhattan without maiming or being maimed. She flashed her ID at the uniformed man guarding the entrance ramp to One Police Plaza, and pulled down two levels to her assigned parking space. Getting out of the car, she handed me an ID badge. "We're one of the few units that doesn't have to go through the front desk for these."

Of course. Internal Affairs often had visitors that it didn't want known to the cops working in the building. I had been in that category once. We proceeded through familiar elevators, corridors, and endless rows of desks. It seemed to me that the palace guard, as street cops referred to their brethren assigned cushy inside jobs, had grown along with the dirt. The floors hadn't been swept very well, the walls had acquired a coating of grime undisturbed by cleaning or painting, and the legions of functionaries were no less sullen than I remembered. This was the heart of the department that provided police protection for nearly eight million people. Occasionally, for brief periods and reasons no one understood, the organization forgot its petty bureaucratic feuds and remembered what it had been hired to do.

"This is Chief Fraleigh," Captain Stephanie Ferrari told a husky young cop in civilian clothes who should have been out on patrol someplace instead of sitting on his ass outside Seymour Gross's office.

He nodded, picked up the phone, pushed a red button, and after a moment said, "Captain Ferrari and Chief Fraleigh are here, sir." He listened intently then hung up. "Chief Fraleigh, you can go in now." Despite myself, I felt the old revulsion come back. I wasn't even in the department anymore, yet the unpleasant feeling about going into an IA interview was strong. I pushed it out of my mind. I had escaped them. Hadn't I?

Stephanie was already walking away. I hadn't noticed any sign of disappointment that she hadn't been invited in. Then again, Gross was the department hangman. Even the pure of heart were uneasy in his presence. He was the man to whom field associates reported. The title *field associate* was Big Brother speak for spy. Field associates were assigned throughout the department, and only Gross knew who they were. Their job was to report secretly on their fellow cops. Somehow, despite this fail-safe system, police scandals popped up as regularly as they had before it existed.

Gross's office on the twelfth floor was respectably large by NYPD standards. It actually had a good-size desk with three comfortably upholstered chairs, bookshelves, and a couch and coffee table along the far wall. The windows hadn't been cleaned for a while, but if you crooked your neck you could see a slice of the East River between two red-brick apartment buildings.

Gross came out from behind his desk and put his arm around me. "How are you, kid? Although it's not *kid* anymore! It's *chief* now, right?" He pushed back, holding me at arm's length, looking intently at me. He shook his head. "Christ. It's still there. How long are you going to keep blaming yourself?"

Somehow I remembered Gross as being much taller. His mere presence in a station house had caused panic. It usually meant a cop or cops were going to be arrested and their commanders demoted. Now, standing next to me in his fancy office, he stooped a little, standing barely an inch taller than I. His tough, stern face sagged, the firm jaw smothered in flesh. He hadn't grown any new hair, and his bald pate called attention to a cheap pair of bifocals. I remembered that they were provided free under the department health insurance plan. Unlike the eyeglasses, his suit hadn't been skimped on, yet the expensive gray flannel didn't conceal the waistline flab. It was more than fourteen years' worth of change, but I knew the kind of work he did.

There had been a time when Gross had been a pillar for me. A strong father to replace mine as he became history. "You look good, Seymour." His first name was strange on my lips. It had always been "Inspector Gross," back then.

"I look good, ha. Sure I do. I thought I had you convinced not to perjure yourself to me." He grinned, then the smile faded. "There are some things I need to tell you. About your father."

I interrupted. "What did you find on Bartlow?"

Gross sighed. "You don't want to talk about your father, or your brother, or the past. I don't blame you. We can discuss it later. Here's the Sixty-one on Bartlow's assault, and two cover-your-ass DD-Fives by the detective who caught the case. As you can see, he didn't do a fucking thing except call Bellevue Hospital to speak to Barry, or as you call him, Bartlow—who refused comment. Notice the name of the investigating officer." He tossed three single sheets at me.

I hadn't expected any more from the UF61, the uniform cop's complaint form, or the DD5, which was the basic report from the investigating detective. I glanced through the papers and noticed that Detective Paddy Fitzgerald had signed the 5. I folded the papers into the pocket of my jacket. "What else do you have?"

"Well, of course, the Anthony Wong in this case is known as Mad Anthony Wong to the cops. He's connected to the Dragon Triad in Chinatown, so we got a shitload of information, most of it the same old useless crap from intelligence. Let's see." He read from a yellow legal pad. "He's thirty-nine. Born in Hong Kong. Came here fifteen years ago with a bunch of young punks thrown out of the Colony. They didn't go for the old ways, respect for elders. They shot the shit out of the old-timers running the Tongs and took over the Dragon Triad. Now they're part of the establishment if not the establishment. Your friend Anthony is also the Democratic Party captain in the district." Gross paused, looking out at me from under his dime-store eyeglasses to see if I had absorbed Wong's political clout. "He's a leg breaker, and a shooter. We locked him up once for murder. Turns out, his only convictions were grand larceny six years ago, and armed robbery when he was nineteen, the year he came from the Colony. The only time he's done was three years in Greenhaven for the robbery."

"That's pretty hard time isn't it for a nineteen-year-old?" Greenhaven was a maximum security prison modeled after Attica, upstate.

"Yeah. But it seems that the cabdriver—the victim— lost an eye. Wong does have a rep for being a crazy. He pistol-whipped the cabbie. Too bad the judge didn't believe in an eye for an eye. Anyway, according to our so-called intelligence experts, Wong has moved into dope with the Colombian Medellín Cartel and the Jamaican Posse here. They've been very big in Florida, but rumor has it that they're shifting operations to California. You heard anything?"

"It could be," I said. "The feds have been putting tremendous heat on in Florida. They've been seizing estates and businesses like crazy under the asset-seizure law. So the shippers have had to go elsewhere. The action has moved to the West Coast. The latest stats I've seen show that the LAPD seized three hundred fifty-eight pounds of cocaine in 1983 and more than thirteen thousand pounds last year."

"Silicon City is way north of L.A., isn't it?"

"Yes, but the picture is the same at San Francisco Airport. There's been an incredible increase in the amount of dope seized. What we're really worried about is San Jose International. There's hardly any security. Big shipments could be moved in easily and sold right there to the hotshots in the Silicon Valley computer industry. They're all so sophisticated, if you know what I mean?"

"I know. Christ, I hope I never need a pacemaker put together by some stoned asshole. But, I didn't think San Jose had an international airport."

"Ha. You're right. You have to know San Jose, though. It dreams of being a real city. A Mexicana jet couldn't land in San Francisco because of fog. It was diverted to San Jose. The mayor rushed out and named the airport San Jose International. But they do get a zillion flights a day from the L.A. area. That's what we're concerned about in the Bay Area. L.A.'s the dope hub."

"One thing you gotta know, Fraleigh. The street's different from when you were here. These guys kill without blinking an eye, and they don't give a shit about hitting cops."

"What about the stockbroker? How is he tied in with Wong, and would he be part of a robbery?"

"Damned if I know. Here's what we got on him. Christopher MacLeod of Brown, MacLeod, and Solomon. These bond-dealer guys are known as Masters of the Universe now, according to some books. They deal in junk bonds. They earn money the old-fashioned way— they scam the suckers. But, they exude respectability, and for your information, MacLeod's brother—who just happens to be the firm's general counsel—was chairman of the mayor's reelection committee."

"What's going on, Seymour? This used to be such a nice honest city."

"Yeah," he laughed, "before my time. We didn't know that MacLeod and Wong were tied in together. On the other hand, there's so much dope on Wall Street, and so much dope money that needs laundering, who knows? There's no doubt that Wong's been big in drugs for years. I passed on the possible connection with MacLeod to intelligence. In another ten years they might get around to looking at it. What do you think?"

"I don't know. We're just beginning this investigation. It involves stolen securities. Bartlow was trying to peddle them. He gave one to our sting sergeant as a sample. Probably the same kind that he had with him in New York. I need to know how he got them, and he probably let that out to Wong and/or MacLeod when he tried to peddle the bonds. Bartlow's brother is a big cheese in Silicon City. On the Board of Supervisors, one of my bosses. I was hoping your intelligence people would have something more on the securities angle."

"'Intelligence,' you say." Gross snorted again. One of his mannerisms, I recalled. Very effective with cops trying to worm out with elaborate lies during interrogations. "You should be so lucky. I could tell you stories about the intelligence unit."

He could tell stories about everyone. Nasty stories. "Is it possible for me to talk to Wong and MacLeod?"

"You think they're ready to do their civic duty and cooperate with law enforcement?" He smiled.

"We're not interested in them. Maybe we can use some leverage."

He was skeptical. "Yeah. Listen, Fraleigh, I put a lot of cops in jail for so-called leverage."

I shrugged. "I'm not your responsibility, Seymour. Just set me up for a meet with them."

He spoke slowly. "I guess I owe you something. That ox, Fitzgerald, can put you together with them. You know the department has to be at arm's length?"

I nodded. "No problem."

"So you say. Fitzgerald has more skeletons in the closet than a med school. He's no grass grazer, you know. He's a meat eater, and I mean the tenderloin. He should have been history years ago, but he's lucky. I reached out for him, but I can tell you, I don't like it. He's in the Fifth Squad, one of your brother's men, although I doubt if your brother even knows what day of the week it is. I got Fitzgerald for you, but the detective bureau don't forget contracts and I hate to think what the bastards may ask in return. It's still the same old cover-up club. You know, the team-player bullshit."

I remembered the bureau's team-player gambit, all right. My brother Jack had been a detective sergeant and had tried it with me when the shit was hitting the fan over the old man. Jack had accused me of not being a team player. We had ended up hurting each other physically that night, and hadn't talked since.

Gross got up and walked to the dirty window. I knew he was about to talk about the old days and I made up my mind to tell him to skip it.

"About your father . . ." The phone buzzer interrupted him.

He ignored the speaker phone setup and put the receiver to his ear. "Yeah, OK." He listened a moment, wiggling his eyebrows at me. "OK . . . All right, already! I understand. Right away," he said into the phone. He hung up and held his palms outward. "What can I tell you? God calls. The meeting was supposed to be in a half hour, but the P.C. says now. So it's now."

"He's not your God, Seymour."

"So you say, but the Jewish precinct captains make sure their commands have the most marchers at the Holy Name Communion Breakfast and Parade every year. The P.C. is God to thirty thousand of us regardless of what religion we practice. You know that. I'm sorry, kid, but we can talk some more tomorrow."

I couldn't help but smile at Gross's view of life in the predominantly Catholic police department. Also, I wasn't at all sorry that he had to leave. I hadn't been looking forward to the conversation about the old days, and it was still early enough to have dinner with Nola, if I could catch her at her hotel. "You'll let me know what time Fitzgerald sets up the meet for tomorrow?"

"Tomorrow! Fraleigh, you forget how we do things in New York. The meet is on for tonight. I had Fitzgerald contact MacLeod, who was listed as a witness on the Sixty-one. Stephanie will take you up to T. J. Brown's. Fitzgerald will be waiting for you. Take care of yourself. And nothing illegal, right?" He patted my shoulder, grabbed a clipboard, and hurried out of the room.

Captain Ferrari was waiting for me when I left Gross's office. I asked if I could use a phone, and she brought me into her cubbyhole of an office which was crowded with plants. I called the hotel and asked for Nola Henderson. Ferrari, who had been listening, smiled and folded her arms. When there was no answer I left a message that I was in New York and would call later.

"She's on the Board of Supervisors in Silicon City," I said to Ferrari, who seemed to be waiting for an explanation. I realized I was starving. I had forgone plane food for great New York chow. Now I was headed to a glorified neighborhood bar where fatty hamburgers and french fries were haute cuisine, if you could successfully fight the crowd and get your order filled. All in the hope that I would be led to a millionaire stockbroker who supposedly helped steal some stolen bonds from shyster Richard Bartlow. It was a crooked world.

Sixteen

HEADING UPTOWN, CAPTAIN FERRARI STUCK WITH FIRST Avenue longer than I would have, but my knowledge of the city's gridlock was fourteen years out of date, and I guessed she knew better. The traffic was probably crawling everywhere at this time of evening. "How did your meeting go?" she asked.

"OK. I expected Fitzgerald would be with us by now."

"Chief Gross doesn't want him anywhere near our office. We'd never live it down. So he and your man are waiting for us at Brown's."

"Where are we supposed to meet MacLeod?"

"There." She smiled slightly at my surprise. T.J.'s was a Third Avenue landmark often visited by celebrities, midtown executives, singles, and make-believe singles—as well as hordes of neighborhood groupies and tourists. It was the last place that I wanted to meet MacLeod. We would have far too many witnesses to put any pressure on him. "He insisted on it," she said. "He doesn't trust Fitzgerald any more than I do. And apparently he lives nearby."

I wondered in which of the expensive buildings MacLeod had his apartment. They were mostly co-ops and went for millions. Being from IA, Ferrari wouldn't put the car on a fire hydrant, although I noticed that a number of civilians were less reluctant. The bus stops were all filled up, too. Finally, she left the car in a red zone, tossed the police ID plate on the dashboard, and we hiked two blocks to T.J.'s.

Normal New York. We had to search for five minutes to find an illegal space.

It was the kind of summer night made for Manhattan. Mild temperatures and unusually low humidity filled the streets with people. And clean air titillated the nostrils. The inexplicable promise of nights like these and the pulsating excitement of Manhattan had always turned me on. But tonight, although accompanied by a beautiful woman, I found my attention drawn to the freaks panhandling, a couple of bag people calling it an early night in their doorways, wall-to-wall hookers, and pushers working every corner. One of the hookers was so stoned she didn't make us as cops. "How about some fun, the three of us?" she said.

Ferrari straight-armed her out of our path. She had been 100 percent tough professional so far. I decided to tease. "Stephanie, you never even asked my thoughts about the young lady's suggestion."

She turned with a surprisingly warm smile. "My apologies." She put her hands on her hips and faced me. "You can pick her up and bring her back to your room after we've finished in the bar." Her eyes returned to brown marble. "Now, let's move it. I want to get there before Fitzgerald passes out."

I laughed. "I'd forgotten how tough you are."

"You didn't forget. You never knew."

I hoped I didn't find out. We pushed our way into the crowded bar. I realized instantly that the air-conditioning had been overwhelmed by the mass of flesh. Good-looking young women smoked incessantly while their male companions in four-hundred-dollar suits and Gucci loafers toughed it out drinking Heinekens out of the bottle next to locals dressed slightly better than the bag people outside. Sweating bodies, air heavily laden with beer farts, expensive perfume, cigars, and the cooking of pure cholesterol hamburgers made it difficult to breathe until you surrendered and became part of the mob. The sly-faced Irish bartenders wore ready smiles, but their washed-out blue eyes coldly followed the flow of cash on the bar.

Following Stephanie Ferrari's lead, I elbowed my way into the center of the room to where the Block and Fitzgerald sat, taking up considerable bar space with their bulk. They were gorging themselves on double-thick hamburgers and french fries smothered in ketchup. A well-dressed black man in his thirties stood at the bar watching them. He was drinking a martini straight up with an olive. I knew the black guy was too old to be a pimp. They didn't live to be thirty in this town. Besides, he had clean-cut good looks which didn't signal crook, although I had been wrong about those things before.

"Hey, Fraleigh," the Block bellowed above the din. "You were right. The food is great." He put the sandwich down momentarily.

I confiscated it and took a bite, trying to catch the attention of one of the bartenders.

"Just like a fucking boss," Fitzgerald laughed. "Steal the food right out of your mouth." I wondered if Captain Ferrari had been kidding about his passing out. His eyes were bloodshot, and even with a mouthful of hamburger it was apparent that his words were slurred. Ferrari rolled her eyes at the ceiling. I wondered whether it was in reaction to my wolfing down the burger or to Sergeant Fitzgerald's condition. It was probably a combination of both.

"Hey sport." The Block had gotten the bartender's attention by pinning his forearm to the bar when he had been careless enough to set down someone's drink within the Block's reach. "We got two new people in the party, and me and Jocko," he leaned his head toward Fitzgerald, "can use another one."

The bartender started to protest his arm being pinned to the bar, but remained silent after taking us in. The precinct cops frequented the place, and given the multitude of violations that would have closed most other bars, the idiosyncrasies of cop patrons were overlooked.

"Plain tonic," Stephanie said, causing the bartender to look twice at her to see if she was really a cop or just a cop's bimbo. She moved closer to Fitzgerald and began to chew his ass fiercely. The noise was so great that I missed most of it, although I heard Fitzgerald saying respectfully, "I'm all right, Captain, honest."

"Chief Gross will cut your balls off and stuff them down your fat throat. That's if you have any balls. And when he finishes with you I'll kick your ass back into the grand jury where we can go over all those fucking lies you thought you got away with. You drink soda from now on." She moved what looked like a double scotch away from him.

The Block stared at her. Turning to me he said, "Jesus Christ. Did you hear her castrate him?"

"You better ease up on the booze yourself, Block, or I'll put her on *you*."

"I only drink beer," he protested. "And I didn't even say anything when you stole my hamburger." He shook his head like I had irreparably hurt his feelings.

I had spoken too loudly. Ferrari had heard my comment to the Block and was unamused. "As you might have guessed by now, Fraleigh, I opposed bringing Fitzgerald in. I know your history and why the chief's so sympathetic, but people like *him*," she nodded toward Fitzgerald who was morosely staring at himself in the bar mirror, "turn my stomach. He shouldn't be on the job." She stood next to me speaking quietly, sipping at her tonic.

I didn't disagree with her, but he was my key to getting to MacLeod and Wong and I didn't want a purist IA captain screwing up the works.

"Chief Gross promised me this asshole will set up the meets. I hope you're not going to let a personality conflict mess up the deal."

The crowd had pushed us close together. She wore sensible medium heels and her eyes were a couple of inches lower than mine. She looked into my eyes and the same beautiful warm smile came onto her face. The same smile she had worn a few moments ago on the street outside when she had cut me down. We were so close I got a little nervous. She would be very good at karate and I was far too near her for defensive purposes.

"Personality conflict! Now listen, you knuckleheaded male chauvinist shithead, I've been saddled with you and that hulk you got off the plane with . . ."

"Captain, Captain." I held my hand up in a sign of peace, mustering my warmest smile. "Truce. Truce. You're right. You got a crummy assignment and everything you say about him," I pointed in Fitzgerald's direction, "and most of what you say about us," I grinned, "is true. But this case is really important. Help me. Let's work together."

She looked at me and finally nodded. "OK. Just remember, it's my job to keep that piece of shit from embarrassing the department. If I can do that and help you get what you want I will, but don't forget who's running the show."

I almost made the mistake of saying Yes, ma'am. Catching myself in time I said, "No problem."

"Yeah. No problem. Don't try to jerk me off, Fraleigh. I know you'll try anything, but just remember what I said. It would give me great pleasure to lock that fat tub up." She pointed at Fitzgerald. I saw that his eyes followed her in the bar mirror and that he had overheard. "And if you and *your* fat tub have to fall with him, so be it." I stopped wondering why Seymour Gross had recruited a beautiful woman to his staff. She moved to the bar and put her drink down. "I'm going to the restroom and then I'll call the office to let them know MacLeod hasn't shown yet."

"I told you he said eleven o'clock, Captain," Fitzgerald said. "It's too early." She walked away without looking at him.

"Hey, Chief." Fitzgerald beckoned to me with his hand. I got close enough to smell his breath before backing up a foot. "I was willing to call in a few chits to help you guys. I'm a team player, and if that's what the bosses want I'll set up meetings, but I'm not working with that cunt. I got a feeling that no matter what I do these meetings won't come off—know what I mean?"

I knew all right. This lush held the cards. He could go through the motions, make sure we failed, and tell Gross he had done his best. He continued in his wheezing bar voice, "No one can tell what these niggers, chinks, or wops are going to do on any given day. That gash is sucking dicks for the brass while I bust my chops in the squad. If she had to put up with the garbage for a day, we'd see what kind of cop she was."

"Look Fitz," I put my hand on his shoulder, "forget her. Set up the meets and I'll take care of it with Chief Gross. Here, finish your drink." I pushed his scotch back to him after making sure Stephanie was out of sight.

"Just keep her off my back, that's all."

Yeah. And how did I do that and keep Fitzgerald on the level? I turned to see where the phones were. I should call Nola. I stepped back from the bar, noticing that the black man had been watching me and listening to our conversation. New Yorkers are adept at avoiding eye contact, but I was out of practice. When our eyes met he said, "You're all cops, aren't you?"

"What makes you ask?"

"All the nigger-calling and cussing."

"How about yourself? What do you do for a living?" I said, because I couldn't think of anything else to say.

"You didn't answer—which confirms my opinion. Look, don't get up-tight. I'm not Mau-Mauing you. It's good for me to hear you honkies once in a while. I grew up in Scarsdale. Was president of my high school class. Went to Yale. I need to get back to reality every now and then." He fumbled with his wallet. "I'm a stockbroker. Very successful." He handed me a business card. "But that woman. I could hardly believe those words came from something so exquisite. Is she really a cop?"

"She's an actress practicing for a part in a cop movie for television." I read silently from his card, Phillip Rogers, Account Vice President—with Merrill-Lynch and gang. Still, cards were cheap. "I've been thinking of some stocks myself. What do you recommend?"

"Sorry. I'm handling only large portfolios now. Can't take any new clients. Besides, never take a stock tip you get in a bar. I knew she was too fine a person to be a cop. But if you want, I can refer you to another broker at the firm. How much do you want to invest?"

We were distracted before I could think of something else to ask which would reveal whether or not he knew anything about being a stockbroker. A young woman to the left of Fitzgerald had cried out, "Oh God. This is too much."

We turned to watch Fitzgerald, who had staggered off his stool, unzipped his fly, and was stirring Ferrari's tonic with his limp dick. "Fucking bitch. This is what she needs, some cock." The girl who had spoken turned away shaking her head. The two guys with her gaped, then started clapping. A bartender pretended he hadn't seen a thing. The Block, who had jet lag compounded by far too many beers, growled at Fitzgerald, "What the hell are you doing?"

"I pissed in it. Let her taste some good Irish cock for a change," Fitzgerald mumbled, putting the drink back on the bar and zipping his fly.

I tried to make my way to the bar to dump the drink without antagonizing Fitzgerald. MacLeod was due any minute and Fitzgerald was the only one who knew him.

"That's disgusting. How could you do that to the lady's drink?" The stockbroker had somehow gotten between Fitzgerald and me.

"What's it to you, Jesse Jackson?" Fitzgerald replied in his own charming way.

"Take it easy, Paddy. You too, Rogers." I had the stock-broker's left arm and tried to move him away from the bar.

The Block leaned over to Fitzgerald. "You know something," he slurred, "you're a fucking bigot." With which he slapped the detective lightly on the cheek. The trouble was the Block's light slaps always knocked people down, and Fitzgerald turned out to be no exception. Going down, he took a bar stool and several glasses with him along with a small man wearing spectacles who was holding a cocker spaniel on a leash. The dog yelped, and barking shrilly, bit Fitzgerald in the leg. Shaking off the dog, he lurched into the girl who had cried out. She won the noise contest easily, screaming so loudly that even people in the front turned to see what was going on. Others added their own yells to the din.

"Well done. If you ever want to open an account, come and see me." The stockbroker gave the Block one of his cards. The bartenders had converged on the altercation and held miniature baseball bats at ready. I tried to move in to help Fitzgerald. Out of the corner of my eye I saw Stephanie Ferrari struggling to get to us through the pushing and shoving crowd. That was the last thing I saw for a while. Something hit me in the back of the head and blackness swept over me.

"Goddamn it. Wake up. We need to get out of here." Ferrari was supporting me, my right arm was around her and her left arm firmly encircled my waist. I had only been out for a few seconds. Groggily, I pulled my nose out of her hair, thinking she smelled good. I unsteadily shifted my weight back to my feet just in time to see a big guy with a red beard advancing on me with a broken bottle at ready. I tried to regain my balance to face him, but Stephanie moved in front of me. She feinted him out of position and then kicked him in the balls so hard that the guy just sank to the floor in amazed pain. He'd piss blood for quite a while.

But I had stared too long. I looked back toward the bar to see how the Block was doing and saw a fist with a huge stone ring headed for my nose. Ducking, I saved my eyes, but the blow crashed into my forehead and the ring opened the skin. Blood gushed into my eyes and I fell back a step. But now I was mad, and I whipped a right into the soft gut of the fat guy who had sneak punched me. Then with three precision punches I broke his nose and jaw. I was going to be inconvenienced by his punch, but he would remember mine much longer as he sipped through a straw for two months.

"For Christ's sake, let's get out of here," Ferrari said to me after I watched her dump another drunk with a hand slam to the throat. I let her shove me out the door. On the sidewalk she produced a hand radio from her bag and calmly called in a signal 10-13—Assist Officer. We were standing there waiting for the magic music of sirens when the floor-to-ceiling side glass window of the bar gave way in a thunderstorm of jagged pieces. We watched the awesome sight of the Block half carrying, half dragging the inert hulk of Fitzgerald through the hole. Steam from the food steam tables swirled around people pouring through the new exit. Fights had spilled all around us on the sidewalk. Clearly, the meeting with MacLeod had gone down the tube.

Ferrari had stopped a cab, but the driver was balking at loading up our bloody crew. She stuck her shield under his nose and said, "Either you or I are driving this hack into the precinct. Now which way do you want it?"

"Jeez. You're a captain. I can't believe it. Hey, no offense. Don't get mad. I meant it as a compliment. I'm happy to take you to the station house."

The first wave of cops was arriving with flashing lights and sirens. New York's Finest began to apply their nightsticks with gleeful abandon. I burst out laughing thinking of the spot Ferrari would be in when complaints of unnecessary force had to be investigated by IA. Hearing me, she said,

"You must have a concussion," which only made me laugh harder.

We were pulling away when the black stockbroker yanked open the door and piled in. His suit was torn and blood trickled from his swollen bottom lip. I noticed that his knuckles on both hands were bruised and bleeding. He had gotten in some heavy punches. I wondered if he had knocked any teeth out. "Hey. That was all right. Can I join you?"

Since the cab was already careening out of the area, his question was rhetorical, but I said, "Be my guest."

"Hey. Where are we going next? I know a fun place up on Lexington Avenue. What do you say?" He beamed at Stephanie.

"What's your name?" she asked.

"My card, lovely one." He flashed a brilliant smile as he handed the card to her. "Where's the party?"

She flashed her own killer smile back and I felt sorry for the stockbroker. "At the Seventeenth Precinct, Mister Rogers. We'll be needing your statement, but it shouldn't take more than a couple of hours, and since I have your card, take your hand off the door handle. I wouldn't want to send cops around to your office tomorrow."

"I thought you said she was an actress," the broker whispered to me.

"She's too fine a person to be an actress," I said.

Fitzgerald grimaced drunkenly at the broker. "Sucker," he said.

Seventeen

WE PULLED UP IN FRONT OF THE GREEN LIGHTS ON FIFTY-First Street identifying the Seventeenth Precinct, or the One Seven in New York cop language. "You and you," Ferrari pointed at the Block and me, "stay in the cab. The driver will take you back to your hotel. I don't want you surfacing in this." Then she swung her finger at Fitzgerald and the broker. "You and you. Out of the cab and into the precinct. I'm going to write the Unusual Occurrence Report. You're going to read it and we will jointly prepare your statements, which you will sign. Fraleigh—Fitzgerald and I are going to have a little chat, and I am more than sure that he will arrange for you to meet MacLeod and Anthony Wong tomorrow without the entertainment. I'll give you a call early in the morning with the schedule." With that she was gone. The cab driver sighed with relief. I think he feared that he too was about to be ordered into the precinct by the Dragon Lady Captain.

As we approached the hotel it occurred to me that I was a mess. The wound on my forehead was forming an angry red scab, my formerly white shirt was caked with dried blood, my tie had disappeared, and my jacket was torn. The Block, who didn't look much better, was snoring unconcernedly in the corner of the cab. The cab driver failed to hide his gleeful anticipation of the hotel doorman's reaction to us when he opened the cab door. I realized how exhausted I was.

I generously gave the driver ten bucks, since he had "forgotten" to throw the meter flag. The hotel doorman's uniform was three times as glorious as my police chief's uniform, but what the hell, he probably earned three times as much as I did after not declaring tips on his income tax. He was tall, black, slim, and about thirty. "Motherfucker!" he exclaimed softly, almost reverently when the Block and I emerged from the cab. I think he regretted not having slammed the door closed on us. I gave him a dollar, and he watched, frozen, as a bellman tried to stop us from entering the lobby. "Sir, I'm afraid. . ."

"Automobile accident." I cut him off, dangling my room key under his nose. All I could think of was a soothing hot shower, two aspirins, a slug of brandy, and an ice pack on my swelling left eye and cut forehead. Walking to the elevators I glanced into the bar lounge and found there were other things I could think of.

There sat Nola at a small table with a flickering candle. She was dressed in a lovely emerald green dress. In the distance she could have been a movie star. Next to her I saw the rear of a well-shaped razor haircut—the kind often seen among overly paid electronics executives in Silicon Valley. His hand was over hers on the table.

"Go on up and hit the sack, Block. I need to make a stop." Yawning like the Grand Canyon, he didn't argue. I headed for the lounge fully aware that people were gaping.

The same overly zealous bellman blocked my way. "Sir, I'm afraid I can't let you go into the bar in your condition. Shouldn't you be seeking medical attention?"

I pointed over his shoulder at Nola. "That's my physician. I'm going to get her advice right now." I pushed him aside before he got his courage up again.

It was dark in the lounge and they only had eyes for each other. As I approached I heard the guy telling Nola, "Well, that's really impressive. You managed to get yourself into a position of power when so many people just complain about things. And as someone doing business in the area, I can't tell you how exciting your ideas are on improving housing and traffic flow. You're obviously a doer."

I fully expected to see Nola's eyes twinkling with amusement over his gratuitous line of bullshit, but when I got closer I saw that he had her full attention. Both had a glass of white wine before them.

Nola's mouth dropped open when I approached the table. The guy swiveled to see what she was looking at and turned pale. I flopped into a seat. "Hi, gang," I said.

"What in God's name happened to you, Fraleigh?" Nola was a mixture of anger and concern.

She wasn't surprised to see me, so I guess she had gotten my phone message. I suppose I did look pretty bad. "I'm working on a case with the New York cops. We went to T. J. Brown's to meet with one of the crooks involved."

"Brown's? Really?" She frowned. "And?"

"Well, the place was jammed. Detective Fitzgerald, the New York cop, was drunk at the bar. He whipped out his dick in front of a bunch of people and stirred this female captain's drink with it. A black stockbroker objected. One thing led to another. The Block called Detective Fitzgerald a bigot and knocked him on his ass. The crowd went berserk and some rat hit me on the head." I touched the back of my head. The wound oozed some blood onto my fingers. Out of the corner of my eye I saw a look of horror cross the guy's face. "But the guy that did this," I touched my forehead, "I taught a lesson. I broke the prick's jaw." I put my bruised knuckles under the boy scout's nose and he recoiled.

"Clark, this is our chief of police. Fraleigh, Clark Massey, CEO of Future Chips."

He had the clean-cut good looks of the up-and-coming tycoon, and I resisted the impulse to shatter his forearm where Nola had touched him.

"Nice to meet you. I don't think I've ever met a police chief before. It must be interesting work." His friendly smile wilted slightly as I put pressure into our handshake. He pulled away from me rubbing his right hand, then, self-consciously, stopped. His eyes were wary, and he leaned away from me as if I might try a bearhug next.

"Clark and I knew each other in college. Now he is thinking of expanding his plant in Silicon City, creating as many as one hundred fifty new jobs." Nola was positively bubbling. "Future Chips has a patent to manufacture the latest RAMs."

"Rams? Condoms?" I said, deadpan.

"Heavens no. RAMs not R. . ." He caught himself while I looked on spellbound to hear about computers from such an important person. "RAMs stands for random access memories, the things that make computers possible."

He had actually said, *heavens no*. "Golly, that is exciting. Well, don't let me interrupt," I said.

Nola's eyes were now very serious. She mouthed the word *asshole* at me when Clark wasn't looking. I gave her a big smile.

"Nola, I've got to make a call." Clark Massey couldn't stand my bloody presence. "I'll be in touch tomorrow." He was on his feet and away.

She hardly noticed. Her chin was cupped in her hands and suddenly she was laughing. "Fraleigh, you're magnificent. Anyone who could present a crock of shit like that with a straight face deserves tender loving care. Poor Clark. He almost wet himself when he got a look at you approaching him. He probably won't sleep all night." Her fingers ran gently over my face and her eyes had a familiar light in them.

My hand under the table slid through the slit in her dress and caressed her wonderfully smooth thigh. "I was hoping that you were getting a little wet yourself."

"You dirty pig. I'm going to make you pay, Fraleigh. First I'm going to clean and bandage your wounds. Then I'm going to unmercifully fuck the truth out of you. Clark Massey may or may not sleep, but I guarantee you won't until I get the full unvarnished story about whatever police escapade you were really involved in."

Eighteen

NOLA *WAS* UNMERCIFUL. AND TRUE TO HER WORD. SHE WAS in the shower and I hadn't slept much when my phone rang at seven A.M. and Captain Stephanie Ferrari told me what the day's marching orders were. Strangely enough I felt great.

Nola came out of the bathroom. "You ravished me all night, you grotesque sex fiend. I'll look exhausted all through the symposium, while you'll merely look like you were run over by a subway train. Let me put some of my makeup over that cut on your forehead so that you don't scare people."

"You look fabulous. Stop beaming, everyone will guess what you've been doing all night. And don't overdo the makeup. I don't want to be cruised by New York gays all day." She did look fabulous. This was the old and new Nola. A mixture of the innocent little girl and the wicked woman. She left for her room insisting that she simply needed an hour to make up before appearing at the official opening of the drug symposium. It was untrue, of course. If she had walked into the meeting room the way she was now, everything would have stopped. She was going to make up to tone it down.

Downstairs at the symposium, Nola and I stood talking to each other when Captain Stephanie Ferrari walked up. I introduced them. I almost felt sparks from the electricity flowing as they sized each other up. Two high-powered women. Nola's cheerfulness subsided and Stephanie's greeting, "Ma'am," didn't help. In the front of the room the keynote speaker was being introduced. He was a gray-haired, eyeglassed scientist who had more degrees than anyone cared to hear about. We were solemnly informed that he was to speak on "epidemiology, anomie theory, differential association, and substance abuse."

"I thought this was supposed to be about dope?" the Block said.

"That's what the man just said, dummy. Come on. I already know all this stuff."

"Yeah. I notice that since you made chief you know everything."

Stephanie Ferrari smiled, but Nola did not. I said good-bye to her and moved toward the door.

We walked out the hotel door just as the Lincoln pulled up. Fitzgerald, behind the wheel, wore dark sunglasses. I could have used a pair myself. The Block got into the front and the two of them nodded cordially, like they hadn't been batting the shit out of each other last night. I got into the back with Captain Ferrari. She wore a dark-green business suit which enhanced her color.

"The meet is all set, Captain?"

"In about half an hour," she said.

"Er, Stephanie, were you planning on being present when we take on MacLeod?"

"Why do you ask?" With a slight smile, she leaned back against the cushions waiting for my answer.

I took a deep breath. "Well, I was wondering what you thought. You know these brokers and their attitude toward women. Then too, I'll have to squeeze him a bit."

"And you wanted to spare me the indignity?"

I grinned. "Actually, I wanted to keep you from breaking MacLeod's neck."

She laughed. "All right. I'll go in with you to make sure everything is OK, then I'll leave. I'm not anxious to be a witness. I don't even want to know how you intend to make him talk."

"Good," I said. "I was hoping you wouldn't misinterpret what I was saying."

"Are you disappointed in having to leave the drug symposium so early?" She changed the subject pleasantly, if abruptly.

"Yeah. They were just getting into epidemiology, anomie, differential association, and substance abuse. Fascinating. It was all I could do to get the Block to leave with me."

She half smiled. "I put up with years of that stuff at John Jay College. I feel the same way he does." I wondered with some unease what had put her in such a good mood. She continued, "We're going to meet MacLeod in his office on Wall Street. It's not far from Forlini's, and if you don't commit any felonies, I'll treat you to a delicious lunch."

"I don't know. I never had any willpower in Forlini's, and I can't afford even the normal calories they serve."

"Don't be so modest. I saw how you moved in T.J.'s last night. You're in as good shape as when you were boxing. Except for your face. Come here." Her fingers reached up and she placed her hand along the side of my face. "Nola's makeup has come off." Her eyes teased. Then she took a little tube and puff from her purse and began to apply makeup to my forehead, keeping her cool left hand on the side of my face as she worked. Her brown eyes were all innocent concentration, but she was anything but innocent. If Nola hadn't screwed me so unmercifully all night, I probably would have tried to kiss her right there and gotten slugged in the process. Or she might have responded. This was a damned interesting woman. Finished with the makeup, she patted my cheek. "No charge, Rocky," she said, her eyes warm and friendly, and last night's sarcasm totally absent.

"These are the people I spoke to you about, Mr. MacLeod," Fitzgerald said. We were on the forty-second floor and MacLeod clearly rated. His office was large with a plush crimson carpet and a great view of the river, Battery Park, and the bay.

I had expected to see a broad-shouldered captain of Wall Street, but the man behind the desk reminded me of Woody Allen. He fiddled with his glasses and smiled at Stephanie as Fitzgerald introduced her. "Also, this is Fraleigh and the Block from California law enforcement," Fitzgerald said, ID'ing us for MacLeod.

MacLeod had regular features and dark hair. He had barely glanced at us, but was openly devouring Stephanie. Stephanie had a slight flush in her cheeks. She was looking back at MacLeod about the same way she had at the guy whose balls she had kicked the night before. I held my breath hoping she'd go, before MacLeod provoked her in some way. Finally, MacLeod looked in my direction. With a slight nod to me, Stephanie left.

I turned toward Fitzgerald. "I want you to leave, too."

"No fucking way, Fraleigh. I stay."

MacLeod's eyes widened. His head bobbed back and forth between us like he was watching a tennis match.

"Get out," I said softly to Fitzgerald without emphasis.

MacLeod turned to see Fitzgerald's response.

"Fuck you. I don't take your goddamned orders, you hick asshole."

The Block and I had set up a game plan. I shook my head *yes,* and he slammed Fitzgerald in the stomach. My full attention had been on MacLeod. I hadn't even been looking at Fitzgerald when I nodded to the Block. I got what I wanted. MacLeod blinked when the Block swung. "My God," he said, "you can't do that in here."

He wrung his hands as the detective collapsed onto the floor moaning. The Block reached under his arms and dragged him out of the room. MacLeod wet his lips. "Please, we can't have that sort of thing here in the firm," he said.

"Yeah, sure." I said. "Look, we're here off the record. We want some information from you and we'll be on the way. The New York cops won't know what was said. That's why I threw Fitzgerald out."

"Won't you get in trouble hitting a policeman like that?" MacLeod looked scared.

The Block had returned. He walked to the desk and leaned on it with his fists clenched. "Did you say something about me hitting a cop, fuckface?"

MacLeod cringed away. "Yes, no—I mean, I didn't see anything. Please, you'll have to leave. This is a very prestigious firm."

"No shit?" The Block sneered at him. "What are you gonna do pal, call the cops?"

MacLeod stood. He was pale, near panic. "I don't understand. I agreed to see Detective Fitzgerald, who interviewed me. Who are you?"

"That's not important, MacLeod. We're not interested in you," I said. "A couple of months ago you did some business with a creep using the name Dick Barry. He ended up in Bellevue Hospital after trying to peddle you and Mad Anthony Wong some bearer bonds. We don't give a shit about Barry or what happened to the bonds. We just want to know where he got them and we know he told you where. Just repeat it and we walk out. You'll never hear about it again."

"I want my lawyer." MacLeod's voice was even higher pitched.

"We're not cops. We're here as private citizens from California," I said.

"I have nothing to say. Why did you hit Fitzgerald?"

What I hoped for was happening. Despite his refusal to talk, he was talking. A combination of ego, fear, and curiosity that I had counted on. Also, I had planted an important seed in his mind for later. We weren't actually cops. We were from California and tough. It was OK to talk to us if there was something in it for him.

"He's a scumbag and he's wearing a wire for the feds." I made up the answer to his question about Fitzgerald on the spur of the moment.

"Feds? What does this have to do with the federal government?"

We had a reaction. "Nothing, if you tell us what we want. If you don't, we'll throw you and your firm into a securities investigation that will rival Ivan Boesky's."

"You can't fool me." MacLeod's face had gotten sly. He was regrouping. "Fitzgerald and I have done each other favors before. He already warned me about you and the lady captain. She's something, isn't she?" An ugly smile appeared on his face. "If I could rent her for a month in my circles I'd never have to work again."

I thought to myself that if she had just heard you, you'd never be *able* to work again. I couldn't let him recover. "Take a moment to read these and I think you may change your mind about working with us." I passed along a phony UF61 crime report and DD5 supplemental investigation report which I had typed out in the hotel before going to be enlightened at the drug symposium.

MacLeod was just dumb and self-centered enough to fall for one of our oldest dodges. I had typed in charges of armed robbery, extortion, and felonious assault, all heavies for a guy like MacLeod. The mere accusation of any one of them would panic his prestigious "firm." On the DD5 the investigating officer stated that he had obtained enough evidence for an arrest warrant and a search warrant to be served against the suspect, Christopher MacLeod, by enlisting the cooperation of his accomplice Anthony Wong, aka Mad Anthony, who had described how MacLeod had engineered taking the bonds from the victim, Dick Barry, by force in the Fifth Precinct. When the victim had struggled, he had been severely beaten and required hospitalization in Bellevue Hospital. The investigating officer was Patrick Fitzgerald, Fifth Detective Squad. I had signed his name with a flourish knowing that he would never have given MacLeod anything in writing, so the handwriting didn't matter. I had another pair of reports in my pocket exactly reversed, indicating that Anthony Wong had been the real bad guy and that the information had come from one Christopher MacLeod.

It was nothing more than an old cop pea game. We played each suspect against the other. The distraction thrown in to keep MacLeod from recognizing it was that we hadn't acted like cops the way we treated Fitzgerald—and that Fitzgerald had signed the DD5. MacLeod coursed the reports. When he came to the caption where he was listed as suspect, he gasped as if he had been hit.

"This can't be true, Mr. Fraleigh. These accusations would ruin me. Fitzgerald told me everything would be all right if I did what he said . . ." He paused, realizing he had said too much.

"We're not interested in Fitzgerald, either. Only where Richard Barry got the bonds."

"I had nothing to do with the assault, of course."

We waited.

MacLeod cleared his throat. "I can't afford to tell you something relative to a client."

I showed no emotion, but I had him. He was going to tell me what I wanted without admitting to himself that he was telling me anything. "Your client is Anthony Wong isn't it? Mad Anthony is sending you under to protect himself. You'll either talk to me or to the local and federal grand juries. Do yourself a favor and put this to bed before it blows up in your face."

"If anyone broke bones, believe me, it wasn't me. You know that."

After being with him for two minutes we knew it, but now we stared back at MacLeod. He continued. "Mr. Wong and I know each other slightly. He's been a client of the firm for years. I only brought Barry to him as a favor. I didn't know what would . . . I mean, I thought Barry was a bit shifty and

I had heard rumors about Anthony, you know." He looked appealingly at me and the Block.

I bet you heard rumors about Wong. I wonder how much of Mad Anthony's drug proceeds you laundered. "Go on," I said.

"Well, it was incredible. Barry had only a couple of sample bonds. But Wong was convinced that Barry had hundreds of thousands of dollars in stolen bonds in a locker at Kennedy Airport, or Grand Central Station, or someplace. He began to beat the man, totally lost control of himself. I ran and called nine-one-one anonymously from a store. If the police hadn't arrived when they did, I believe he would have killed him. I told Fitzgerald all this. He said it was better to report that no suspects were known. It would keep the firm out of it. I have no desire to have someone like Anthony Wong after me." MacLeod was sweating. "I haven't spoken to Wong since this happened. I gave his account to another broker."

I looked skeptical. "Then how come he's laying such heavy shit on you?"

MacLeod wiped his forehead. "Orientals—who knows? They have centuries of these intrigues—Tongs, Triads, you know. I'm an honest Christian businessman. I feel better telling you this. I've been worried sick."

I wondered how much of what MacLeod had told us was true. I suspected that the basic story was. He had simply left out that Wong supplied cocaine to his circle, and that he handled his drug money. When Bartlow approached him with a shoddy deal, MacLeod saw a way to make a bundle. He would go through Anthony Wong for the purchase cash and not involve the "firm." He hadn't counted on Anthony going crazy.

I asked, "How did Bartlow come to contact you?"

"This is a well-known, reputable firm. He must have read about . . ."

"We don't have time for bullshit, MacLeod," I said.

MacLeod broke eye contact with me. Lowering his eyes he said, "A man I once dealt with by the name of Lee Bronheim called me from California. He said Bartlow was his attorney and wanted to sell a large number of bonds. He referred him to me. That's what we do, after all."

"Sure," I said, pleased that Charley Thompson's info on Inky Lee Bronheim confirmed what MacLeod was telling us. "So, you knew all along that Barry was a phony name?"

"Many clients use different names. We're not in business to cure them of their eccentricities."

"Where did Barry say he got the bond?"

"From an old folks' trust in California. He bragged that he could get plenty of them and they were nontraceable. His brother is a powerful politician and got him appointed someplace as a conservator."

"What was the name of the trust?"

"Heaven or something."

"Heaven?" I frowned. "You're a broker. You'd remember the name of a trust."

"You're right. But I ran. I think Wong would have killed me, too. I never did hear Barry's complete information."

"Who'd he say appointed him conservator?"

"A judge, someone who knew his brother the politician."

"Let me give you some advice, Christopher. If Anthony Wong, Detective Fitzgerald, or even your mother wants to talk about what happened, don't. There's a chance that we can keep your name out of it if you keep your mouth closed."

"Just a chance?" he whispered. "You said you . . . What sort of chance? What are the probabilities?"

"About the same chance as the market closing up tomorrow. Fifty-fifty," I said.

He winced. "No better than the market?"

I laughed. "Hey listen, MacLeod. You haven't exactly been a bundle of help. Especially for a broker. If you were a plumber I could understand that you wouldn't have paid that much attention."

"If I were a plumber I'd have security. People don't understand how volatile this business is. Er . . ."

"Yes?"

"Barry did hint that the funds came from some electronics companies' pension investments."

"Which companies?"

"I don't know. It was a grouping. Named the Silicon Valley Consortium."

"Can you find out by tomorrow which companies are involved?"

He looked pained. "Tomorrow? We're not quite that bad." He turned to a computer terminal next to his desk and began to play with it. After a couple of minutes of fooling around with the keyboard he pushed a button and a printer across the room began to clatter. His personality had changed. He strode purposefully across the room and tore a sheet from the printer. "Here are the eleven companies. I trust this ends our business, Mr. Fraleigh."

"Don't put your trust in very much nowadays, MacLeod. Things are too volatile," I said.

We left him pouting behind his big desk staring down at his plush carpet.

Nineteen

"SO, HOW DID YOU MAKE OUT? I TRIED TO READ YOUR face. Nothing. The Block's face, nothing. Both of you are poker players," Stephanie said.

We were in a booth in Forlini's on Baxter Street, a block from the Tombs Jail and Centre Street courts. On the edge of Little Italy and Chinatown, it was a favorite eating place of cops, lawyers, judges, affluent defendants, and occasional mafiosi. The appeal of its robust Italian cuisine had created a kind of sanctuary for combatants of New York's criminal justice battles. Many a deal had been cut over the antipasto.

Stephanie had dispatched the Block and Fitzgerald to a nearby beer hall to have lunch while we ate in a luxurious setting. I wondered about their compatability, but the two of them had been chatting affably enough. The Block had apologized for having belted Fitzgerald "to make it look good," and the detective, rubbing his sore stomach, had shrugged it off. I suppose he didn't have much choice. In answer to Fitzgerald's question, the Block had said, "The little wimp didn't tell us shit."

"It worked out just the way I hoped," I said to Stephanie Ferrari.

"Really? I'm intrigued. If you didn't commit too many felonies, tell me how you got that jerk to talk. I thought you were dead in the water when I saw him sitting there doing a two-bit imitation of the tycoon."

She had ordered an Italian white wine for us. I had preferred a California Chardonnay, but one didn't argue too much with Stephanie Ferrari. At least she had let me order Clams Oreganatto to begin and Veal Ambrosiano for an entrée, when Frank, the owner, suggested them. She skipped an appetizer, ordering pasta with clam sauce for her main dish. Without an invitation she had taken one of my clams and was delicately sighing over it.

"These helped." I pushed the phony UF61 and DD5 toward her and sipped the wine, which turned out to be excellent.

"You forged these." She looked up from the forms.

"Of course."

"Even so. I can't believe he fell for the old 'your partner gave you up' routine," she smiled.

"He was thrown off when the Block slugged Fitzgerald."

"That was clever. My only complaint is that you didn't let me do it."

"Maybe next time. How come you're so relaxed and friendly today, and why did you send those two off on their own for lunch?"

"For one thing, we can't talk in front of Fitzgerald. Never trust him, Fraleigh. Secondly, I don't enjoy being around him and . . ." She turned on the full smile, but this time I enjoyed its sincerity. "You were nice this morning. You knew that the interview wouldn't have worked if I was present, but you worked hard to get me to say it, not you. You could have gone over my head to Chief Gross and just told me, here's the way it is. It was sensitive, and I don't see that very often on the job. And I guess your battered face is growing on me. It goes well with hearty peasant food."

"Thanks a million."

"Did MacLeod give you all you need?"

"I'm not sure. He gave up Wong quick enough. Said no way would he, MacLeod, be into violence. Therefore, Wong must have done it. On the bond, all he could remember was that it came from a senior citizen trust, and the first name could have been Paradise or Heaven or something like that.

The trust tied in to a consortium of Silicon Valley electronics firms. When we check in California I hope that it will be enough to identify the fund and trace the stolen bonds."

"He put the whole job on his partner." She laughed. "Honor among thieves. Always touching. I have to admit, Fraleigh, I thought you would come up empty. Still, you'll never get any of this into court. The forged reports, slugging Fitzgerald. . ."

"I know. But the beauty of it is we won't need any of it in court. Once I know where Bartlow stole the bonds I can nail him with the sting videotapes in court."

"So we can skip Mad Anthony Wong? I worked in Chinatown during the Tong wars. I wasn't looking forward to going back."

"No. I'm afraid we need to confirm MacLeod's story with Wong, and maybe he can remember more about where the bonds came from than MacLeod did. And, who knows, he may tie in Bartlow's brother, the politician."

"You really want the politician, don't you? Why is that?"

"He's just another crook as far as I'm concerned."

Stephanie laughed. "Sure."

"Well, maybe I have sounded like I'm after him. I guess it always bothers me when someone thinks they've got so much clout that they can get away with whatever they want, and to hell with the cops. The cops are too stupid to catch them. Or if they aren't, then the cops will be told to go investigate someone else, or cops on the inside will leak stuff, and . . ."

"I'm sorry I asked." She smiled. "Tell me this. How are you going to get Mad Anthony to talk? He's too smart to do what MacLeod did."

"You're right. We need different tactics. Like this." I held up my thin dictating recorder. "I had this in my pocket." I looked around to make sure we couldn't be overheard, then turned the machine on. Its quality was surprisingly good. MacLeod's high-pitched voice came through clearly.

I fast-forwarded the tape to make sure it had the part where MacLeod was clearly pinning the whole deal on Wong. "Wong should enjoy listening to that."

"You're too much, Fraleigh. I'm sorry we lost you to California." She looked at me in a way that a lot could be read into what she had just said. I was beginning to enjoy the Big Apple again. I found myself smiling back at her. Suddenly, thinking of Nola and last night, I got back to the case.

"The trouble is I'm not sure this will be enough to get Wong to open up. I need another gimmick."

"Knowing you, you'll improvise. Try to stay away from felonies though. I still need four more years to start collecting my pension."

Stephanie Ferrari, after witholding it from me yesterday, had just very deliberately told me her age. She now watched to see how I reacted. You had to be twenty-one to join the department and normal retirement was possible after twenty years. So she was thirty-seven. A little younger than I am. She looked ten years younger, while I was beginning to look ten years older.

I almost said that she didn't look a day over forty until I remembered that women have absolutely no sense of humor over age. "They let you on the job when you were fifteen?" I said.

She flushed a little. "Don't overdo the corn. I'll accept it as a compliment."

"Anyone as beautiful as you, and as good at what you do, doesn't need to hear compliments."

"Um. Maybe I could allow you a couple of small felonies, at that, in Chinatown."

Stephanie hit the ladies' room and I buzzed our hotel. "How come you're not dazzling them at the conference?" I said, mildly surprised that I had caught Nola in her room.

"I came up to powder my nose, detective. What marvelous clues have you uncovered today?"

"Go ahead and laugh, but I have something that I think you'll find interesting—what a stockbroker said about the Bartlow brothers."

"Really? Incriminating? Bond scams? Tell me."

And suddenly I hesitated. "Not on the phone. Look, I have to go to headquarters. I'll be back at the hotel around six. I'll tell you about it then."

"But, you said it's something really good. Give me a hint."

"I'll give you more than that, but let's save it until later."

"You are a rat, Fraleigh. Are you with that pretty captain?"

"Off and on," I said, watching Stephanie come out of the ladies' room.

"Well, try not to let her get you beaten up today."

"Nola?" Stephanie smiled as I hung up the phone. "Isn't that a bit of a conflict of interest for you and her? Romance in the boardroom?"

"Just professional," I said.

Stephanie laughed and patted me on the chin. "I saw you together this morning. Don't try to fool a woman about these things, Fraleigh."

Leaving the restaurant, where she had insisted on paying the bill, Stephanie Ferrari impulsively squeezed my arm. "Everyone needs to hear compliments. Especially a woman in this job. You're a good guy underneath the macho."

We walked along Canal Street to a lot where the Lincoln was parked. "Did MacLeod have anything to say about me?" she asked.

My inclination was to let it go. She was very professional, but . . .

"Oh, come on, Fraleigh. Did he say anything about me?"

"Yeah, but . . ."

"Tell me. I'm curious."

I remained silent.

"Come on, Fraleigh, I want to hear."

"He said that if he could rent you for a month in his circles he'd never have to work again."

Ferrari whirled in front of me hands on hips. The old full-beam dangerous smile was on her face. "You know something. You can't stand acting human for an hour without reverting to your true asshole status." She turned and walked stiffly to the car. I followed, wondering how you win. If I had refused to tell her, she would have been mad as hell. I tell her, and she's mad as hell.

At headquarters, I found that my request for information on the bomber, Mel Zale, had been passed on to less-than-enthusiastic Detective Marvin Fisher. "No way did Zale do your bombing," the detective said, scratching himself vigorously about the groin. Fisher was a husky twenty-five, and convinced that he was the best detective in New York.

"I'm telling you, Zale has been washed up for years. No one takes him serious anymore. He's turned into a lush. Word is they would have taken him out except his cousin, Big Augie, is capo. But, the real reason he's not history is that they know he can't even remember his own fucking name, let alone any jobs he did for them. He's a nothing mutt."

"We came all the way from California, Fisher. I don't doubt what you say, but, I might as well talk to him as long as we're here."

"Don't make no difference to me," Fisher said, although his face indicated the opposite. He was pissed at being told in no uncertain terms by Stephanie that he would cooperate. I left with his promise that he would find out where Zale was hanging out and take me there as soon as possible.

Looking for a cab to take us back to the hotel, I wondered why I was uneasy about telling Nola that MacLeod had confirmed that the Bartlow brothers had pulled a big rip-off and were trying to sell the loot. Had she been a little too anxious on the phone? The stalemate over the chief's job had put me somewhat on the defensive with her, but layers down, my cop instinct had come to life. I was suddenly cautious.

Every cab we sighted was occupied or off duty. "The hell with it," I said to the Block, "let's take the subway. It's probably faster anyway."

We walked a couple of streets to the Lexington Avenue line. I approached the booth and gave the clerk two dollars in exchange for two tokens. He paused as he was pushing them toward me from under his grilled barricade. He was a heavy-set black man with short-cut gray hair. I turned toward the platform to see what he was peering at above his wire-frame glasses.

Five teenage black kids were sauntering along in a diamond formation. The tallest was in the lead. I saw that all of them wore expensive tennis shoes. The guy in the booth shoved the tokens at me and picked up the phone. People heading for the turnstiles gave the kids a wide berth without meeting their eyes. I handed a token to the Block as the noise of an approaching train rumbled inside the station.

The cruising teenagers were about to come upon an elderly woman from behind. Unaware of their presence, she opened her purse for a token.

"Come on. We'll miss the train," the Block said, pushing the kids aside.

"Block," I tried to warn him as he shouldered the kid in the lead out of the way.

Almost instantaneously, the blade of a Swiss army knife appeared in the leader's right hand and flashed upward. The Block, who hadn't seemed to be paying any attention to what was going on, hit the kid with a right hook that sent him crashing into the turnstile and to the ground. The knife bounced away.

"For Christ's sake, Fraleigh, do you want to make this train or not?" The Block was inside the turnstile, the train's doors were open, and people watched the action. The kid on the ground stirred. The others stood quite still, watching the Block. I put my token in and walked toward the train.

As he turned to join me the Block pointed at the kids. "You little shits better hope that the doors don't close before I get on because I'll come back and wipe the fucking platform with you."

The guy in the booth gave me a thumbs-up sign as the subway car's doors closed behind us. The Block straightened his jacket. "How many stops do we go?" he asked.

The people in the car began to applaud. The Block leaned close to me. "What's going on?" he whispered.

"Nothing," I said, "you've just been named Subway Vigilante of the Month. That's all."

As we jolted along I stopped listening to the Block's comments about how the BART (Bay Area Rapid Transit) system back home didn't have graffiti all over the cars and stations. It also didn't have several million riders and thousands of miles of track that the New York subways had. I scanned the list of small-to-moderate-size Silicon Valley electronics companies MacLeod had provided, not expecting to recognize any, since I was familiar with only a few of the Silicon Valley giants like Hewlett Packard in Palo Alto and IBM in San Jose. They were too big to be on the list. Halfway down the list I swore.

"What's wrong?" the Block said.

"I'll be goddamned. Future Chips is one of the companies on the list."

"So?"

"When I met Nola last night in the bar, she was with the CEO of Future Chips."

"Nola. Not Supervisor Henderson. I wondered why you picked this hotel. You're up to your old tricks again, Fraleigh. Although, I got to admit she is a looker. And you got your eye on the Ferrari broad, too. I doubt if you can handle all that action. Just remember, I'm standing by to help a friend out if you need me."

"Block, you're too much. I tell you something important and as usual, you're talking nonsense."

"Yeah, nonsense. Sure, Fraleigh."

Back in the hotel I called Paul English.

Twenty

"HOW'S THE HERO CHIEF BEING TREATED IN THE BIG Apple?" Paul English said.

"Hero? I thought I was the villain for roughing up Zorro?"

"Ah, that was yesterday. Today, three women's organizations are suggesting that you get a medal, and the newspaper even ran an editorial in your favor saying that violent rapists don't deserve public sympathy. Fritz Gerhart stuck his foot in his mouth at a press conference by publicly hoping that the prosecution against Zorro wouldn't be harmed by your 'actions' when arresting him. Nancy Pellow, the deputy D.A. carrying the case, criticized Gerhart for making a 'dumb' statement. She said that she had reviewed the arrest and that the chief of detectives ought to be aware that police officers are allowed to use reasonable force in protecting their own lives when arresting violent felons. Even better, the preliminary hearing is over. Zorro's attorney is looking to cop him out with the best deal he can get. It won't be necessary for you to testify."

"Great. Yesterday, I was a bum for using force to keep myself from getting killed. Today, I'm a hero because they think I brutalized a guy who deserved it."

"Mark how fleeting is the estate of man."

"Paul, this is long distance on the taxpayers. How about we get back to police work? What's new at the sting?"

"Well, Lofty Chief, I gave you the good news first. We took Luther Banks to the hospital yesterday with chest pains. The doctors think he had a mild heart attack."

"Heart attack? How old is he?"

"Thirty-one."

"Jesus. He's going to be OK?"

"They think so. They'll let him go home tomorrow. But no more sting. When he comes back to work it will be modified duty. The other thing you should know about is that Hector Gonzales surfaced yesterday for the first time since he escaped and shot up the police car."

"He did? Where?"

"Would you believe, The Blue Mirage Bar?"

"We nailed him?"

"Unfortunately, no. Art Estrada was on the bar. He didn't make Gonzales immediately and by the time he did, Hector was long gone."

"He didn't make Gonzales? What the hell was he doing?"

"Actually, he was on the phone conversing with the chief of detectives."

"Damn it. I knew you and the Block screwed up putting Estrada in the sting. He misses Gonzales and spills his guts to Gerhart. He's the leak."

"I don't think so, Chief. First of all, Art came on board after the leak on Bolero. Secondly, he politely told Gerhart to check with you for any information he needs. Gerhart is furious at him. The other thing is that Art was out of town on an investigation for a month around the time Gonzales escaped. He's not that up on him, and Gonzales was in and out within a couple of minutes. We're lucky Art put it together later on. Or maybe we're unlucky. Nunzio about flipped when he heard it. I think we may have to move him out. He's on the edge."

"So Gerhart is on to The Blue Mirage. How did that happen?"

"I'm not sure, but we'll find out eventually."

"Well, it better not be too eventually because the estate of acting police chief is very fleeting. Is that the end of your good news?"

"Afraid not. Manny and Mary are becoming increasingly incompatible and I can't seem to do anything about it. We need the Block back here with his basic personnel skills of threatening the safety of anyone who gets out of line. We can't afford to lose anyone else from the sting. When will you two be coming back?"

"We need another day or two. I got some information from the stockbroker MacLeod. I want you to look into these companies he mentioned." I gave Paul the names of the Silicon Valley Consortium. "Another thing, Paul, see if you can nose around the legal community without it getting out. Find out if a judge appointed Attorney Bartlow conservator of an estate. It may be where he's stealing the bonds."

"Good idea. I've been doing some research on the bonds."

Paul never did investigation. It was research like he was still studying at Stanford. "What did you turn up?" I asked.

"Municipal bearer bonds up until 1983 were issued without requiring information on the buyer. It saved the municipalities a lot of money in administrative costs. The bond that Bartlow gave to Manny was issued in 1976. It has no record of ownership. A thief's delight."

"If it's so easy to dispose of them, why does he need Manny at all?"

"Internal Revenue now requires the buyer or redeemer to record the social security number or tax identification number of the seller. If you have any significant number of bonds, you would have to find a way to launder them."

"Paul, another thing. I'm concerned about Nola Henderson. She's hanging out with some of these big-money people from Silicon Valley including a guy by the name of Clark Massey who is CEO of Future Chips."

"Ah. That's one of the companies you just gave to me."

"No one could ever say you weren't a brilliant detective, Paul."

"I'm astute enough not to ask about you and Nola."

"Paul, if you can wrench your mind away from your favorite subject for a minute, you might be interested to know that NYPD intelligence says that Mad Anthony Wong, whom I hope to interview tomorrow, is deeply involved with the Florida cocaine trade through the Columbian Medellín Cartel and the Jamaican Posse here in New York."

"Do you think Wong may be joining those fleeing the federal heat in Florida and reorganizing in California?"

"Could be. You better check with local FBI and DEA people to see if they have anything on Wong."

"So all you expect me to do is solve three major whodunnits without letting the chief of detectives find out about it. Do you have any methodological suggestions?"

"Yes. Proceed cautiously and have all the answers by the next time I call."

I gave Nola a call and invited myself to her room for a drink. "I'm in eight-sixteen, and the password is Springtime in Manhattan," she said.

"So, things are going well for you in New York," Nola said after admitting me. "Last night you were awfully vague about the case you were working. How about telling the truth tonight?"

"Nola, you were fucking me unmercifully last night. I couldn't remember my own name."

"Is that so?" She put her hands on my shoulders. She was in one of those fluffy white robes that the hotel provided. I always thought they were tacky until I saw Nola wearing one. "Are you pleading for mercy tonight?" She undid my tie and tossed my jacket on the floor. I didn't even think about picking it up.

An hour later in bed she propped herself on one elbow and ran her finger along my chin. "You didn't even shave for me, you bum."

"I'll shave and we'll do it again."

"Let's be civilized and order dinner by room service first."

Room service is almost always a mistake in New York hotels and this was no exception, but we were in a good mood and had a nice bottle of wine. I felt ashamed of my earlier suspicions of Nola until she said, "Give, Fraleigh. You hinted like crazy last night about a big case, one big enough to bring you to New York. Then you clammed up. I want to know what's going on."

"Nola, we have a whodunit. We suspect Duane Bartlow's brother Richard of selling hot bonds. The thing is we don't know where he got them."

"Richard's the lawyer. I know him slightly."

"Maybe you can help us. Could you quietly find out if Clark Massey and the other companies in the Silicon Valley Consortium have been doing business with Bartlow?"

"Me? You want me to become a police agent?"

"We weren't thinking of deputizing you. Citizens do occasionally cooperate with the police."

"There's a difference between cooperating as a witness and becoming an undercover investigator. As both a lawyer and public official I find your suggestion offensive."

"I guess the thought of people finding out the truth about them could be threatening to both lawyers and politicians."

"I didn't say I was threatened. I said I was hurt that you thought I'd spy for you."

"I give up. I apologize for thinking that you might be interested in seeing justice done."

"I am interested in justice. And, I'm also interested in civil rights and what kind of methods the police use." Her cheeks were red. "In fact, my job as a supervisor requires me to oversee your operations and I'd like some information right now on what you're up to."

"Well, I can give you some information. We're involved in a criminal investigation that involves Bartlow and possibly your friend Clark Massey, so I suggest you not mention anything about it to anyone or you may be defending yourself against a charge of obstruction of justice."

"That's a threat. You can get the hell out of my room right now." She was mad enough to spit. We didn't even finish the wine.

I had a way with women all right. Within a couple of hours both Stephanie Ferrari and Nola Henderson had gotten sore enough to slug me.

Twenty-one

IT WAS SEVEN O'CLOCK AND MY EVENING WITH NOLA HAD ended unexpectedly early. However, when I got back to my room I found a message to call Detective Marvin Fisher. I did. "Chief Fraleigh? I ran down Mel Zale. If it's convenient, I can come by in about half an hour to pick you up, if you still think it's essential to see him."

"OK, I'll wait in front of the hotel for you." I hadn't missed Fisher's sarcasm with the words *convenient* or *essential*.

We got into the Lincoln. Paddy Fitzgerald was behind the wheel and Detective Fisher next to him. The car was silent as Fitzgerald took us across the Williamsburg Bridge into the Bushwick area of Brooklyn. I rehashed my conversation with Nola. Her loyalty to me had certainly lessened as she had gotten involved with the big-buck makers in Silicon Valley.

On a side street off Bushwick Avenue I met Mel Zale holed up in a dingy furnished room. Fisher pointed him out and went back to the car to wait with Fitzgerald. It took me five minutes to realize that Fisher was halfway right. Zale was out of his head, but it wasn't just booze that did it. He was a speed freak. Totally zapped.

On the way back to Manhattan I said to Fisher, "You're right. He can't even remember his name."

"That's what I told you in the first place," he said, without looking up from his copy of the *Post*.

Fitzgerald stopped at One Police Plaza and Detective Fisher vanished into the bowels of the red-brick fortress, neglecting to say good-bye—no doubt preoccupied by the many cases he was carrying.

It was nine-thirty by the time I let myself back into my room. My message light was blinking.

I dialed the message center, but the gal who answered didn't speak English too well. A characteristic of New York hotel operators and cab drivers which had evolved since my departure from the Big Apple. It took me three tries before I realized she was saying to call Miss Henderson in room 816.

I wasn't anxious for another confrontation with Nola. Half the time I couldn't keep my hands off her. The other half I was ready to make her a suspect in the case. I dialed room 816.

Her voice sounded strained. "Fraleigh, I think you better come here as soon as you can. Someone sent me an anonymous package."

"Don't touch it," I said.

"It's not a bomb, or at least that kind of a bomb. How soon can you come? You'll understand when you get here."

In her room I stared at a nondescript manila envelope. She was pale, her only makeup a light coral lipstick, and she wore the white robe that still looked great. Her feet were bare. "It came Federal Express right to my room," she said.

I read the Federal Express envelope. It listed the sender as John Smith with a Silicon Valley address. I didn't have great hopes of finding a John Smith at that location. Handling the package by the edges I saw that it had her name typed on the front. The package had been opened, and typewritten on a plain piece of white paper inside was a note that said: IS THIS WHAT YOUR POLICE OFFICERS SERGEANT HERRERA AND POLICEWOMAN FLACONE ARE DOING INSTEAD OF THEIR JOB?

Gingerly, I took a videotape from inside the envelope making sure that I didn't smudge any possible prints on it.

Nola's television set was on and so was a VCR that hadn't been in the room when I had left. We were in a fancy hotel that rented VCRs. I put the tape in and hit the play button. The picture tube flashed with interference for about twenty seconds before the picture cleared. I was jolted to see that it was a sting tape. Sergeant Manny Herrera sat on the familiar couch in the back room of The Blue Mirage. All sting tapes show a date and time of day in the upper right corner of the screen. This tape had been recorded at 0400 hours the previous Saturday morning. A time when the operation was supposed to be closed tight.

The security of the sting had been blown. My mind tried to cope with it. Who the hell had managed to get hold of this tape and mail it to Nola? And why would any tape have been made at that hour?

On the couch, Herrera sat with his eyes closed, but not asleep. A full minute went by while my misgivings increased. There was movement on the screen. Police Officer Mary Falcone entered the room and stood above Herrera. She wore faded blue jeans and a brightly colored blouse which was tied so that her midriff was bare. Remembering the look that had passed between them, I tried not to imagine what we might see next, and avoided looking at Nola. I would obviously have to tell her something about the sting, but I wasn't yet sure what I should say, so I continued to watch.

Manny Herrera reached up with both hands and untied the knot holding Mary's blouse together. She wasn't wearing a bra. To my surprise I saw that her breasts were as big as Nola's. The blouse fell to the cluttered coffee table. Herrera's right hand slowly rubbed her breast in a circular motion as his thumb manipulated the nipple. Mary's sharp intake of breath was clearly audible. His mouth closed over her other breast and he noisily sucked on it. After a moment he released it from his mouth and began to rapidly tongue the nipple while his thumb continued to massage her other nipple. Mary gave a long "Oh . . . oh . . . Manny."

I turned to Nola. "Nola, I think I should tell you . . ."

"Wait, there's more." Her eyes were fixed on the screen.

I could guess there was more. I felt like a voyeur. I had seen this kind of stuff before, but now I knew the people, and they were cops who worked for me. The camera angles were perfect. Mary had moved closer to Manny and was rubbing her hands through his hair as he continued to work on her breasts. Her head was tilted back and although her eyes were closed, her face left no doubt about the emotion she was feeling.

Abruptly, she went to her knees knocking beer cans and ashtrays from the table as she pushed her rear end against it to give herself room. Kneeling, she unzipped Manny's fly and placed her mouth over his erection and began to move her head up and down. Despite myself, I had grown hard and I turned so the bulge in my pants wouldn't be visible to Nola. Goddamn Manny, what the hell had he been thinking of? I reached for the switch to turn the machine off, composing in my mind what I was going to tell Nola about the sting operation, but her hand stopped me from pushing the off button.

"No." She held my hand firmly.

We had been watching the tape for about five minutes. Her eyes met mine and they were intense. Her cheeks had the slightest hint of color. Was she still angry? I sat back resigned to watching the rest of the tape. Nola had been standing behind me and when she reached to stop me from pushing the off switch, she had briefly swept against me. As she released my hand, hers had ever so lightly brushed against my own erection. I flushed in embarrassment and looked sharply at her, but she was staring at the screen.

Mary had discarded her jeans without stopping her rhythmic head motions over Manny's groin. She swung herself onto the couch, squatted over Manny and lowered her thick bush down onto his face while she continued to suck on him.

Her bare bottom facing the camera was now in considerably more motion than it had been when she was waving it at us in the observation room. Finally, she got off Manny; he shed his pants and got on top of her on the couch and they climaxed quickly. They held each other tightly, and I hoped that we would finally turn off the tape.

"We might as well watch the rest. It's only another few minutes," she said.

During the final segment, Manny and Mary repeated much of what had gone before. The only difference was that they had remained naked in between. And I noticed that the time on the videotape showed that it had been turned off for an hour, before being reactivated for the final fifteen minutes.

I rewound the tape, ejected it from the machine, and in case there were fingerprints, carefully dropped it into the mailing envelope. I got ready to talk to Nola, but she had other ideas. She joined me on the couch and put her lips to my ear. When her tongue followed I quickly got rid of her robe. Two hours later when we finally began to talk I realized that we had in fact duplicated everything that we had viewed on the screen.

"Who the hell could have sent you that tape, Nola?"

"You tell me. And while you're at it, how about the truth."

"It's a sting operation. That was Sergeant Manny Herrera and Officer Mary Falcone."

"So, despite my warning to keep a low profile, you started another sting operation and those were two police officers. Your sting certainly doth weave tangled webs. You'll have to shut it down, Fraleigh."

Her head was on my shoulder, and it was quite damp with perspiration. Looking toward the foot of the bed I could see both of our bodies wet from exertion. "There would be problems doing that right now."

"You don't understand," she said. "Neither Sally Fenton nor Laura Kadisch would approve of a sting. They'd regard it as police spying and would blame you for it. You can't afford to lose either vote. I'm certain that Bartlow's favorite candidate, Captain Gerhart, would be more than willing to swear that he would never allow such techniques. I'm not crazy about them myself. And I remember you telling me of your own misgivings when we talked after the raid fiasco where the naked gunman escaped. Have you caught him yet?"

"No." I got up on my elbow and looked down at her face. "Law enforcement stings go on all over the country. Besides, we're too far into it. A murder may be involved."

"Was it that car bombing?"

"What makes you think that?" My tone was sharp. Were there even more leaks than I suspected?

"My God. Relax. I'm just guessing. That was the most recent murder I remember reading about. The point is, this tape is dynamite. A policewoman and a sergeant on duty. The fact that we don't know who recorded it. Who sent it to us. Who else might have received a copy. And as I said, the mere existence of another sting would be enough for Sally and Laura to change their votes. I know you love cops and robbers, but the sting has to go if you're to have a chance at the job. So, a few cases don't get made. It's not the end of the world."

"Nola, your colleague Duane Bartlow may be involved."

"What? Bartlow in a sting? Somehow, I just can't picture him popping in to sell a hot TV. Or, do you mean? . . . Ah. This is where Richard Bartlow showed up with the bonds you think may be stolen. At the sting. And you think Duane is involved?"

"I don't want to tell you more than you should know about the case, but my guess is that the two of them are in on it together."

"You know something, Fraleigh? You know how to titillate. Supervisor Bartlow going to jail. That would be very interesting. Still, we have to distance you from the sting, in case it's exposed. And the tape scares me." She stretched her hand, slowly drawing it across my chest, lightly stroking the area of my right nipple.

"Nola, once again, I ask you to work with me."

"I don't know, Fraleigh. Duane Bartlow isn't one of my favorite people, but I can't picture him involved in a theft. Do you have evidence to back up your suspicions?"

I hesitated, still not wanting to tell her too much. "We have some hearsay from his brother, but it's strong." I was about to tell her the other hearsay about a judge being involved, but the phone rang.

"Yes, Clark, how are you?" She rolled on her stomach and I contemplated her lovely ass and tried to figure a way to convince her to get information from him. "No, I'm going to bed early tonight." She winked at me. "Tomorrow's a big day, as you know. Fine, I'll speak to you in the morning. What?" she laughed. "You don't give up, do you? I'll see you tomorrow—good night, Clark." She was wiggling her rump. When she hung up she said to me, "Why do people always call just when I have to pee?"

She bounced out of bed and went into the bathroom. I got up to stretch and see if there was another sip of wine in the bottle on the dresser. I decided that it would be worthwhile checking with the local Federal Express office to see what time the package had arrived from California and any other details they could provide. I opened the top dresser drawer where the phone directory had been located in my room. Just a little simple act that changes lives. There were three telephone message slips stuck into the phone book. As I poured the remaining wine into a glass, I glanced at the one on top not really intending to read it, but the name across its face caused me to spill some wine. The message had been that Duane Bartlow had returned her call. It listed his number for a return call. Looking at the time listed, I realized that she must have called Bartlow and missed his return call during the period that I had left and come back to her room. The other slips were from an aunt in Brooklyn and a cousin in Scarsdale. I wiped up the wine, closed the drawer, and got back into bed.

Nola came out still naked. Slowly she walked to me and put her arms around me. "Stay with me tonight, Fraleigh." She kissed me lightly on the lips while I tried to control my face.

"Unfortunately, the Block and I are getting together to sum up the investigation so far and to plan tomorrow's work," I lied.

"It doesn't seem like much to sum up from what little you were willing to tell me." She picked her robe up from the floor, put it on, and went back into the bathroom.

I dressed and waited until it was clear that she wasn't coming out. "Good night, Nola," I said through the door.

There was no answer. I went to my room knowing that sleep would be elusive.

Twenty-two

I CALLED PAUL ENGLISH AT HOME AT 0730 HOURS THE next morning. A sultry-voiced female answered the phone. "This is Fraleigh. Put Paul on, please," I said.

She hung up. I dialed again. "Fraleigh, has anyone ever explained to you that when it's seven-thirty A.M. in New York, it's four-thirty in California?" Paul English said.

"That's a new voice answering your phone, Paul."

"Forgive me if I'm not dazzled at this time in the morning by your powers of observation."

"Forgiven, but go out to the extension. I don't want your lady friend to overhear our conversation."

"I'm in the other room. Cynthia is sound asleep, but I know there's no point in arguing with your paranoia. I was going to call you later. I faxed you yesterday afternoon's front-page headlines and story. Why have you called before yon dawn breaking?"

"Paul, someone sent Supervisor Henderson a porno tape of Manny Herrera and Mary Falcone. It's on our equipment at the sting and shows them fucking merrily away from four to six o'clock last Saturday morning. Do you have any idea who made the tape, who sent it to Nola's hotel room, or what the hell is going on with Manny and Mary?"

"Last Saturday? Well, the path of true love is never smooth. They certainly have had a falling out since then. I have no idea who did the tape or leaked it. It's weird. I'll sniff around."

"I suggest you start with Art Estrada. How is Manny doing with Bartlow? Or is he too busy to fit in any police work?"

"Fraleigh, Art Estrada is a good man. I don't think you have to worry about him. Manny's been under a lot of strain, but he's still doing some great stuff. Bartlow's due in again this afternoon."

"You better tell Manny to push Bartlow harder. Try to complete the buy on tape. It's clear that The Blue Mirage's days are numbered. What else is doing? Were you able to find out anything yesterday?"

"Yes, I have some surprising information for you. Are you sitting down?"

"Get on with it, Paul."

"Well, I spoke with a buddy in the D.A.'s office. She's been active in the local bar association so she hears what's going on in civil as well as criminal circles. It seems that legal tongues wagged over Richard Bartlow's appointment as a conservator for Paradise Retirement Trust. A kind of senior citizen's retirement home for millionaires. Only it's not really a home, it's a huge estate, luxurious, et cetera. I'll find out more about it. But what Pam, the D.A., told me was that Richard Bartlow is regarded as something of a sleazebag in legal circles, so his appointment by an above-reproach jurist was surprising."

"That's interesting, Paul. You found out quicker than I thought possible."

"I lucked out. Pam is someone I know very well and she fortunately was in a position to help. But the big news is that the distinguished judge who appointed Bartlow is the Honorable David Henderson of the Superior Court. Does that name ring a bell?"

I sat with the phone in my hand.

"Fraleigh? Are you still there?"

"Yes, Paul." Nola's father. Jesus Christ, and I've been telling her about the sting and the bonds.

"I was shocked, too. Pam, by the way, thinks Nola Henderson is a superstar and she likes the judge, too. He's known as Maximum Dave for his sentencing, so he's understandably a favorite in the D.A.'s shop. I have another little tidbit for you. I got intelligence to do a name check on Mad Anthony Wong. They talked with the FBI and DEA. Both of them have information that Wong has visited San Jose Airport six times within the last two months. They think he's setting up something in Silicon Valley because of the Florida heat. They also think his aka is for real. He's crazy. Enjoys blowing people away."

"Paul, I want you to get me everything you can on Judge David Henderson. Pick him up in the morning and put him to bed at night. I don't have to tell you to be careful who you use. I especially want to know his regular habits, like where I might casually bump into him during the working day. In the meantime, go back to sleep so that you'll be alert later."

"No way, Fraleigh. I'm wide awake. I'm going to wake Cynthia so that we can experience the sunrise together."

Twenty-three

AT BREAKFAST, I TOLD THE BLOCK ABOUT THE VIDEOTAPE. "Goddamn. Who the hell could have done it? And what's wrong with those two jerks—shitting where they eat?"

I dispatched the Block to see if he could learn anything from Federal Express about the package sent to Nola. I called Stephanie Ferrari, who told me they were still trying to set up a meet with Mad Anthony Wong. I asked if she could arrange for me to meet with someone who could give me an intelligence briefing on Wong.

An hour later she called back saying that she had set up a meeting with Deputy Inspector Kevin Dougherty, who headed up the criminal investigations and security unit of the intelligence division. I went back to One Police Plaza after lunch and sat in a chair to the side of Dougherty's desk surrounded by other desks and cops coming and going. Dougherty didn't rate an office, but he was true to the department's tradition of not giving information. A close-to-the-chest, sallow-faced Irishman, he took two hours to tell me just about what Seymour Gross had said in two minutes.

The additional details were that most cops believed that Wong was top gun in Chinatown, although there were a couple of other major players. The cops felt that given Wong's penchant for offing people, the other players wouldn't be around very long. Wong had been in the Tong wars years earlier. He was one of the young Turks who had arrived from Hong Kong prior to the Chinatown wars. Chinatown had plenty of crime. Dope, gambling, white slavery, and loansharking, but the ancients had ruled through tradition and tribunals of elders.

Neither tradition nor tribunals had been much good against the machine guns of the young Turks. Wong was the most feared because of his daring and cruelty. Over time he had emerged on top. The intelligence unit was sure that Wong was bringing in Cartel dope from Colombia through a network of Marielitos in Miami and New York. They were the Cuban prisoners from Mariel that Fidel Castro had sent Jimmy Carter for a present. They killed with a casualness that made the Mafia look like wimps. Whole families, wives, children, and mistresses all died when someone was foolish enough to stand up to them. Wong must have really hit it off with them.

As I was about to leave, Dougherty got a phone call for me. It was Stephanie. The meeting with Mad Anthony Wong was set for tomorrow afternoon. The Block and I would be picked up around noon at the hotel.

Back in my room I sat at the desk writing down notes of where we were. So many things had happened since shyster Bartlow had shown up at the sting that I covered two pages.

Item—Richard Bartlow, an attorney of dubious ethics, shows up at our sting to peddle a large amount of hot bonds. Item—Bartlow was referred to the sting by Charley Thompson, a crazed hype. Item—Thompson learned that lawyer Bartlow was robbed of sample bonds in New York after unwisely relying upon the advice of his client Inky Lee Bronheim. Bronheim, a con man and check forger, referred Bartlow to crooked broker MacLeod, who brought in Mad Anthony Wong with violent results. Item—Lawyer Bartlow, who uses the alias Dick Barry, tells everyone who'll listen that his big-shot brother, Supervisor Duane Bartlow, is involved in the deal. Item—Supervisor Bartlow, a longtime sleazebag, is trying to get his buddy Fritz Gerhart appointed police chief. Item—righteous Judge David Henderson,

Nola's father, appointed attorney Bartlow as conservator of a trust. The bonds may well have been stolen from the trust by Bartlow. Item—The trust is owned by a group of companies. Clark Massey, CEO of one of the companies, is with Nola in New York. Item—Nola had called Duane Bartlow yesterday shortly after I had told her that it looked like the Bartlow brothers were up to their eyeballs in a bond theft. Writing it down hadn't made it easier to understand. My phone rang.

"Fraleigh."

"Fraleigh, this is Nola. Do you have a few minutes to come up? There are some things that we should clear up."

So I went back to Nola's room. A grossly fat man with a full gray beard was vacating 814, the room next door to Nola's. I had to step aside in the hall and wait for the bellman to get all of his luggage past. Two pretty teenage blond girls were with him. They both giggled when they saw me looking, but stopped abruptly when the fat man turned and frowned at them.

Nola was dressed in a light-blue, flowered dress and was wearing medium-high heels. She was polite and subdued. I tried not to let ugly suspicions show on my face.

"We don't seem to be communicating lately. I didn't do a good job explaining why I can't do what you asked or in convincing you that you should be sharing information about what the department is doing. And I mean that for your sake as well as mine."

"I don't want to fight with you, Nola."

"I know. Let me explain that I'm making major efforts to get the businesses in and around Silicon City to help in curing our traffic and housing problems and to help improve the city's tax base. In previous years the board projected an antibusiness attitude. So industry and other lucrative tax sources located outside city limits. The board gave away the store to developers of residential housing who made a fortune but left the city with a couple of hundred thousand new residents who needed police, fire, and other services for which there was no revenue. Clark Massey is a leader in the group I've been asking for help."

"What brings him to New York?"

"There's a computer convention here this week. All of Silicon Valley companies have sent people."

It was impossible not to believe her. She was open, sincere, and irresistibly desirable. I sat there feeling my hunger for her winning out over suspicion. "Nola, I can't argue with what you said. Forget that I asked you."

"No. I won't forget. I'm not going to start probing, but I promise to keep my ears open and share anything I hear that sounds fishy."

"Great." On the spur of the moment I said, "How about dinner at Windows on the World and some nightclubbing tonight?" We could talk in a reasonable manner. Maybe she could clear up the mystery about the relationship between her father and attorney Richard Bartlow.

She smiled. "Thank you for the invitation. I was beginning to wonder when you didn't even mention my hair. Here, I spend two hours in the chair and you didn't even notice."

I should have noticed. I smiled in apology.

"I'm sorry, Fraleigh, but I have plans for tonight."

"And, I'm not in them."

"No, but you will be tomorrow. Now that I've explained about the business group, I hope you'll be candid about what the police department is up to. I'm not being nosy, but you have to be reporting to someone higher in government, and as Chair of the board, I'm temporarily replacing the mayor."

"What's doing tonight?"

"Are you going to continue to stonewall me?" Her good humor was wearing thin. "What I'm doing tonight is none of your business, but I'll tell you anyway. I'm meeting with the group of businessmen I told you about. I hope to persuade them to form a permanent political action committee for

Silicon City. Now, why don't you let me in on what you're doing?"

"Me, I'll probably watch a movie and go to bed early."

"That's not funny, Fraleigh. I'm not going to let you defy my authority just because I'm a woman."

"And the business executives tonight include Clark, no doubt?"

"Yes, although that too is none of your business. Let me remind you that you do report to me." Her fists hanging at her sides were clenched.

"How could I forget it? What I'm beginning to forget is the innocent prepolitician, Nola." I was losing it. My voice had risen.

She got up and walked to the window. Looking out at the airshaft didn't calm her down. Her voice was shrill. "Fraleigh, I'm not kidding, I won't allow you to defy my authority."

"You're even more beautiful when you're angry."

"Get the fuck out of here. I'm not going to stand for your male sarcasm. I'm one step away from calling the board in California and firing your ass right now. In fact, I'm expecting a couple of calls from there and just may discuss that subject. I'll speak to you tomorrow and you had better be prepared to tell me the truth."

"Give my best to Clark and the gang, Nola. If they come up with the dough, will it be attorney general first, or will you go straight at it—the first woman governor of California?" I closed the door gently on the way out, but my hand was shaking with anger when I put the key in my door. I sat on my bed for five minutes going over our conversation. It seemed incredible that I had been on the verge of trusting her again. But one thing she said moved me to action. She said she was expecting calls from California. Something was going on. I went down to the lobby and to the front desk.

A young woman at the desk asked how she could help me. "This may sound kind of foolish, but I'd like to change my room from four-thirty-six to eight-fourteen."

"May I ask why?"

I smiled, but her eyes remained questioning. "I was about to give you a big story about being superstitious, but the truth is I met the woman of my dreams last night, Nola Henderson in room eight-sixteen." I reached across and pressed her hand. "You understand, don't you?"

She smiled, and palmed the folded twenty-dollar bill I had slipped her. After surreptitiously reading the bill's denomination she said, "It's still the same old story. A fight for love and glory." She handed me a new registration card to fill out.

Twenty-four

IN ROOM 814 WAITING FOR THE BLOCK, I TRIED HARD TO be unemotional about Nola. By the time the Block arrived, I had made a decision.

"You look like shit, Fraleigh. And what the hell are you doing sitting in the dark? Trying to save the hotel money? Forget it. The place is so fancy it has phones right next to the toilet, but if you're taking a crap, you got to break your back to reach the toilet paper. Another thing—no wonder you left this town. People been punching holes in you since we got here, to say nothing of what I think those two dames been doing to your constitution. Still, if you got to kill yourself, what a way to go."

The Block was in his usual form. He had eaten like a pig, knocked several people out, drank everything New York had offered, and done any number of other things I didn't want to know about. I slumped in a chair and admitted that he was more or less right. Why had I come back? New York had kicked me in the teeth once and seemed to be repeating the process. Now Nola had joined in.

"Block, I've been racking my brains for an hour. I need some eavesdropping equipment, and I don't know who to ask for it."

"That broad Ferrari looks at you like she'd be happy to do whatever you wanted," he leered.

"She'd lock you and me into an airplane to California if she even knew what we were thinking about."

"How about your old buddy Gross?"

"Seymour would die of a heart attack. All he can think about is retiring."

"I don't think you ought to ask your brother, since you're not talking to each other. And Fitzgerald is the kind of guy you can't trust in church. How come one of these field associates don't turn him in?"

Fitzgerald. Everyone said the same thing about him. Don't trust him. That is, everyone but Christopher MacLeod. He trusted Fitzgerald for good reason. They had done business together. And I hadn't gotten around to mentioning to Stephanie or Gross that Fitzgerald had persuaded MacLeod to withhold evidence in the Bartlow robbery investigation.

"Call Fitzgerald and tell him to get his ass up here."

"You sure, Fraleigh?"

I took a deep breath. I was sinking into a sewer, but I had no doubt Paddy Fitzgerald would do what I wanted when he heard the tape of MacLeod telling how Paddy had convinced him to cover up Mad Anthony Wong's robbery and near murder of Richard Bartlow. And there was no time for other methods. Duane Bartlow might call Nola again any minute. I needed to hear what was said.

The Block accepted my plans to bug Nola's room without comment, but bitched like hell when I asked him to get me some chow. I had decided not to involve him, and to do the listening myself, but he wasn't grateful.

"What the fuck do I look like, a delivery boy?"

I had instructed him to go to the Stage Deli for two corned beefs on rye and a six-pack of Miller Lite, warning him not to belt the waiters when they insulted him. It was simply a local custom.

By the time the Block returned and surlily deposited the food, forgetting my change, Fitzgerald had come and gone twice. The equipment was on the floor and Fitzgerald's words still resounded in my head.

He had, of course, protested his innocence. "It's bullshit. But if you really believe it, what does that make you? You're

so anxious to bug someone's house [I had disguised my
target] that you're willing to deal off robbery and attempted
murder?" He paused in the doorway and leered at me. "When
you needed help you came back to a standup guy, a detective.
Not one of your humps from IA." He closed the door and I
went into the bathroom and washed my hands.

Lying on the bed a few feet away from Nola, separated
by the hotel wall, I reflected that she had every right to
be pissed at me for not filling her in on the sting. And it
was true that she was too sharp to fall for my double-talk
about what was going on. Yet, the message slip about Duane
Bartlow's call and the information from Paul about her
father and Richard Bartlow and her relationship with Clark
Massey, whose company just happened to be mentioned by
Christopher MacLeod, had convinced me that her eagerness
for information was more than idle curiosity. Then too, I had
never determined why Bartlow had provided the necessary
third vote for her appointment to the Board of Supervisors.
Did she owe him a favor?

The sting investigation was at a crucial stage. Any hint
to the Bartlow brothers could undo the whole thing, maybe
even endanger the cops. I simply had to find out what Nola
was up to. Perhaps it was all harmless. But, I couldn't take
a chance. No. And if it was all innocent, then what I was
doing didn't do any harm, did it? No one but me would
ever know. So why did I feel like such a shit?

I waited for her to leave. Her phone rang three times, I
prayed it wasn't Bartlow trying her again. The walls were
too thick for me to hear what she said. A couple of minutes
later her door opened and closed. She had left, and I guessed
that Good Old Clark had called to take her to the political
shindig. It was time for me to go to work. I got off the bed
and put on rubber gloves.

With a Phillips screwdriver, I quickly removed the plastic
cover from my wall socket. As I had hoped, our pricey hotel
had saved a few bucks on construction by putting the room

sockets back to back. Otherwise, I would have had to use the drill to make a hole through my wall into hers. When I had done these things as a New York plainclothesman I didn't care about leaving evidence of drilling holes after checking out. Now that I was working without a court order, I did.

I was installing a tube mike. A microphone had been built into a small sealed box. A long thin piece of plastic tubing came out of it. The mike in the box would only pick up sound traveling through the tube. Using magic glue, I adhered the end of the tube against the back of Nola's wall socket with the open end, and the exposed mike, facing into the room. The mike was sensitive enough to pick up any sound in the room. It wouldn't provide the other side of phone calls, but without committing a full-scaled burglary into her room, I couldn't do any better.

The box was on the end table next to my bed. I took off the rubber gloves which had prevented me from being electrocuted had my fingers slipped working in the open electrical socket. I hooked the box to a set of earphones and to a tape recorder. I wasn't sure how much time I'd need, but out of habit, I set the recorder at slow voice speed, which would give me four and a half hours of recording time. It wasn't likely that I'd need more than a few minutes of her conversation with Bartlow, but it didn't cost any more to be careful. I finished the whole hookup in ten minutes.

I dialed the hotel's number on an outside line and when the operator answered, I asked for Nola Henderson. My equipment picked up the ringing phone quite clearly. When the operator came on to announce that there had been no answer, I left a message to call Duane Bartlow immediately and gave the same number for him that I had seen on Nola's message slip. Then I started on the first beer and sandwich. It might be a long night. Knowing that I would hear Nola's door opening, I turned off the lights and set the TV dial to a cop show that was beginning. I kept the volume very low.

The other sandwich was gone and I was down to my last beer. The detective sergeant on television had kicked the shit out of at least four bad guys, shot two armed robbers to death, groped a couple of different gals, and, in general, acted like an asshole between commercials.

Voices in the hall jerked me awake. Looking at the clock I realized that I had slept three hours. The last couple of days had caught up with me. A new cop show was on the tube with a shootout resembling the battle of Inchon. I zapped it off with the remote control, and after a last moment of soul-searching, activated the tape recorder and put on my earphones.

Nola's voice came through loud and clear. "Clark, I really appreciate your assembling that group. They're certainly impressive."

"Fortunately, everyone is in New York this week for the computer conference."

"Oh, oh, a message," Nola said. I heard her gown rustling as she picked up the phone and dialed the operator. Fitzgerald had provided good equipment.

"It can wait. A call from California, but it's three hours earlier there, no rush. Clark, it was sweet of you to bring that bottle of champagne from the reception, but I've really had enough wine. Please don't open it. It's too good to waste."

Nola was on a high. It wasn't the wine. She must have wowed them at the shindig and was feeling pretty good about it. And why not? She was light years ahead of the politicians I had met. The bozos should have been impressed by her.

"The champagne certainly isn't wasted on a lady like you. Who knows? I may be sharing it with a future governor of California."

"Now, Clark. You and your friends say some nice things, but let's not lose track of reality."

"Don't be coy, Nola. We all know how strong you are politically in the region. Those computer CEOs didn't get to where they are by backing losers."

He paused then continued, "But tell me more about this silly investigation that's upsetting you. Frankly, that police chief fellow doesn't inspire confidence. I have some friends who practice law and have contacts. Maybe I can help behind the scenes. We don't want anything to interfere with a great future in politics. You deserve it. Look what you have going for you. The money this new political action committee will give you, the publicity that you and your programs on roads and housing will get—and let's face it, you're the most beautiful politician in the country."

"Clark, stop it. I'm already flying from meeting all those people tonight."

"Nola, I'm not just blowing smoke. I'm serious. Your father's reputation with the people forming the PAC committee—and his political influence in California—doesn't hurt a bit either. Let me open the champagne. We'll drink to an exciting future."

I didn't like this one bit. I had expected Nola to jump on the phone to Bartlow. Then I'd know which side she was on right away, but this asshole Clark had other things on his mind. Things with Nola that I didn't even want to think about, let alone listen to.

"Let me make a call before you open the bottle, Clark."

Thank God, I thought. *Get Bartlow on the line. Get the show on the road*. Nola called the operator and asked for me. I almost jumped out of my skin when my phone rang. Jesus! She had called me, not Bartlow. I began to sweat. I almost picked up the phone on the second ring. Maybe Nola and I could talk this out. Who knows? Why was she calling me? On the fourth ring my hand reached for the phone. Five rings. What had Clark said about an investigation, a scandal? Nola must have discussed Bartlow with him. And perhaps the sting as well? Six rings. I couldn't take anymore.

I started to lift the phone just as I heard her hang up through the earphones. I placed the phone back on the cradle.

"OK. Open it up. Let's drink to Silicon City."

"No. To your future, lovely supervisor."

I sat knees up on the bed, earphones on, cursing Bartlow. Come on, you miserable bastard. Call. Call her.

"Clark, you must be the golden boy of Silicon Valley."

Nola's voice had slurred just a bit. Twenty minutes of mutual admiration had gone by as the champagne was consumed. "I mean, establishing your own company at your age, thirty-four, into one of the most dynamic in the industry."

"Wait until next year, Nola. If I can pull off those two mergers . . . well, the possibilities are simply incredible. But tonight's your night."

Clark's voice had grown husky, how much from the wine and how much from something else I could only guess, and I didn't like what I guessed. The room was identical to mine, so I knew they were sitting on the couch, the champagne probably on the coffee table in front of them.

"Oh shit, I knocked over my glass—that good champagne."

"No problem, Nola. Here, let me pour some more."

"I've had enough. When I start to waste it . . ." She laughed, "Clark what are you doing?"

"I think you got a little on your dress, I'm just using the napkin to dry it."

"Are you sure? You were being awfully thorough if that's what you were doing." She laughed, "Stop, you're tickling me. And I'm in a giggly mood. You're taking advantage. Clark, um, Clark, I don't know—you're not tickling now." Nola took a deep breath. They were kissing. I heard other sounds, the rustling of Nola's gown.

"Um, Clark. I don't know if this is a good idea."

"I can't think of a better one. Remember how close we were in college? And your lips are as delectable as the rest of you."

The CEO line of the year. No wonder the computer industry was in trouble. Another five minutes went by during which there was more kissing and a steady rustling of Nola's gown. I wiped some sweat from my forehead.

"Clark, hold on now." Even to my ears it sounded like a weak protest. Breathing and rustling noises indicated that Clark wasn't paying any attention to it. "Hey, come up for air. Give me some more wine, you evil man."

I heard him pour the wine. Choke on it, Clark, you phony bastard. Have a fucking coronary. We'll bury you surrounded by computers. There was only a little sipping before the kissing and gown rustling began again. I couldn't sit still. I walked as far as the earphones permitted.

"Nola, this dress looks too superb on you to let it get all wrinkled. Why don't you get more comfortable." Another line of the year. If I had owned computer stock, I would have dumped it immediately.

"You're a smooth devil, but you're nice too." Her voice was soft and a little more slurred. I heard Nola get up. The gown was apparently coming off. I tried not to visualize the scene and the look that I knew was in Nola's green eyes.

"My God. You're magnificent, Nola." The son of a bitch was right. And I felt the corned beef rolling in my stomach. "Come here. To the bed." His voice was husky, the phony bozo cadence, gone.

Sitting in the darkness, I shut my eyes and began to take the earphones off when a loud whirring noise made me jump. My first thought was that Clark had a bug detector and that it had discovered my mike. Computer companies were paranoid about security of company secrets. Then, Nola giggled. "Clark. Where in the world did you get that thing?"

"It's one of the latest. Have you ever used one?"

"I refuse to answer on the grounds of . . . of . . . " The whirring noise continued, not quite drowning out her voice. "Oh, Clark. You thought of everything, you sweet man."

I took the earphones off and sipped from the last of my beer. It was warm, just the thing for an upset stomach. Sitting there in the dark, blocking out the sounds from the next room, my mind floated back to when I had become a New York cop.

Twenty-five

I WAS TWENTY-ONE. MOM HAD DIED YEARS BEFORE. THE old man, my older brother, Jack, and I lived in a two-family detached brick house in Queens. One or two black or Puerto Rican families had moved into the neighborhood within the last year, but it was predominantly Irish Catholic, with a sprinkling of Italians and Germans. Feeley's Tavern was the gathering spot after the last Sunday Mass at nearby Saint Matthews. The bar wit who cracked "Cops and firemen are the principal industry in this neighborhood" wasn't far wrong.

Our family didn't see much of each other. For one thing, Jack and I never got along. He constantly berated me in front of the old man, and ignored me when we were alone. Also, we were all busy. I was at college much of the time. Jack had made detective recently and put in long hours, although judging from his condition coming home, it appeared that a lot of them were in bars.

My father was an up-and-coming assistant chief, working all the time. A cop's cop. A tough old detective who was also a college graduate. Although he never said a word about my not going to church, he was a leading Catholic layman, Past Grand Knight in the Knights of Columbus, the whole bag. He was the big shot of our neighborhood, and a power in the police department. His name frequently got mentioned as a future police commissioner. Some said he was wired right into Cardinal Kelly's empire, the chancellery on Fifth Avenue. The cardinal didn't have the clout to name the next

201

P.C., but he did have unofficial veto power over the mayor's selection.

The old man never commented on any of it, and he had a presence which stopped people from asking personal questions. But he had his fan club, all right. Cops would pat me on the back and say, "Your old man will be the last Irish Catholic police commissioner, and the first Christian one." It was a wry commentary on how political power had shifted away from the Irish in the city, and a bitter observation on the brutal discipline handed down by the unbroken string of Irish Catholic P.C.'s.

My father never encouraged or discouraged me from joining the department. I remember being disappointed when he didn't praise me for doing well on the entrance exams and in the police academy. But he had given me a big grin and a hug at graduation. Of course, Jack hadn't been able to be there, which hadn't bothered me at all.

The old man took me to the Irish Pavilion on West Fifty-seventh Street to celebrate. It was one of the few times that just the two of us had done something together. Yet, we were hardly alone. My father was a borough commander, and a steady parade of people came by to say hello to him. It was one of the best days of my life.

The old man didn't discuss my assignment with me. I would have gone anywhere he said, but despite his power, he simply stayed out of it, and I drew the Twenty-eighth Precinct, central Harlem. "With your old man's pull, he let you come to this shithole? What's the matter, he pissed at you?" cops said. But I loved my year in Harlem. It had the most police action in New York. Word was that if you wanted to be a doctor, intern at Bellevue, you'd see everything—and if you wanted to be a cop, rookie in Harlem. You got experienced fast, or else.

I spent a lot of my time in court with felony arrests, grabbing a meal at Forlini's during the court's lunch break. I didn't think about it, but my arrest record was building a solid reputation. I wasn't just a top boss's son. And, the reality of Harlem was also forcing itself through my bigoted parochial school consciousness. White Harlem cops either hated blacks or began to develop sympathy for the conditions they had to live under. I wasn't a hater.

Then, one night as I drove into work, I stopped on a deserted side street for a red light. It was a Monday in early February and cold as hell. I was doing a late tour, and at eleven P.M. a gust of wind howled through my half-open window as I sat waiting for the light to change. Reaching to wind the open window closed, I found myself looking into a brightly lit bodega. A little sixtyish man in a white apron was screaming at two customes, and as I watched, one of them pulled a sawed-off shotgun from under his coat.

I switched off my motor and headlights, and as quietly as I could, left the car. Crouching down behind a beat-up Ford parked at the curb, I wished in vain for a police hand-pack radio to report an armed robbery in progress. Never taking my eyes off the store, I drew a Smith & Wesson Chief's Special, a favorite off-duty gun of cops because it's small and concealable. But now, as I watched the second customer pull out a forty-five-caliber semiautomatic handgun, I was acutely conscious that my gun held only five rounds. I tried to plan. The only tactic that would give me half a chance against all that fire power was to take them coming out.

The owner picked up a big butcher knife. Oh, no, mister. Please. Don't be stupid. Put it down. Give them the dough. How much could it be?

The guy with the shotgun was enjoying himself. A smile crossed his face. He slowly raised the gun. It was too far a distance for me to be accurate with my shot, given the short barrel and lightness of the Chief's Special. On the other hand, the owner with his raised knife and the guy with the shotgun had closed out my options. I drew a bead on the shotgunner's head, a smaller target than the chest, which we were trained to shoot at, but a hit to the body wouldn't prevent him from pulling the trigger and killing anyone close to him.

Despite the cold, a drop of sweat ran into my eye making me hesitate to shoot. Then the shotgun went off and I lost my sight picture completely, looking in horror as the owner was blasted against the back wall and blood from his head and chest splattered all over the counter. I was frozen. My gun hand shaking. With a wail, the owner's wife ran to her husband. She screamed and threw a can of soup at the shooter, who thought that was very funny. The woman looked at him with hatred, picking up the knife at her husband's side and getting to her feet. She moved forward as if she had all the time in the world. This too struck the shooter as amusing.

Still smiling, he slipped two more shells into the shotgun and snapped it closed as the woman shuffled toward him. I took a long breath and somewhere deep inside my twenty-two-year-old body an icy calmness took over. I steadied my aim and fired just as the shotgun was leveled at the woman. The round was a trifle high and to the left, singeing the killer's eyebrow, but not really hurting him. He turned toward me when my second shot caught him in the chest. The shotgun went off and blew out the front window. He was on the way down when my third bullet crashed into his left eye.

The other guy jumped over him and ran out of the store right toward me. My next round caught him in the chest. As he fell against the wall, I squeezed off the last shot and hit him between the eyes. Five shots. Four hits. Unbelievable. Then, I holstered my empty gun and pinned my shield to my outermost garment just like they said to do in the academy.

I walked over to the hysterically screaming woman and tried to comfort her. When she saw my badge she reached out and touched it, and suddenly threw her arms around me and sobbed into my shoulder. That's how the squad-car cops found me. Numb. Holding the hysterical woman, three dead bodies on the floor, and blood all over the fucking place, except in my face, which was chalk white.

They parked me in the corner of the detective squad room and provided hot coffee. I wanted to feel the warmth go down my throat into my belly, but my hands were shaking too badly to pick up the cup. The place was bedlam because of the shooting. The owner's wife was crying at top volume. A uniformed policewoman fruitlessly tried to comfort her. People were hustling all over the room because of the robbery. Gradually, I started sipping the coffee, spilling some of it on my fingers. After another ten or fifteen minutes I noticed a detective whispering to the squad sergeant and looking over in my direction. He and the sergeant both turned away when they saw me watching them.

What were they saying? Looking into the empty coffee cup, I went back over what had happened. I should have yelled, or maybe fired a warning shot. Maybe the old guy would be alive. And, I never had given them a chance to surrender, but it would have been suicide with that shotgun, and the way the guy had killed the owner, smiling. No, I didn't have any regrets over him. The other kid, though. Jesus! That's right. His terrified face looking at me as he tried to run. He had only been a kid. I turned quickly and saw the two cops again looking at me. Abruptly they walked over to a desk and picked up some papers. Were they saying I had panicked, killed a kid?

About twenty minutes later I found out that they had been thinking of a way to tell me that the second guy had been a fifteen-year-old. His forty-five automatic, a realistic toy replica. I had killed an unarmed boy.

The detective told me as sympathetically as he could and provided a pen and paper for me to write out my report. But I sat there holding the pen in mid-page trying to get the boy's face out of my mind. Going over again what the gun had looked like. It had looked totally real—or had it? I had written exactly five sentences. I don't know what made me turn around then, but in the far corner of the room I saw my father being briefed by the squad lieutenant. My old man's eyes were on me, and there was a look in them that I had never seen before. Only later did I realize that it had been pain. Pain over his son's loss of innocence. The job wasn't always cops-and-robbers fun. Tragedy and agony also came along with the badge.

My father came over and put his hand on my shoulder. "Are you all right, Finny?"

I nodded, too down to react to my hated first name. Finnbar Fraleigh. It had actually gotten me into boxing. As a kid, my protests over its use often led to fights. I got into amateur boxing to learn how to protect myself. Obscure Irish poet or revolutionary, or whatever ancient Finnbar had done to leave me with his cursed name, only my father used it, and somehow, I never minded when he did.

A fat detective came over and said to me, "Congratulations. You did a great job. The guy with the shotgun was good for four other jobs, and the kid, well, you stopped him before he got started. And look at it this way, there are two less niggers around."

My father was a big man. He actually picked the detective off his feet and slammed him into the wall. The room fell into stunned silence. "If you ever talk to my boy again, I'll have your shield and beat you to a pulp." I had never seen him angry. It was awesome. No one moved in that room until he stalked out. The detective straightened his shirt and left without a word.

As a result of stopping the robbery, I got a medal and assigned to plainclothes vice duty as a prelude to being promoted to detective. The grand jury ruled that my shootings had been justifiable homicide. But, my old man had been right. Police work had changed forever for me that night when my gunsights had zeroed in on a fifteen-year-old boy.

Twenty-six

IT HAD GONE DOWNHILL QUICKLY FROM THERE. PLAIN-
clothes was lousy duty. Instead of going after rapists, robbers, burglars, and thieves we pursued hookers, gamblers,
and homosexuals. I was no cherry. I knew that some of
my colleagues were getting paid off. But I kept my own
nose clean and they were careful to leave me alone. It
was unpleasant work, but the real nightmare began the
night we went on a routine bust of Gloria Fell's call-girl
operation.

I was one of three on the arrest team. Barney Krewuski
had come up with a tip on the operation. Later I learned that
Gloria had been paying him off for years, but had refused to
jack up the price when Barney asked for 25 percent more. It
was his last year in clothes. He was going back into uniform
and was trying to score a final year nest egg from all of his
"contacts."

Gloria was a beautiful dark-haired woman in her mid-
thirties, her figure only slightly softened by passing years.
She was pissed when I slammed her door chain off with
a sledge hammer. Barney had learned the password of the
apartment. He used it to get the door opened a crack on
the chain. I banged it completely open with the hammer
before they could dead-bolt it again. I hadn't meant to, but
I knocked Gloria down with the door. A couple of young
hookers screamed and ran into the next room.

"You son of a bitch." Gloria had regained her feet and
turned on me.

Then, before I could apologize, Krewuski did something that changed my whole life. He slapped Gloria Fell in the face. "Shut up, douchebag. Who the fuck do you think you're talking to?"

She lost her cool. "I'm talking to motherfuckers who took my money for years. I've got names in my book that will sink your miserable asses. You'll be freezing in uniform in Canarsie."

"Fraleigh, why don't you hit the other room before they start destroying evidence. I'll take care of stuff in here," Barney said, but there was a funny look in his eyes, as if he was sorry he had started something.

Gloria's original calling was as an accountant. She was keeping the books for the operation when the madam died of a heart attack. Gloria gave management a try and made a hundred and fifty grand her first year. Five years later she lived in a plush East Side apartment and socialized with some real big shots. She had never been busted before. Being hit and called a douchebag by a crooked plainclothes cop had sent her over the edge.

I was just as happy to get away from Gloria. Barney was trying to apologize to her, but she was ripping. I had only taken a couple of steps toward the other room when she stopped me with a yell.

"Fraleigh! You're his son. You look just like him." She broke away from Barney who was trying to soothe her. "You better clean up your act, young Fraleigh. You two crooked bastards aren't going to push me around. There are brass and politicians in here along with your dad." She waved a small black address book at me.

Flushed, but holding on to my temper, I started around her toward the other room. She waved the book again. "This will fix your ass, and your father's too."

Even then I was prepared to ignore her, but she brought her knee up sharply into my groin. I turned just in time, taking it on the thigh instead of getting hurt.

That did it. I don't know if I was more furious at her or at Barney. I was pissed at her for mentioning my father as well as attacking me physically. Everyone knew he had never taken a dime in all his years on the job. I flipped her onto the couch, handcuffing her behind her back. I picked up the black book. "This is evidence now, Gloria. Call all the fucking politicians and brass you want." She was suddenly silent, looking questioningly at Barney.

In the station house, Gloria and Barney talked before she was searched and lodged into a cell by the matron. He came over to where I was filling out the arrest cards. I ignored the worried look on his face. "Listen, Fraleigh, Gloria ain't a bad gal. She just lost her temper because of the door. She wants to apologize, and if you forget the book, there's something in it for you."

"Fuck her and you. It's all going in exactly as it went down, including what she said about the book."

"Come on, be reasonable. The book could hurt a lot of guys, including some good bosses."

A guy wearing a suit and tie had been filling out some forms at the same long table we were using. I assumed he was a precinct dick. "What's going on, Officer?" he said, with a friendly smile.

"Nothing," I said.

"I doubt that very much from what I just overheard. Let me introduce myself. I'm Lieutenant French from the Internal Affairs division."

He began to read us the Miranda warnings. Barney looked sick. I was annoyed. This bullshit arrest was now going to take a couple of extra hours. Little did I know.

Lieutenant French faded from the picture quickly as Inspector Seymour Gross took over. I never did see what was in the black book, but I assumed that there were plenty of big shots for someone of Gross's reputation and rank to have taken over the case.

From the beginning we got along. He sized me up right

away, appealing to my sense of professionalism instead of fear. He knew that I didn't want to give up any cops, even though I didn't have much sympathy for guys like Krewuski. And I didn't really have much more to tell than what they already knew, what Lieutenant French had overheard.

After some minor fencing, I simply told Gross to the best of my recollection what had happened in the raid on Gloria's pad. It didn't surprise me that Gross kept going over and over what she had said. It was standard practice for call-girl operations to list top politicians and top brass, whether or not they had ever met them. It usually stopped the list from being published if the operation got busted. Gross wanted to protect the department by making sure that none of it was true—that the department would not be embarrassed by leaks to the press that some top brass were dirty.

I did resemble my father, and given Gloria's "contacts" with people in the vice unit, I had assumed that she was just shooting her mouth off. It didn't occur to me even for a moment that the old man had known her. I didn't get suspicious even when Gross moved from my police work to questions about the family. How long had my mother been sick before she died? Had my father dated while she was alive? After she passed away?

I told the truth. I didn't know. I had never thought about my father's sex drive and the problems not having a wife created for a highly visible police commander. Then Gross asked, "How do you think Gloria Fell got your home number and your father's work number?"

I said, "Why the fuck don't you ask him, Inspector?"

Gross was smart enough to realize that the questions were over. Krewuski was suspended. I had been assigned to debriefing at Internal Affairs. I was taken in through back entrances, and actually put up in a hotel room at night in the company of IA personnel. During the few days this was going on, my father was in Washington, D.C., representing the NYPD at a U.S. Department of Justice conference. I had been given a written order by Gross not to contact him or to discuss the investigation with him should he contact me. As soon as I got near a public phone unobserved, I left a message at my father's hotel that he should call me.

On the third day, Gross called me into his office. "Kid, we're sending you back to work. I want to thank you for being honest. We need people like you in the department. You're going to be harassed. Don't let them get you down. I want you to call me, any time day or night, if they threaten you." He actually gave me his home telephone number.

Gross appeared to be sincere, but I thought he was bull-shitting me a bit to dramatize his own importance. What the hell had I done? Krewuski's big mouth in front of an IA lieutenant had gotten him into trouble, not me.

I was totally unprepared for my reception when I got back to work. There was a terrible smell around my locker. Opening it, I gagged. A rat that had been dead for a while hung from a clothes hook. Every uniform I had was slashed beyond repair. I looked around for someone to beat the hell out of, but the locker room was empty.

My eye caught a sign painted in red on the wall opposite my locker: ONLY SCUMBAGS GIVE UP COPS. ONLY SUPER SCUMBAGS GIVE UP THEIR FATHERS.

Marty Brady was my sergeant in the unit, and a nice guy. We had drunk a lot of beer together and played in a weekly poker game. I went into his office. He looked up at me, his face expressionless.

"Sarge." He just looked at me. No *hello*. No *How's it going?* I broke the silence. "Some asshole put a dead rat in my locker and cut my uniforms to shreds."

He picked up a blank UF61 complaint form. "If you want to make an official complaint, fill out the Sixty-one. I'll bring it to the lieutenant's attention."

"For God's sake. I didn't turn anyone in. Krewuski shot off his big mouth in front of an IA lieutenant. I didn't give them anything that they didn't already have."

"Officer, you're discussing an ongoing official investigation. That's against IA rules. You work for them. You should know better, so don't try to discuss the case around here."

Officer. In the months I had worked for him he had never called me or anyone else *officer.* His eyes had expression in them now, total contempt. If he hadn't been a sergeant, I would have knocked him through the wall.

I went to the desk we used. There were six cops in the squad room. Not one of them looked in my direction. The desk had a sign on it: CONTAMINATED: FOR USE BY FRALEIGH ONLY. It went on that way for two days. I kept leaving messages for my father in Washington, but he never called back. I finally decided to take the next day off and fly to D.C. on the shuttle.

That night, I was watching the eleven o'clock television news when Jack came home. Despite our differences, I was going crazy. I needed someone to talk to. Taking one look at Jack's flushed, drunken face, I turned back to the screen.

My own face flashed on while an announcer said, "The police commissioner and special investigating prosecutor tonight praised the courage of Plainclothesman Finnbar Fraleigh for uncovering a corrupt alliance between the police and Gloria Fell, a madam running a police-protected prostitution ring. It is widely believed that the officer gave information despite the fact that his father, Assistant Chief Patrick Fraleigh, may be involved. Chief Fraleigh is the highest ranking officer ever to come under suspicion in scandals plaguing the department in recent years. It is particularly embarrassing to the department because Assistant Chief Fraleigh has often been mentioned as a possible replacement for the present police commissioner when he retires next year."

"Well, you should be proud, you courageous scumbag. You're a real team player. Gave up your own father."

"Jack, you don't know what the hell you're talking about."

He hit me before I could get out of the chair. I fell back against the wall, regaining my balance as he came at me. He was heavier and stronger and the cluttered living room gave me no opportunity to outmaneuver him. But a week's frustration boiled up in me. I moved toward him. I finally had someone to hit, my brother.

Jack and I stood toe to toe, slugging it out. We had each gone down a couple of times during a few minutes of heavy punching. My knees were wobbly as I circled, deciding where to hit him. He was too exhausted to lift his arms in defense, but I knew he was maneuvering to grab me in a crushing bear hug. In the back of my mind I was aware that someone was ringing the bell and pounding on the front door. Both Jack and I turned when we heard the glass in the vestibule shatter. We stared as Seymour Gross and two precinct uniform cops walked into the living room.

"For God's sake. Are you two crazy? You should be supporting each other at a time like this." Gross's face was somber.

"Who the fuck gave you permission to break in here?" Jack said.

Gross looked at me. "We had a call from the Washington, D.C., police. I've been trying to get in here for quite a while. You guys were making some racket. I finally had to call a squad car."

I took deep breaths trying to pull myself together. Gross breaking in. A call from Washington, D.C., cops. My father hadn't answered my calls.

"Your father's dead. I'm sorry."

"Dead? The old man?" Jack was suddenly sober. Paying close attention to Gross.

"The D.C. cops are listing it as a suicide. He used his service revolver. I'm terribly sorry. I don't know of any easy way to tell you."

Jack fell into the armchair. "Terribly sorry? You slimy Jew bastard! You killed him. You and this courageous scumbag."

He began to cry like a baby. Instinctively, I put my hand on his shoulder. He shook it off.

"It wasn't my fault or yours," Gross said. "Your father pulled the trigger, not us." He was trying to convince himself as much as me, and not succeeding in either case. Jack got up and stormed out. It was the last I saw or heard from him.

I didn't sleep that night. At eight-thirty the next morning I went into the local precinct and turned in my gun and shield along with my resignation. Two hours later I flew to California to start all over again.

Twenty-seven

NOLA'S PHONE INTERRUPTED MY REVERIE. I HAD HEARD her door close earlier and guessed that Clark Massey had left. I slipped the headphones back on in time to hear Nola answer the phone.

"Daddy, I'm so glad you called. Yes, I'm fine. The meeting with Clark Massey's group went well."

There was a long silence before Nola spoke again. "Yes, you were right. They're the top people in the industry and are willing to contribute to a political action committee. Not just willing, Daddy. I'm trying not to let it all go to my head, but their reaction to my plans was terrific . . . Yes, I know you always say those things about me, but you're biased," she laughed.

She was quiet for a moment then said, "I don't know about the investigation." Her voice had lost the buoyancy. "He's interviewed some broker and was excited about what he found out, then suddenly wouldn't tell me anything. I guess you were right—he's taking advantage of my getting too close to him, but I can't undo that, it just happened . . . I know what you said at the time, yes, but . . ."

Nola coughed, then said, "No, I don't want you to discuss it with him. I'm furious. He wouldn't defy a man this way. But I'll take care of it myself. I know, Daddy. There are disturbing civil rights aspects to it, but I'm not sure about what you're suggesting. I need to think about it, and there

are other ways of dealing with Duane. I'm flying back
tomorrow. I'll try to convince Fraleigh to be honest with
me before I leave."

Now I really regretted not hearing what the judge was
saying. It sure sounded like his advice had something to
do with the sting.

"I love you too, Daddy. Bye, bye."

She hung up. I heard steps and then water run in the
bathroom. Then she came back and picked up the phone.
Clearly, she had discussed the sting with her father, the
judge. I didn't approve of that, but I suppose it wasn't
that unusual for someone in her political position to discuss legal and civil rights aspects of a sting with a judge.
And if the judge was your father, that would give you
all the more confidence in his discretion. But this judge
had appointed Richard Bartlow as conservator of Paradise Trust.

"This is Nola Henderson calling Duane Bartlow. Yes,
I'll hold."

Her fingers nervously tapped the table. "Hello, Duane.
Thanks for calling me back."

She listened for a moment, then said, "Yes. New York
is always exciting, but you're right, I wouldn't want to live
here. I'll take the earthquakes over the muggers and rapists.
Duane, I called for a couple of reasons. You and I seem to
be opposing each other an awful lot since my appointment.
I wouldn't be on the board if it weren't for you, and I'd like
us to get along better. I was wondering if we could meet to
discuss some things. I'd like to find ways we could work
together."

So, the third and crucial vote had come from Bartlow,
not Kendle. Interesting. I wondered what the trade-off had
been. She sure had crossed Bartlow by not appointing Fritz
Gerhart as chief.

"Well, no one has ever accused you of not being blunt,
Duane." Nola's short laugh seemed forced.

Bartlow's reply was so loud that I could hear the noise if not the words. When he paused, Nola spoke persuasively, "OK, OK. I'm not arguing with you. It *was* quid pro quo. You did keep your word and vote for me. You don't owe anything. All I'm suggesting is that we might find some other reasons for you to change your mind about opposing my father's appointment. Who knows? Your brother may need another favor. And some things have happened here in New York that you might be interested in."

I heard the bed squeak. After a moment she said, "Yes, you're right. We shouldn't discuss this on the phone. I just wanted to get to you before you called Senator Horace about my father's appointment. I'll call you tomorrow when I get back. We can meet in your office."

Bartlow was still talking. Nola answered, "OK, Duane. We can discuss the police department also, if you'd like. I'm very interested to hear about this new development you mention. If it's relevant to the appointment of the chief, I promise to consider it. OK, good-bye."

When I heard Nola's shower running, I turned on the light and quickly disconnected the mike. I rewound the tape, and, once again sitting in darkness, put on the earphones and played it back, trying to make up my mind whether there was any evidence of a crime other than the one I had committed by eavesdropping.

Nola's father had appointed the crooked attorney Richard Bartlow conservator apparently in return for Duane's vote to put Nola on the Board of Supervisors. We had heard enough from Charley Thompson during the sting, and from the broker MacLeod here in New York, to be pretty sure that this appointment enabled attorney Richard Bartlow to steal the bonds from Paradise Trust. But even if that was true, there was no evidence that the judge knew about the thefts or even suspected Bartlow of something crooked. So, it was all questionable, but probably not illegal. Politics as usual.

Nola had discussed unknown aspects of the sting with her father and Clark Massey. Questionable, but again probably not illegal. Politics as usual.

Nola was clearly trying to butter up Duane Bartlow over something to do with her father and Senator Horace, who was our area's state senator in the California legislature and very close to the governor. It sounded like Judge David Henderson was trying to step up the judicial ladder. Maybe an appellate or state supreme court slot? Or who knows, the brass ring—an appointment to the federal bench? Lifetime.

Whether or not this horse trading was legal depended on how far Nola and her father went to secure Bartlow's favor. Any disclosure that Richard Bartlow was under investigation would constitute obstruction of justice, a felony. But, I was uneasy remembering the judge's mention of civil rights violations. If someone's rights were being violated by the cops, then it would be perfectly OK to warn them—wouldn't it? I shook my head. It could be argued both ways.

Nola was willing to discuss the "new developments in the police department" to see if they were relevant to the chief's appointment. I supposed that this was a reference to the headline story about me and Nunzio in the diner. It was ironic. After the way I'd clammed up about the sting, I was sure I'd lost Nola's vote. Next Friday the board would meet and I would no longer be chief. But Nola would have finessed Duane Bartlow into supporting her father in return for dumping me, when Bartlow could have gotten that one free. Government of the People, by the People, and for the People sure took some interesting turns.

The bottom line was that we had a horse race. The sting and I would soon be out of business. Would there be time enough to complete the case against Richard Bartlow? And if warranted, against his brother, Supervisor Duane Bartlow?

Twenty-eight

STEPHANIE FERRARI DIDN'T UTTER A SINGLE WORD DURING the five minutes it took Fitzgerald to get us to Chinatown, and that suited my mood. I was concentrating on figuring out how to break down Mad Anthony Wong. The meeting with Wong was at his headquarters, a narrow shop selling jade and ivory jewelry. The store was located south of Canal Street and our large car made its way slowly through the crowded hundred-year-old tenements. The tiny streets were jammed with Chinese pedestrians forced into the roadway by vendor stands tumbling over each other on the meager sidewalks. They were doing a brisk business in fish, vegetables, fruit, and housewares. The outdoor telephone booths had pagoda tops and except for a stray Kentucky Fried Chicken sign, all the shops were labeled in Chinese.

Once off busy Canal Street, the air was filled with Chinese language. In the largest and most important Chinatown in the United States we were the only whites, and our presence was ignored by the mass of people surrounding the car. But, of course, we had been noticed. Chinatown's homogeneous secrecy made it largely immune to law enforcement because outsiders were quickly categorized as tourists, business people, police, or, occasionally, mafiosi from adjoining Little Italy. A human chain of workers spread the word of our progress through the streets many times faster than we moved.

Fitzgerald found a gap in the street stands and pulled the large vehicle halfway up onto the sidewalk. It was clear he would have to stay with the car since a truck of any size would be unable to pass.

"How will we know Wong if Fitzgerald doesn't come with us?" I said.

"I'll know him," Stephanie said. "I busted him a few years ago when I worked here in plainclothes during the Tong wars. He's a stone killer. Now he has so much money he thinks he can do anything and buy his way out afterward if he needs to." The Block stared at Stephanie. I also found it hard to picture her in this area during one of the bloodiest gang wars in history.

Fitzgerald sat behind the wheel picking his teeth with a matchbook cover. He wasn't a bit unhappy about staying with the car. Wong's store was only a short block away, but I didn't like the idea of us walking there. Chinese gangs were heavily armed, and Stephanie, the Block, and I were a distinct minority in a community where no one ever saw anything to report to the police.

"At least you ought to supply us with weapons."

"No can do, Fraleigh. You know that. Scared?" Her eyes canvassed the street.

The Block had moved out of hearing range. He was perched on the fender of the Lincoln waiting for a command decision.

"Scared? Are you out of your fucking mind? Of course I'm scared. You worked here. You've known Mad Anthony's reputation and the kind of mutts he has working for him. You're not scared?"

"I'm terrified. What do you want to do?" Her face was expressionless. She could have been pulling my leg, but I didn't think so.

"You have your radio. You can call for help if we need it. Let's chance it." I waved the Block over so we could get started.

"Hey, Captain, mind if I ask you a question?" the Block said before I could explain the game plan.

"Sure, Block." She smiled. For reasons beyond my understanding the Block had grown on her.

"Well, you know . . . with all these field associate guys around, how come the one working near Fitzgerald doesn't report him?"

A good question I thought, momentarily distracted from our dilemma of how to reach Wong's headquarters.

Stephanie flushed. Given our predicament, she hadn't anticipated the question. She looked away, embarrassed. Slowly it dawned on me.

"Jesus Christ, Stephanie, you don't mean to tell me . . ." I said.

Now she was angry. "I'm not telling you anything. Either of you. And you should realize that whole area is off-limits."

The Block had looked on during the exchange. Now he said, "I'll be goddamned. He don't get reported because he is the field associate. A dirtbag like him. No wonder the NYPD got problems."

People always underestimated the Block's intelligence because of his appearance and speech, but he had added two and two together more quickly than I had. He had also pissed off Stephanie, who didn't appreciate being surprised into giving something away.

"Are we going to discuss police ethics or visit Mad Anthony?" she said.

We started down the sidewalk. "Even if you call in a Ten- Thirteen, the cars won't be able to get to us through these streets," I said. Signal 10-13 was assist police officer. Cops would come flying from everywhere, hoping that they would be in time, and with the thought in the back of their minds, next time it could be me.

"They won't try very hard anyway," she said.

"What?"

"Ten-Thirteens from IA personnel go over like a lead balloon."

Great. It was like a scene from *High Noon*. We were strolling down the unfriendly sidewalks alone. Of course, they would make us immediately as cops but wouldn't know that the Block and I were unarmed, that only Stephanie was carrying. A temporary advantage at best. It was bright daylight, maybe we wouldn't have any trouble. Sure.

"There have been improvements in technology since you left, Fraleigh." Stephanie spoke as if we were still enjoying ourselves in Forlini's, but the sweat was dripping down my back, and the temperature wasn't that high. I saw what she meant. One of the kids on a stoop across the street was speaking into a hand radio. In my day lookouts had whistled or yelled, and had been working for hookers and gamblers, not crack dealers. The boy with the radio was about twelve years old. The American entrepreneurial spirit at work.

I saw a flicker of movement ahead of us which I assumed was in response to the radio signal. A kid who looked like he was fourteen slowly descended the steps of a brownstone. He wore white tennis shoes and a nice-looking English-style raincoat which reached his knees. His sallow face was without expression and his right hand was buried in his pocket, which would be slit to allow him to draw his Uzi or sawed-off shotgun.

Stephanie didn't carry a purse. I wondered where she carried her gun. I hoped it wasn't one of those dainty five-shot models. We were about ten feet from the kid, who was now lounging against an iron railing on the stoop. I saw something in his eyes as he began to straighten up. I guessed he was about to whip out whatever was under his coat. We were too far away to rush him so I got down and slowly began to untie and tie my shoelace. Stephanie stopped with me, turning as if she was fascinated by my loose shoelace. She slipped a thirty-eight-caliber Colt Police Special from under her suit jacket. The Block meantime kept plodding straight ahead as if he hadn't noticed or didn't care about us stopping. In the bright, sunny silence that had grown, the kid on the stoop hesitated.

Suddenly, he realized that the Block had gotten quite close. He whipped an Uzi out of his coat. But it was too late. The Block, with surprising speed from someone his size, was on him. He took the gun away so swiftly that Stephanie and I running forward didn't catch up with him. In one motion the Block ejected the clip and raised the gun above his head. Every eye on the street watched. Then he brought it down with such force on the railing that the firing mechanism bent. A piece of metal fell to the ground with a clank. The Block grabbed the stunned boy by the shirt collar. "These things can be dangerous for kids your age. Now go on home before I have to slap you." He gave the kid a shove, tossed the useless weapon into the street, and continued walking.

We caught up with him, and I kept telling my back to relax. We were past whatever they had been guarding. A dope or gambling house? They wouldn't shoot now. Would they? "Nice work, Block," Stephanie said. She had slipped the Colt back under her jacket and I doubt if anyone but me had seen the gun. We finished our walk without further incident.

Mad Anthony Wong was taller than the people we had passed in the street. He was slender at five nine, but the eyes under his jet-black hair were intense. Very intense. "You!" He looked at Stephanie in a decidedly unfriendly way. "Where's Fitzgerald?"

"I had him stay with the car, Wong. This is Fraleigh and the Block from California. They want some information that won't cost you a thing. We're not interested in you. You help them, and we'll be out of here in two minutes."

"It's good to see you again, Captain." Wong had a big smile on his face that I didn't like. Something was wrong. He was too confident. He bowed, then held out his hand Western style.

"Let's stop the bullshit, Wong. This isn't a social visit. They want to know about Dick Barry and the bond. These are the complaint and detective investigation reports." She handed them to him, which saved him the embarrassment of having to retract his unshaken hand. But he wasn't at all embarrassed. A young muscular Chinese man with a shaven head stood in the rear, his eyes focused on Wong for a cue to action. Despite the day's warmth, he wore a three-quarter-length black leather coat. His right hand was buried in the pocket and I wondered what kind of weapon it was resting on.

Wong turned to me. "This lady arrested me a few years ago. Even after the charges were dismissed, she was most bothersome. It cost me ten thousand dollars to have her transferred. And now she's back." He shook his head at me, laughing silently.

I picked up the reports from his desk. "These are going to be even more bothersome, Wong." I pointed to a paragraph on the DD5. "Your friend MacLeod puts the whole job on you."

"Mr. Policeman from California, I have experienced police tricks since before you were born. Too bad you didn't bring Fitzgerald with you. He could have told you Wong is no fool." He spoke softly, but his English was perfect.

"This is his signature on the report. Fitzgerald obtained court arrest warrants for you based on what MacLeod said."

Frowning, he picked up the report. "So you say."

"If you give my friends a couple of harmless pieces of information, Wong, I tear up the warrants. We're not interested in some john getting ripped off in Chinatown, as long as these men get cooperation," Stephanie said.

"You expect me to believe this nonsense?"

"No," I said. "But I expect you to believe this." I held up the recorder and played the part in which MacLeod denounced Orientals and identified himself as a Christian businessman. Wong didn't even blink at the racial insults, but his eyes widened when he heard MacLeod give him up. "All I care about is where Dick Barry told you he got the bonds from."

Wong looked at me bitterly. "Then why don't you ask the stockbroker MacLeod, the Christian businessman? I will tell you nothing. And you, Captain Ferrari," he pointed at Stephanie, "you have been most unwise. You are from Internal Affairs. No policeman will lift a finger to help you, yet you bring these men here. I heard you removed a machine gun from a corrupt child on the way here. You know how many more disturbed young ones are out there? Do you really think you will get out of this street alive?"

So that's what was behind his confidence. He figured we couldn't get out in one piece. I pushed the thought that he very possibly was right out of my mind, but it took a little pushing. I wondered if visiting Wong just to confirm MacLeod's information that Richard Bartlow had stolen the bonds from Paradise Trust was worth it.

"There's another thing I'm obliged to tell you, Wong. The law now requires the police to warn people when we learn that a contract is out on them," I said. It wasn't quite true, but I bet MacLeod was *thinking* about a contract on Wong, and Wong still needed prodding.

"Contract?" I had Wong's attention now. "Who put a contract out on Wong?"

"The same guy you heard on the tape—MacLeod."

"Don't buy any green bananas, Wong," the Block said.

"Green bananas? I do not understand."

"You may not be around to enjoy them by the time they get ripe," Stephanie said with quiet authority.

Wong was angry, but not enough to talk. I tried a new tack. "We're not interested in your drug business either, Wong. Of course, if you don't give us the information we need, we'll keep looking, and maybe the deal you're cooking up in California will get burned." Not interested until I got this sting over with. Then Wong would find out that we were very interested.

Mad Anthony Wong's intense eyes now had a mad look about them. I had touched a nerve. He spoke, trying to control his breathing. "I did Mr. MacLeod a favor. You should ask him what happened to the white man from California."

This wasn't getting us anywhere. I decided to put on more pressure, and made a mistake. "We don't care about what happened—all we want to know is where he got the bonds." Wong just smiled at me. "From now on, you won't move in California without me behind you. I'll know every time you visit San Jose airport, what credit card you use, what bank you're dealing with, and who you're talking to. You won't be able to run a red light, let alone do a dope deal."

Wong blew. I hadn't realized how on edge the mention of dope had made him. He pounded the table. "You fools will not interfere with my plans. You are nothing here. I say what is the law and now I say that you are finished." He stood and nodded toward the guy standing behind him, who reached out and touched a switch on the wall. I heard chimes ringing throughout the house.

"No hard feelings, Wong." Stephanie's killer smile had come on. She held out her hand. I got ready. With a condescending look on his face, he took her hand. She stepped close to him and with her other hand swung her revolver up to his left eyeball. "Tell the kid to freeze, Wong."

The bodyguard had been quick. He had produced a sawed-off shotgun from under the leather coat. It was trained at Stephanie, but only for an instant. She moved quickly behind Wong. The kid moved too, trying to cover her. He came too close. I grabbed the barrel of the shotgun, pushing it upward, and hit him flush on the side of the cheek with a left hook. The gun went off with a roar and a flash of heat made me let go of the barrel, but the Block had lifted the bodyguard off the floor from behind, and I chopped the gun out of his hands easily. The kid sank to his knees. He was out of it, but there would be more where he came from. Our ears were ringing, there was a huge hole in the ceiling, the room stank of burnt gunpowder, and we were far from out of it.

"You forgot that I worked here, Wong," Stephanie said. "I remember your famed good-bye chimes, but we won't be waiting for your goons to surprise us on the way out."

"You will never get out," Wong said.

Stephanie moved in front of him switching the gun to her right hand, with the barrel pointing between his eyes. "We don't get out, you don't. You'll be the first to go, Wong. I promise you."

I believed her and I guess Wong did too. "Ten thousand dollars to get rid of a crazy woman and she returns."

The door opened and several of Wong's people cautiously looked in. They were heavily armed. "Go," he actually yelled. "I believe we have a stalemate, Captain. No one will come to help those from Internal Affairs. You will not kill me without provocation and I am prepared to wait with Oriental patience. You are not."

Stephanie, with her gun steady on Wong, used her left hand to produce the small hand radio she had used at T. J. Brown's. Wong smiled. "Signal Ten-Thirteen in the Fifth Precinct. Shots fired. Ten-Thirteen shots fired," she repeated, giving the address of Wong's store.

"What unit is calling a Ten-Thirteen? Identify yourself," the dispatcher said, and Wong's smile broadened.

Shit, I thought. Since cop ambushes had been occurring, the communications unit had verified calls for assistance. Stephanie was right. They wouldn't respond when they heard IA.

"This is shield Forty-one Forty—Fifth Squad."

"Ten Four, Forty-one Forty."

We heard the broadcast and almost simultaneously sirens, as all cops within hearing turned their cars toward Big Wong's.

"Fifth Squad. You are not from the Fifth Squad. You are from Internal Affairs. You lied. She lied," Wong said to me, disappointment covering his face.

"Nobody's perfect, Wong," I said.

Twenty-nine

THE FIFTH PRECINCT ON ELIZABETH STREET WASN'T ANY different from its grim replicas throughout the city. Weeks of old litter fluttered around our knees when a sudden breeze kicked up as we mounted the front steps. Wong had been through the drill enough times with members of his gang to have booked himself, but like us and the young uniformed cops who had provided transport, he allowed Captain Ferrari to lead the way. She walked past the desk officer without deigning to flash her tin or speak to him, knowing full well that a cop from the street had already phoned in about the "cunt captain from IA" who was bringing in Wong and one of his flunkies on a weapons charge. The rescuing cops had been pissed when they found out that Stephanie had used Fitzgerald's shield number, but they couldn't very well unrescue us.

Wong could probably have escaped had he thought about it, because the cops following Stephanie up the stairs ignored the prisoners and kept their eyes on her shapely legs, nicely displayed by her blue skirt. In the squad room on the second floor, she reached over the railing and pressed the little catch which allowed the gate to open.

"Whatcha got, honey?" A slender blond detective in his mid-thirties gave Stephanie his best smile. It wasn't good enough.

"I'm Captain Ferrari, IA. What's your name, Officer?" Her brown eyes killed his smile and stopped him in mid-step. Meantime, I noticed a dark-skinned, heavy-set guy with a sergeant's shield displayed in his shirt pocket staring at me. He scooted into the lieutenant's office in the corner of the room, closing the door behind him.

"Detective Harris, Cap," the former lady killer said softly to Stephanie.

"Detective Harris, search those two prisoners thoroughly and put them into the cage. I'll fill out the arrest cards and then you can stand by as a witness while I Mirandize them and see if they want to make a statement."

Harris was herding Wong and his accomplice over to his desk when I heard the lieutenant's office door open behind me. I turned slowly to see how the lieutenant in charge of the squad would react to Stephanie.

I found myself looking into my brother Jack's face. My mind coolly accepted that Jack was apparently now the commanding officer of the Fifth Squad, but my stomach churned, and my Adam's apple swelled so that I couldn't speak. He was two inches taller and still about twenty-five pounds heavier than I. His eyes burned into mine and the only sound in the squad room was the ticking of the large official clock on the wall.

Oh, hell, I thought, this is stupid. All these years and two brothers, the only ones left in the family, not even talking to each other. I found my voice, but it was barely audible with the swelling in my throat. "Jack." I put my right hand out for a shake. A peace offering.

His eyes bulged, and what I'll never forget is that he slowly extended his hand. When I moved forward to take it, he swung at my head. Jack knew well that with my ring experience he could never land a sucker punch so he had drawn me off balance. I rolled with the punch the best I could, but it caught me high on the forehead. I slid to the right and crouched, anticipating Jack's rush. With his strength it was all over if he grabbed me. Sure enough, he charged like a runaway locomotive. I caught him with a straight right that didn't travel more than eight inches to his solar plexus. I never hit anyone harder in my life. My fist didn't find any softness, but no one alive can take a shot like that.

Jack fell gasping into a chair. The swarthy sergeant jumped toward me with a blackjack in his hand, but Stephanie stepped in front of him. "All right, Sergeant. Help the lieutenant into his office." She turned to me. "You're bleeding again. Go into the washroom and see if you can stop the blood." Leaving the squadroom I noticed that Wong's gloom had vanished. He wore a big smile. Cops were punching each other out.

Jack's ring had made an ugly wound high on the left side of my forehead. The side that had escaped the brawl in T. J. Brown's unscathed. Apparently men's rings were big in Manhattan. After inspecting the cut in the stained and cracked mirror, I searched the washroom in vain for paper towels, finally settling for cheap toilet paper to wipe the blood from my face. In one of the open cubicles a black man sat on the toilet and the combined smell of his winey breath and defecation caused me to gag. A white uniformed cop leaned expressionless against the far wall, taking me in while never losing sight of the wino, who was apparently a prisoner.

"Man, we got to put a stop to this police brutality. They even whipping white ass now. You want a witness, brother, I'll go all the way to the Civilian Review Board with you," the black man said.

"Wipe your asshole, asshole, before I come over and flush you away. This place stinks almost as bad as you do." The cop spoke out of the side of his mouth, never quite making eye contact with me. I ran cold water on the wound without slowing the bleeding very much. A couple of more days in New York and I'd be nothing but scar tissue. After a while, the blood seemed to ooze a bit slower as I dabbed the wound with toilet paper.

"You heard him cuss me, mister. I'll be your witness. You be mine. We got civil rights in this country. These honky motherfuckers think they can do anything. What do you say, brother?"

"Don't waste your breath, asshole. This dude only rats on cops he's related to."

Like Jack's punch, the words caught me by surprise. Looking up from the washbowl, I found his eyes meeting mine in the mirror and the familiar venom hurt as much as it had when I was in the department. I didn't recognize him, but the speckling of gray in his hair indicated that he had probably been on the job back when my picture had been front page. No doubt word had already flashed through the precinct that I was in the squad room. The intensity of his gaze hypnotized me. Only the flushing of the toilet caused him to break it off and look toward his prisoner.

Stephanie walked into the men's room. She pushed away my hand filled with bloody toilet paper and peered at the cut. "Goddamn it. That's a nasty cut. You may need a stitch. It was totally uncalled for." She wrinkled her nose, looking around. "Let's get out of here. It smells."

"Hey, lady," the wino cried out.

She glanced at the wino, now handcuffed to the water pipe. The cop had been waiting for her to turn in their direction. He unzipped his fly and exposed a fat, circumcised dick which he waved at Stephanie before she could turn away. "Mornin', Captain. How's everything in IA nowadays?" He made no move to turn away from her toward the urinals. Furious, she looked him in the eye.

"Lady—captain? You from IA. You got to stop this brutality. I'm a witness. This officer beat that poor white man until he bleed. Right brother?" the wino said.

"Let's go, Fraleigh. I've had enough of cops today," Stephanie said, looking at the patrolman, whose smile mocked her as he stood there with his genitals cupped in his right hand.

She walked from the washroom handing me a beige lace handkerchief for my forehead. It had the fragrance of her perfume. I took a deep breath and tried to put the smell and pain of the Fifth Precinct and New York out of my mind.

Captain Ferrari left the Block and Fitzgerald in the squad room to make sure the routine of the arrest was followed. I closed my eyes and listened to the continuous chatter of the police radio as Stephanie drove us: a Signal Ten-Thirty, felony in progress in the Seventh Precinct; a Ten-Thirteen in the First Precinct; a possible jumper in the Fifth; Ten-Thirty shots fired in the Seventh; a sergeant in the First was trying to get additional units for traffic control at a two-alarm fire. There was no letup. Things hadn't changed in New York any more than the way the cops regarded me had changed. I was light-headed, bone-tired. I wondered without really caring where Stephanie was taking us.

She pulled into an underground parking garage on East Seventy-third Street. It was a residential complex and we walked to an elevator. Neither of us had said a word since leaving the precinct. On the fourth floor we got off and walked to the end of a corridor where she went through the New York apartment owner's ritual of opening thirty or so locks before we finally went into the apartment. She quickly moved away from me in the foyer to the kitchen. Following, I saw her disarm a burglar alarm.

"Life in the Big Apple." She shrugged, motioning me to come with her. In the bathroom she took out a first-aid kit and soaked a piece of cotton in peroxide. I thought of what the bastard cop had done in the men's room. Technically, she shouldn't have been there. He knew that he could escape any attempt at discipline by claiming that he had merely been surprised as he had gone to take a leak. How many other humiliations had she suffered during her years as one of New York's Finest?

"This will sting a bit," she told me, like I didn't know about those things. She kept her left hand on my cheek and tenderly cleaned the wound, wiping away the crusted blood.

"You do good work." I gave a half-hearted grin.

"I'm sorry, Fraleigh. Your own brother, and you reached out to him. Gross told me what happened. Your father wasn't your fault, but they blame you. The fucking police department."

I saw that her eyes were moist. "The fucking police department," I said, thinking of the way we had been treated in the Fifth Precinct, having to use a trick to get assistance to keep from getting killed in Wong's pad. Then the squad sergeant and Jack acting like assholes. And the jerk detective's and uniformed cop's treatment of Stephanie. And Nola and Clark Massey and . . .Stephanie reached up, taking one last dab with the cotton. I put my arms around her. She dropped the cotton on the bathroom floor and slipped her arms behind my back, putting her head against my shoulder.

We just stood close like that for a while. Suddenly, I realized that she was crying. I could feel her deep sobs. I held her firmly, not knowing what to say. I felt as low as she did. In a few minutes she quieted in my arms. She looked up and very tenderly put her lips on mine. I returned the kiss, and feeling her against me, felt a warmth pushing away the week's ugliness. Her kiss moved us from tenderness to desire quickly, and within minutes we were in bed.

Her body was a combination of muscular toughness and a soft femininity. Given my earlier lethargy I wondered if I was wise to be attempting romance, but within minutes her open hunger kindled my own passion and our sex was rich and breathless with a raw edge of pleasure that peaked with incredible sharpness. She clung to me afterward, and I kept my arms tightly around her, making an effort to keep the real world from creeping into the room.

Our tranquility was broken fifteen minutes later when her beeper sounded. Stephanie moved from the bed to the phone on her dresser and dialed. Sensing my attention, she half turned and ran her eyes over my body; by the time they reached my eyes I was beginning to feel a tingling in the groin. But when she got on the phone, she was all business. I didn't catch the other end of the conversation, but was disappointed when she said, "OK. We're on the way."

"Duty calls. Chief Gross wants to see you. We'd better get going." She came back to the bed and touched her lips to mine. I caressed her breast. She sighed, "I'll give you a half hour to cut that out." But she wasn't serious. Within fifteen minutes we were in the elevator heading down to the garage. We made pretty good time going south against the rush-hour traffic heading north. No words, but she kept me from sinking back into the depression that had covered me since bugging Nola's room.

The desk outside Gross's office was deserted. Darkness had closed in, obscuring the grime of One Police Plaza's windows. The rows of desks were empty. Stephanie waved me to a chair, knocked on Gross's door, and entered. About ten minutes later she opened the door and beckoned for me to come in. Gross's briefing had been completed.

He looked very tired. The lion of the department, a shrinking man in his sixties sitting behind a big desk. "Stephanie tells me that you've accomplished pretty much what you came for with MacLeod, Wong, and Zale. The other stuff—don't be too harsh on the department, Fraleigh. Oh, I know. They're bastards sometimes, and they'd steal a hot stove if we weren't here, but look what they're up against every day. Sometimes I wonder. I'll have to retire soon. Nobody's going to say, 'Good old Seymour.' All these years locking up cops for one ungrateful P.C. after another, and I won't ever be able to show up at a cop function. You can bet your ass the people I worked for won't be calling me to come to dinner or some racket. No. They'll still sit at the head table, but me . . ."

A sightseeing helicopter whirled south over the East River heading toward the Battery and Statue of Liberty. The pilot was probably pointing out police headquarters to well-heeled tourists, but just the exterior of the building. Outsiders didn't get to see what went on inside the organization. The kind of stuff Gross was discussing.

"Captain Ferrari's been terrific, Seymour. The other stuff—well, I didn't expect anything to be different," I said.

"It should change! You'll end up like me. A lifetime cop that cops won't even talk to. And in your case, it's bullshit. It wasn't your fault, and that fucking nitwit brother of yours knows better. I'll take care of him if it's the last thing I do."

"I don't want that, Seymour. It wasn't easy for either of us losing our old man that way."

"What way? That's what I wanted to tell you the other day. Your father didn't shoot himself because he was dirty and you gave him up. Jack knows that. Why the hell is he still persecuting you?"

"What are you saying? I don't get it."

"OK. Remember Gloria Fell, the hooker you busted? She implied that you better let her go because her gals were putting out for some big shots. No cop could have taken a chance on not reporting that. It might backfire. Besides which, hookers don't give cops ultimatums. Oh, I know we portrayed you as a fearless foe of corruption, but I knew all the time where you were coming from. You were no reformer, and you had no idea your father had slipped a little after your mother went into a three-month coma. Actually, the first time he shacked with Gloria he didn't know who she was. It didn't last long and was no big megillah. Everyone knew he never took a nickel or lifted a finger to help Gloria. It was strictly a stiff dick with no common sense. If we applied the same standards to the politicians and judges, there wouldn't be anyone to run the city."

"Then why did the department make such a big fucking deal of it that he committed suicide?"

"Your so-called exposé was chickenshit stuff, Fraleigh. It had nothing to do with him committing suicide."

"What?"

Gross stood up and walked to the dirty window. "Your father had been diagnosed as having the big C. In the liver. Terminal. He didn't want to be a lingering invalid like your mother. He was really in Washington getting a second opinion at Johns Hopkins. It confirmed what his doctor here said. He went back to the hotel room and killed himself. He never even knew about you busting Gloria."

Manhattan's darkening sky was broken by friendly lights coming on in apartment buildings. Despite the warmth of the scene, I shivered. All the years of guilt. It had been cancer. "Why the hell didn't I know about this?"

"I was ordered under pain of demotion not to tell you. I'm not proud of myself, but I'm no hero."

"I don't get it, Seymour. Who ordered you not to tell me? Who the hell would have cared one way or the other?"

"Think back. Remember the scandals. One after another. Plainclothes corruption. Sergeants' and detectives' pads. The narcs stealing dope and selling it. There was enormous pressure on the mayor, the special prosecutor, and the P.C. to do something. You were ideal. The new-breed policeman. Your father was already dead. Let people think what they wanted about him. The media would have ignored the petty bullshit you had exposed if they knew your father had checked out because he had cancer. The story was the suicide of one of the top brass whose corruption had been exposed by his own son. It gave the P.C. and all the politicians a chance to hold righteous press conferences. You were an honest cop. A hero. And we needed one just then."

Thirty

I SPENT THE NIGHT IN STEPHANIE'S ARMS. IT WAS A NIGHT of wine and lovemaking. We awoke early, almost simultaneously. In the harsh light of dawn filtering through the blinds, Stephanie's face for the first time showed her age. I held her tighter.

"How is it that some guy hasn't captured you by now?" I asked over breakfast.

She poured me some orange juice. "Not surprisingly, most of the guys who tried were cops, and although a couple of them were nice, I just didn't want to be that tied to the job. Some of the other business types and lawyers who were interested finally gave up. I was too independent. Too career oriented. Too assertive. Too much a cop. Always too something. Now I feel too old to have children, so the appeal of marriage has diminished. And you?"

"Oh, I tried it once. That was more than enough."

"I saw the way you looked at Nola at the symposium. Are you sure?"

I glanced at the tiny television set on the counter. One of the early morning shows was doing national weather. It was sunny and warm in California. How could I explain Nola to Stephanie when I couldn't to myself?

"Well, your face is quite an answer, Fraleigh. Here I go again," she said, her mouth puckered unattractively. "My luck. Catch them on the rebound. I thought something happened between you, but I preferred to believe that my charms had become irresistible."

238

"Stop bullshitting, Stephanie. You're dynamite, and you know it. Do all you women need constant stroking? Your new hairdo is magnificent. Your career arrests are fantastic. Your housing programs and road programs are marvelous. You're all absolutely great. And then, if we say it as often as you want, you get suspicious. We must be wimps. If we don't say it enough, we're male chauvinists, and some other phony with a spiel talks you into the sack. Make up your minds."

"Who was it? Who's the guy you're jealous of? I knew you were down."

She was smart and I was transparent. "I didn't mean to sound off. You've been terrific," I said.

She moved the table so that she could sit in my lap. Putting her arms around me she said, "I'm going to call and be late for work this morning, Fraleigh. You need a good send-off to California."

"You're pretty assertive. Don't think I'm so easy," I said, untying her robe.

"Good-bye for now," Stephanie said, dropping me at the hotel an hour later. A truck horn blared behind us. Blocking a midtown sidestreet at nine o'clock in the morning was grounds for justifiable homicide. "Stay in touch, or I'll come out to Silicon City with a warrant for your arrest." She touched her left hand to my cheek and lightly kissed me on the lips.

The same doorman who had opened the cab door the night the Block and I returned from the brawl at T. J. Brown's winked in approval. Stephanie turned heads.

I showered, shaved, and packed. It was two hours to flight time at Kennedy. I would be early, but with New York traffic you never knew, and I needed to get back to Silicon City before it sunk into an anarchy of police civil war. I called the bell captain and told him to send someone up for my bag in fifteen minutes.

Two minutes after I hung up, there was a knock on the door. New Yorkers couldn't stand to wait, I thought, but my bag was zipped up and I was ready. I opened the door. Stephanie stood there with a look on her face that I hadn't seen before.

"You've come to take me to the airport?"

"I'm not sure where we may take you, Fraleigh, but it won't be to the airport." She stepped in, and her eyes swept the room. "Where's the equipment?"

"Equipment?" Ironically, during my time in the department I had never feared IA, but now I knew what that coldness in the bowels felt like.

"Damn it. I told you not to trust Fitzgerald. He got busted last night on a stolen property charge that's been pending for months. He's been busy all night giving people up left and right, including you on the eavesdropping paraphernalia."

"Help yourself, Captain. Look around." I waved my arm in a circle. After I'd taped Nola's conversations I had cleared the room of the equipment, putting it into a locker in Grand Central Station and mailing the key to Fitzgerald in the Fifth Squad. There was no way it could be traced to me. Nor would Ferrari's scrutiny of the walls yield evidence. I hadn't drilled any holes and had replaced the socket carefully. Fitzgerald's word alone was worthless, but the cassette tape in my pocket was evidence of a Class E felony under Section 250.05 of the New York State Penal Code.

"No. I didn't think we'd find the equipment. You're too good a cop for that, but did you do anything to the wall? A little drilling? And the tape, what did you do with that?"

"Is this the part where you strip me naked like in the *Maltese Falcon*?" I laughed or tried to, and with an effort kept my hand from the tape.

"Two male detectives from IA are on the way to do that. Here's the search warrant."

I pretended to study it. They had me. It was all over when the two detectives arrived. Should I throw myself on her mercy, ask for a chance to get rid of the tape? I tried to gauge her expression. It wasn't anger. It was sadness. She knew I was going under. She was the professional now; it was no use appealing. I sat in the armchair to wait for the dicks.

"I warned you to play it straight. You can't say I didn't," she said.

"Oh, for God's sake, Stephanie, don't ask for absolution. IA has to enforce the rules. Cops have to try to catch the slimebags despite the rules. We don't expect IA to understand."

She flared. "We're not team players like you. Is that it, Fraleigh? The inherent corruption of detectives. You're allowed to do anything to make your case. Well, it stinks. Using me is one thing, but knowing what Fitzgerald is and still dealing with him? And Nola. As close as you've been with her." She nodded toward the wall. "Did what you hear send you flying into my bed? Was she making love? Committing treason? Would you do the same to me after last night? Don't bother to say anything. I know the answer."

"I'm after a murderer and crooked politicians. You can't always catch them playing by IA rules. If I taped Nola, is it really that different from what you're doing now in the line of duty—the professional IA bloodhound? At least I'm not about to lock Nola up."

"You know damned well it's different. I'm doing what I'm supposed to do. You were committing a felony."

"Yeah. The killers and crooks in office applaud your integrity. They go on forever, and if any cops try too hard to nail them, the cops go to jail."

"I've heard all the bullshit before, Fraleigh. Tell it to the judge."

A bell sounded in the hallway indicating the elevator had stopped on this floor. It was probably the IA men. I began to think about a lawyer. I didn't know anyone in New York anymore. God! The news media—they would have a field day: REFORMER COP WHO CAUSED HIS FATHER'S SUICIDE ARRESTED FOR HIS OWN CORRUPTION. Stephanie got up to answer the knock on the door. It was the bellboy.

"He's not checking out right now. There are no bags for you."

He was a young black kid and the disappointment showed in his face. No tip. And he had missed another call coming up here. Maybe a big tip.

"Hey, come on in," I said reaching for my wallet. "It's not your fault. I did call for someone to take my bag. Take this." I took a couple of bucks from my wallet.

Stephanie was watching from the doorway. I found myself looking into those beautiful brown eyes again. I couldn't read them. Suddenly, just at that moment, with me standing with my wallet open, she chose to go into the bathroom and close the door behind her.

I took a twenty-dollar bill from my wallet and gave it to the bellboy, whose eyes glistened. "This is yours. I want you to do me a favor. You know the Federal Express office on the corner?"

He nodded. "Sure do."

"Well, send this tape to me at this address." I handed him my business card, the cassette, and fifteen bucks to cover the Federal Express cost.

"Man. You're police chief. This is undercover, right?"

"Right. Now listen. Hold the receipt for me, but don't give it to me if anyone is watching. This is just between us. There's another twenty for you when I pick up the receipt. OK?"

"Great, man. You don't need the other twenty. I'll work with you."

Stephanie came out of the bathroom as he was leaving. Two detectives from IA stopped him. They were big. The larger of the two flashed his tin and said to the slender bellboy, "You're not taking anything out of this room are you?"

"No sir. The lady said to come back later for the bag." The cops turned toward me, missing his wink. But Stephanie saw it.

"We'll do the bag and room first, then I'll wait in the hall while you search him. He's seen the warrant and been advised of his rights," she said. She hadn't given me Miranda, but I didn't think it was time to get technical.

The search was brief and unpleasant. It was the first time I had been strip-searched. "He's clean, Captain," the bigger cop said. I wondered if the other one was allowed to talk.

We went down in the same elevator. I carried my bag. The bellboy I had given the tape watched us. Outside, the doorman got me a cab. Stephanie stepped close, out of earshot of the two dicks. "Do the world and yourself a favor, Fraleigh. Get out of police work." She turned and joined the detectives. Walking toward Fifth Avenue, she looked small and fragile between them.

Three streets from the hotel I told the driver to swing back, I had forgotten something. I scanned the area to be sure that Stephanie and the IA cops were gone. Inside the lobby I traded another twenty for the Federal Express receipt.

"You don't have to do that, Chief," he said, while burying the cash with that sleight of hand unique to New York. "Were those cops, you know—dirty?"

"The woman was all right. The other two—who knows?" I went back to my waiting cab.

Thirty-one

EVEN THOUGH I WAS GLAD TO BE BACK IN MY OWN BED, I didn't sleep well that night. I should have felt relieved about my father, but I kept waking from nightmares. I dreamt that my blood had been drained in a New York emergency room. Later, people were pushing me around the city's streets, but without blood I was weak, powerless to resist. Then the scene shifted. Catherine Mendez was in the emergency room berating me because her husband had been shot. She said he would be in a wheelchair for the rest of his life. But when they wheeled him into the room, it was me in the wheelchair. I was clammy with sweat and the sheets were wet when I got out of bed.

Back in my soon-to-be-vacated office I was groggy. Things seemed hopeless. There was a good chance that Nola was going to expose the sting immediately. Even if she didn't, we only had three days until the Board of Supervisors' session, and the existence of the sting was sure going to get blown then. Then too, it was almost certain that Fritz Gerhart knew about it by now, and I had no doubt that he'd leak the information.

Denise fussed over me and served me a cup of coffee and a doughnut I didn't want after I had been foolish enough to admit that I hadn't had breakfast. I drank the coffee hoping the caffeine would unglue my brain, while I nibbled at the fried dough. I was staring glumly at the wall when Lieutenant Cathy Stevens tapped on my open door and walked in.

"Chief, I've been designated to tell you that most of us around here want you to hang in there. We heard of the Board of Supervisors delaying the vote last week on the chief's selection. We probably don't say things like this often enough, but you turned some people on when you hung tough on Mayor Middleston's investigation."

"Thanks, Cathy."

"Don't get me wrong. I plan to retire next year. I'm not bucking for anything. I'm happy heading up the sex crimes unit. Still, I hope those fools who run the city give you the chief's job." She paused. "Is anything wrong? You really look down. I know we all expected you to be appointed last week, but the info is that it's just a technicality and the appointment will go through. No?"

"I have something else on my mind, Cathy." That was putting it mildly. My mind was buzzing with Nola, the Bartlow brothers, and the sting. Was she dirty? Would those two crooks beat the rap simply because we ran out of time? "Frankly, I don't know what the Board of Supervisors will do, and I'm not sure I care that much."

She sat down. "Look, there are ups and downs. It's a tough job, but we have become more professional around here because of you. If Gerhart gets the job, it will be a disaster—the same good-old-boy cliques will come back. Hang in there. It's important to a lot of us, and if there's anything I can do to help, I'm here."

"I appreciate what you're saying, Cathy." She had put an idea in my head. "Look, I have a real crisis on my hands and maybe you could help."

"You name it, Chief."

I took the envelope containing the sting tape of Falcone and Herrera from my drawer. "Cathy, be careful of the envelope and the tape cassette. They haven't been dusted for prints. The tape runs about twenty minutes. Look at it in my conference room. There's a VCR hooked up to the TV. And lock the doors. I don't want anyone else seeing that tape."

I watched a guarded expression cross her face. She had made a sincere offer of help but had never dreamed that it would be accepted. Now she was properly cautious about what she was getting into.

"Don't forget to be careful about the prints," I said as she went into the conference room.

"I'll try to remember, sir," she said, looking at me like I was a civilian for daring to remind her.

She returned about twenty-five minutes later, carefully placing the tape on my desk. Her blue eyes held fire. "I'm assigned to the sexual assault unit, not Internal Affairs, and from what I could see, there was no sexual assault since both parties seemed to be acting freely, to put it mildly."

I remembered that she had been married to the same guy for twenty-three years and had raised three kids who had stayed away from dope and out of jail.

"I guess maybe you're right to be ticked off at me for involving you in this, Cathy, but I don't know where to turn, and you did ask if you could help."

"I'm not a swinger, and I personally resent looking at that stuff. It's not part of my job."

"You're right. I'll find someone else to get to the bottom of this, Cathy. I don't have to tell you to keep it confidential."

She sat there looking at me for what seemed like a full five minutes. "OK, you must have had some reason for asking me to view the tape. I'm willing to listen."

"You realize by this time that the tape is from our latest sting at The Blue Mirage, which is supposed to be secret. I have no idea who recorded it. The operation should have been closed during the time shown on the clock. In addition to that mystery, someone mailed the tape of our cops' sex life to Nola Henderson, chairman of the Board of Supervisors."

"Chair*person*," Cathy said absently. "This is really crucial to your appointment then, if the board has the tape?"

"Not the board, just Nola."

"Nola . . . you mean Supervisor Henderson? She's beautiful, isn't she?"

I was conscious of my flushed face. "Cathy, you're absolutely correct. I have no right to ask you to take on this assignment, yet it's crucial to the department. I need to know who made those tapes and who sent it to Supervisor Henderson."

"And to your appointment as chief."

"True, but that's not why I asked you to investigate it."

She frowned. "Do you have any fucking idea of how tired we get of hearing that something is a woman's job? I don't want to get involved with whatever problems Mary Falcone's got at the moment. And outside of the female angle, I don't see any reason why you asked me to look at the tape."

"I asked you because you're one of the best investigators I have, and I trust you completely."

"And, of course, the fact that I'm female had nothing to do with it."

"I didn't say that, Cathy. When we get to the bottom of this, and we have to, I won't have any trouble understanding male behavior, but I'd feel better if you were able to explain what the hell was going on from a female's perspective."

She looked at me so long that I was sure she was composing a speech about why she wouldn't handle the investigation. Finally, she said, "Who else knows about this tape?"

"Let's see, I had to tell the Block and Paul. Supervisor Henderson has seen it, and whoever made it and sent it out."

"Well, I guess I appreciate your confidence. I want the confidentiality to continue along with a promise on your part that Mary Falcone will not be judged by different rules than apply to the rest of the force. I'm not going to be part of making her a scapegoat, and I want a commitment for what resources I need for the investigation."

"Thanks, Cathy. Whatever you need, just ask."

"We'll have to close the sting soon." Paul English rubbed his head. His responsibilities during my few days away had erased some of his laid-back casualness. I had played only that part of the hotel-bugging tape for them that contained Nola's phone conversations.

"I agree. We only have a couple of more days. Tell me what you came up with on Judge Henderson, Paul," I said.

"In relation to your request of his daily activities, there are a number of possible ways for you to meet him casually. This afternoon he's the main speaker at the California Department of Justice's annual symposium on criminal law at the Saint Francis Hotel, in San Francisco."

"I don't know. It might look funny my just popping in."

"I took the liberty of enrolling you. You'll be expected."

"Good. Anything else before we move on to Herrera and Falcone?"

"Yes. The judge is interesting. For someone supposedly nonpolitical, he's extraordinarily active."

"Just tell us whether the asshole is dirty or not. Fraleigh ain't got all fucking day to listen to you, English. This place is sinking right from under him."

"Thank you, Block. I'll do my best to be succinct if you can keep from interrupting. Judge Henderson is one of the major partners in a redevelopment project downtown which received substantial loans from the city. He holds twenty percent of the project ownership. It's a limited partnership. The general partner is Harley Curtis Developers, who yesterday hired Duane Bartlow's real estate firm to do the exclusive sales on their west-side housing project—two hundred seventy-five units priced at a half million bucks and up. Of course, it's totally separate from the redevelopment project."

"So what else is new? They covered their ass," the Block said.

Paul continued without a pause. "The commissions should be enormous. It is also rumored that the redevelopment project is ready to go into Chapter Eleven bankruptcy. If it does, the partners lose their money, but the city has indicated it will go for another three-million-dollar loan to keep them solvent. Nola Henderson will be ineligible to vote because of her father, but supposedly it's still in the bag."

"Very fucking interesting, Paul. Now Fraleigh and me can get our real estate licenses."

"Patience, Block. The juicy item is that the judge didn't put up a nickel of his own money for the investment. Harley Curtis accepted a promissory note. Very questionable indeed, since Curtis has one civil case and two criminal cases pending in this Superior Court district."

"Paul, as much as I hate to admit the Block is right, this stuff is getting us nowhere. If it's not actually illegal, why bother?"

"You asked what we uncovered—I'm reporting. There is one other serendipitous thing. We ran the judge's name and date of birth on our computer. Do you remember the case we made against the Deluxe Escort Service last year?"

"It was a big one, wasn't it? Four million bucks a year and johns from all over Northern California—Forty-niners and Giants as I recall—along with some pols. I don't remember Henderson handling the case, Paul."

"He didn't. He handled the merchandise. His name showed six separate tricks within four months."

"Only six? What a wimp," the Block said.

"These outfits always put a lot of names of prominent people down so that we don't dare publish the lists. How good is the stuff on Henderson?" I said.

"Their records list his home address in Saratoga."

"Still inconclusive."

"Not when we have these." Paul wore a big smile as he handed me copies of six credit card slips. "Don't bother to ask. It is his credit card number and signature. We got them from the escort service with a search warrant. It's an interesting question as to why the D.A. let Deluxe cop out to a fine, isn't it?"

"Yeah. Interesting just like why the D.A. wouldn't prosecute our former mayor. These politicians all shit in the same pot. And from what we heard from his daughter on the tape, she's gonna close the sting before we nail her old man's buddies the Bartlow brothers. Chances are she already blabbed about the sting to them. Whatcha think, Fraleigh?"

"I don't know, Block. As many times as I've gone over the tape on Nola's calls, it's not certain. Has Herrera made any more progress on Bartlow, Paul?"

"Yes. The deal is almost ready to go down. Bartlow will sell a half million dollars of bearer bonds on a forty percent discount, and another two million two months after the first deal. The same terms."

"Forty percent amounts to two hundred grand. Where will we get that kind of buy money?" I asked.

"It's all academic if you don't stop Nola from exposing the sting within the next day or two. You have to convince her to give us a week. However, I suggest you not mention that we know her father, sitting as surrogate judge, appointed attorney Richard Bartlow as conservator of the Paradise Hills Trust."

"I wasn't about to. What have you learned about the trust?"

"Well, Chief," Paul said as he slipped back into his professorial role, "Paradise Hills was incorporated twenty years ago by George Spencer, now deceased. It's a huge senior citizens' retirement village catering to elderly people without families. The residents signed over their property to Spencer in return for a lifetime guarantee to stay at the home. Spencer formed the trust and invested a great deal of the money in bearer bonds, and the trust is now owned by the Silicon Valley Consortium as a business enterprise."

"No wonder Bartlow was so confident that the bonds wouldn't get hot. I'll be damned—it confirms what Wong and MacLeod said. And owned by the Silicon Valley Consortium. But let me ask you, Paul, just how do you suggest that I get Nola to allow the sting?"

"Yeah. It looks like she kicked Fraleigh out of the sack when she found him balling the New York captain," the Block said. "You oughta keep that thing in your pants for a while, Fraleigh, you're messing up our political relations. Still, you should have seen Captain Ferrari, Paul. Fabulous, and tough. She looks like a movie star, but she kicked one guy's balls right over his shoulder in T. J. Brown's."

"Fraleigh's way with women has caused us trouble through the years hasn't it, Block? Or I should say his absence of a way with women has."

"What you *should* say, Paul, if anything at all, is that I was out of my head to let you two talk me into this sting. I can't think of one good thing that it's accomplished. And Block, if Captain Ferrari heard you mispronounce her name, she might give you the same treatment as the guy in the bar."

"Don't forget the sting probably got asshole Thompson wasted. It did some good right there," the Block said.

"Have we checked to see if that California suspect— what's his name, Golta—is still in the can?"

"Strange that you should mention that, Chief. You're not as senile as people say."

"He ain't senile, Paul. He's all fucked out. Those two women almost killed him."

"He does look knackered," Paul continued in his unique style of briefing the police chief. "Ken Matsukowa pursued it. Boom-Boom Golta has been out of the joint for three months. His conviction is on appeal. And guess who his lawyer is, Fraleigh?"

"Richard Bartlow."

"Absolutely correct, Chief," Paul smiled, his report completed, finally.

Thirty-two

JUDGE DAVID HENDERSON WAS A HANDSOME MAN, AND his pinstriped suit fit his lean features and graying hair. Just what everyone expected a distinguished jurist to look like. He stood to deliver his address with the assurance of a man who knew he would be listened to. Known as Maximum Dave, he got strong applause from the mostly law-and-order audience.

I found a row that had been reserved for police chiefs of the major cities in the Bay area. I sat next to the chiefs from San Francisco, San Jose, and Oakland. The moderator had announced our presence just prior to introducing the judge as keynote speaker. Henderson's glance had briefly flickered in my direction when I was introduced. The hook had been baited.

I'm not sure that the other police chiefs were that appreciative of the judge's strong criticism of casual and continuous violations of civil rights by police, but I hung on every word and gesture. If all went well, I would be taking on David Henderson within the next hour. Listening to him issue his closing challenge to the police to live up to the ethical standards of their office, I tried to anticipate the most successful strategy for confronting him. I didn't for a moment doubt what I had heard. David Henderson possessed one of the most brilliant legal minds in the country. He wouldn't be easy.

Henderson gracefully acknowledged the applause following his speech. The moderator announced a fifteen-minute break before the next speaker. I drifted along with the other chiefs toward the coffee table set up in the corridor, knowing Henderson was watching. The meeting rooms were on the second floor of the luxurious old hotel. Securing my fix of steaming caffeine in a Styrofoam cup, I wandered back to a crack in the open door, watching the judge separate himself from the crowd of ass kissers surrounding the podium. I positioned myself at a display of criminal justice publications and was intently studying the crap as he came through the door.

He made right for me. "Chief Fraleigh."

I tore myself away from a volume detailing the history of strict constructionalist legal theory to see who was speaking to me. "Judge Henderson. I enjoyed your speech," I said with complete truth. It had given me time to assess the bastard and plan his downfall as the means to continuing our sting.

"Thank you. You know, for some time I've wanted to meet with you. I wonder if you have a few minutes?"

"Of course, Judge." I stood still in the hallway as crowds surged around us, knowing that he wouldn't want to chat under these circumstances.

"It's a bit difficult to have a conversation here. Perhaps we could go down to the lobby lounge."

"Sure, Judge."

He touched my arm. "Chief, why don't you leave your coffee here. We can get some more downstairs."

"OK." I put the Styrofoam cup down on an antique table as he winced, then tagged along behind him looking thankful that I had someone to keep me from making a fool of myself in this elegant hotel.

In the lobby he headed for the Compass Rose Lounge. "It's almost deserted at this hour. We can take a table in the corner."

We walked up the carpeted stairs and stood between the twin eighteenth-century delicately carved blackamoors. A slim young blonde was playing the harp to our right.

Huge black marble pillars reached up to the thirty-foot-high ornate ceilings. "Let's sit back there." The judge headed toward the opposite end of the room while "Greensleeves" floated through the air. We strode past one of the two large cloisonné vases produced in Korea during the nineteenth century. Rare, Middle Eastern, lavishly carved mirrors inlaid with mother-of-pearl threw our reflections back at us and reminded me of another time here with a lovely woman who had identified for me the various art objects in the room before demonstrating her own artistic talent in one of the sumptuous upstairs suites.

The judge ordered a dry sherry. "I'll have a light beer," I said to the waitress, pretending not to notice Henderson's disapproving expression.

"First of all, let me congratulate you on the fine work that you've done in the police department. I know you've taken a hard line on corruption and brutality, and you've shown great courage in investigating political corruption." Stroking his chin, he added, "Of course, I'm not in a position to comment on your methods, but I certainly believe that we must insist on high ethics in politics."

"Yeah. I feel the same way, Judge."

"Yes. Actually, there was another reason why I wanted to meet with you."

I reached into my jacket pocket and turned on the recorder. Unlike the one in my hotel room in New York, this recording was legal.

"It's a delicate matter, but I know as a policeman you appreciate bluntness. It's about Nola. I understand that you've been seeing each other."

Shit. This wasn't what I had been hoping for. "Yes, Judge, we have."

"I hope that you won't take this the wrong way. Nola is my only child. She's poised on the brink of a great political career. Oh, I can understand how young people like yourselves throw caution to the winds, but it seems to me that your relationship with Nola can only hurt both of you. You're a professional policeman. Of course, there's nothing wrong with that."

Like hell there isn't, Judge. You wouldn't have come down from your throne to work me over otherwise. "I'm glad you feel that way, Judge."

"Yes, but having said that, Fraleigh, let's face it. You and Nola have traveled in different circles all your lives. Those influences aren't dissolved by moments of passion. In addition, both of you have a clear conflict of interest. She's your superior, and it's basically unfair to her. It puts her in an impossible position. I know this is distasteful for you, but I think you're man enough to realize I'm speaking only out of love and concern for Nola. I hope you'll consider what I've said, and if you have real feeling for her, consider what impact you're having on her future."

"That's fair enough, sir. I appreciate your frankness, and I'll really think about what you've said. I certainly don't want to stand in Nola's way." *As if I or anyone else could.*

"That's very good of you."

I looked away, afraid of what he'd see on my face. I needn't have bothered. Henderson was holding his sherry up to the light admiring its amber glow. I found my voice. "Judge, you know, I was impressed by your speech, but the ethical standards you were proposing seemed very high for the police service."

"Well, I'm afraid that the police must raise themselves up to the same standards that those of us in higher office hold. It is, after all, a privilege to serve the public, and those of us who are engaged in enforcing the law have not only to obey it ourselves, but to avoid even the appearance of impropriety. That's why I'm so concerned that Nola not be caught in an embarrassing situation."

"That's what I mean, Judge. You're an expert on law. Us cops aren't. Sure, we arrest people, but we rely on D.A.s and judges to rule on this stuff. My father's dead now, but once he got into a lot of trouble when he was an assistant chief in New York, even though he never broke the law."

"I was unaware. What was it all about?"

"Well, he got involved with a madam after my mother died."

"Yes, Fraleigh, but I'm afraid a man who pays for sexual services is equally guilty under the law as is the prostitute."

"Oh, my dad never paid or gave any official favors. It was a brief fling. I guess he was just lonely."

"That's the point I was trying to make, Chief. Although there was no evidence of crime with your father, a man in his position should have realized that he was disgracing himself."

"That's the way I felt at the time, Judge. Lately, though, I've been thinking. My mother went into a lengthy coma, then died. My father was a lonely man with normal sexual urges—was it so terrible that he went to bed with a woman if he didn't pay her or do any favors for her?"

He licked his lips before answering. "Fraleigh, believe me. I have no desire to add to your grief, but people who accept high public position have to accept higher standards. Your father's weakness was human, certainly, but at his rank he had to be like a judge, above reproach."

"Like a judge. It's a strange coincidence, isn't it, Judge. Like my father, you lost your wife. It must be lonely at times." I held my breath. Henderson was not only a sharp lawyer, he was a judge—surely he was going to see through my ploy.

He signaled the waitress for another sherry. I hadn't touched my beer. The waitress returned with the sherry. Picking it up he said, "When we hold high office we have to accept high standards."

"Did you accept them when you called the Deluxe Escort Service to send hookers to your house?"

He put down his sherry and glared at me. "How dare you? You're not dealing with some plainclothes cop. I regard what you just said as an insult to be reported to your superiors."

"Nola is my superior, as you mentioned, Judge. Do you really want to report it to her?"

Henderson was so angry that he could hardly speak. So far, I had lots of hypocritical bullshit on tape but nothing incriminating.

"Nola is sophisticated. You won't turn her against me because of your petty report. She's enlightened enough to recognize that the tide is turning in this country. Victimless crimes like prostitution are going to be looked at quite differently. My casual sexual encounters with the girls from the escort service aren't going to shock her the way you think they will."

"You mean your paying of prostitutes will be looked at quite differently from my father's case?"

"Fraleigh, I'm going to give you a friendly warning. Don't try to smear me. I'm not a vindictive man, but if you breathe one word of that rumor to anyone I'll destroy you."

"Your destroying days are all over, Judge. At this point I have to remind you that I'm a police officer and that anything you say can be used against you in . . ."

He laughed. "I can't imagine what Nola ever saw in someone as stupid as you. Do you think for one moment anyone would ever believe your word against mine? If you even suggest that this conversation took place, I'll see to it that your minor-league career is over. Let me have the check, waitress." His face was flushed.

I sat still while he produced his credit card for the waitress. The judge was above carrying cash, which was fine with me. She was right back with the slip. When he signed it, I picked up his card and the credit slip he had signed. "What are you doing? Give me back my card."

"Judge, I insist. The treat is on me." Looking at the bill, I saw that he drank the best sherry. I gave the waitress twenty-five bucks and told her to keep the change. "I wanted to make sure we have the same card and signature." I pulled the six copies of his credit card slips signed to the escort agency from my jacket and compared them with the one he had just signed.

"Fraleigh . . ." He had turned pale.

"They all appear to be the same, Judge. I'll mail you an evidence receipt for your credit card. Have a good day." I had hoped to get him to say something about appointing Richard Bartlow conservator, but you have to take what you get in this business. It was obvious that the judge didn't have anything else to say to me. I left him staring across the room at the harpist. She was playing Gershwin's "Someone to Watch Over Me."

Thirty-three

LIEUTENANT CATHY STEVENS CAME INTO MY OFFICE, GIV-
ing off a chill that almost turned my coffee cold.

"Good morning, Cathy."

"I've finished my investigation of the sting tape that you
assigned me. I'm ready to report."

"That was quick. Go ahead."

She shuffled through some papers and pulled out a single
sheet. "I found that on numerous occasions Sergeant Herrera
and Police Officer Falcone engaged in sex acts at the sting
location as well as other places. Some of these took place
on duty. It appears that these acts were initiated by Sergeant
Herrera." Lieutenant Stevens again shuffled through her
papers while I contained an impulse to tell her to get on
with it. She was obviously uptight.

"Both Policewoman Falcone and Sergeant Herrera were
unaware that their activities were being taped."

"Both unaware?"

"Precisely, Chief. Shall I continue?" Cathy's blue eyes
behind her reading glasses weren't friendly.

"Please."

"Officer Falcone says that Sergeant Herrera frequently
made sexual overtures toward her. Her own marriage was
experiencing some difficulties, and she was confused over
her relationship with Herrera. He was her supervisor. She felt
apprehensive about resisting his advances at the same time
she experienced increasing tension from the sting operation.
She was coming into a good deal of contact with very

aggressive criminals and believed she depended on Herrera and the other male officers for protection. An undercover operation puts all of the officers under great stress, but especially Mary."

I remembered Mary Falcone wiggling her ass at the guys in the back room when she didn't believe I was there, and the way she had fended off Charley Thompson. Was this the same gal being described by Cathy?

"Did you have a question, Chief?"

"Yes. Did you find out how the tape came to be sent to Supervisor Henderson?"

"I can only guess. I had the package dusted for fingerprints. It was wiped clean. However, the tape itself had a single print. I had the fingerprint unit run it against police personnel prints. It came back positive. It's Sergeant Myers's thumbprint. He was smart enough to wipe the package, but careless enough to leave a print on the tape itself."

"That was fast work, Cathy. How did Myers come into possession of the tape?"

"I can only speculate. I decided not to interview Myers until you approved. But I did find out that he had been designated by his lieutenant to inventory all sting records, tapes, and evidence vouchers. They've been producing a hell of a volume, and the records lieutenant put Myers on it to free up the other people and probably to get rid of him. You know what a jerk Myers is."

Damn. We had of necessity alerted the records lieutenant to the deluge of reports he would be getting. Never in a million years did anyone think he would tell Myers about the sting. And I was pretty sure Myers had provided Fritz Gerhart with the report of the incident in the diner. Gerhart had probably engineered the whole thing and sent the tape to Nola to get her to vote against me. Never underestimate the capacity of the bureaucracy to fuck up. Maybe Murphy's Law should be changed to Fraleigh's Law.

"Yes, I know Myers, Cathy. No one cleared with me telling him about The Blue Mirage. Did Myers actually go to the bar?"

"Yes. Mary told me that they all thought you had sent him. Myers talked up how close he is to you. It's common knowledge that Sergeant Herrera and Mary are involved with each other. My guess is that Myers hoped sooner or later he'd catch them. He probably hid in the recording room and made the tape himself. He's found lots of excuses to spend time back there alone. Everyone avoids him for obvious reasons, so he's had a free run of the place."

"Cathy, what the hell is going on with Mary that she let this happen? She's married, isn't she?"

"Chief, I told you when I took this assignment I wouldn't stand for Officer Falcone being made a scapegoat, and you promised agreement."

"A scapegoat? She's part of a porno tape session at our secret sting location and a tape of it gets sent to the chairman of the Board of Supervisors—and she's a scapegoat?"

"Chair*person*. Have you ever placed yourself in the mind of a twenty-two-year-old officer coming under great stress?"

I remembered my own experience in New York. The bodega shootings, arresting Gloria Fell. My father's death. "No. But I'll try, Cathy. Go on."

"Mary Falcone has had the misfortune to have gotten involved with two real losers. First her husband. Then on the rebound, Manny Herrera. She's very young and confused. Her husband has openly been carrying on with other women. When she complained he told her to leave if she didn't like it. At work, her supervisor who's married and has three young kids was hitting on her. It's not her fault that you can't control the male nymphomaniacs we have as supervisors."

"I take it you got all this from Officer Falcone?"

"Yes. Sergeant Herrera refused to make a statement to me. I want him suspended, and both of them removed from the sting immediately."

"We'll see about the suspension, but both of them will be out of the sting soon."

"I recommend now," Lieutenant Stevens said.

"Has Herrera severed his relationship with Officer Falcone?"

Cathy shifted in her seat. "He and Mary have set up house together."

"What? Cathy, I appreciate the job you've done, but honest to God, it doesn't read like Falcone is an innocent victim in this."

"I knew the male establishment would close ranks. Get someone else to do your dirty work." She placed the file on my desk and started to walk out. In the doorway she paused. "Another thing. You've got to take Nunzio Papa out of the operation. He's a basket case. Hector Gonzales has been around The Blue Mirage. Once he went into the inside. Fortunately, Nunzio wasn't there. Unfortunately, Gonzales left before reinforcements arrived."

"I know."

"And those jerks are still doing Hector jokes on Nunzio. Not only that, but Gerhart is on Nunzio's case about you and him in the diner. Whatever you two were doing together it ended up in the newspaper and Nunzio can't cope. To make it worse, his colleagues are now engaging in their sick humor by asking every night if he's going out drinking with you."

Despite myself, I smiled. It was a mistake.

"God, you're just like them. I give up." She slammed the door on the way out.

Denise buzzed me. "Chief, Supervisor Henderson would like to see you in the mayor's office."

Thirty-four

THAT NIGHT IN THE BACK ROOM OF THE STING WE OBSERVED Sergeant Herrera work an Hispanic burglar-hype. "Man, we're *hermosos*—brothers. Not like this Anglo cunt." The squat dark-skinned crook pointed to Mary Falcone, who showed no reaction.

"Amigo, I can't give you more than fifty bucks for it." Herrera pointed at an Uzi assault rifle. "I got to earn a living too. And you got a hot serial number there. I can't sell it to some guy like I'm his local gun store."

The give and take had been going on for about twenty min-utes. I watched Herrera and Falcone, two skilled cops, talking to the crook, always for the tape. They had maneuvered him into bragging about where he had stolen the gun, as well as about two other burglaries he had committed. They were gathering just as much evidence as the crime scene tech crew or interrogating dicks were. Why then were the sting people under so much more stress, as Cathy Stevens said? Maybe because they had to play the part. Why did a third-generation Mexican-American professional like Manny Herrera, whose father was a dentist, care to be called brother by a dope addict, thief, and potential killer? And how did he feel about Mary Falcone, the woman that he had left his wife and kids for, being called an Anglo cunt? And how did she feel? Yeah, being in the same room with these characters was stress all right.

In the back room, we sat in darkness broken only by the green video screen and dimly lighted recording equipment being monitored by Nunzio. I wasn't sorry that the darkness covered his increasingly twitchy face. Paul and the Block had convinced me that pulling Nunzio right now would really crush him, but we would have to watch him closely. The sting was racking up police casualties. Luther Banks, our only black cop working the sting, was on sick leave with a heart attack. He was thirty-one years old. Mary Falcone and Manny Herrera were hardly the mental-health models of the year. The sting was running out of cops, as well as time.

I had a tape recorder in my attaché case, and cassette tapes of Nola's phone conversations and my session with Judge Henderson. I had come here to steel myself to do what was necessary to convince Nola to let the sting run at least until the board meeting. My appointment with her was first thing in the morning. I was getting in the mood.

Herrera got rid of the hype and we went into the other room. He hadn't been at all friendly when I greeted him earlier. He knew he was in trouble, and was guarded if not downright sullen. On the other hand, he was quite nice to Falcone, who wouldn't even look in my direction. It didn't appear that Herrera knew about the videotaping.

"Bartlow is due the day after tomorrow with the first installment of the bonds. He wants to see the dough. All of it. I think we can get a sale by flashing the two hundred thousand. Then I'll offer him twenty grand or so for a portion of the bonds. He'll scream for the rest, but once we have the sale on tape, screw him," Herrera said.

"Sergeant, I don't want you to take Bartlow lightly. This is confidential, but we think after he got ripped off in Chinatown he's covering his tracks. He may have blown Charley Thompson up as part of the effort."

"Since you ain't got any fucking intention of paying Bartlow, Chief, let alone the dough to do it, what's the difference?" the Block said.

"Chief, I hear we're closing down. What's the truth?" Herrera asked.

"The truth is that so many people know about the sting that we'll have to close it soon. Hopefully you can finish Bartlow before we do," I said.

Herrera shook his head. "I don't see how we can nail Bartlow tight without another week of dealing."

"I'll try my best to get you three more days, but this is beyond my authority now."

He scowled at me. "You mean, Chief—you told some of the politicians?"

"*I* didn't, but at least one supervisor knows. I don't think the Bartlows do yet. As soon as we see signs that they do, we close for safety reasons."

The next morning, walking to Nola's office, I kept fingering the tapes in my pocket, wondering if I could bring myself to use them. Could I actually deal off her father in return for keeping the sting going? To let the bastard go on to the federal court?

Yes, I could deal him off. Who knew—maybe his ethical hypocrisy would fit right in on the court. The real question was whether I could take the reflection of me that I would see on Nola's face when I played the tapes. That's why I had gone to watch the bruised and battered cops at work— to listen to them ask for more time to risk getting blown away by dirtbags. Marquess of Queensbury niceties weren't going to nail murdering crooks like the Bartlow brothers. I was prepared. I felt the cassettes.

I hadn't seen Nola since our angry confrontation. I was braced for a fight, but she glided toward me with nothing but affection on her lovely face. She wore a blue business suit that underemphasized her curves in a way that only made them more alluring.

"Fraleigh." She brushed me on the lips and stood back studying me. "I missed you."

I fought, but the familiar spell was beginning to take hold. "Yeah." I walked to her window to look out at Silicon Valley.

The empire of the Clark Masseys.

"Hey, you're still pissed at me. I guess I climbed all over you when you were under a lot of stress."

My suspicions were building. What the hell was going on here? Her mood was unexpected.

"Fraleigh, I have some big news. You know I'm scheduled to run for election in two months?"

"Yes."

"Well, I made a decision this morning. I'm not going to run."

"What?" I came back from the window to look at her. She was serious. "Did you get some kind of appointment?" That was it. Her father's connections had probably gotten her a bigger job.

"No, no," she laughed. "You're so cynical. My father called me this morning. No one knew about this, Fraleigh, but he was in line for an appointment as a federal judge. A lifetime appointment. He told me he withdrew."

I sat down, remembering Henderson staring into space when I left him in the Compass Rose.

"He simply didn't think all of the behind-the-scenes dealing and politicking were worth it. Daddy thought it wasn't in keeping with the dignity of the court. I know how much he wanted it, and the prestige. I'm proud of him for having the character to make the decision."

"I had a drink with him yesterday in San Francisco." I watched her face for the slightest sign that he had shared any of our conversation about the Deluxe Escort Service.

"Yes. He told me." She came over and took both of my hands, sinking to her knees so that her green eyes were level with mine. "I'm so ashamed that I never got up the courage to tell you that my father had been pressuring me not to see you. You should have heard it from me, not him."

"That's OK, Nola." I was totally confused. Not even Meryl Streep could pull off this good an acting job.

"My father's going back to New York. He's resigning from the Superior Court to teach legal ethics at New York Law School."

"Yeah. I heard him speak yesterday. He'll be good. Maybe he'll invite me as a guest lecturer."

"I know you're hurt," she said, "but don't be so bitter, so down on everyone including yourself. You *could* give a lecture on ethics. It was your conduct as much as my father's that made me realize I was becoming like Bartlow and Kendle, wheeling and dealing, letting personal ambition cloud my judgment. You're so uncompromising on policing, unwilling to yield to political pressures. I've decided to join a public interest law firm in the city. I'll just be another lawyer on the staff, but I'll be doing good things instead of some of what I've been doing lately in this job."

I sat there feeling like shit, seeing the old Nola come back, and wondering what she'd think of my ethics if she knew about the tapes in my pocket or the truth about her father's decision. "Maybe you ought to think this over a bit, Nola."

"Oh, I have. I feel a tremendous weight off my back." She put her hand to my cheek. "Don't worry though. I'll still be in office on Friday to vote for you."

"Nola, I don't give a damn about that. I need five more days for the sting."

"I don't see how you can pull that off. Today is Wednesday. You'll have to respond to Bartlow's questions on the diner incident during the supervisors' session Friday. If you don't satisfy Fenton and Kadisch, you'll lose their votes. I think you'll have to be able to say that the undercover stuff is over."

"You know, the so-called diner incident is a phony, Nola. Nunzio Papa and I were on the way to the sting. Gerhart leaked a distorted version that would never stand up in court. We weren't drinking. Nothing really happened."

"The trouble is, this isn't a court and they're really gunning for you. You can't talk about the sting unless you've ended it, and you can't evade the questions or they'll appoint Gerhart. You've got no place to go."

"Nola, think with me. You're smart as hell on this political stuff. Come up with a stall for the board."

"You know I've never been crazy about the entrapment possibilities of the sting. If I hadn't been so blinded by my own political desire to get something on Duane, I probably would have insisted that you close it down."

"Just five more days, Nola. We're talking about a murder as well as a massive fraud."

She shrugged. "I don't know. That sex tape, the whole thing. I'm not sure it's fair even to the cops to have them work under that kind of pressure. Have you reassigned any of them?"

"No. It will all be over in five days. I've come here with their request to ask you to give them a chance to finish what they started. After all, they've risked their lives and are close to nailing some bad bastards. And the fraud Bartlow is pulling off will leave quite a few old people destitute."

"The cops have put a lot of pressure on you and it's showing. I've never seen you this way. The way you were in New York. You're on the edge. You've got to face reality, you'll never be able to right all wrongs."

"Five more days, Nola. Please?"

She shook her head. "You're persuasive. If I can think of something, I'll try to get you more time—but it's a long shot."

Thirty-five

MY BEEPER WENT OFF AS I CROSSED THE LOBBY OF CITY hall. I stepped around to the corner exit where the public phones were located, and called Denise, as I had been instructed. I chose the public phones knowing the city hall operators passed the dull moments away listening to extension calls on the city lines.

"Chief." Denise was excited. "The Block said it was urgent to let you know that Mario Golta, the bomber, has been shot. It just happened. The ambulance is on its way to the Medical Center's emergency room."

"OK, Denise. I'll be there in five minutes."

"That's too soon for that distance. Be careful in traffic, Chief, a few more minutes won't make any difference."

I was still shaking my head over her unsolicited advice when I pulled into the emergency-room area. A marked police cruiser and the electric-blue Trans Am that the Block had taken a fancy to were parked in the red zone. I joined them and went into the hospital.

In the emergency treatment room Golta was surrounded by people in white. A small young Hispanic woman wearing glasses applied a stethoscope to Golta's chest while a tall red-headed guy checked the electronic equipment hooked up to him. A skinny Oriental man hooked an intravenous feeder into the patient, who had his eyes closed and was taking deep breaths. It took me a moment to figure out which one was the doctor. The Block stood against the wall chewing gum and joking with a young uniformed cop. I joined them.

"He stopped a couple of slugs, but unfortunately, he's going to be OK. That is, if the female sawbones knows what she's talking about. Golta's scared though. He never knew what hit him. He stopped for a signal light and a car pulled up next to him and started blasting. He took one in the chest and one in the shoulder. He got a better deal than all the poor bastards he sent on their way with bombs—although the world is probably better off without them. The doc thinks he's coming out of shock now. You want to talk to him?" the Block said.

I went over to the gurney. "Mario, I'm Fraleigh, police department. How are you feeling?" I had learned never to ask permission of the doctor before questioning a suspect. Given a chance to think about it, they'd routinely tell you *no questions*. The doctor glanced at me from above her surgery mask, then she continued exploring Golta's bloody shoulder wound.

"I'd feel better if they had a white man working on me. Goddamned hospitals. Save money. Hire spicks and gooks. The hell with the patients."

Neither the doctor nor the Oriental nurse reacted, but the red-haired orderly said, "Why don't you stop being an asshole and keep your mouth shut?"

"That's enough, Roger," the doctor said firmly. The orderly grunted, but closed his trap, which was OK with me.

"Mario, we'd like to get the guy responsible for shooting you up. Did you see the guy who did it, or get a license plate number?"

"Fuck off, copper. I want a lawyer."

"Sure, Mario. But, I have to give you what we call a dying declaration. Do you believe you are about to die and have no hope of recovery?"

"What? What the fuck are you talking about?"

The doctor rested her instruments and shook her head at

me. Golta momentarily raised up from the table and looked at me before sinking back with his eyes closed. I held my hand up in silent warning to the doctor.

"Mario, we both know that you've sent many people on their way through the years. I know you would normally plan to blow up whoever shot you, but you're not going to be able to get even on this one." The doctor turned and looked at Golta to see if he was going to protest his innocence. "We can do it for you. Why don't you tell me who did it?" I said.

"Drop dead. Leave me alone."

The doctor had resumed work on his shoulder, but when Golta whined to be left alone, she looked up at me and once again started to speak. I held up my index finger. One more question.

"OK, Mario—I'll call your lawyer for you. According to our records he's Richard Bartlow, right?"

Golta jerked upright on the table. "That little scumbag! I don't want no part of him! Get me *anyone* else!"

"Did he have anything to do with the shooting, Mario?" The doctor was letting me continue, but I suspected she was going to chase me any second.

"Get my brother in here. His name's in my wallet. He'll handle this for me. I'll even the score. It may be the last thing that I'll do, but my lawyer will be paid in spades."

"Did this have anything to do with the car bombing on Broad Street two weeks ago? The Ford Galaxie that went up with Charley Thompson in it?"

"Doctor." The white-coated Oriental pointed at one of the instruments that indicated God knows what. My questions had caused a reaction, all right.

"That's all for now, Officer." The doctor was just as firm as she had been with the orderly. She moved quickly to Golta's other side, held up a hypodermic needle to the light and sprayed a little liquid upward, then injected the rest into his arm.

"You're not as dumb as you look, copper. But I'm still going to take care of this myself," Golta said.

The doctor jerked her thumb at me. No appeal this time, but I wasn't going to get any more out of Golta, anyway.

The Block and I walked into the hall. "That was slick telling him he was croaking, Fraleigh. It got him to open up a little. Of course, if he keeps making cracks about the doctor and the nurse, it may turn out to be true. But he sure sounded like he was putting the bombing and the shooting on shyster Bartlow, didn't he?"

"Yeah. But he didn't give us much for court, Block."

"I know, but who would've thought that little wimpy attorney would turn into a homicidal maniac? What's got into him?"

"I could never figure why he was willing to involve a two-bit fence like Bolero in a big securities deal to begin with. Then, Charley Thompson—who's the only connection between him and Bolero—gets taken out. Now, the day before the securities deal is to go down, someone attempts a hit on Golta, the only contact between Bartlow and the bombing."

"If you got the right scoop, Fraleigh, Bartlow picked Bolero because he figured he could off a two-bit fence without any big deal. We better get Manny out of circulation before he's next on the hit parade."

"Manny's safe until he pays off Bartlow, but we need to put a guard outside Golta's room. Also, let's apply for an order to bug his room. I'd love to hear the conversation between him and his brother about Bartlow."

"A court order? Getting legal all of a sudden, ain't you, Fraleigh? But, I guess you had no choice in New York. There was no time, and those New York cops would've said no if you asked them to apply for a bug license."

"I don't know what I'd do without your analysis of the case, Block," I said, scowling at Paul English coming through the automatic door of the emergency-room entrance.

Judging from the look on his face, he wasn't bearing good news. Then again, I couldn't remember the last time I had heard any good news.

"Did you get anything from Golta?" Paul said.

"Yeah. After Fraleigh violated his rights by giving him a phony dying declaration, Golta let it slip that the little shyster weasel Bartlow was behind the bombing of Charley Thompson, and probably the attempted hit on Golta. We think Manny's next, as soon as he pays off Bartlow on the bonds."

"I wouldn't be at all surprised—but I wonder if we'll ever pull off the transfer? I've got bad news, Fraleigh."

"When have you ever had any other kind?"

"Now, Chief, you must be supportive of your subordinates under stress. Do you want the good news first or the bad?"

"Knowing you, it's probably bad and worse, so go ahead in any order."

"Very well. The good news is that Manny has Bartlow coming in to do business at fourteen hundred hours tomorrow. I don't think he's ready to sell, but we'll have to figure the money soon."

"Money? What fucking money? Fraleigh is lucky he can scrape together twenty grand let alone two hundred thousand."

"Precisely, Block," Paul said. "That's what I'm trying to explain to him. Manny and I are convinced that Bartlow won't sell any of the bonds unless he sees two hundred thousand and believes that he'll soon be getting the whole amount. Manny's plan to get him on tape selling twenty thousand worth of bonds won't work if we don't have two hundred thousand in flash money. And we may be finished anyway. Nunzio Papa flipped out last night. He took his wife to dinner to celebrate their anniversary. He looks so scroungy the waiter refused to serve him and made a crack about his wife. Nunzio blew and belted the guy. A brawl ensued and our gendarmes took Nunzio in. Captain Toll suspended him after he started yelling and screaming at headquarters. He's in no shape to participate, and as you know, Luther Banks is out with a heart attack. And oh, I almost forgot to mention that Sergeant Myers in records reported all this to Captain Gerhart. And guess what? Duane Bartlow has called a two o'clock press conference to discuss serious misconduct in the police department."

"This is the good news?"

"I'll leave it up to you to interpret, Chief. I've solved another mystery. I checked with Sacramento. The computer searches on Bolero were done from Sergeant Myers's terminal. As you know, he is quite friendly with Captain Gerhart. Also, I found out Myers turned the report on you and Nunzio over to our friendly captain just before the story ended up in the paper."

"Well, the public has a right to know—and all that stuff, Paul. But getting back to continuing the sting, the three of us can cover Mary and Manny from the back room if we can hook the Bartlow brothers into a meet."

"I don't see how we can nail them. Myers is reporting everything to Gerhart and if he discovers Bartlow is endangered by the sting, he'd warn him rather than lose his clout at city hall."

"You're right, Paul, but we have to assume that Myers hasn't yet figured out that Dick Barry and Richard Bartlow are one and the same, so he hasn't blown the whistle to Gerhart yet."

"Yeah, the chief is right, Paul," the Block said. "Myers is dumb. A real asshole. He ran to Gerhart with the diner fight and is probably all excited about the fucking and sucking tape. I bet he ain't tumbled yet to the main event on Bartlow. And Gerhart's another asshole. He can't add two and two if it's right in front of him. He's getting his jollies off nailing Fraleigh on the diner caper and I'll bet my paycheck *he* mailed the cop porno tape to Nola Henderson. He probably thinks he's knocked Fraleigh out for the count. I bet the jerk is studying how to sound smart for Friday's interview for chief, figuring Nola and the other two gals have backed away from Fraleigh, which is probably true anyway."

"Hmm, do I detect some devious Fraleigh strategy emerging?" Paul said.

"Block, take Myers out for a few beers. Keep him away from the sting and complain that I shut down The Blue Mirage yesterday and started a big new sting in a gas station on the other side of town. You know—bitch like crazy that the bar sting was just getting started."

"Do you think he'll fall for it, Chief? You know I hardly ever complain," the Block said.

Paul choked. "Despite your uncharacteristic complaining, Block, I don't see it working. Even if Gerhart only informs Bartlow that a bar sting is closed—wouldn't it warn them enough?"

"One other thing you will let slip, Block, is word that there's an investigation beginning next week into some kind of a multi-million-dollar theft of bearer bonds," I said.

"They'll go apeshit trying to close with Manny before the investigation, right?"

Paul said, "Perhaps, Block, if all the other ifs are correct—but the real bad news, Fraleigh, is that Mary and Manny have split. He's gone back to his wife and she to her husband. They're not talking to each other, so I'm not sure how we can let them do Bartlow."

"I don't give a goddamn what the state of their romance is! They're cops and if they want to continue to be cops, they'll damn well do their job."

Paul held up his hand. "If you yell any louder there won't be any job—everyone in town will know about the sting."

"Paul, I'm not kidding. That tape puts both of them in deep trouble, and if they let the sting down now, I'm not going to lift a finger to save them. I want you to personally convey that message to them. You, and I, and the Block can cover them from the back room for the meeting with Bartlow. In the meantime, I'll call Daddy Warbucks. If he's available, the Block and I will drive up to San Francisco and take him to lunch."

"I don't know if even Warbucks can get the FBI to come up with that kind of cash at the last minute, Fraleigh."

"Neither do I, Paul, but if you have a better idea, let's hear it."

"How about we go back to New York and hold up MacLeod and Mad Anthony Wong?"

"I'm glad you find this so amusing, Block. Jorge Mendez is in the hospital shot full of holes. I'm about to get fired. The sting is going down the drain, all the cops who worked on it are going down the drain, and the Bartlow brothers are going to walk. It's hilarious."

"Lighten up, Fraleigh. You been sour balls since New York. I was just trying to cheer you up."

"The Block is right, Fraleigh. You shouldn't take all this so personally. Remember Shakespeare: None of us should see salvation in justice. Your troubles are not going to be vanquished by convicting the Bartlows."

"I really need you reciting Shakespeare right now, Paul. Try some of it on Herrera and Falcone to get them back to work."

Thirty-six

I SPOKE BRIEFLY ON THE TELEPHONE WITH SENIOR SPECIAL Agent Warbucks, who indicated that it would be his pleasure to be taken to lunch at the Washington Street Bar and Grill in San Francisco. When the Block and I arrived, I could see why. It was the kind of ambience a guy like Warbucks enjoyed. He was a presence. Six two, shaven bald head. A linebacker in college twenty years earlier, who had stayed in shape. The patrons of the restaurant delighted in rubbernecking for celebrities, as much as in consuming the good food and expensive wines. They were looking for local politicians, visiting movie stars, or national big shots. None of them made Warbucks for being FBI. He was obviously Hollywood. An actor, maybe a producer. If they gave him a chance, he would be whatever they fancied him to be. But this afternoon he was himself. One hundred and twenty percent FBI. His fellow agents who had read Orphan Annie comic strips had nicknamed him Daddy.

"Ah, Fraleigh. Such a pleasure to enjoy fine food on you locals. And you brought the Block along. Wonderful. He's guaranteed to eat more than I, so no one will be horrified when I gluttonize myself on Silicon City."

"Fuck you, Warbucks," the Block said, downing a long swig of Heineken from the bottle while Daddy savored his favorite drink, an extra-dry Beefeater martini.

A fifteen-year member of the local bureau, Warbucks knew San Francisco Bay Area politics and crime backward and forward. He had been an invaluable partner in nailing

278

the previous mayor of Silicon City. There were never any illusions that you split the credit fifty-fifty with the FBI. Or for that matter the lunch bills. The bureau got 100 percent of the credit for cases and we locals got 100 percent of the lunch bills. But when you needed a shylock, there wasn't much choice.

"Well, Fraleigh. What new troubles do you have since we helped you depose your mayor? And what new requests do you have of your beneficent federal government?"

"We're running a new sting operation, Daddy. We've got a big one going down tomorrow and I need some flash money."

"That should be no problem, provided what you're doing is halfway legal and the bureau can take most of the credit for making the case. How much dough do you need?"

"Two hundred grand."

Warbucks spit out a significant portion of his extra-dry Beefeater martini. "Jesus Christ. You're serious. And all these years I thought you were rational."

"I'm hungry. Let's order some grub before you two start duking it out," the Block said. "I got to warn you, Warbucks, last couple of weeks Fraleigh's gotten back into punching it out."

"I can see that," Warbucks said, staring at my forehead with what I thought was very bad taste.

"Don't kid yourself. He can still hit, and he's sneaky fast like all the boxers. He got lumped up in New York because he had his eye on women instead of his opponents."

"An understandable if serious weakness," said Warbucks, watching a young blonde in a miniskirt walk to the bar. "However, I assume that you failed to duck a real haymaker, Fraleigh, if you're serious about us coming up with two hundred grand."

The waitress took our orders, blinking only once or twice when the Block and Warbucks ordered two of everything and more drinks.

"Daddy," I said, "don't be too hasty in your judgment. The flash money is to allow the brother of one Duane Bartlow, who sits on the Board of Supervisors, to sell us stolen bonds. The same Duane Bartlow who tried to block your indictment of Mayor Middleston. The same Duane Bartlow who would dearly like to appoint a chief of police who would screw up the case against Mayor Middleston . . ."

"Hold on for a minute, for Christ's sake. OK. You got my interest. But, as you well know Fraleigh, it is unconstitutional to visit the sins of the father upon the son, let alone the sins of a brother upon a brother."

"Not these brothers, Daddy. Duane got his brother appointed a guardian to a senior citizens' trust. The brother's an attorney who is stealing bonds from the trust. We've got him on videotape and I confirmed all of it in New York where he made his first attempt to peddle the bonds. In addition, we think these two fine citizens of Silicon City probably had a hype by the name of Charley Thompson blown up to cover their trail on the bonds."

"So why do you need me? It sounds like you nailed the bastards."

I sighed. "Remember our D.A., Daddy?—the guy who wouldn't prosecute Mayor Middleston? We need just one more session. All we have on tape so far is Bartlow giving us one stolen bond. The D.A. insists on at least two buys to avoid entrapment defenses, and unless Richard Bartlow sees the whole nut, we're not going to get him tight enough so that our fearless D.A. will prosecute."

"That sounds fairly legit. Maybe I can help. When will you need the money?"

"Tomorrow morning."

"You have been sparring without your headgear. It would take a week or two if I can pull it off at all."

"Trouble is, Pappy, that when I go for the chief's interview on Friday morning, the sting will be blown. Tomorrow is our last chance."

"Blown by a certain captain, right?"

"A captain who may be the next police chief, yes. We probably have enough now to arrest Bartlow, the lawyer, but I think the brains behind him is the politician—and if we don't get the flash money for tomorrow's show on candid camera, we're finished."

"Hm . . ." Warbucks thoughtfully chewed a piece of his large T-bone steak while signaling the waitress for another martini. "For some reason, my boss is a great admirer of yours, Fraleigh. Of course, we both know he's an egotistical paper-shuffling asshole, but he and our illustrious U.S. Attorney would love a big news conference telling the world how they were cracking down on political corruption. They might even allow you to lurk in the background for some of the TV shots."

"I don't give a shit about the publicity. They can have it all. Do you think you can get the dough by tomorrow morning? Bartlow is due in the afternoon."

"Well, what gives us a chance is that you guys have done all the work, and these are local politicians. The big crooks in Congress are off-limits after what they did to the FBI budget and charter subsequent to ABSCAM. It is also convenient that local politicians are almost invariably in the opposite party to this administration. Not that such things ever influence law enforcement decisions, of course. I'll do my best, but to be honest, Fraleigh, you may have wasted a lunch. It is a lot of cash."

"How soon will you know?"

"By tonight. I'll give you a tinkle. You know that if we do come up with it, our team will be there to make sure it doesn't get ripped off from you local yokels."

"That may be a problem, Daddy. We can accommodate you in the back room provided you don't eat another lunch like you just had, but it's too small for anyone else besides Paul English, the Block, and me."

"We'll bring Wheeler. He's a pain in the ass, but he's skinny. They'll never let that kind of dough out without at least two of us being present."

"Isn't there anyone else besides Wheeler?" Bobby Wheeler had wounded the victim and a cop in a robbery hostage escapade we handled the previous year.

"Hey, he's a fully qualified special agent of the Federal Bureau of Investigation. I can't allow you to criticize him. For your information, I'm stuck with him. Orders from Washington. My experience and steadiness will help Agent Wheeler to overcome his inclinations toward hasty action in combat situations. Unquote."

"Make sure you load his weapon with blanks, Daddy, or I'll have to slap him down when things get going," the Block said as he drained the last of his beer and began to look for the waitress.

"I may incapacitate him myself, Block. Not to worry, Fraleigh. We'll muddle through," Daddy said.

"Sure we will," I said, as my beeper went off with the message that I call Denise immediately.

Thirty-seven

I DIALED DENISE ON THE CAR PHONE AS THE BLOCK NARrowly missed an elderly female crossing the Embarcadero. She flipped us the finger while Denise was informing me that Supervisor Henderson had requested my presence in her office immediately. I told Denise that I would be there in forty-five minutes.

"I'll get you there in nothing flat, Boss," the Block said.

"Take it easy, Block. There's no hurry at all," I said, as he forced a Volkswagen filled with young children passengers onto the shoulder of the freeway. There was one thing to be said for the Block's driving. It didn't give me much room for worrying about the summons to Nola's office.

Forty minutes later, her male secretary announced me over the intercom and then indicated that I should go right in. She sat behind her desk and studied me, her tinted glasses propped back into her hair. She wore a pale-green business suit and a matching scarf which called attention to her lovely green, and totally unreadable, eyes.

"Sit down, Fraleigh."

I obeyed, and she handed me a letter. "This came in the morning mail."

The letter was on New York City Police Department letterhead. I skipped the text and looked down to the signature line. It had been signed by the commanding officer of the One Seven Detective Squad—the precinct where our hotel had been located. The letter said that pursuant to New York State law, the victims of Penal Code Section 250.05,

Eavesdropping, had to be notified, and that the enclosed crime report constituted such notification.

Feeling her watching me I used all of my willpower not to reach up and dry the film of sweat starting to appear on my brow. In turgid bureaucratic prose the letter went on to inform her that investigation had not yielded sufficient information for a prosecution, and that unless she came forward with further evidence, the case would be considered closed.

I read the copy of the UF61 which had been enclosed. She was listed as the victim; the place of occurrence room 818 of the hotel; and the time of occurrence between 1900 and 1000 hours on her last day in New York. I hadn't fooled Paddy Fitzgerald at all with my ploy about bugging a house, and he had been more than cooperative with his interrogators by supplying Nola's name, room number, and California address. The UF61 listed me under the caption, *suspect*. The narrative section indicated that the information had come from statements made by Paddy Fitzgerald during his interrogation for other crimes. The report concluded that no other evidence had been found to corroborate Fitzgerald's statement that he had provided eavesdropping equipment to me in my hotel room.

I took a deep breath and looked up at Nola. Her glance riveted me. I gently put the letter and the 61 on her desk.

"Jesus Christ. You really did it. You bugged my room. I can't believe I'm going through this scene, Fraleigh." She picked up the 61 and read it, putting her finger on the caption containing the time and date of occurrence. "That's when you began to act funny. When you spoke to me on the phone you were excited about information MacLeod had given you about the Bartlows. Then suddenly you were cagey, picked a fight with me, and stormed out."

I shifted in my chair, looking past her out the window. For once the sky was pure blue and the bay shimmered in the late afternoon sun. The kind of day that made Northern

California special. The lunch I had enjoyed in San Francisco had turned to lead.

Her eyes widened and held mine, even though I tried to look away. "That was the night. . ." She was silent for a long moment then said, "Did you peep through the keyhole too, Fraleigh? Maybe got some videotapes of Clark and me screwing? What did you do with the recordings? Take them back to your cop friends in headquarters for a showing? A beer party with lots of laughs? I'm trying to understand. Was I some kind of suspect? Or is this pathological with you? A kind of fanaticism like you have about this sting operation. Do you guys get off looking through the one-way windows trapping people, even each other, in sex acts?" She paused for breath. "Are you just going to sit there, Fraleigh? Not even say a word?" Her voice had risen.

"You're not all that innocent are you, Nola?" I found my voice, but it was flat, exhausted. "You did discuss the sting with Clark during your political wheeling and dealing. And with your father, didn't you?"

"My father? My father is an expert on law. A man of integrity. I hate to hear someone like you even mention his name. Someone like you, slinking around spying on people. I wish I had listened to my father about you."

"Your father . . ." I caught myself. There was no point in hurting her more.

"Go on, Fraleigh. You were about to say something about my father. What was it?" She was furious.

"Nothing."

"I can't wait until Friday morning for the pleasure of voting you out of office. If you had any decency, you'd resign now and save the department the ordeal."

"The ordeal for the department will come after you and your colleagues appoint some crook you can control. Everything will be nice and cozy for those criminals who are close to the pols. The only losers will be the honest cops and the taxpaying slobs who get ripped off by thieves with political connections."

"Oh, yes. And you'd prevent that, wouldn't you, Fraleigh. Stings and videotapes and recorders and spies everywhere. You'd run a police state—but you're not going to get the chance. I'm curious to see if you have the nerve to show up Friday. Even the cops won't support you when they find out the truth."

I got up and leaned on her desk, feeling my face flushed. "I'll be there Friday. I'll own up to anything I did, if you'll admit what you spilled and to whom about a confidential fraud and murder investigation. Let's see who the public supports—me, or you, with all your righteous bullshit that just happens to provide perfect cover for crooks in public office. Oh, and the cops, I don't have any illusions about the cops. Most of them will cheer you on. They never support the boss until they see what you politicians replace him with. But nothing will keep me from being there Friday. It will be an honor to be fired by people like you and Bartlow."

I had been shaking with anger, but walking away from city hall it hit me. I had gotten used to the chief's job. Making things happen. Picking out good people and giving them assignments that would help their careers. Helping them send crooks to jail. But I was about to be fired. And I had lost Nola. That ache went much deeper than the job. How had it happened? All of it had come inexorably out of the sting. What had Nola said?—"Your sting weaves tangled webs." No one had gotten more tangled than I, and despite my bravado with Nola, I was filled with a sense of loss. A sense of failure.

Thirty-eight

"MYERS ATE IT UP. HE COULD HARDLY GET AWAY FROM me fast enough to pass everything on to Gerhart. And your strategy worked, Fraleigh," the Block was crowing. "Manny got a call from shyster Bartlow. Bartlow was trying to play it cool, but he was pissing in his pants to get the deal done. He must of swallowed the story of the bond investigation beginning next week. So instead of some more dicking around, we got a sale this afternoon. Even the fucking FBI is on time for once. Nice going Warbucks."

Warbucks had seen a lot of action for an FBI agent. We had been in a shootout together a year before, and he had pissed ice water. But now he was nervous. Somehow he had secured the money. He opened an imitation leather attaché case containing two thousand one-hundred-dollar bills. It was just like the FBI to use a Woolworth's container for all that dough. The Block, Paul English, and I crowded together with Manny Herrera and Mary Falcone to gaze down at the neatly bound and stacked bills. Even cool Paul English was impressed. He whistled. "Man, that would buy a nice week's sailing off Maui, Daddy."

"Listen, you guys, my ass is grass if this dough isn't resting back in the safe in the Federal Building tonight, so let's not screw up." Warbucks was uncharacteristically serious—a mistake with this crew.

"Yeah, Manny," the Block improvised, "don't let them walk off with this loot like you did with the twenty thousand last month."

"That wasn't my fault—you let the crooks in with machine guns. Besides, my fat Mexican ass is worth more than a lousy twenty grand."

Mary Falcone's eyes twinkled. "Yeah. And that was real money. Local money. This is fed. Monopoly stuff. They only start to count in billions. They'll probably be sore at us if we send back a few bucks like this and screw up their accounting."

I let them go on, pleased that morale was high. Whatever Paul had recited to get Mary and Manny back to being a team had worked.

Warbucks grinned, realizing what he had started. Bright-eyed Bobby Wheeler however, was oblivious. "Gentlemen, and lady," he said, "this is an official FBI operation now. Agent Warbucks and I are responsible for these federal funds. They will not leave this premise under any circumstances." He brandished an Uzi loaded with a thirty-round clip.

"That fucking Uzi is leaving the premise right now or I don't go into the ring. We'll all be dead if anyone starts shooting one of those in here," Herrera said.

He was right. We were in the tiny transaction room. Any gunplay at all would be deadly. And those of us observing from the back room were no safer. The walls of plasterboard were easily penetrated.

"This is my official weapon this afternoon, gentlemen and lady," Wheeler said, his eyes glowing a little brighter.

"Wrong, Bobby. That goes in the trunk. This is our operation and you'll obey orders like everyone else or you can wait in the car," I said.

Wheeler looked to Daddy for support, but Warbucks was expressionless. I knew he was enjoying Wheeler making an asshole of himself. Wheeler lapsed into a Clint Eastwood lisp. "Well, if anyone would like to try taking . . ."

His eyes bulged when the Block lifted him off his feet from behind, pinning his arms. Herrera walked over and removed the Uzi from Wheeler. "You want to store this in your trunk, Warbucks?"

"Sure, Manny. No problem." Daddy said.

"Sarge, I'm not telling you how to do your thing. You're better than anybody else at it," I said, "but I do have to tell you this is your last go at it. The Board of Supervisors is meeting tomorrow morning and I'm pretty sure some of them know about the sting and will order us to close it." The understatement of the year. "So, you're going to have to take some chances. Maybe force things a bit. Try to get him to accept twenty or thirty grand good-faith money when you agree that the turnover will take place at a spot he chooses."

"Five grand should be enough," Warbucks said.

"At least fifty to make it look good. What the hell, it's only our taxes," the Block said.

Bobby Wheeler said, "I'm not sure that we should allow . . ."

I interrupted. "Use your own judgment on the cash, Sarge. We'll have to play it by ear whether or not we bag him before a turnover or go through with it. We'll see how the setup looks when we know what he's proposing. The main thing is his brother, the supervisor. We need to know . . ."

"Chief . . ."

"Yes, Sarge?"

"You were gone, so maybe you haven't heard how much I pushed him during our last session." Herrera looked at Paul.

"You're right. I haven't had a chance to brief him," Paul said. "Manny pushed him a little further than any of us were comfortable with, Chief, although the good attorney gave him an opening by mentioning that his brother was one of the biggest politicians around here and that he had his protection on the deal. Manny asked him to bring his brother along for this session, and . . ."

"And he agreed?" I broke in on Paul's monologue before he started quoting Homer. We didn't have much time.

"Not exactly. As I was saying before you interrupted, he was cagey, but said he would bring Manny all the proof he needed without actually making a commitment that the supervisor would be along."

"What do you make of that?" I looked at Herrera.

"Damned if I know, Chief. He's one strange dude."

I frowned.

"What's wrong, Fraleigh? You ought to be happier than a pig in shit to be nailing another one of your political superiors," Warbucks said.

"This has been a strange one right from the start, Daddy. Bolero was set up to be a small-time fence. We were surprised to see Bartlow approach him with such a big money deal. We pretty much believe that Attorney Bartlow plans on eliminating all of his connections as the deal goes along. If he really is so willing to incriminate his brother, that means he's very dangerous right now. And we can't have Sergeant Herrera sitting alone with two hundred grand. Someone is going to have to ride shotgun right here on the couch."

"Normally, Nunzio would do it, but he's out of action. Or we hope he is. He was seen yesterday hanging around outside like he's staking out the bar waiting for Hector Gonzales to return," Paul said.

"Goddamn it. I don't like that one bit," I said. "Paul, as soon as the meet with Bartlow is over, I want you to get Nunzio. I'll tell him in no uncertain terms to cool it. But right now he's unavailable and we need someone else." There was silence as we looked around the room. The Block, Paul, and I were out of the question. Our pictures had been in the local papers from time to time. Wheeler broke the silence. "I'm the logical one. I'm not known locally, and this is bureau money. I'm sworn to protect it."

No one paid any attention to him. My eyes settled on Daddy. He wasn't known and his presence with a loaded shotgun would certainly be a deterrent in case Bartlow thought he could pull an easy one. But he would be a new player, and Bartlow might be reluctant to talk in front of him, and we definitely needed more on the tapes. I looked at Mary Falcone. She had been in the back room with Bartlow on occasion. She wouldn't inhibit his conversation. Would she inhibit his inclination for a rip-off murder?

"What do you think?" I asked her.

"Sure. No problem, Chief." Officer Falcone picked up the sawed off shotgun in the corner, jacked two rounds into it, and put it on her lap. She looked like a tough gun moll. She would do.

"I can't believe this. They intend to use a woman. You better straighten them out, Warbucks. If anything happens, I'm going to put it all on you," Wheeler said.

Warbucks had sized up Mary. "It's OK with us, Fraleigh."

"Good." I looked at my watch. "We better get into position. Bartlow's due in fifteen minutes."

"I'll bring a couple of pitchers of beer into the back. No telling how long we'll be stuck back there," the Block said.

The phone rang as we entered the back room. Paul picked it up. After listening for a couple of minutes he said, "OK, Captain—I'll tell him," and hung up.

"Chief, that was Captain Toll. One of our patrol units spotted Hector Gonzales about twenty minutes ago in a yellow Mustang. Gonzales was a passenger. The officer was ramming the Mustang off the road, but he lost control of his car when Gonzales opened up with a machine gun."

"Your men are too hasty, Chief—taking on someone like Gonzales alone wouldn't be allowed in the bureau," Wheeler said.

"Is the cop hurt, Paul?"

"No. He's shaken up, but isn't injured. He lost Gonzales a few miles from here. Toll has set up perimeters and they're doing a search. The helicopter is up."

The door to the bar banged open. "Here we go." The Block came in with two foaming pitchers of beer. "We can drink to success this afternoon."

Thirty-nine

ATTORNEY RICHARD BARTLOW, AKA DICK BARRY, ENtered the back door and shook Herrera's hand. Bartlow wasn't in a suit and tie this time. He wore a dark running suit, which looked totally incongruous with his soft physique. I studied him intently, looking for bulges that could be concealed weapons, but the outfit was too loose for me to spot anything. He was carrying a small brown paper bag that was too flat to contain a weapon.

"What's she doing here?" Bartlow pointed at Falcone sitting on the couch with the shotgun in her lap. It wasn't exactly pointed at Bartlow, but with the slightest movement would have covered his chest.

"No offense, man. But with this kind of dough around I wouldn't trust my mother." Herrera nodded toward the closed attaché case.

Bartlow regarded the case like a starving lion eyeing a crippled zebra. His effort to be cool brought a smile to my face, but not to Warbucks, whose gaze never shifted from the attaché case.

"You know, Bolero, by this time we should be trusting each other."

"Yeah, I know. But I don't see your big-shot brother here like you said." Manny was following my directions to push the lawyer into giving us evidence that would incriminate his politician brother.

"I didn't say he'd be here. I said I'd prove to you that he's one hundred percent behind the deal. I got the proof right here." He held up the brown bag.

Manny was openly skeptical. "Yeah? I still don't see nothing."

Bartlow nodded toward the case, unable to contain his eagerness any longer. "First, let's see the money."

Manny shrugged and opened the case after being careful not to walk between the shotgun and Bartlow. I noticed that with the case open Falcone now had the barrel right on Bartlow's midsection. He, however, was completely unaware of that. His eyes were gleaming, and he actually reached out and stroked the stack of bills.

"OK," Bartlow sighed, "get me a VCR and I'll show you the proof you want." He took a video cassette out of the paper bag.

Herrera was as excited as we were, but he moved with his usual slowness, poking around among the two or three VCRs in the corner. I knew he was thinking that he wanted to set it up so that it would show on our camera hidden in the back room. Bartlow fidgeted. Finally, Manny got the VCR placed so that we could view the screen as easily as he could.

Bartlow handed him the tape and the screen crackled for a few seconds before a picture came on. Both Bartlow brothers were in the supervisor's office and both wore wide smiles. The politician spoke. "Hello, Bolero. Dick Barry, my brother, has told me all about you. I'm sorry I couldn't be with you in person, but I want you to know I'm one hundred percent behind the bond deal."

My heart was racing. This was unbelievable. Christmas in summertime. The supervisor had even used his brother's alias. What evidence! I glanced back to make sure our own video was getting it. Bobby Wheeler was frowning, fiddling with the dials. "Paul, for Christ's sake, make sure we're getting this," I yelled. Paul had been absorbed in watching the action through the window along with the rest of us. He hadn't noticed Wheeler touching the equipment.

"Wheeler, what the hell?" Paul said.

"I was only trying to clear up the picture," Wheeler said.

"Are we getting this, Paul?" I said.

"No. Hold on. I'll get it back."

Meanwhile, Bartlow, the politician, held up a fistful of bonds on the videotape. "These are as good as gold, Bolero. And I guarantee you there's no risk involved." He was positively beaming like he was giving a political speech. The VCR screen flickered and went dead.

"There. I got it back on. You must have touched the record button, Wheeler."

"You fucking asshole, Wheeler. You blew the whole thing. You're dead if we don't come up with the original tape."

"Take it easy, Block," I said, although those were my sentiments as well. We were still in the midst of an operation and couldn't afford a fight. But what luck. It was unbelievable. Wheeler should be burned at the stake.

"You don't have the bonds with you, I suppose," Manny said to Bartlow.

I jumped as the phone rang behind me. The Block picked it up. "Yeah?" he said with his own style of telephone courtesy. "The Chief's busy right now, Captain, but give me the info and I'll pass it on."

I wondered what additional bad news was coming from Captain Toll while I tried to concentrate on the exchange between Herrera and Bartlow.

"Jesus Christ. What do you mean the lieutenant lost him? What the hell did he do, turn invisible? The chief ain't going to like this one bit, Toll."

The Block slammed the receiver down and said, "Chief, you won't believe this. The zone lieutenant was taking part in the search for Gonzales and he kept driving in wider and wider circles until he drove by here. Who does he spot sitting in his car staking us out, but Nunzio! The dumb fucking lieutenant turns the corner and calls Toll for instructions. Toll tells him to collar Nunzio, but by the time he gets around the corner, Nunzio's car is empty and he's nowhere to be seen. What kind of fucking cops are we promoting to lieutenant these days?"

"Paul, check around outside. We don't want Nunzio barging in right now," I said.

Later, as we reconstructed events, we realized that the coffee Nunzio Papa had consumed during his stakeout had worked on his stomach. He had been using the corner gas station to take occasional leaks, but its men's room was filthy. Not at all suitable for a bowel movement. Leaving his parked car as the lieutenant was calling Captain Toll, Nunzio decided to take a chance and pop into The Blue Mirage Bar and Grill where he knew the toilets were cleaned once in awhile. Nunzio hadn't been himself for some time, or he would have noticed the yellow Mustang turning the corner when he entered the bar. Just as Nunzio walked in, the fill-in bartender, Art Estrada, was bent over in the unfamiliar task of tapping into a new keg of beer. Nunzio's soft-soled running shoes carried him into the men's room without a sound before Estrada straightened up to fill the glasses of the bar's only customers, auto mechanics taking a beer break.

Detective Paul English beckoned Estrada to the end of the bar and asked him if he had seen Nunzio. Getting a negative reply Paul told Estrada, "If he should come in, don't let him near the back room—and buzz me right away."

"Art Estrada hasn't seen Nunzio, Chief." Paul had returned. "I told Art to keep him out of here and buzz me right away if he shows up."

I nodded, hoping nothing was going to interrupt as we finally seemed to be getting the evidence we needed.

"You remember what I said," Bartlow said, unable to take his eyes off the money. "We do the exchange on a neutral spot in one hour."

"Here. Count it. Each bundle has the same dough." Manny casually handed Bartlow four packets, each containing ten thousand dollars. "I trust you. You can stick them in your pocket for an hour until we complete the deal." I felt Warbucks next to me wince. "Where you wanta meet?"

I appreciated Herrera's attempt to disarm Bartlow enough to give away the location. But it didn't work. Bartlow stuck the video cassette in the left side of his jacket and the forty thousand dollars in the right. I wondered what he was carrying in his pants pocket. He said, "No way, Bolero. Just like you have your girlfriend here for security, I'm being careful, too. I'll call you ten minutes before we meet. Just you. Or you can bring her if you like."

And at that moment Nunzio Papa burst from the bar into the sting room. As we watched, horrified, Nunzio clawed for his gun. It caught in his right-hand pocket. Beyond him was Hector Gonzales and an Uzi-toting friend.

Before we could even move I saw Bartlow's rodentlike face tighten. He reached into his running suit and pulled a handgun. Coolly, he fired at Nunzio. Papa crumbled to the floor. Behind him was the terrifying figure of Hector Gonzales leveling an Uzi. His eyes were mad, and he was laughing hysterically. I could see saliva dribbling onto his chin from his bloodless lips. He jerked the Uzi and put a burst through Bartlow. Bartlow's body jumped and twitched. Bright-red blood spurted from his running suit as the high-velocity rounds tore into him. The room was filled with the flame and the acid smoke of gunfire.

Falcone had covered the opening door with the shotgun. Recognizing Nunzio, she held her fire. She hadn't seen Bartlow pull the pistol. As soon as he fired she started to cover him. But Bartlow slumped against her, dead. She shook him loose and trained the shotgun on Gonzales. He screamed, "Hold it motherfuckers," and held up his left hand, which contained a hand grenade.

The Block jerked open the door of our observation room. He, Warbucks, and I collided in the open doorway trying to get a bead on Gonzales. "Jesus Christ. He's got the pin out of the grenade!" the Block yelled. We froze. Helplessly, we watched.

Nunzio, wounded in the leg, was crawling toward his gun two feet away from him on the floor. Hector focused on the money in the open case. "Payday, amigo!" he shouted to his friend standing next to him. "But first . . ." He straddled Nunzio as he had during the raid, "I've been looking for you, *maricon*." One-handed, he pointed the Uzi at Detective Papa. Papa's bulging eyes looked upward in terror.

Mary Falcone had been swinging her weapon back and forth covering Gonzales and his friend. Now she steadied it on Gonzales. She let Gonzales have both barrels of the shotgun in the chest. Once again the small room was filled with the roar and belching flame and smoke of a powerful firearm. Crazy-eyed, Gonzales slammed back against the wall and with his last breath hurled the grenade. It bounced off the opposite wall and rolled toward us.

"Hit the deck! It will take us all out!" the Block yelled.

He didn't have to tell me. I knew the shrapnel would tear through us and begin a deadly ricochet around the room. I hit the floor first and almost expired when the Block and Warbucks landed on top of me. The grenade concussion was terrific. I was having trouble breathing, which was understandable with two hulks on top of me. But it slowly dawned on me that something was wrong. Smoke was everywhere, but no metal had been whistling around us.

"It was only a smoke grenade! Get off me you assholes," I yelled.

We jumped up in time to see through the smoke that Herrera was sneaking a handgun out from under the cushion. He was bringing it to bear when the guy with the Uzi opened up, spraying the room with abandon. We all tried to hit the deck again, but it was carnage at that range. I felt fire in my shoulder as I hit the floor, my eyes catching sight of Bobby Wheeler still prone on the floor in the rear room with his hands over his head in the position he had assumed upon hearing of the grenade.

The hated hammering of the Uzi finally stopped. I lifted my head to see the kid who had been with Hector backing out the side door with the attaché case. My right hand had no feeling in it and I didn't know what the hell had happened to my gun anyway, so I just watched as Warbucks limped to the door and got off a shot. Paul English pushed him out of the way and fired a burst of three shots before the Uzi replied. He ducked back inside while the bullets showered us with glass and plaster.

I crawled over to Bartlow's dead body, saying a silent prayer that the videotape hadn't been damaged. With one hand I pushed his bloody corpse on its side and reached into the jacket pocket where he had placed the tape. I pulled it out. It was OK. I smiled. Warbucks had been watching.

"I'd hate to have you after me, Fraleigh," he said.

The smoky room looked like a scene from Beirut. Bullet holes everywhere. Plaster hung from the ceiling, and there was a carpet of broken glass. Except for Paul English, who had fled after the money-carrying bandit, and Bobby Wheeler, who was cautiously emerging from the back room, we were all bleeding. Mary Falcone kept saying, "It's all right, Manny. It's all right." Herrera was holding his stomach with one hand, and with the other was brushing blood from Falcone's face cut by flying glass. "Are you all right, baby?" he said. Nunzio was moaning on the ground holding his left leg. The Block had been grazed by a bullet and was trying to staunch the flow of blood from a wound on his forehead. Warbucks had taken off his belt and was applying it as a tourniquet to his right leg. Art Estrada ran in from the bar. Gently he led me to the couch. "You're losing too much blood from that arm, Chief," he said and started to make a tourniquet.

I put my head back as the room started to spin. Paul came back in. "He and Hector must have left the car with the motor running. He was pulling away in a yellow Mustang by the time I got to the street. I'll call in the alarm." He went out to the public phone in the bar. The money was gone, Bartlow and Gonzales were stone dead, and five of us were wounded. Quite an impressive sting operation I had run.

The last voice I heard before passing out was Bobby Wheeler. "Two hundred thousand in federal funds gone. There'll be hell to pay over this," he said.

Forty

THE NURSE'S FACE WAS FLUSHED. SHE WAS SO ANGRY SHE stuttered. "That is out of the question. You're already violating regulations by changing out of hospital attire."

It was the day after the shootout and I was sitting on the side of my bed, and with Paul English's help, trying to tie my necktie. The nurse had barged into my room to take my temperature or check my insurance or something and had paused in mid-stride, outraged when she saw me in street clothes. In answer to her question of what in the world I thought I was doing, I had replied truthfully that I had to go to a meeting.

My right arm was bound up in a sling, and a bandage covered the left part of my face where last night the doctor had had jolly good fun fishing out broken glass. Fortunately, my eye hadn't been seriously cut, but it too was covered by the bandage. My knees were wobbly, and I had a splitting headache.

At first, I had no thought of going to the Board of Supervisors session to be a witness to my own firing. But then I remembered my defiant promise to Nola. Nothing would keep me away. Of course, it was stupid. Mentioning to Paul my intention to go, I waited for him to talk me out of it so I could get some sleep. To my surprise he had volunteered to help me dress, which meant I couldn't back out.

"We'll see about this," the nurse said, stomping out. Five minutes later I heard her high-pitched voice outside the door,

"You can't go in there. The room is already too crowded and the doctor is coming."

"Bullshit." The strong male voice was familiar. "That's my kid brother, the chief, in there, and I want to see how he's doing."

I gaped as Jack pushed his way in, the nurse unable to slow his big frame. He was clean-shaven and his eyes were clear. Jack was on the wagon. I had a lump in my throat. He came to the bed, taking in the bandages that threatened to smother me. Jack's eyes watered. He took my good hand.

"Jesus, Finney, what did they do to you?" he said softly.

It was all I could do to mumble "Jack," and squeeze back with my good hand. He had always called me kid. Hearing him say "Finney" brought back memories of the old man and got me even more choked up.

It turned out that my shooting had made the national news. Jack had taken the first available plane. Paul was finishing bringing Jack up to speed on the details of the sting when the young doctor summoned by the righteous nurse arrived. He was pompous. "I'm afraid we can't be responsible for you if you leave the hospital, Mr. Fraleigh," he said. He made the Block seem like Mother Teresa.

"Hey, he does what he wants, Doc." Jack approached the doctor who moved to the other side of the bed.

"Mr. Fraleigh, you have a number of serious injuries and are on medication. The hospital cannot be responsible if you choose to leave," the doctor said, watching Jack.

"I understand. I'm not asking you to be responsible. I'll sign forms to that effect. I'm only going out for a couple of hours."

"We're preparing the forms now. However, if you leave, you're discharged, and will not be readmitted for twenty-four hours."

"OK, Doc. If it satisfies your concern for my health that I stay out twenty-four hours instead of two, I'll just have to party the rest of the time before checking back in."

Jack grinned, and I felt a little better.

On the ride to city hall I wondered if I should have listened to the nurse and doctor. I alternated between chills and sweating fits, and found it hard to concentrate. At one point I made the Block angry by breaking into an uncontrollable fit of giggles looking at him. He had suffered a concussion along with cuts, and wore a huge turban of white bandage on his head. He looked like something out of a science fiction movie.

Paul had briefed me on the aftermath of the bloody shoot-out, but it was kind of fuddled in my head. Miraculously, Bartlow and Gonzales were the only fatalities. Nunzio had a broken leg, but had been in gleeful spirits after finding no pulse in Hector Gonzales. Herrera had a stomach wound. He was going to have to lay off the chili for a while, but would be OK. Falcone had some cuts from broken glass, and Daddy Warbucks had been lucky. The Uzi slug had gone through his thigh without hitting bone or artery.

Paul had turned the original tape of Supervisor Bartlow over to the FBI, retaining a copy. He was putting together the state case, but after talking it over with Warbucks, he had decided to delay turning over evidence to the local D.A.— given that official's coziness with the political machine and Duane Bartlow. Warbucks had confided in Paul that the bureau, worried over the two-hundred-grand flash money, had gotten a Title Three telephone tap on Duane Bartlow's office. Naturally, Bobby Wheeler had forgotten to check the log.

Bartlow was on the telephone tap with Gerhart who, sure enough, had passed on information about a big bond investigation. Fortunately, Gerhart was unaware that Richard Bartlow was attempting to peddle hot bonds at The Blue Mirage. In sucking up to Bartlow, Gerhart had never gotten around to mentioning the sting other than to talk of an undercover-police sex scandal. The lack of a warning about the sting had been fortunate for us and fatal for Richard Bartlow. Supervisor Bartlow had, no doubt, urged his brother to sell the bonds quickly before the police investigation began.

The feds had really hit pay dirt with Bartlow's call to his brother, the attorney. They had both agreed that in light of the pending police bond investigation, the deal with Bolero had to be completed and Bolero "retired." God knows what murderous plans they had been laying to eliminate various witnesses. If we had heard the tapes, the final sting would have been unnecessary. There was plenty of evidence, but Bobby Wheeler had been too busy checking out his Uzi to listen to the tapes and inform Warbucks.

I learned that Paul had mumbo-jumboed the media on the sting. They hadn't minded a bit and weren't impressed that forty thousand dollars of federal money had been recovered from Bartlow's body. It had given the media a perfect excuse to present us as trigger-happy Keystone Cops who let one hundred sixty grand be ripped off while we blasted everyone except the thief. Another item for the Board of Supervisors to cite when they sacked me. As if they needed another item. I was so tired of it all that I started to tell Paul to turn the car around and take me home, but by that time the car was pulling up to city hall.

We were ten minutes late, which meant that there was a fifty-fifty chance that the board was ready to sit down and conduct business. Jack helped me onto the elevator to ride to the second-floor chambers for public hearings, the same place where the interviews for chief had taken place.

We entered the front set of double doors and Jack guided me along the guardrail that separated the elected from the peasants. I looked up and saw that four supervisors were seated. Duane Bartlow's chair was vacant. Nola was looking at me curiously. It occurred to me that I must be a sight—unable to navigate on my own, my arm in a sling, and half my face covered by bandage.

As we slowly proceeded I glanced toward the public seating, expecting to see the same few bored reporters and political-science students. Instead, the three hundred seats were almost all taken. TV crews and news media were in full attendance.

I stared at the people in the audience and stopped walking. It was incredible. They were almost all cops. Some in uniform. Some were accompanied by wives. There were detectives, their sergeants and lieutenants. Captain Toll and uniformed supervisors and patrol officers of all ranks. Male and female, black, brown, yellow, white. Captain Gerhart sat next to Sergeant Myers and a guy I recognized as Bartlow's aide. The sons of bitches had all turned out to see me get canned.

For a moment, an intense rage hit me. I almost flipped them the finger, but my right arm was in a sling and the left held firmly by Jack. What had I said to Nola . . . ? That the cops would cheer her on when they fired me? But I had never thought they would do it personally. Sure, I had fired a couple of cops and tightened discipline and raised standards a little. But California cops were supposed to be different from New York cops.

It was also true that I was responsible for a sting operation that had turned into a battlefield leaving two dead and a lot of cops wounded, and one hundred sixty grand getting ripped off—and I hadn't even gotten a shot off. As chief, I shouldn't even have been there, but the DOAs were bad guys and I had been fighting for the cops against the pols, and . . . Oh, what the hell. It was no use. You never got a chance to explain. I felt the bile rise in me the way it had in New York. I looked back at Nola to see if she was gloating. She looked away and dabbed at her eyes with a tissue.

I realized that a noise had been trying to break through into my consciousness. Then it penetrated. There was a rhythmic applause coming from the huge audience, the cops. I glared at them. "What the hell are they clapping for?" I said to Jack.

"For you, Finney," he whispered.

"They're clapping for me?" I said in disbelief. "Why?"

The Block had joined us. "Because you're a dumb asshole cop just like them and this is the last chance they have to do it before you get canned," he growled.

We continued along toward our seats. I couldn't believe it and kept sneaking looks at the crowd, but the applause continued. Finally, I shook my good arm loose from Jack and raised it in recognition to them. My vision was a little blurry and it wasn't because I was dizzy from my wounds. The volume doubled with my acknowledgment. They cheered and slowly began to stand, one section of the room joining the other until they were all on their feet.

Supervisor Kendle, presiding over the meeting, kept pounding the gavel. "We won't stand for this!" I heard him say over the public address system. "This board will not be swayed by a mob. Keep quiet or I'll have the chambers cleared."

I sat down. It had touched me, but now it was time for the real stuff to start—my dismissal. But the noise continued and each time Kendle pounded the gavel, it got louder. Paul leaned over to me. "Fraleigh, you're going to have to stand up and ask them to keep quiet."

I got up and made quieting gestures with my left arm, urging the audience to sit down. Eventually, they did, and the noise only flared up again when Kendle said, "That's better. We won't tolerate hooligans whether they wear police uniforms or not."

This time they began to stamp their feet as well as yell. Kendle was quite a statesman. I got up again and went through the same motions asking for quiet, and gradually they settled down.

"I hereby call this meeting to order. Let the record show," Kendle intoned, "that the Board of Supervisors is reconvened to finish the business of appointing a police chief from the meeting which was postponed for legal reasons three weeks ago. Let the record also show that Supervisor Bartlow is excused from attendance because of a death in the family."

I held my breath, but aside from a few snickers, the chamber remained silent. Kendle bared his teeth at the audience. "However," he said, "the audience should know that Supervisor Bartlow has provided his proxy vote to me in a form supervised and approved by the city attorney. For the information of the audience and the press, the city attorney has ruled that there is no discussion on this particular vote, since that was concluded in the previous session."

Behind me I heard hissing as a lot of people in the audience bared their own teeth back at Kendle. He banged the gavel again until there was silence. Then, with a smile he said, "The motion left on the floor three weeks ago was, I quote, 'Should Acting Police Chief Fraleigh be confirmed as the permanent appointment to the position of police chief?' Supervisor Bartlow left his proxy on that vote and also in favor of another candidate on a subsequent motion when— excuse me—*should* the original motion fail. I now will register his vote on Mr. Fraleigh."

Kendle pressed a button on his control panel and to no one's surprise a bright red light indicating a negative vote lighted up next to Bartlow's name on the huge voting board displayed in the front of the room. "I also vote against Mr. Fraleigh."

The two red lights gleamed out at us and everyone realized that it took only one more for me to be officially fired. Kendle spoke again. He was really enjoying himself. "I now ask the other supervisors to vote by pushing the appropriate buttons on their control panels."

There was moderate applause when Sally Fenton's light turned green. The crowd knew the eventual outcome as well as I did. Kendle stared expectantly at Laura Kadisch. She looked him in the eye then poked at her control panel. A bright-green light joined the others. The crowd again applauded politely. Two reds and two greens. I found myself a little disappointed in Nola. In a way, I could understand how she felt about me, but to drag it out in corny dramatics that we all knew were phony? She stared down at her panel and total silence enveloped the room. I wished she'd get it over with so that I could get out with the Block, Paul, Warbucks, Jack, and maybe a few of the cops and have a beer and joke about it, but she really drew it out.

Then, incredibly, the green light lit up next to her name on the display board. The crowd went berserk, jumping and yelling. I sat, unable to comprehend. Kendle pounded the gavel. "The vote is not final! The vote is not final!" He yelled over and over until finally the crowd stilled. "I want each supervisor polled by the clerk."

I sensed an ugly mood coming over the audience. They were suspicious of Kendle. The clerk said, "Supervisor Fenton, do you vote *aye* or *nay* to appoint Mr. Fraleigh to the permanent position of police chief?"

"Aye," Sally Fenton said.

"Supervisor Kadisch?" the clerk said.

"Aye," Laura Kadisch smiled.

"Supervisor Henderson," the clerk said.

"Aye," Nola said loud and clear, looking at my band-aged face.

Once again the crowd cheered. Kendle threw the gavel onto his panel and walked out of the room.

"Congratulations, Chief." Daddy Warbucks hobbled up to me on crutches. I had been so out of it I hadn't even seen him sitting in the crowd.

"I'm sorry about the dough, Daddy. Any news yet on getting it back?"

He shook his head from side to side, looking embarrassed. "Fraleigh, I wonder if you'd do me a favor. Do you think you could have Paul or the Block drive you up to our office in San Francisco, Monday?"

"Sure, Daddy, no problem," I said, even though I didn't really feel like going through some three-hour FBI inquisition on how the money had vanished. But Daddy was in trouble. It wouldn't do for us to be reluctant witnesses.

"Is Uncle Sam going to grill us about the dough?" Paul English said.

Daddy's face turned red. "Actually, my boss asked. The Attorney General and director of the bureau are coming into town to give me and Wheeler a medal. The boss really wants Fraleigh to be there."

Paul smiled.

Daddy said, "It was either fire us or give us a medal. We didn't know which way it was going to go until Washington sent a telex at eight o'clock last night."

I burst out laughing. "You lost one hundred sixty grand and get a medal. I'm about to get fired and have a sting operation turn into Nam, and get appointed police chief instead of getting fired."

The Block walked up as the two of us were guffawing. "What the hell is so funny, Warbucks?" he asked.

"Law enforcement, Block, law enforcement. It's hilarious," said Special Agent Warbucks.

Epilogue

JACK AND I WENT TO SMALL'S FOR LUNCH. IT WAS A PRICEY restaurant across the street from city hall. I had wanted to go with the Block and Paul English to the Peace Officers Association Hall where they were having a reception in my honor. But Jack had insisted on buying me lunch. He had a plane to catch.

The restaurant was surrounded by palm trees too big for its modest-size lot. The food wasn't that great either, but the location drew the movers and shakers and made people willing to take crap from a snotty maître d' in order to be seen among the important folk.

The dark-complexioned matred wore a tux and had slicked-down black hair. He'd always reminded me of a guy in a grade-B *Godfather*-type movie. He looked askance at my bandages and steered us toward a back table. "Hey," Jack said, "this is your new police chief. We want a nice table."

The maître d' froze in his tracks. "Chief, I'm so sorry. I didn't recognize you. I read all about it in the papers. You'll have the front table."

Given my appearance, it was the last thing I wanted, but my protests were to no avail. He seated us at a large table commanding a view of the front entrance.

"You sure you should be having that with all the medication they gave you in the hospital?" Jack pointed to my glass of Chardonnay. He was having Perrier water.

"For a guy who used to drink double bourbons like water, that's rich."

He laughed. "Those days are gone forever. Although once in a while on a special occasion like this I get tempted."

"Forget it. If you order any booze, I'll have you thrown out. You can see I have a lot of influence in this town."

He grinned. "It's a shame the old man isn't here to see it."

"Yeah." Jack's comment got me a little choked. It had been an emotional morning. He saw my reaction and was silent for a while.

"Neither of us will be the man he was, Finny, but you've done real good."

"You know, Jack, I'd rather be over at the hall hoisting a few with the cops than be in this fancy restaurant."

"You're the permanent chief now. You can't afford to go drinking with the troops. Oh, they'll buy your drinks and pat you on the back, but don't kid yourself—they really want you to be above that sort of stuff. I never had any respect for a boss who drank with us. It's better that you sent the Block and English to represent you."

"I'm going to drop in at the reception after lunch."

"And so you should. But remember, you're the guy who gives assignments, promotions, discipline. They'll be watching to see if you're impartial. You can't get too close to anyone. You'll even have to watch yourself with the Block and English."

"Jack, for Christ's sake, those guys have been with me all the way. We were almost killed a couple of times. They're my best friends."

"That's fine. And you should use them. You can trust them to be loyal to you. Just keep your distance. They're both way-out characters in their own way. If they get into trouble on their own, you have to make sure there's enough distance between them and you. You're the chief. You've got to be whistle-clean."

I picked at my food. This was a hell of a celebration. Jack's comments had depressed me. The Block and Paul were probably having a few laughs while my brother told me the facts of life. Looking up I noticed a crowd at the entrance waiting to be seated. Nola Henderson pushed through. Raising her index finger she caught the maître d's attention. He rushed forward and, with a bow, led her into the restaurant. She wore the emerald-green dress that fit her like a shrouded negligée.

My depression vanished. I'd ask her to join us. Introduce her to Jack. I felt a warm rush. God, I wanted to put my arms around her. Let that beautiful brown hair rub against my cheek. Feel her breasts against my chest while I inhaled her perfume, letting it seep through me until my hardness pushed against her crotch and caused her to give that tiny gasp that drove me up the wall.

No one entering the restaurant could fail to notice our table. Nola slowly scanned the room as she was being led in our direction. She saw me and I smiled. I braced my hand on the seat to get up. Her green eyes locked on mine for an instant. The smile froze on my face and I slumped back.

There had been no reaction. I might have found some hope if she had shown anger or even contempt, but it had been dead. The good-bye look. She didn't even turn her head in our direction when she passed the table.

Jack hadn't missed the exchange. "That's another thing that goes with the chief's job, little brother. You have to keep your distance from politicians."

He punched me lightly in the arm. "Come on. It's time for you to take me to the airport."

ABOUT THE AUTHOR

Joseph D. McNamara, police chief of San Jose, California, started his career as a beat cop in Harlem, New York City. He is the only police chief in the United States to hold a Ph.D. from Harvard University. As a very vocal national spokesperson for Hand Gun Control, Inc., McNamara has been profiled in *Time, Newsweek,* and *The New York Times*. He is the author of two other Fraleigh novels, *The First Directive* and *Fatal Command*.